CW01658629

THE QUEEN OF AHL

The Paranormals of Ahl Book 4

ML CONKLIN

The Queen of Ahl (The Paranormals of Ahl Book 4)

For information contact :

MLConklin@MLConklin.com

Sign up for the newsletter for updates and information on new releases:

http://www.mlconklin.com

Cover design by Getcovers.com

ISBN E-book: 979-8-9928787-0-7

ISBN Paperback : 979-8-9928787-1-4

First Edition: May 2025

A Note from the Author

Hello, Reader.

I'm so happy to share this entire series with you! The Queen of Ahl is the fourth and final book in the Paranormals of Ahl series. I suggest you start with The Dragon Problem and read the entire series, including books 2.5 and 3.5, which are shorter books from Lily's perspective. If not, you'll be lost.

Trigger warnings and heads-up:

- This book is heavy on the politics of Ahl.
- There are demons.
- For all other trigger warnings, see:
    - The Dragon Problem (Book 1)
    - Bug Magic (Book 2)
    - The Mage Vampire Hybrid (Book 2.5) – Lily's POV
    - Crowns and Curses (Book 3)
    - The Hybrid Heir (Book 3.5) – Lily's POV

Chapter One

Grief doesn't fade with time, like some will have you believe. It changes and settles into your soul. Some learn to cope, while others hide it. But it's always there—a constant ache in your heart or a thought in the back of your mind. Sometimes it punches you in the gut, making it hard to function, but the world won't wait for the pain to subside. Because even while dealing with the most crushing grief, the living must move on. Grief isn't something you can ignore, shed, or escape, so you must learn to cope. And everyone deals with it in their own way.

After my brother's death, his match, Emine, withdrew from society while I threw myself into my work. When I returned from Drake's horde, my assistant had a mountain of paperwork waiting for me. So it was the logical thing to do. When the griffin matriarch, Helen, forced me to rest, my mind would replay that terrible, awful day. It always started with Mat's death. Then came the plethora of other lives lost during my war against the Bellicose. When they melted away, I saw Drake drenched in blood as I fought and failed to save him. They weren't worse nor better than the nightmares I suffered my entire life, but equally awful. So, I worked.

Which is why I sat in my usual spot in the Council chambers with my chin resting on my hand and my eyes drooping. Movement to my left startled me, and I rubbed my eyes.

The Ogre Queens elbowed each other as they settled into chairs beside me. The one-eyed queen won the seat and beat her chest when she noticed me watching. "We are prepared to slaughter your enemies and bathe in their blood, Your Grace."

Great. More blood. "Thanks."

I glanced at the spelled windows overlooking the arena-style room. Mat and I used to stand inside and watch everyone. I couldn't deal with the emotions it brought to the surface, so I took my usual seat while the leaders settled in for the first meeting since the battle. Some went straight to a chair, while others wandered around the circle of desks, trying to find the perfect spot.

When I first rearranged the seats into a circle, I assigned them to stop the status games. Before my interference, they arranged themselves based on perceived power and influence. Everyone shared equal status, in my opinion, so I shook up their order. It amused me how careful some were about following my instructions, while others were resentful of the arrangement.

The doors behind me flew open, and I twisted in my seat. My heart skipped a beat when the most beautiful man I'd ever seen stepped through. His green eyes locked on mine and heated, and my stomach turned to jelly. He strutted in my direction, ignoring the people scurrying away from him. I tried not to show my sheer joy, but based on Drake's smug expression, he could feel it.

Hello, Jenella. His smooth voice rang through my mind as he took his place beside me.

"Hey. What have you been up to?"

"Visiting your sister." A smile ghosted across his face. "Has Tarquin updated you on her recent antics?"

Besides a text saying they couldn't make the Council meeting, I hadn't heard from Quin or Ara since my return. "No. Do I even want to know?"

"Perhaps not right now." Another wry grin.

Lily wasn't the kind of person to stay idle. I heard she recently challenged a dragon to a race up the side of a building. Bastien had to step in and break it up before a drunken brawl broke out. If it were up to me, I would have let her win. Especially since I used to long for that kind of freedom and understood hers wouldn't last long, being the heir to the throne of Umbra. "Now you've made me curious."

"It can wait until there are fewer sensitive ears present."

"Is it bad?"

"Undetermined. It may be a positive."

I groaned as my attention turned back to the arena. Holograms popped up, revealing the leaders who lived in other pockets or couldn't be present. A few stragglers raced towards empty chairs. I activated the projection spell. "Let's begin." The room fell silent. "During my recent sabbatical, my assistant carried out orders in my absence. Orders several of you questioned or ignored." I rested my hands on the desk. "We're here to clear up any confusion."

The Kelpie Queen leaned forward. "You left at a critical point in the war without explanation. This proves your lack of decision-making skills."

"The decision was mine." Drake made eye contact with the more problematic leaders. "If you wish to question it, you will address me."

Several faces paled. The Kelpie Queen's eyes darted around. "We only wish for an explanation, Sir First."

His eyes lit with green sparks. "No."

The Chimera King flew out of his chair. "She may wear the crown, but we are also leaders. It's our responsibility to ensure the coalition has adequate leadership. The girl has proven more than once that she isn't capable."

I snort-laughed. "You weren't worried about leadership when your people kidnapped all those paranormals and dragged them to Hospa. Nor were you worried about it enough to join our battles." I pointed at the Kelpie Queen. "And you can't even negotiate a truce with the trolls. Your quest for better leadership should start by looking in the mirror." I squared my shoulders. "You will address me as 'Your Grace' and not 'the girl' or any other derogatory term."

Drake leaned back and crossed his arms. "If you ignore my mate's orders, you will deal with me."

The room fell silent.

Jonas cleared his throat. "There are more pressing matters than Her Grace working remotely. Like the human authorities flooding the valley and trying to dig up evidence of our existence."

"What have you learned, Jonas?" My casual use of names without titles when I addressed my friends made some leaders bristle. Most ignored it, but some looked appalled. The other Firsts and my closest allies found it amusing.

"Federal agents are scouring the ruined Bellicose apartments. There have been incidents at several gates where paranormals are being shot at. The hybrid leader's business was attacked shortly before your return. My son believes disgruntled hybrids are working with the human authorities."

There wasn't enough time or energy to deal with an additional threat. My mind went back to all the times I argued with Mat about how boring and restrictive being a queen sounded. I wished he were around so I could apologize for my ignorance. Grief punched me in the gut, and I almost flinched. "How many hybrids still live in the valley?"

"Too many," Drake said. "They have built lives outside the pocket and don't want to abandon their businesses and human friends."

I scanned the room looking for Dale, but he was absent. "Where is the hybrid leader?"

Jonas shifted his weight. "He's dealing with the fallout from the attack on his bar."

And no doubt, he didn't have the patience for the harassment from the other leaders. *Is your team still monitoring the situation?* I asked in Drake's mind.

Yes. However, Roman's vampire house is under government surveillance, so they're unable to help.

Thanks. It felt like a lifetime since I'd visited the battle site, so I added it to my mental to-do list. "We have eyes on the situation, and I'll contact Dale."

Jonas inclined his head. "Thank you, Your Grace."

My lips twitched. I adored Ann Marie and Jonas. They were the definition of good people. I wanted to be like them if I ever got my head on straight. "Who here, aside from The First, Jonas, and the Sorceress Ann Marie, understands one or more of the human cultures and governments?"

A few hands raised.

"We'll need to study the various governments and cultures before we're forced to reveal ourselves. If you understand anything about them, contact my assistant to schedule a time to teach a class. I'll see if the recovery teams will help. Let's learn how they operate, what they want, their strengths, weaknesses, and anything else we can learn. Use their internet if needed, but make sure you're well-educated before you teach the rest of us."

The meeting continued for another hour. My fatigue made my brain foggy, and I fought to remember everything. Luckily, my overly efficient assistant, Verity, used a monitoring spell I could reference later. I was about to end the meeting when Razazia the First stood. "Your Grace. The Firsts would like a private chat before you leave."

Ugh. More meetings. "Okay." I glanced around the room. "Meeting adjourned." I leaned toward Drake as the leaders filed out. "What's this about?"

He feathered kisses along my knuckles. "They didn't include me in their scheme."

Of course not. The Firsts always rejected Drake. My eyebrows drew together, and I extracted my hand. "Let's find a more private place."

The room overlooking the arena hadn't changed since Mat's death. I could almost imagine him standing in his usual spot, watching the leaders assemble. When I blinked, the vision was gone.

Drake's warm hand landed on the small of my back, and I shuffled to a chair. Gorman slipped inside after the other Firsts, his smile looking extra fake. I didn't like the First, because he came across as disingenuous and worked with the Bellicose at one point. Though he claimed it was by force, he did what he needed to do to save his own ass. The only reason he was still alive was because I refused to become my mother. I already killed his match, Cynthia, which was punishment enough. The nightmares caused by her death would plague me for a long time.

Razazia flapped her translucent wings and folded her hands in her lap. "We believe there is one more First who Anitta put to sleep."

"Tracy and I researched it using a reliable source. Gorman and Cynthia were the last."

"We believe Celia was her first victim."

I swung toward Drake. "Didn't you say she died?"

"Correct. Celia chose permanent death."

Gorman lifted a finger. "Untrue. Anitta started the rumors of Celia's death. One reason I took part in her plans despite her weakened magic was because she claimed she could find other Firsts to replace me. She brought up Celia's name more than once."

My stomach fell. After Gorman and Cynthia's involvement with the Bellicose, I had no desire to wake another First. "Was it before or after I woke Drake and Razazia?"

"Both."

I didn't trust Gorman. It wouldn't surprise me if he came up with the idea for me to chase after Celia, only to claim plausible deniability when his intel was wrong. Still, if she were sleeping, I had to wake her. It was one of my first promises to Drake, and I intended to keep it. "On a scale from one to ten, how sure are you that she's alive?"

"Eight." He didn't hesitate.

"Do you believe him, Razazia?"

"I wouldn't be here if I didn't."

Of course not. Razazia was a shit-stirrer but took her oaths to the coalition seriously. If she thought Gorman was being deceptive, she'd say so. "Jonas?"

"He's not lying. But there are more urgent matters. I suggest you delay looking for her until we deal with the humans."

"And the Bellicose," I mumbled.

"What Bellicose?" The gleam in Razazia's eyes reminded me of bloodlust.

"I don't think Morten led them."

"The strange magic?" Drake asked.

"Yes."

Jonas rested his elbows on his knees. "Lily says she no longer senses them in the valley."

"It's possible Anitta brought in some outside help when she rekindled the Bellicose." Everything about the coup led back to my mother. "If she summoned demons, she'd make a deal with anyone to further her goals."

His eyebrows drew together. "She's gone. Why would they still work on her behalf?"

"If I knew that, they'd be dead, banished, or captured. If the Bellicose are gone, why are there so many human authorities in the valley, and who gave them the location of our gates?"

Drake's chair creaked as his weight shifted. "You think they're working with the humans?"

"No. Yes." I threw my hands up. "A memory surfaced of a demon. His magic wasn't like any other demon we've come across. He referred to Jacques as his son."

"The strange power coating the pyramid wasn't from a demon."

"No, but if she slept with a demon to have a son and tried to kill her own children, what else would she do for power?" I swallowed back bile at the thought.

Gorman's face hardened. "She would do anything. I witnessed it first-hand."

"Yes, she would. The question is, who did she work with?"

"It doesn't matter." Jonas rubbed his chin. "Let's develop a strategy to deal with the humans before they drum up enough hate to isolate us."

My list of life-threatening problems grew every time I talked to some-one. "I agree."

Razazia stood. "When will you resume in-person hearings?"

I frowned. "I changed the format to electronic or hologram. It saves everyone time."

"Do you not wish to connect with those you rule?"

"I do. But the only paranormals who come to hearings are the disgrun-tled ones." And they were tedious. When Mat held them once per month, people loved to show up and waste our time with unnecessary complaints.

"It's also a good way to build trust and showcase your leadership style."

Good point. "I'll consider it."

"I'll text you if I learn something new about the federal agents," Jonas said.

"Thanks."

Gorman opened his mouth to speak, but Razazia shoved him out the door.

I watched them go. "I suppose I should get to work."

Drake took my hand. "You cannot do a good job while exhausted."

"Sure, I can." Working was better than hellish nightmares.

He stood and helped me to my feet. "I can feel your fatigue. I'll stay with you and help with the nightmares."

Peaceful sleep while wrapped around Drake sounded great. "I can't leave Verity to fend for herself again, or she'll quit."

"Then give her the remainder of the day off. The Coalition won't fall apart if you take a nap."

Chapter Two

My eyes snapped open, and I launched myself from the bed.

"Where are you off to?" Drake's voice held a touch of amusement.

"I have to pee." I raced to the bathroom while pondering why my healing magic didn't take care of it for me. Probably a lack of intention on my part. When I returned, Drake sat on my bed, wearing nothing but a pair of boxers. His hair was smashed on one side, and his scars were pink where he lay on them. My stomach fluttered as I drank in his disheveled appearance.

"If you keep having those thoughts, you'll never make it to the office."

Fire erupted through my body as I sauntered toward him. "Oh?"

He lifted his head. The glowing burn made my knees buckle, and my sexy march turned into a stumble. His smooth laughter as he steadied me made it worse. "As much as I'd love to ravish you, I must check in with my team." He pulled me onto his lap, and his soft lips met mine.

I struggled to keep from drowning in desire as my fingers traced the prickly stubble on his jaw. "Can they wait?"

Another laugh rumbled through the room. "As long as you keep looking at me like that, everyone can wait."

I laid my head on his shoulder and soaked up his heat. "Thank you."

"For what?"

"Last night was my first good sleep since we left your horde."

"You needed it."

I pulled back. "What about you?" He spent the entire night holding me and using his mental magic and our bond to chase away the nightmares.

"I can sleep anywhere. I often take small naps throughout the day."

"Do you have nightmares?"

"Everyone has nightmares. The key is to learn a coping mechanism. You're doing better, but you haven't found it yet. I'll help you sleep until you do."

His words stayed with me as I marched into my office with renewed enthusiasm later that morning.

Verity wasn't at her desk, but Charlotte's wings buzzed as she hovered above her chair. "Umm...Your...Jenella. May I ask you a question?" Her gray skin flushed.

"Sure."

"When will you and Consort Drake have a match ceremony?"

My heart almost choked me when it leaped into my throat, and I had to lean against the desk so I didn't fall. "We haven't discussed it."

She nodded. "My grandmother suggested that it would help bring the factions together if you had it soon."

"Right. Um." I shuffled toward my office. "I'll talk to Drake."

A shy smile formed on her face. "I'll inform the other sprites you're working on it."

I rushed in and plopped into my chair. In all the time since I'd acknowledged our bond, a ceremony never once crossed my mind. But it should have. An official match ceremony with my chosen consort was expected. Everyone overlooked it because of Drake's First status, so I wrongly assumed I didn't have to have one. I loved Drake with an intensity equal to the sun. But it still terrified me.

I dismissed the thought and eyed my to-do list. Two difficult tasks needed my attention while I was well-rested. I stood and straightened the wrinkles in my suit jacket as I worked up some courage. Once I felt steady, I marched out of my office.

Several heads lifted when I entered the palace guard area. I ignored them as I stayed focused on reaching what used to be my brother's office without falling apart. I stopped outside and stared at the closed door.

"Your Grace, if I may?" Pablo, Mat's assistant, reached around me to open it.

"Thank you." I poked my head inside.

Mat's scent still lingered, along with some residual magic. Even though we transferred his workload to my office, his desk still looked the same. The dark hardwood floors gleamed. A war room table with several chairs took up one side, and a serviceable desk on the other. My glassy stare landed on the circular purple rug with our family crest in the center, and tears stung my eyes. I blinked them away.

Pablo often worked with Verity, but hadn't moved his things. He insisted on staying at his post outside Mat's office until I appointed another person to take over the palace guard. The idea of replacing my brother in any capacity cut deep, so I'd been putting it off.

He rested a gentle hand on my arm. "I will clear it out so you can focus on more important matters." As a boggart, Pablo could read emotions and anticipate needs. His statement made me wonder what he had picked up—probably the same sense of perseverance rolling off him.

More tears threatened to fall. No way I'd allow myself to cry. I'd already cried and screamed and cursed many times. It didn't accomplish a single thing. What I wanted more than anything was to heal. "Thanks, Pablo. But I should handle this. How about I take care of his personal belongings and you sort the business stuff?"

He searched my face before nodding. "I see. Of course. May I ask about your plans for me?"

My eyebrows slammed together. "What?"

"I've served Mathias for many years. Will you employ me elsewhere, or should I make other arrangements?"

"You can work in my office. If Verity agrees, you'll become my second Chief Aid. We've taken on a lot more work and need your help. The two of you can arrange your schedules, so you both have some days off."

A sad smile settled on his face. "I will discuss it with The Juror, Verity."

Gathering Mat's things broke my heart all over again. And I wasn't alone. When my eyes became weepy, Pablo handed me a handkerchief and squeezed my shoulder. When I heard him sniffle, I created a similar one and gave it to him. We worked in silence, packing away my brother's life.

When we were done, griffins swept in to move the boxes to storage, or Pablo's new work area near my office. When it was empty, I swallowed back the pain and forced my expression to remain neutral. "Put the rug with the family crest in my office, please." As I turned away, I felt hollow. But I wasn't done. I still had one more task, and it was a doozie.

The mage district's houses were brick and had three exterior styles. Small attic spaces with one window above the front porch made the one-story houses look like clones. The two-story houses were tall and skinny, with pop-out picture windows in the front. And the largest houses had multiple levels and more than one chimney. They all had pitched roofs and black shingles peeking through the snow.

I lowered my eyes and made sure my hood was in place as I walked. Everyone within a few miles could find me, thanks to my power radiating like a beacon, but the hood made me feel less exposed. Steam from my uneven breath rose in the chilly air as I drew closer to my destination. Even with the cold, there were still a few mages outside doing snow removal spells, and coming and going from the district. Some ignored me, while others stopped to gawk. Out of habit, I sipped their power.

The mage leader's house was a replica of the others, with its tan bricks and multi-layered roofs. I stopped outside, straightened my spine, and touched the wards.

The door opened, and a dark-haired woman appeared. "Well, hell. I wondered when you'd track me down."

I couldn't help but smile. "Hey, Emine. Mind if I come in?"

"Not if you're going to ask if I'm okay."

My mood sobered. "I don't plan to ask questions I already know the answer to."

She flashed to the wards and tugged me through. "Good. Because if one more well-wisher or pity-faced person shows up, I'll shoot first and ask questions later."

"As you should." I scanned the neighborhood and followed her up the steps. "So, are you planning to live here?"

She motioned for me to take a seat and closed the door. "Miss me, little sis?" The usual lilt of snark in her voice was absent.

I missed everything from her commentary to helping me break protocols while Mat lectured me about them. "Yes. And I need to know where you're at." As her eyes narrowed, I threw a hand in the air. "I'm not asking how you are. I meant I need to make sure the enforcers and mages have a leader."

She sighed as she plopped into a chair. "I don't have ruling magic, so I can't lead the mages." She scanned the room. "Rayar built this place for me and Mat. I suppose I'll need to sell it to the next leader."

I didn't understand how the passing of ruling magic worked, but my grandmother could grant it to people. "If you had ruling magic, what would you do?"

"Not gonna lie. I like leading the enforcers. But if I had ruling magic, I'd prefer to live here and whip the mages into shape." She rubbed her sad eyes. "I'm not moving back into the palace. I can't."

"You live where you want. If anyone gives you trouble, we'll team up and go all bank dragon on their ass."

The statement dragged a small cackle out of her. "That was a fun day."

It wasn't for me. I was working on my first case, and she inserted herself into an interview with the manager at The Bank of Mahri during my coronation week. We fought a dragon, where I bumbled my way through, and Emine fought him like an equal. "Yeah."

Tears filled her eyes. "I suppose you have a way to give me ruling magic?"

Technically, she was already the leader of the mages by default, since it was Mat's role, and she was his match. If she wanted to keep the position, I'd need to appoint a new head of enforcers and learn how to give her ruling magic. "No. But I'll work on it if you choose to lead the mages."

"I do. There are so many underutilized skills and a lack of cohesion. It might take time, but I have nothing better to do these days."

When I was a teenager, Mat used the house to try to coax me to unwrap my magic without prying eyes. I had fond memories of him trying to drag me out of my protective shell, while Bastien stood nearby and growled. The house was too big for one person. "Helen's going to have some griffins nest here when she decides you're ready."

"Fine by me. I miss the griffins. They're a hoot to mess with."

"Yeah." I wasn't sure how long I could sit in silence with her without drowning in my grief. My eyes darted toward the door. "Emine?"

Sheer pain reflected in her eyes as she twisted her head towards me.

I held her gaze so she could see my pain, too, and maybe feel less alone. "Losing Mat sucked and caused you a bunch of emotional shit. But news flash, we all have shit to deal with. And moping around avoiding everyone, you're just more shit. Is that what you want to be?" I repeated the words she said to me after I threw a childish tantrum. Though she delivered the line with confidence, where I barely choked out the last question.

Her eyes flashed. "So, you're saying I should get off my ass and deal with it?"

"Yes. And if you want help, find me. I'll be glad to cry or spar with you. I don't care how you handle it, but stop bottling the grief before it drags you, and everyone you care about, down."

"Stop. Being. Shit." We said in unison.

Emine cackled and stood. "You waited a long time to throw that back in my face."

"Too long." I climbed out of the plush chair. "I suppose I should head back before the entire castle descends on you with pitying looks."

"I've already warned everyone I'll shoot them. Before you go, I want to show you something."

We stepped inside an unmarked office building deep inside mage territory. Heads turned as Emine led me downstairs to a basement area. I gasped when raw mage magic choked my senses. "This is where the tech mages work?"

"Some. Most work from home and are scattered throughout the pockets. We also have four factories where they infuse human technology with spells. Any witch or mage can work there. But this is where they create spells and monitor the important stuff."

As we moved across the open-concept office, I noticed one witch and one mage sat at each workstation. Several heads turned our way, their eyes glowing from their work. "Is everyone creating spells?"

"No, ya idiot. These amazing folks work in intelligence."

A nearby mage flinched at her abrupt tone. I had to smile as a bit of Emine's personality peeked through. "We could use their skills to learn what's going on in the valley."

"Duh." She motioned me forward. "Ara said the Feds are watching Lily and Alex." She stopped next to a mage with dark hair. "This is Bree. She runs the tech mage operation. Bree, this is Her Grace, Queen Jenella."

"Hi, Bree." I managed an awkward wave as I began taking sips of magic from everyone in the room.

Intelligent brown eyes assessed me. "Your Grace. I was the prince's primary contact here. My condolences for your loss."

"Thank you." A foggy memory surfaced where Mat said something about how he worked with tech mages, but it was just out of reach. I'd need to read his notes or ask Pablo.

Emine saved me the embarrassment. "Mat had them tracking Bellicose activity. I requested they pivot toward humans after..." she trailed off.

The crack in her voice mixed with the sheer sadness rolling off her broke my heart as I leaned down to examine Bree's set-up. "I'm taking over Mat's duties, but Emine will still lead the mages. How difficult is it for you to gather information about government operations?"

She touched the screen, and deep blue magic activated an app. "Humans aren't like us. While we inject magic into our tech and rely on spells for security and innovation, they rely on things like encryption and have entire information security plans. Larger businesses teach their employees basic internet safety. The ones who work in cybersecurity practice hacking to become more skilled."

"Okay."

"Sorry. I'm rambling." She brought up a screen. "My point is, in the past, we could magically hack into many of their systems. Over the last year, they've pivoted."

"Pivoted how?"

"They're using magical security."

My heart raced as I spun toward Emine. "How does this affect us?"

She shrugged. "Unknown. But if they have access to tech mages and witches, they can block us from gathering so much information."

"Is it something we can work around?"

"Not without alerting them to our efforts."

I sighed. "Human agents are gathering information at the ruined Bellicose apartments. They have mobile devices."

Bree cocked her head. "We're on it. Lucky for us, their magical systems aren't well-developed yet, nor are they widespread. The challenge is to determine which systems and devices are unsecured. Sometimes, they hide magical traps. If we trip one, they throw us out. It's a time-consuming game we don't like to play."

"Can we alter our magic to circumvent their safeguards?"

"Sure. The witches are working on spells, and our top mages are absorbing and testing them in a sandbox."

Whatever that meant. "Thanks, Bree. Contact Pablo if you find anything about the agents."

"Will do." She turned back to her screen.

Emine tugged me toward the door as my mind reeled with the new information. If humans were using magic, someone was helping them. Probably someone who once worked for the Bellicose.

Emine pulled her gloves on. "Whatcha thinkin'?"

I pulled my hood over my head. "We need to learn everything we can about humans. They're resilient, and unlike us, aren't stuck in the past, clinging to protocols."

"Well, yeah. And they're always developing super fun new weapons. Unlike us, they don't have a choice but to move forward if they want to leave their mark on history, because they die so damn fast." Her voice hitched, and she fell silent until we stopped outside her wards. "Tell Helen she can send some griffins."

"Okay." I kicked a clump of snow and blinked back tears. "Please don't drift away from me. You're the only family I have left."

"A ton of people care about you."

"Yeah. But they're not you and Mat."

She lowered her head. "I'll do my best, but it hurts. I can't look at you without seeing him."

A tear streaked down my cheek. "Neither can I. Everything I do is because of Mat's influence. Drake says I'm lucky because he will always live through me, and I should cherish it. But it's hard when I can barely look at myself in the mirror without falling to pieces." I swiped a sleeve across my face. "So I guess we both have a lot to work through."

Emine squeezed my hand and strutted back through her wards. When she reached the door, she paused. "Don't let that dragon make you become too careful. You're more fun when you wing it."

Chapter Three

A few days later, I sat in the office I once dreaded and tried to focus. I remembered telling Mat how being a queen seemed like a cage. Back then, I didn't realize I had boxed myself in by being so stubborn. Since taking the throne, I'd never been so free. When I first noticed the shift in my attitude, I thought it was because Drake made sure we did something fun at least once per week. But I soon realized it was because I started to believe I could do whatever I wanted, and in the process, freed myself.

The piles of work Verity organized for me during my absence dwindled. But there was always more. As I trudged through a proposal from the Trolls to make their placement under human bridges permanent, my senses picked up a mass of power heading my way fast. I marked my place and lifted my head as the door slammed open.

The First Jonas stormed in and jabbed a finger towards the human television. "Turn it on!"

I folded my arms. "Why?"

"Turn. It. On!"

Alarm bells rang at the anger rolling off him. Not wanting him to shift into a dinosaur in my office, I raced to the conference table and grabbed the remote.

Verity stomped in. "Family or not, you don't get to bypass me and interrupt Jen whenever you're in a tizzy."

His eyes flashed amber. "The human authorities have taken my kids."

An electric jolt of fear raced through me. Alex could kill with his mind, and Lily was too fast to catch. I found it hard to believe anyone could trap them. "Wait. What? Who?"

Verity pulled the remote from my hand and smashed the power button.

Jonas tossed a phone onto the table. "Ann Marie found this inside Alex's car. They allowed themselves to be arrested."

"They have a ton of power, so why not use it? Especially when half the police force works for you. Or me."

The TV came to life, showing a house on fire near downtown. *The cause of the fire is unknown. Police are investigating the incident and believe it's arson. Three persons of interest are in custody.* The camera zoomed in on the fire before pictures of Lily, Alex, and Elsie appeared on the screen. *Thirty-one-year-old Liliana First, twenty-five-year-old Alexander First, and thirty-five-year-old Sharon Baxter were spotted entering the residence moments before the house exploded.*

I swung to Verity. "Have Pablo contact our plants inside their government. Force the authorities to let them go."

"On it." She raced out.

Jonas grabbed the phone and hit 'play' on a video. It started with Alex's voice warning Lily not to do anything other than request a lawyer. A cop tapped on the window, and Lily complied without a fight. A woman said something in the background as they searched the vehicle.

"What are you thinking, Jonas?"

"You have the power and resources, so use them to save my kids. Something spooked Alex, and I will not lose another child to this war."

"You think I should flash into a jail blind, find three people, and make them disappear?"

"Yes."

"I'm not very good at flashing to places I've never seen. Even if I were, I'd need to consider the consequences before rescuing them." I tapped the phone. "You heard Alex. He picked something alarming out of their minds. Stop looking at me like I'm prey. I'm right."

He planted both hands on the conference table and took some deep breaths. "So, you won't rescue them?"

"I didn't say that. But I need to think before I act." My hands shot into a defensive gesture when he growled. "I'm trying to be less impulsive. And if any situation has ever called for a pause and think moment, it's this one."

He jammed the phone into his pocket. "Fine. Let's think fast and get to the part where you save my kids from walking themselves to their deaths." Pure anguish reflected in his eyes. "I can't lose another child. If anything happens to them, you'll need to put me down."

I could never work up the courage to kill Jonas. "We'll save them."

Drake rushed in my direction, and I glanced at his office as Verity popped her head through the privacy spell. "Pablo convinced them to declare the explosion a gas leak."

"A what?"

"Humans use what they call natural gas to heat their homes. It's highly flammable. If there's a leak, it can explode."

"Okay. As long as the humans release them."

Drake emerged from his office, fire in his eyes. "Jonas." He somehow made Jonas's name a warning.

A warning Jonas ignored. "Drake."

Bastien slipped in behind him. "Glacintial believes the human authorities are moving them to another location."

A popping sound came from Jonas's knuckles when he clenched his fists. "Where?"

Drake positioned himself between us. "It doesn't matter. They're highly capable, and we have eyes on them. I've sent one of Lily's dragon friends to help Glacintial. They'll intervene if needed."

Jonas unclenched his fists. "I'm going to find the god. He's been sniffing around my daughter and might have the skills to retrieve them."

"I've already notified him. Cavil has retrieved several of our people caught up in government sweeps."

It was news to me, and I wondered what Drake had been up to while I buried myself in work and grief. I didn't care if he made decisions without me, but I needed to know what was happening. An old scab from Mat withholding information festered. Instead of letting the anger rise, I focused on Jonas. "If he can rescue them, he will. If not, we'll do something else." I still believed Lily and Alex would rescue themselves, but everyone needed help sometimes. "Bas, find out why Alex allowed their arrest."

"Of course." His black eyes stayed glued to the angry First.

Jonas ignored the scrutiny. "Text me their location when you find it." The door slammed behind him.

Bastien tore his eyes away. "I'm going to discuss solutions with my mother. Be careful around him, Jenella."

I leaned against Drake to soak up his warmth and confidence. "Sure." When he launched from Drake's balcony, I sighed. "I won't allow them to hurt my sister or take another child away from Ann Marie and Jonas. But we need to be smart about how we handle it. The government is already blocking the tech mages and looking for hybrids."

Ara breezed in, her long ponytail swaying behind her. Dark circles lined her eyes. She waved Verity off. "It's fine, dear. I'll only be a few minutes."

"We need to establish better security before I drop people at your door," Verity said through clenched teeth.

"Sure." I separated from Drake and motioned for her to sit. I'd never seen Ara look so ragged, so I waited for her to speak first.

She smoothed her T-shirt. "I need to inform you of Quin's and Lily's recent antics."

I had no idea what she'd say next, but I knew I wouldn't like it. "Oh?"

"My love is trying to train Lily, and they have turned eight federal agents."

"What!?" I swung toward Drake. "Did you know about this?"

He refused to meet my eyes. "Yes."

My mouth hung open, and I clenched and unclenched my fists. "Great. Is that why the humans kidnapped her and Alex?"

Ara held up a hand. "Of course not. The first one was an accident. The rest were going to die. Lily has three under her power, and we absorbed the rest. I have Lily's feral one under my control. Once he learns his place, the entire batch will make excellent vampires."

I rubbed my eyes. Vampire turnings weren't my business if they didn't break coalition law. As the Queen of Umbra, Ara chose who they turned. The only time I could involve myself was if they exposed their actions to humans or another faction filed a complaint. And I wasn't sure if the situation qualified. "Right. I thought Lily didn't want a house."

"She does not. However, it is inevitable because of her base instincts. But I am not here to debate semantics."

"What *are* you here to discuss?" I should have thanked her for the information, but I didn't have it in me.

"Lily and Alex's arrest. I believe my brother, Roman, was involved."

My shoulders slumped. "He betrayed her?"

"Perhaps. I have yet to hear from him on the matter." She paused. "Lily cannot let this stand without appearing weak to the other masters."

"What does 'let it stand' mean in vampire terms?"

"It means she will need to eliminate or blood bond him." She smoothed her skirt. "I am quite anguished about how this has turned out. I wished to ease my granddaughter into vampire politics."

"Yeah. It's not right to force her into running a house. If he kills her, I'll crush him." Thoughts of what I'd do to the guy flooded my mind, and I shook it to clear them.

Ara stood. "Do not worry, dear. Lily will win. Though less experienced, she is more powerful, thanks to her lovely mage magic. Tarquin turned five vampires, and I took in Lily's rogue. I must return before he kills them." Ara paused. "Will you keep me updated on their escape?"

Too deep in thought to respond, I nodded. The moment she disappeared from my senses, I spun to Drake. "You're keeping secrets from me."

"Secrets?"

"Cavil retrieving our people? Or how about Lily turning federal agents?"

Drake's eyes heated. "*You* approved the government rescues and Cavil's involvement. And I asked Lily to contact you because it wasn't my secret to tell."

My gaze landed on the desk. "Oh. When did I approve the rescues?"

"Most likely when you were half asleep." Drake stood and extended his hand. "Which is why I will stay with you every night."

"What? No. You shouldn't upend your life because of my nightmares. I've dealt with them forever." Though I had to admit, it sounded like pure bliss. The old and new nightmares didn't dare show themselves when Drake was around. "I haven't heard from Lily since we returned. Why didn't she text me?"

"Perhaps she's busy."

Or she didn't want me in her life. After all, Verity dragged her to Allure to do my job. And before she even knew me, I took her to a jungle to wake her first and planted a pocket in her backyard. "I'm grumpy and off balance."

He pulled me to my feet and feathered soft kisses down my temple. When a tickle of breath touched my ear, he pulled back. "You're used to Mathias withholding information. Must I remind you I am not him?"

Good point. I was used to living in a pattern that no longer existed. My breath hitched at the thought. I'd give anything to storm into Mat's office and argue with him. I rested my forehead on Drake's massive chest. "There's no mistaking you for anyone else. So, you think I need a babysitter to help me sleep?" I sent lust through the bond.

He sucked air between his teeth. "Not a babysitter, no." Drake lifted my chin until our eyes met. "But I can no longer leave you alone with the torment your mind creates when it relaxes."

I kept my gaze locked on his while I thought through the arguments I could make. "Thank you. If we can't sleep, I have some ideas about what we can do."

A suggestive grin spread across his face. "As do I."

I dragged him toward the adjoining door to his office. "Like planning our match ceremony and your coronation."

He groaned, then flipped me around and pulled me against him by the ass. "We don't need a ceremony. We have a dragon bond."

I rubbed myself against him and trembled when my desire threatened to burn me alive. "Tell royal protocol and your adoring masses we don't need one. I dare you."

His lips touched mine. When I tried to deepen the kiss, he pulled back. "We will discuss it later, when we're *not* sleeping." He released me and continued toward his desk. "Oh, and Jenella?"

My eyes trailed over his hard body as I drank him in. "Yes."

His lips twitched. "Pull your mind out of the gutter."

I chuckled as he launched from the balcony. That dragon had me hook, line, and sinker.

It took three days for Glacintial to report back to Bastien on Lily's whereabouts. Meanwhile, I'd been to her house to talk to Ann Marie and Jonas twice. "Third time's a charm," I mumbled as I materialized outside the wards in the colorful hybrid pocket. Pride swelled inside me when I saw how well-coordinated the bright colors were, even if they were odd. I tapped the wards.

The god, Cavil, appeared beside me and patted his messy hair. "Hello, Jenella."

"Cavil. Were you able to get inside the prison?"

"Yes. Lily won't leave. She believes Alex has a plan."

"Did you visit Alex?"

"Yes. He believes Lily has a plan. It's maddening. But I won't give up on Lily, not only because I am oath-bound, but because she is my soulmate."

"Sure." A million questions were on the tip of my tongue, but I swallowed them when Ann Marie appeared with one of Lily's dragon buddies.

She pulled us through. "Where are they, Cavil?"

He shrugged. "She wouldn't come with me. Lily fears that if they disappear, Jenella will blame her for the fallout."

"That's ridiculous," I said. "Humans are already searching for us. It's how they found Lily."

"She assured me she'd wreck the place and escape should they hurt Alex or Elsie."

"Good." The urge to pace was almost overwhelming. "How many humans are in the building?"

"Many. I warded the office areas to protect them, but what will happen when she uses her magic is unknown."

Lily's magic liked to do dark things, and she only partially controlled the violent little surprises. "I'll work on protecting the humans. You work on convincing her to leave."

"It's my sworn duty to protect Lily." His eyes trailed over me. "Release some magic before you explode. Have you learned how to control the powers you've absorbed so you can mimic?"

"Somewhat." Not really. I hadn't lifted a finger to learn my magic other than when I released my ever-present ball of anger by pounding on rocks. "I have an idea, but I need to run it by Lily when she gets back."

"If," Ann Marie interjected. "Don't underestimate the power and reach of the world's governments."

Her words stung, but I didn't comment because, like everyone, she knew more about it than I did. "That reminds me. Are any hybrids willing to teach council members about human governments?"

She shrugged. "I'll ask Dale."

"Thanks. If Lily and Alex don't escape soon, I'll order the dragons to act."

"Good. I sent some of our lawyers, but they weren't allowed past the lobby."

I flashed to the circle at the palace and rushed to the back door. It swung open as I approached, and a stately older gentleman's blue eyes settled on me. "Welcome home, Jenella."

A smile lit my face. "Hello, George. It's good to be home."

The conversation between Tracy and Quin halted when I entered my office. My eyes narrowed. "Verity, call the surrounding pockets and explain how destructive Alex and Lily can be. Send teams to the area to save as many people as possible."

"On it." She motioned toward my friends. "Quin already alerted the local vampires, and we have a group of healers nearby."

I focused on my friends. "Does healing magic work on humans?"

"Potions don't," Tracy said. "At least one ingredient is always grown in the pockets. A person needs to have magic for it to activate."

"Yeah. I've never tried to heal a human."

Verity squeezed my arm. “I’ll ask the healers about it. Chances are, some of them have tried.”

“Thank you.”

Quin emerged from his vampire stupor. “I wish to make a request.”

I plopped into a chair. “Oh?”

“Do not look at me that way.”

“Like what?”

“I simply wondered if you would grant Lily clemency for her transgressions.”

I bit back a laugh. “Do you mean for turning three federal agents, or what she’s about to do? Because vampire turning doesn’t fall under my jurisdiction. And we’re sending in teams to minimize the damage.” My attention turned to Tracy. “She wouldn’t leave with Cavil because she’s afraid I’ll blame her for confirming our existence.”

“It’s a valid concern. I mean, she’s going to open a lot of eyes when she escapes.”

“Yeah.”

“Unless the turning causes issues for the coalition,” Quin continued, as if the other conversation didn’t happen.

“If anyone questions it, I’ll take the blame.”

“How?”

“It was my fault we took so long to clear the area. You and Lily used the opportunity allotted to you by the predator laws to bolster your numbers. If you don’t exceed the number of vampires lost in the previous two battles, it’s a solid legal argument.”

He tilted his head. “There is one more issue.”

“Issue?”

“I believe Roman had a very specific reason for his antics. He portrays himself as a kindly gentleman, but I guarantee you, he is not.”

“Again, not my jurisdiction.”

He leaned forward. "Yes. Let's pretend you are not concerned about your sister."

"Of course I'm concerned. But Lily's tough, and I can't interfere with vampire disputes unless another faction is affected."

"Lily is a mage of Ahl and a vampire. A hybrid. She fits into three factions."

True. "So, you're saying everything she does affects three factions?"

"Perhaps you should try to use your critical thinking skills."

"I'm all out of those, so you'll need to clarify."

"Should Roman hold her territory, which if he wants to, he will, she will never again trust a pureblood. Including you."

"So, you think I should rig the fight in Lily's favor?"

"She would not forgive you if you did. But perhaps you could speak to Roman. My love has already tried, and he won't listen to her."

I scratched my head. "How about if I bully him into letting Lily win?"

"Perhaps I have not made myself clear."

"I'll do what I can to protect Lily. But why would Roman listen to me?"

Tracy scooted her chair out. "I mean, her territory is for hybrids, and he doesn't qualify, so he can't hold it, right?"

"It depends on the contract he made with Jonas. If his house is part of their community, he can."

Quin jumped out of his seat so fast that I flinched. The TV's volume increased.

The screen showed a multi-story building swaying. Golden flames shot into the air as people on the ground sprinted away. My heart pounded as it imploded, and dust plumes cascaded through two city blocks. As it settled, people stumbled around, dazed. When a reporter came on, I braced myself. No matter how we tried to spin it, we could not cover up the use of magic. It was time to face the humans.

Chapter Four

My advisors filtered into the conference room as Thaddeous and his expanding group of leprechauns finished setting up the catering.

Deva leaned down and kissed Drake's cheek. The sadness that plagued her for months was still present, but had faded a bit. "Hello, love."

"Hey, Deva. Have you heard from Glacintial?" He was near Lily and Alex when the building imploded. We hadn't heard from them, but I hoped they made it out.

"I'm pleased to announce our two heroes are safe inside a pocket and awaiting transport. My dragons are watching over them."

My shoulders relaxed. "Thank you."

"Of course. It is the least I can do after you allowed me the freedom to hunt my enemies." She referred to how I set her loose on the Bellicose after the battle that killed my brother and almost took out her and Drake.

Drake squeezed my hand. *Are you ready for this?*

We planned for this when we fought the Bellicose inside the city.

Razazia flittered in and settled beside Olwen, the Snow Elf King. He glowered at her before turning his attention to me. "After the meeting, I'd like a word with you."

"Sure." Olwen was one of my most reserved advisors and one of my original allies. If he needed something, I'd do my best.

Emine strutted in silently and took the chair to my left. I ignored the sheer pain emanating from her, because I understood. The entire palace seemed hollow without Mat storming through it, barking orders.

After everyone settled, I rested my hands on the table. "As many of you are aware, the humans have learned about us. They detained Lily and Alex First a few days ago. The two broke out of their prison this morning."

Razazia smirked. "Interesting way to describe Lily's spectacular display of power."

I shrugged. "We understood something like this might happen when we waged war in a suburb. We're here to decide what to do about it."

Jonas rubbed his tired eyes. "We can't start a war with the humans. They outnumber us and have weapons capable of our destruction. Even if they didn't, the Firsts are oath-bound to protect and help them."

"Oath or not, I agree," Emine said, her voice void of emotion. "We're gathering more information about their weapons."

I nodded in agreement. "We need creative solutions."

"You're going to want to see this." Verity projected the image from her tablet to the TV.

The entire group turned and watched as one of our transports blinked into existence, then faded. It came back into view a split second before it exploded, spreading a long line of fire through a snow-covered field. Human authorities descended on it from every direction.

My heart thundered as I hopped to my feet. "Tell me Lily wasn't on the transport."

Deva's eyes took on a bronze glow. "They were on it. Glacintial and Lyran witnessed them leave the area. Should I send the dragons after them?"

I wanted to say yes, but had to consider the other passengers. Lily and Alex could escape, while other paranormals couldn't. "No. Have the dragons help the others."

"Of course, love."

Ann Marie tapped on her phone with a shaky hand. "I'll see if Cavil can track them down."

"Ara, can the local vampire house help evacuate?"

"Yes."

I squeezed Drake's shoulder. He was unusually calm, considering the situation. I wanted to ask him why, but decided it could wait. "Verity, have Pablo ground all transports until we figure out what happened. I need updates on the status of the passengers when you have them. Please."

Ann Marie took Jonas's hand. "Yes. We're going to stay at Lily's house until she returns. The climate in the hybrid pocket is...tense since Roman moved in, and she has two new vampires who need guidance and protection."

"Thank you." I watched them disappear. "Anyone who wants to work on crisis management, grab a sandwich and head to my office." I breezed out the door.

Drake followed me out the door. "It will be okay."

"Will it? Because it didn't look okay to me. And why are you so calm?"

"Because it will be okay."

"Bullshit. You know as well as I do what this means."

"Yes. It was inevitable since Anitta built the pockets to isolate us under the guise of our safety. The segregation was never going to last."

I stopped and swung toward him. "Explain."

His eyes flicked towards my advisors, who followed us at a respectful distance. "I'll explain when we have more privacy."

I continued down the hall when he sent calm reassurance through the bond. "Verity, contact the Leadership Council and ask them to brainstorm creative ways to reveal ourselves to humans. We need to control the narrative as much as possible. Also, let's start our lessons. I don't care how confident the leaders are, they need to take part." Some of them would proclaim themselves experts without a shred of knowledge. "If they resist, ban them and their people from leaving the pockets." I swung toward Deva. "Too harsh?"

A wry look settled on her face. "They've come to expect extreme actions from you when you stand on principle, love."

After Verity asked a few questions for clarity, I scanned my advisors. "Start brainstorming."

As we reached the stairs, guards scrambled to push a tour group back. A man pulled two young hybrid girls towards the door. His intentions didn't sit right with me. Deva's head snapped to them, and she veered in their direction. It was a reminder of how much trust I put in her. I didn't even notice when she read my thoughts. I needed to work on blocking her and Alex automatically, like my defensive magic once did.

Several hours later, my phone pinged, interrupting the meeting. I pulled up the text from Ann Marie and sighed in relief. "Cavil has them. They were in awful shape, so he's giving them time to recover. They'll be here tomorrow."

Razazia leaned forward. "And what about the other seventy-two passengers? Or are we no longer worried about them?"

I glared at her. "I don't have the patience for your snark tonight."

Deva stood. "Thanks to my dragons and the local vampire house, the passengers are safe. The self-destruct system on the transport worked as planned."

"Thank you, Deva." I tapped my foot and tried to clear my foggy head. "Let's call it a night. The Council meets tomorrow. I'd like to hear what they come up with, and what Lily and Alex discovered before making more decisions."

"Excellent. We will return in the morning." Ara and Quin vanished.

The others filtered out until only Tracy, Drake, and Olwen remained. "What's up, Olwen?"

"Your avoidance of Mage Mountain offends the Rübezahl. I've also heard from the Sasquatch King. He asked me to inform you he didn't authorize his tribes to work with the Bellicose."

I'd completely forgotten about the Rübezahl and Sasquatches. Too many other problems were weighing me down. "I'll contact them once we handle the immediate crisis."

Drake covered his mouth with his hand. Probably to keep from telling me there was always another crisis.

Tracy had no such filter. "I mean, it's probably never going to calm down."

I shut my eyes. "Right. I'll set aside some time after I meet with my sister and the Council."

He bowed his head. "Thank you. Razazia does not condone my involvement in the Mage Mountain communities and didn't want me to pass on the information."

"Why?" It didn't sound like her. She loved to stir the pot and the weirdos who lived in Mage Mountain were ripe for the picking.

He sighed. "Something about the mountain bothers her. She's afraid the odd magic has influence over us."

The magic from Mage Mountain was strange, colorful, and beautiful. It was almost certainly my grandmother's resting place. "What does the mountain have to do with you passing the message along?"

"She won't discuss it. It's been the home of my tribe my entire life and I have experienced nothing but repulsion from the magic within the mountain."

"The pocket also bothers me." Drake's voice sounded bland and uninterested. "I'll discuss it with Razazia."

"Thank you. And if you could contact the two factions, I would appreciate it."

"Sure."

As soon as Olwen cleared the privacy bubble, I swung back around. "Razazia knows it's my grandmother."

Tracy shook her head. "I mean, it's easy to piece together. Your magic feels so similar, only a fool would think otherwise."

I blinked. "Which means more people have noticed."

"Perhaps, but it is a desolate pocket with a small population, so it won't be many." Drake stood. "I'm going to eavesdrop on the human agents. Notify me when you hear from Lily." He tapped his temple.

"Okay." I turned to Tracy. "I have three goals to meet before summer."

She rested her chin on her hand. "Let me guess. You want to reach out to your grandmother, learn everything you can about humans, and do some other insane thing while dragging me with you."

"Close. The first two are right. The last is to go to Mahri to find the last First. It's not necessary for you to tag along. And everyone needs to learn more about humans." Though most paranormals were miles ahead of me in that department, including Tracy. I'd need supplemental classes.

"I mean, there's no way Drake and Bastien are going to let you go alone."

"Drake will. Or he'll let me have the illusion of going alone." I stood and stretched. "I hate Mahri, but need to visit the castle every year now that Mat can't do it for me. And we already suspect Celia is resting there."

"No, we weren't sure because we were too busy looking for Gorman." She shuffled toward the door. "And you're my best friend, so I'm not letting you go alone. If you leave me, I'll slip you a potion that will give you excessive body hair."

A bright smile lit my face. I didn't mind going alone, but always preferred having Tracy with me. "We'll go when our schedules allow for a quick trip."

She sighed. "If I can get away. Deva insists I learn all I can about dragons, and now that we're not discriminated against as much, Bastien wants me to spend more time with them."

"They're fun. Lily has several dragon friends."

"Because she's a drinker. And I adore dragons. But I'm a witch. I want to create new potions and spells with my dad, run my business, and guard you when you do crazy stuff."

"Deva and Bastien are trying to discourage you?"

"Only about you doing crazy things. But they take up a big chunk of my time. I mean, I like Deva, and Bastien has my heart. But I'm not a dragon. I'll need to set some clear boundaries. Which, as you found out the hard way, is hard to do when Deva's involved."

"Yeah. She'll roll right over you if you let her. You can come here if you need a place to hide so you can think."

She almost blinded me when her face lit up. Not because she had light magic like Cavil, but because my BFF was perhaps the most beautiful being alive. "I will. I better get back to my dad. He's already trying to create healing potions that will work on humans. Shoot me a text if you need anything."

"Tell him I said thank you." I turned back toward the TV and pumped the volume up.

Three hours later, Verity came in, saw what was on the screen, and laughed. "I thought you were watching the news."

"They were repeating the same stuff, so I changed the channel. I thought this might give me some idea about human culture."

"It's an old sitcom and things have changed, so it'll be wrong."

"No kidding? Huh. It's funny."

"Yes. Most sitcoms are."

I pushed a button on the remote. "What do you make of this?"

She leaned in for a closer look. "It's blurry."

"Hang on." I boosted the enhancement spell and pointed at three places on the frozen picture. "There, there, and there."

"It could be the way the light's reflecting."

"The flames are gold. Those bystanders have red eyes."

"Vampires?"

"Or demons. I sent it to Ara for her opinion."

Verity straightened. "Interesting. How about a human lesson in the morning?"

She had spent most of her life believing she was human and was an excellent teacher. "You already have too much work."

"Says you. Come in an hour early so we aren't interrupted."

"Deal. But only if you go home and relax."

"I was coming to tell you we have the Council working on developing lesson plans. They'll present them at the meeting."

"Thank you."

The savory aroma of food cooking made my stomach growl as I wandered toward the table where Emine, Mat, Drake, and I used to gather for meals. I'd been eating in my apartment since Mat's death because I couldn't stand being anywhere that reminded me of him. Drake made sure I ate at least some food, but I'd lived on snacks, rather than full meals.

The kitchen doors opened as Helen burst out of it. "Jenella. Have a seat and I'll bring your dinner."

A sense of loneliness almost drowned me. "No, thank you."

"Nonsense. Sit and eat. I insist." She pulled a chair out and disappeared into the kitchen.

I tiptoed toward the chair, half expecting Mat to come stomping in to lecture me about my duties. At least it was dead center, instead of on the end. I scooted forward and blinked back tears.

Helen returned with a heaping plate of food. One of her sons followed and poured wine and water. When he left, Helen and George sat across from me.

A single tear escaped, and I used my napkin to catch it. I noticed the extra plate beside me. "Drake's in the valley tonight."

"Oh, don't you worry."

The bond lit up when I checked it. "I see."

A smug expression appeared on her face as she sipped her water. "I'm always aware of where the members of my nest are. And in this kitchen, no one eats alone."

I somehow forgot how insistent she was about sitting with anyone who needed company. "Thank you, Helen. For everything you've done for me."

"None of that, now." She twisted in her chair as Drake appeared. "It's what family does."

I didn't respond. Partially because I didn't have words, but mostly because my thoughts scattered when I spotted Drake.

He slid his chair in and sipped his wine. "You outdid yourself again, Helen."

Her face flushed. "Thank you. But I can't take the credit. George cooked this meal. It's his specialty."

The spicy barbeque was delicious, and the company even better as the four of us ate as a family. It felt like my world wasn't tilted sideways, which was rare since Mat's death.

Chapter Five

Learning about humans was a lot of work, I decided as I flipped through the civics book Verity brought with her. "So, this is an overview of the federal government?"

"Yes, if you ignore the backroom deals and pandering for money that takes up ninety percent of the elected officials' jobs." She tapped the hologram, and a basic model popped up. "Other countries don't allow businesses to inject money into their elections, but in the U.S., it's a complicated and ongoing argument."

"It's also not my business. I only need a basic understanding."

"Good. When you learn structure, we'll move on to law, and Titus will take over. He's a licensed attorney. As far as teaching you culture, it varies widely throughout the country, so I need time to create a lesson plan."

"You could recommend videos for me to watch. I only need to learn enough not to be completely ignorant."

"I'll talk to Titus. Now, let's begin."

Even though the book was boring, I found the lesson fascinating. If I had studied it a few years earlier, I would have proposed a new form of government to Mat as an alternative to my taking the throne. He would have clenched his jaw and explained the differences between the coalition and human governments. When I mentioned it to Verity, she laughed because, without a strong power structure, the most powerful would bully an elected mid-level paranormal into doing their bidding. Verity said it happens with humans, too. But their perception of power was different and often revolved around titles, money, and charisma.

As we finished for the day, Drake strolled in, peered over my shoulder, and laughed. "If you want an accurate representation of how they operate, you will not find it in a book."

"Oh?" I snapped the book closed. "Verity mentioned backroom deals. I'm not sure if I could stomach listening to those."

"You wouldn't like them, no. Moving in the shadows isn't your preference." He squeezed my shoulder. "Speaking of which, Alex and Lily are due to arrive soon. Would you like to fly?"

My stomach churned with a delicious blend of anticipation and excitement. One of my favorite things was flying with Drake. "Absolutely. I need to grab a coat." I was good at creation magic unless making detailed items like clothes. The baggy, casual ones were passable, but the more tailored clothes still came out a little lopsided. I made a note to practice like I did building structures, which I was great at.

Pablo cleared his throat as we passed him. "Mistress Ara will meet you at the gate."

"Thanks. Any updates on the casualties from the implosion?"

"Our people were in place and minimized the damage. The enforcers, along with the god Cavil's preventative measures, were effective. The current death toll is nineteen. We suspect they were targeted deaths."

"Targeted?"

"Yes. Approximately five fell victim to mental magic, and the rest were crushed. The team of enforcers who witnessed the incident said Lily used her magic to protect some, but not others. Our team evacuated the ones she spared." Pablo shifted his weight. "There was an incident outside a pocket near the transport crash site where a group of militia shot at something but cannot remember who or what."

I rubbed my face. "It had to be Alex."

"Or dragons," Drake said.

"Are the humans okay?"

"Yes, though they are now convinced aliens abducted them."

I suppressed a laugh. "Thanks, Pablo."

"You're welcome. I will continue to monitor human activity surrounding the pockets."

"You have my permission to deploy resources as needed. Also, call Emine and Calvin. See if they will work together to better hide our transports."

He started to bow, thought better of it, and inclined his head. "Of course."

I turned to Drake. "Ready?"

Icy air sliced across my cheeks as we descended toward the gate. I leaned against my favorite spike and surrounded myself with a warm air bubble. The clothes I wore were spelled for warmth, but the wind still cut to the bone. A few gate guards watched us approach, their eyes wide. I spotted Ara and Quin near the entrance. Quin had his nose in his phone, a deep scowl on his face. Ara leaned against him, watching the gate.

I flashed to them as Drake circled the area one more time before cloaking himself. "Hey, Ara. Quin."

Quin lowered his phone. "Jen. What is your First doing?"

"No idea." I leaned forward to see the gate better. "Are they here yet?"

Ara clasped her hands. "They should arrive shortly."

"Good. Any word on why Roman targeted her?"

"Yes. But I cannot disclose his reasons. Nor can I fight him on her behalf. Even if I want to."

"That makes two of us. I keep telling myself it's none of my business."

"Unlike other members of her family, Lily can take care of herself," Quin said.

"Rude."

"Sometimes, blunt is the optimal way to emphasize a point. I shall rejoin you at the palace." He vanished.

I will also meet you there. Drake flew away.

I waited until they faded from my senses. "What's up with Quin lately?"

"His protective instincts irritate him. My love has spent a thousand years without creating a single vampire or caring about anyone but me. Now, he has five new vampires who require constant care, and he wishes to protect you, Tracy, Lily, and Alex. He cannot be everywhere at once and believes he let Lily down."

I knew Quin considered me and Tracy his. He even said as much. And he'd spent an awful lot of time with Lily. Like me, he understood he couldn't claim Lily without also claiming Alex. "Can I help?"

"Do not worry about him. He will adjust like he always does, dear."

"Since I have a blood bond with him, can I send him energy or reassurance?"

Her tinkering laugh sent shivers down my spine. "No. You may give him orders, monitor his feelings, and find his location. Unless you issue an order and enforce it, you cannot help."

"Not interested."

"Think of it as a lifeline. Like your dragon bond, you can always use it to reach out for help. Otherwise, it is best ignored."

I doubted Quin ignored it. As a matter of fact, I was almost certain he monitored me. Drake assured me that I was the master, and Quin couldn't feel much. It still bothered me.

Cavil appeared beyond the gate with Alex, Elsie, and Lily. They looked rumpled and exhausted. "What are they doing?" I asked as they moved to the back of the line.

Ara sighed. "Lily refuses to acknowledge her title, and the others appease her."

"Huh." I would, too, if I still wore glamour.

The gate guards glanced at us. When we didn't respond, they sped up their check-in process, barely stopping to ask questions.

Ara wrapped Lily in a hug as soon as she stepped past the gate.

Alex came through, talking excitedly with Glacintial and a silver dragon. Elsie hung her head as she hovered behind Lily. No one needed healing.

Cavil detached himself from a small group of admirers and raised a hand in greeting.

I lifted a hand to wave back when I noticed Lily's eyes on me, so I slammed my fists on my hips. "What did the humans do to make you blow up their building?"

"They tore out a fang." She pointed at a missing tooth. "I restrained myself at first. Then they drugged, tortured, and threatened Alex and Elsie, and I lost my shit."

I pretended to be confused. She was unaware how involved we were in finding them. "Holy hell. Why did you let them close enough to take your fang?"

"Humans aren't acting alone. Several men were there with some kind of odd magic, including the guy with the spelled pliers. When we escaped, they sent humans coated in magic into a nearby pocket to shoot up the transport station."

"I heard. Did you read them?" Lily couldn't read intentions like me, but she was excellent at assessing magic level and type.

"Yeah. Sort of."

I noticed Alex smirking at me, and bit back my own smile. The guy always figured out how to read my mind. "Let's go somewhere more private to go over the details."

As we rode the palace's elevator, Lily stared at her feet. "So, how much trouble am I in?"

"Trouble?"

"Yeah. For exposing us to humans. Last I checked, it's against coalition law."

A million answers came to mind. But I didn't think she'd appreciate how Deva, Ara, and I worked to shield her, so I hesitated. Thankfully, the elevator beeped and saved me.

Verity noticed the look on my face as we passed. "Need me for anything?"

"No." I nodded as subtly as I could. "Unless you want to know what the humans are doing?"

She pressed her lips together. "I do."

Alex snorted.

After we settled, I examined Lily's wary face. "To answer your question, you're not in much trouble. It was my decision to expose us to humans, and Roman chose to blow up his house when he knew they were watching. You did what you needed to do."

"And you did it spectacularly." Ara beamed with pride. Vampires admired violence more than most. "Now, tell me. How did you end up in a federal facility?"

They *let* themselves be arrested, believing Ann Marie and Jonas would use the human legal system to save them. Alex read the humans and decided it was the safest way to handle the situation. But the humans had other ideas. The moment we convinced the authorities it was a gas leak, they whisked them across the country where they met the people with strange magic.

Alex and Elsie had videos and took notes on their phones. It was excellent intelligence, but I hesitated to say so. Alex picked up my thoughts and agreed to send me the information.

Lily shifted her weight. "That reminds me. I left my phone in Alex's car."

"Glacintial saw the whole incident. Jonas recovered Alex's car and your phone." Lily's magic flared, and I blanketed her with my senses to study it. "What did they do to your magic?"

She wouldn't meet my eyes. "Other than ripping my fang out by the root and collecting some spit full of blood, they didn't do anything. I got the fang back."

"Our blood registers as human," Ara said.

Lily nodded. "The magic on the guy who took it felt inverted, and he looked grotesque when he shifted."

"It may be from the realm of Gartolia. They are a warring realm that enjoys invading lesser societies. Your description is in line with one of their weaker factions," Cavil explained.

Drake, who'd been listening from his office, joined us. "What did you say about Gartolia?"

Cavil held out a stack of foreign money. "I took these from the facility."

Drake took the money, examined it, and handed it to me. "What did you learn, Alex?"

I half listened to Alex's explanation as I studied the coin. It seemed wrong. Almost as if infused with foreign magic. Close to the stuff I'd come across twice, but not quite.

"...it's almost like they're being fed false information on purpose."

My attention snapped back to Alex. "We haven't heard from our contacts. Was there any sign of them?"

"No. A few guys in the lower level were pondering the mechanics of magic scanning devices. Others were thinking about a few of your people who work in the government. They were arrested but disappeared when the guards left them alone."

Cavil nodded. "I rescued them. I offered to do the same for Lily, but she declined because she worried about exposing her magic."

Lily stiffened, and her head swung toward him. "Why didn't you tell me others had disappeared? If I'd known, I would have left with you in a second."

"I tried to tell you, but you said Alex had a plan. No one expected you to destroy the entire building."

"Yeah. I lost my temper."

Alex cleared his throat. "When they arrested us, I had a plan. Once they transferred us, it wasn't an option. I knew Glacintial followed us when we were on that airplane. If Lily didn't destroy the building, the dragons would have. He was waiting for permission from Deva."

I kept my eyes on my sister. She had sharp critical thinking skills. It surprised me she didn't understand what Cavil was trying to say. My eyes darted toward him, then settled back on her. "I gave her the green light to get you out after they turned Ann Marie's lawyers away." Lily's magic flared again, and my brow creased. "Why does your magic feel different?"

"None of your business."

When she taught me to access my magic, she fought to keep from using the power of Lilith. But it was more blended or something. I paused so I didn't laugh. "You accepted your darker side."

"I don't have a dark side."

"Do, too."

"What are we, twelve? No, I don't."

Alex kicked her. "Don't mind Lily. She's used to being the one who makes childish arguments."

"I do not."

"Do too," Alex and I said.

A laugh escaped before she caught herself and rubbed her temples. "When I lost my temper, I forgot to be careful with my magic, and it did something."

"There was never anything wrong with it," Cavil explained in his teaching voice. "You are a dark goddess who embraced her night magic for the first time. Now you can choose which nasty surprises you cast."

Her face scrunched. "When can we go home?"

I admired the abrupt change of subject. "You can go as soon as we're done here. A group of agents has already raided your human house. Ann Marie removed or warded everything, so they didn't find a single piece of evidence you're anything other than human."

I needed to be at a Leadership Council meeting in an hour, so I was ready to move things along. But Drake had other plans. As they explained how they became terrorists in the eyes of humans, he interrupted. "Your failure to follow my orders and stay in the pocket caused this incident. Had you listened, none of this would have happened."

I started to defend them, but remembered Drake didn't admonish people unless he had a good reason.

Lily's brow creased. "I forgot you said that. A group of hybrids attacked us when I was training Elizabeth and Spencer. When the dragons surrounded them, they said they wanted the agreement with the coalition revoked. They've been talking to the feds, and said they told them about Roman's house. He didn't answer the phone, so we went to warn him. It was supposed to be a quick trip."

Intrigue seeped through the bond, as did Drake's predatory tendencies. "Is that so?"

Lily either didn't notice the fire in Drake's eyes, or she didn't care. "Yeah. Dale knows about the rogue hybrids. They're the same group who shot up his bar. But he might need your help with them. Why did Roman frame us, Meemaw?"

Ara shrugged. "He claims you simply arrived at an inopportune time."

"And you believe him?"

"Of course not, dear. I believe Roman used your visit as an opportunity. He did not intentionally set you up."

I could almost feel the wheels turning in her mind. "You said I'm your heir, right?"

Ara's muscles tensed. "Yes."

"Does that mean I outrank Roman?"

"You outrank everyone except me and your grandfather. Why?"

Her eyes flicked to me. "Because Jen made the pocket for us, not the purebloods. And I wanted to warn you I'm going to revoke his permission and banish his house from it. They are no longer welcome in my territory."

Ara's tinkling laugh sounded forced. "Do you understand the implications of such a drastic action?"

"Yes," Lily said with certainty.

I tried not to jump when Quin appeared. "You are not as ignorant as you led us to believe."

"Oh, no. Ignorant is my middle name. But I've known you were my grandparents for most of my life, and my mom has an extensive library. I researched your abilities after I escaped from Jed's clutches. Until recently, I didn't know I'd inherited them. Then I didn't want to step on any toes." She paused. "If there's one thing this family has taught me, it's how I can't trust any of you. So I don't give a shit about your toes anymore."

Her words stung. We worked hard to make her and Alex feel welcome. I started to say so but hesitated when I realized she wouldn't believe anything I said. "Um."

Quin leaned forward. "And what have I or your grandmother done to prove ourselves untrustworthy?"

"You haven't given me a single reason not to trust you. But then, neither did Roman until he fed us to the humans to save his own ass." She folded her arms. "My adopted family would never consider throwing me under the bus like that. I have their support, so I don't need yours. Especially if you plan to stab me in the back."

I almost drown in Drake's rage. I braced myself and switched to mind talk. *Be careful. She has every reason to feel that way after what Anitta and Jedediah did to her.*

You are not Anitta or Jedediah.

Lily doesn't believe it. Not yet.

Bullshit. You forget I can read her mind.

I didn't forget. I just want her to give us a chance.

Then follow my lead.

He leaned forward. "I swear I will never betray you, Alex, or anyone you consider family."

I couldn't help but smile. Drake was the most amazing person I knew. I repeated his words and was surprised when Ara also repeated them.

Quin wasn't having it. He leaned forward. "You will need to learn to trust me."

"Fair enough." Lily paused, then apologized.

Ara waved a hand. "It is of no consequence, dear. We love having a spirited granddaughter. Your ability to create and enforce boundaries in violent ways is a breath of fresh air."

Chapter Six

The main square was busier than usual as I exited the flashing circle. I spotted the same two young hybrid girls who visited the palace perched on a bench as they watched mages appear and disappear with wide eyes. When I sensed a cloaked dragon behind them, I headed in their direction. As always, I sipped magic from those who bowed and made a mental note to work harder at learning to use it.

As I approached, the elf-shifter hybrid stepped protectively in front of her friend. "We're not doing anything wrong and have every right to be here."

The girls hadn't used cleaning spells or showered in a while. They looked like pre-teens to me, but I was terrible at guessing kids' ages. The second girl, a mage-shifter, bunched her muscles, ready to run. Understanding the urge, I had to be careful. I gestured dismissively. "I wondered what you think of Allure."

"There's a lot of snobs."

I grinned. "Yes." I motioned toward my favorite alley. "Have you tried the deli down the street? A leprechaun owns it, and the sandwiches are the best in the world. Looks like you could use a little luck."

The mage-shifter scowled. “We’re hybrids and kids, you idiot. We don’t have money.”

Her anger masked the underlying fear. They radiated a terrified yet hopeful feeling. “Do you have human money?”

“None of your business.” She used extra bravado.

“So, no. I’ll tell you what. Let me buy you sandwiches at the deli, and we’ll talk about the money and housing situation. Maybe I can help.”

The elf-shifter crossed her arms. “Why would you help us?”

The mage-shifter nodded. “We’re not supposed to go with strangers.”

Impressive how well they pretended not to recognize me, even though they were at the palace a few days earlier. My eyes scanned the blank space where I sensed a cloaked dragon. “Has anyone tried to abduct them?”

A lime green wyrm dragon appeared and melted into a man with a loincloth.

The girls screeched and raced to hide behind me.

An exasperated expression ghosted across the dragon’s face. “No. They told off a gate guard and ducked under the legs of an ogre who did not appreciate it. I ran interference, so he didn’t kill them.”

“Thank you.” Something about him seemed familiar. “Are you Kalth?”

He bowed. “At your service. Your...erm, ma’am.”

I grinned. “You lost the race with my sister. Had Bastien not interfered, she would have had you.”

His toothy grin made him more handsome. “I guess we’ll never know.”

“No, we won’t.” I flipped my hood over my hair and turned toward the girls. “We won’t hurt you without cause. Let me buy you a meal, and I won’t ask for anything in return. I swear it.” I headed toward the alley and started walking as the magical contract zinged across my head. When the young ladies followed me, I motioned toward Kalth. “No need to guard us. I’ve got them.”

"Of course." He cloaked himself and followed at a respectable distance.

Used to being guarded against my will, I shifted my attention to the girls. "How long will you be in Allure?"

The elf-shifter shrugged. "It's complicated."

I wondered why they were alone when they were with an adult at the palace. Based on their body language, they'd been together for a while. Their bond reminded me of Alex and Lily's. I'd almost bet they were placed with the same hybrid parents. And if they ran away to Allure, something had to have gone wrong. "I bet." When we exited the alley, I pointed at Dragon Headquarters. "Dragon Headquarters is the tall building. They made the dragon glass themselves. There's a hotel across the street from the main entrance. If there's space, they'll give you room and board. Tell them Jen sent you."

"Dragons can read minds, so no thanks."

I swung toward her. "What do you have to hide?"

"We're hybrids, lady. Hiding is our thing."

"And our biological parents were dicks," the mage-shifter added. "We're not old enough to have secrets of our own. Doesn't mean we want some green dude scouring our minds. There're memories I want to keep to myself."

"Okay." I knew exactly what she meant. I'd kept so many things to myself until Drake exploded into my life and cracked my psyche wide open. "Well, then we'll start with sandwiches and see if we can find a more suitable place for you."

"FYI, people don't say words like suitable in the real world."

My lips twitched. "Noted."

"They don't say 'noted,' either."

I stayed silent during the remainder of the walk. The scent of pickles and fresh-baked bread washed over me when I opened the door to Thaddeous's deli. The girls failed to hide their hunger as they shuffled inside and sniffed the air.

"Jen! I heard you were headed my way." Thaddeous sounded much too excited to see me.

I took my gloves and hood off as I navigated around the girls. "Hey, Thaddeous. How are you?"

"Doing well. I have someone I want you to meet." He disappeared into the back and returned with another leprechaun in tow. "Meet my daughter, Liza. Liza, this is Jen."

Liza's eyes widened as she scanned my face. "Daddy, that's..."

"Pleased to meet you," I interrupted. I didn't want to out the girls' reluctance to acknowledge my title before I learned why they were wandering around Allure, filthy and unfed.

"Erm. Yes. Me father says you are good luck and convinced the entire family to move to Allure."

I almost argued the point. Leprechauns could sense luck and gravitated towards it. Although I had a hard time seeing myself as lucky, I chose not to contradict Thaddeous. "How do you like it?"

"It's crowded, but lovely."

"Jen is trying to change the world. Those types are always good luck." He winked at the girls. "Name a sandwich and it's yours, ladies."

I stared at Liza, and she returned my gaze with a puzzled expression as the girls ordered. When they were done, I dragged my attention away from her. "I'll have the special." I scanned the seating area. "Is Sylphira hiding somewhere?"

"Nope. Haven't seen her. Are you meeting with the other..." his eyes darted toward the girls. "Your friends?"

"Only a couple." The Centaur and Minotaur Kings were supposed to show up, but neither seemed eager. I needed to be a better friend. For starters, I could stop thinking of them by their titles and use their names.

"I see. Well, have a seat. Liza and I will bring these right out."

"Thank you." As we settled at a table, I tried to come up with a way to make the girls confide in me. I was reluctant to pry, but I also wanted to learn their story. "So, why are you here and so reluctant to take my help?"

The elf-shifter stood. "We need to wash our hands before we eat."

I dug in my pocket and slid a potion bottle toward her. "We use cleaning potions. One drop on each hand will clean your entire arm. You'll find them available in every restaurant and at every food stand. There are more potent ones for cleaning your whole body and clothes. You can find those at any office run by the crown or the witches."

The girl's bravado deflated. "The food stand guy wouldn't let us have a hotdog."

"I'm sorry. Sometimes paranormals are cruel." And I was probably the worst after everyone I'd gotten killed over the last couple of years.

"I'm Olivia and this is Tasha. We ran away and are hiding." The mage-owl said.

The elf-shifter, Tasha, stiffened. "Quiet!"

I ignored her. "Who are you hiding from?"

"Our adoptive dad," Olivia continued. "He's okay, but after our mom died, he started working with some humans who made us nervous, so we left."

"Ol-iv-i-a," Tasha said. "Shut up. It's none of her business."

"You shut up, Tasha. She's nice enough to buy us lunch and give us a place to sleep. I'm sick of sleeping on the ground."

"Where have you been sleeping, Olivia?" I kept my voice even.

"In the forest. We're both part shifter. But I'm a bird of prey. I hate staying on the ground and can't fly in this pocket without someone attacking me."

I couldn't imagine Drake being grounded and unable to spread his wings. It would kill him. "I see. Have you contacted Jonas and Ann Marie?"

Tasha gasped. "We would never bother a First."

"Right." I forgot how privileged I was to contact anyone I wanted. "We'll think of something. But you're *not* sleeping in the forest anymore." I refocused on Tasha. "How old are you two?"

Her shoulders slumped. "Seventeen."

My eyes rolled before I could stop them. "You're shifters, so you understand how dumb it is to lie to paranormals."

She shrugged.

"We're eleven," Olivia announced with confidence.

As I suspected. Their unique heritage meant they were born with the ability to shift, but their magic hadn't manifested yet. And wouldn't for several years. It horrified me how they were thrown out so young. Ann Marie had explained it, but until then, I didn't fully understand. "You're going home with me."

"No way," Tasha protested.

I gestured towards her. "You are too young to be wandering around on your own. So, yes, you are."

"You can't make us."

"Yes, I can. You're not living on the streets."

Olivia shot out of her chair. "Purebloods don't do that! They'll kill you for helping us."

I rubbed the thin line where I'd cut off my own hand to save the coalition. "Oh, honey. You have so much to learn. Sit."

The Minotaur King clomped in, Sylphira perched on his shoulder. He scanned the deli with his usual hard expression. It melted into a genuine smile when the girls twisted to see who I was looking at.

Sylphira zipped toward us, buzzed around the girls' heads, and landed. "Where did you find hybrid kids?"

"Hey, Sylphira. These are my new friends, Olivia and Tasha. Girls, this is my good friend, Sylphira. She's a pixie."

Sylphira bowed. "Pleased to meet you, friends of my friend. The big, scary guy's name is Orellion. Don't let his grumpy demeanor scare you. He's a teddy bear."

I stifled a laugh. The Minotaur King was many things. But I'd never call him a teddy bear. "After we eat, I plan to take them home with me."

Being one of the smartest people I knew, Sylphira played along. "You will love it. Jen has lots of spare space and a big backyard. She often allows my pixies to live in her trees."

Allow was a stretch. It was more like the pixies snuck in and tried to spy until the griffins moved them to a more private area of the forest.

The two girls pretended to be uninterested, but hope peeked through their hard shells.

Orellion shuffled toward us. "Well, aren't I privileged to have a meal with four lovely ladies?" He set a large tray down. "Help yourselves." He gave me an inquisitive look. "So, *Jen,* how are you on this fine day?"

"Excellent. And you, *Orellion*?"

"Very well." He took a bite of his sandwich to hide a grin. I pulled mine closer and offered it to Sylphira. She took a hunk and set it on her tiny table. Orellion leaned toward Tasha. "Has anyone ever taught you about the minotaurs of old?"

She finished chewing before answering. "No. It's not relevant to my life."

"Blasphemy. The minotaurs of old are relevant to every paranormal. Many years ago, a family of malevolent gods moved to this realm...."

I planned to talk to him and Sylphira about human culture. They were creative and probably had some great insight. Instead, I spent the entire lunch mesmerized by his stories portraying minotaurs as great heroes who saved the coalition many times. Even though the girls tried to look uninterested, they hung on his every word.

When our plates held nothing but crumbs, Sylphira filled two glass to-go containers with orange pixie dust. "Use this as a last resort to defend yourselves. It's potent and will disable your opponent long enough for you to escape. Be careful with it because it will also harm you."

Orellion opened the door. "Do you ladies need an escort home?"

"No, we're good," I said as I waved at Thaddeous. I adjusted my hood and lowered my eyes, hoping the dragon, Kalth, didn't give me away as he slipped out of the crevice between the deli and the neighboring building. "Thank you for another enchanting lunch."

The Minotaur King gave me a slight bow and disappeared into the crowd.

Sylphira fluttered to my ear. "My pixies will be glad to help monitor them."

"Thank you." I led the girls back toward the flashing circle and tried to ignore Kalth as he slithered along the sides of the buildings in his wyrm form.

The girls huddled closer to me as we entered my favorite alley. Olivia rubbed her arms. "Someone's following us, but I can't see them."

"It's the dragon who chose to protect you. They are loyal and take their duties seriously, and he won't hurt us." Not when they were with me. I suspected the uniqueness of the hybrids also intrigued him because of his friendship with Lily. I pointed toward an opening. "That way."

It took me a while to convince the girls to flash with me. They were as naïve to our world as I was to the human one. When they gave in, we appeared behind the palace.

"No," Olivia said. "We can't stay here."

"Sure you can. And stop pretending you don't know who I am. I saw you touring the palace the other day."

Her head twisted, taking it all in. "We were told not to acknowledge you or you'll kill us."

A clipped laugh escaped. "I have no desire to kill kids, so you're safe."

George and Helen stood nearby, their arms linked and hopeful expressions on their faces. Helen leaned forward. "Oh, my. What beautiful young ladies. Come. Let's get you some cocoa and warm you up."

Heavy wing beats behind us made my heart skip a beat. I pushed the girls towards Helen and turned toward the sound. Green and black scales shimmered, looking spectacular against the heavy gray clouds. Drake landed a few yards away. His enormous, razor-sharp teeth filled my vision in what I'd come to understand as a dragon grin before he stretched his massive head forward. His scaly nose touched mine. *Boop.*

The girls scrambled behind George and Helen.

I kissed the massive snout and patted his cheek. "Funny."

He shifted and winked at the girls before his sparkling eyes focused on me. "I think so."

Thankfully, he'd glamoured clothes on himself, I thought. "I've offered these young ladies food and shelter."

His rugged face softened. "Naturally." He nodded at George and Helen before addressing the cowering kids. "Has Helen offered you treats yet?"

Tasha's eyes slid from him to me. "Yes."

Helen made hot chocolate, and Drake created a bowl of extra marshmallows. The girls were too quiet as they sipped their drinks with pale faces.

How do I make them feel at home? I asked.

They've been told we'd kill them. Their foster parents hate what they called fullbloods. It will take time and patience.

I doubt they'll stay. If so, will you be okay with them hanging around?

I love kids and wish to help them as much as you.

Thank you.

For what?

Being you.

Laughter and love flowed through the bond.

We took the elevator to my suite. I had a couple of guest rooms and wanted to keep the girls close until they felt comfortable. The suite had a sitting room, mini-kitchen, and dining area in the center. My room was off the dining area, and the spare rooms were off the sitting room. Helen had already set them up for the girls. She even left a few changes of clothes.

I showed them the cleaning potions, then settled on the sofa and flipped on the human TV to study culture. Drake came in and joined me. He pulled me to him, and I snuggled closer. "Are we doing the right thing?"

"Yes. They need love, and we have plenty of it around here."

"I'm going to get so much shit from the council for this."

"Since when do you care what they think?"

"I care when I need to. The hybrids are still a sore spot." I tapped his thigh. "I need to tell Ann Marie and Dale about them."

"It can wait until morning."

The girls spent the evening with Helen, ordering clothes and other supplies. Afterwards, they curled up together and criticized the shows we tried to watch. Eventually, Olivia shoved her phone in my face, and we watched videos, laughing at the antics people posted online. It was as fun as it was addictive, and I downloaded the app and spent most of the night scrolling before Drake pried my phone out of my hand and insisted I sleep.

Chapter Seven

The next morning, Olivia and Tasha trailed me like little ducks. Drake walked behind them, scanning the area like the Bellicose hid around every corner.

Olivia stopped. "You make me want to shift. Will you walk beside me or something?"

Drake laid a hand on her shoulder. "You're wise not to trust a predator at your back. But you also need to learn control. I won't hurt you."

Verity raised her head as we approached, and her eyes settled on the girls. "I heard you found some strong young ladies." She stood. "I'm Verity. The sprite is Charlotte, and the boggart is Pablo. We run the queen's office."

I nodded. "They're the keepers of the coalition, and we'd get nothing done without them."

The girls gave them an awkward greeting and followed me into my office, where Helen and a couple of her daughters were setting up breakfast on the conference table.

Goosebumps coated my arms, and I swung my head towards my desk. Quin sat in my chair, his brow furrowed. "Stealing children from their homes is an outdated practice."

"Hey, Quin. Why aren't you with Lily?"

"She is a housemaster with several high-powered vampires."

"So, you can't get close to her?"

"Oh, yes. Let's pretend they can sense me when even you cannot."

I grinned as I settled into the chair next to Drake. I'd missed Quin. "Want to join us for breakfast?"

"I am not one to bask in domestic bliss." He appeared beside Tasha.

She jumped, then attempted to scowl at him.

"This is Quin. I consider him one of my closest friends. Quin, meet Tasha and Olivia."

He inclined his head. "Princesses."

Alex strolled in, scanned our group, settled beside me, and filled a plate like he owned the place. "Hey, Jen. Mom will be here in a few minutes."

"Um. Okay."

Quin went deathly still. "Who is watching over Lily?"

"She chose her own path." Alex's voice sounded bitter. He lifted his fork and motioned toward the girls. "Have you read these two, Drake?"

"Yes. They plan to gather information and report back to the man who adopted them," Drake said. "Though Tasha is less likely to follow through than Olivia."

Both girls paled.

I took a bite of toast, but didn't comment. Drake already told me, and we hoped they'd come around.

Alex shrugged. "It's odd how Jen doesn't care about things like possible treason."

"Don't talk about me like I'm not here. They're just kids and deserve a chance."

"You knew?" Tasha's voice was barely a whisper.

I nodded. "Kalth, the green dragon, followed you the entire time you were in Allure. As I told you at the deli, dragons are loyal. The Pixie Queen gave you dust because she wanted to help you escape his control."

Her eyes were as wide as saucers. "Pixie Queen? Sylphira?"

"It's safe to assume anyone hanging around Jen is important," Alex explained. "And, as someone raised by a First, I suggest you not try to lie or deceive them. If my dad found out what you planned, he wouldn't bother giving you a chance. Drake is more patient."

"My patience is not a weakness, but a blessing," Drake said.

I pointed at Olivia. "The man who adopted you is using you. It's his bad luck and your good fortune that I found you and not a less tolerant leader."

Ann Marie shuffled in, scanned the room, and her eyes landed on Olivia. "Are these the rescues?"

I sipped my coffee. "They haven't decided if they want to be traitors or rescues. I suspect they're torn after we took them in and offered them the world."

Ann Marie picked up a bagel. "I bet there are several displaced hybrid children. Some might even be coerced to turn on or kill their own."

Olivia jumped out of her seat. "We didn't kill anyone! I swear it!"

"Sit down." I kept my tone neutral.

Tasha stood and linked arms with Olivia. "You're a liar. You pretend to be nice, but you're not."

Alex set his fork down, and his muscles bunched, as if he were ready to pounce. "You really think she didn't read your intentions or have a mind conversation with the dragon who guarded you? Or did it never occur to you that the Dragon First would read your thoughts the moment he laid eyes on you?" He pointed at me. "Jen's the Queen of Ahl. She could have waved a finger, and you'd be at The Cauldron waiting for the Crown Juror to assess your guilt. Instead, she gave you a safe place to sleep, clothes, and enough food for ten shifters to gorge themselves."

Tasha pumped up her bravado. "You're an idiot. Fullbloods are the enemy."

Ann Marie cleared her throat. "Jenella and Drake have done more for hybrids in a year than anyone else has done in the last thirty. We would have never placed you with Shumer if we knew he'd poison you against the crown. But we did. So, now you need to make some choices. You can stay here, move into the shifter compound with me, or live a life running from the coalition with Shumer. Choose wisely."

Tasha's face flushed. "He said the hybrids would die if we didn't help him."

"Did he?" Drake's voice was too calm. I shivered.

Quin's eyes flashed red. "Jenella."

"Drake's fine." I didn't take my eyes off the shaking girls.

Olivia wrung her hands. "No way I want to live at the Cauldron."

"Smart. How about you, Tasha?"

"What's the shifter compound?"

"It's across the small forest behind the palace. Jonas will treat you like part of the pack, and you can learn from other shifters."

"What about Helen's lessons?"

"You can still come for lessons," I said. "Either option is better than becoming traitors or living on the streets."

Tasha blinked. "I want to live with other shifters, but they'll think we're freaks."

"Jonas and I won't allow you to be disrespected."

"If we don't like it there, can we come back to Jen?" Olivia asked.

I nodded and attempted to keep my disappointment from showing. "Of course. You're always welcome here."

"Then we'll stay with the shifters."

Ann Marie held out her hand. "Great. Give me the phones." After they handed them over, she stood. "Let's head over and get you settled in."

After they left, we continued eating in silence. Drake rose from his chair. "I'll watch them."

I nodded. "Hey Alex, look at this app." I showed him the one the girls installed on my phone.

"It's an app most humans watch videos on, if that's what you're asking. Not magical."

"Thanks. Is Lily okay?"

Pain flashed across his face. "She's fine, I suppose."

"What does fine mean?"

"It was stupid for her to fight Roman. And to believe Elsie when she insisted she had to take over his vampires and property."

"I thought she won?"

"Roman's the oldest vampire on the planet, and as natural born as Lily. The only way for her to win that fight was for Roman to let her. She knew it, too. But she fought him anyway because she convinced herself it was the only way to protect me." Alex met my eyes. "In case you haven't noticed, I don't need protection."

I nodded. "Yeah. But she's part vampire, so she will die to protect the people she loves." I wasn't even a vampire and understood.

"Stupid. He could have killed her. But he didn't. He fought her hard enough to make it look legitimate, and just handed everything over to her, and she ate it up. Now she's living in his ugly mansion and prancing around like some kind of..." he trailed off.

"Princess," I finished for him.

He rubbed his eyes. "No offence, but yeah. She doesn't belong there."

He missed his sister. Grief stabbed me in the chest. "Why does she need to live there?"

"Because she took over Roman's house, and we don't have space for them. And because I can't live with so many people without their thoughts bombarding me."

Quin snapped out of his stupor. "So, you came here to mope."

"No. I need time to think and hope to work with Deva. She said she will help me block thoughts."

"Deva and Drake will both help. I bet Lily's not happy running a vampire house." My sister had no desire to have more power. She was happy with her life until the Bellicose interfered.

"Yet she chose to take one over without so much as a conversation with me."

"It is in her blood," Quin said.

"Bullshit. I have instincts, too, but I'm not taking over a lion pride."

"Yet. You are barely a babe."

"I agree with Quin," I said. "What would you have done if your lion family framed you into taking over their territory?"

He sat back and folded his arms. "I would have at least had a conversation with her and Dad before sacrificing myself."

"Are we pretending you did not intend to protect Lily by allowing yourself to be arrested?" Quin stood.

"That's different. You forget I read minds. Including Roman's. That guy is twisted as fuck. I knew what he was doing and made the best decision possible."

"To protect Lily," I added.

"To give her time. She's been off since you crashed into her life and tried to take it over. She's never liked her darker side and wasn't ready to be a leader." He pointed at Quin. "But you kept pushing, and she respects you. When the cops pulled us over and had information about us that they shouldn't have had, I used the opportunity to help her." He sighed. "And now I've lost her."

"Ah, so we are also pretending Lily appreciates others making decisions for her."

"Like how you manipulated her into turning federal agents?"

"She made her own choices."

I picked up my tablet and stuffed it in a bag. "It doesn't matter. I have experience fighting with a powerful sibling, and this is fixable. Let's take you to Deva. When you master blocking, we'll talk about how to reconcile with Lily." I paused. "What exactly was Roman's plan?"

"He didn't build a house full of powerful vampires for himself. He always planned to turn it over to Lily."

Quin materialized in front of him. "Explain."

Alex didn't even flinch. "I caught odd thoughts a couple of times since he started hanging around and ignored them because his mind is like our maze in the DMZ. But it was crystal clear when we showed up at his house to warn him. He spent all that time building a house to push her into her rightful place. He believed he was doing her a favor. The only vampire he planned to keep was Folomi. And that's more of a match situation."

My glowing golden eyes met Quin's shining red ones. "What a crock of shit." I started pacing. "If that presumptuous asshole were here now, I'd kill him." If Lily found out, she'd kill him herself. "Does she know?"

Alex shrugged. "She suspects he let her win the fight, but I doubt she's pieced together why."

Quin's face darkened, accentuating its sharp features. "I must report this to my love."

"Ara's hard to read, so I couldn't confirm if she was in on Roman's plans."

"I assure you, she was not." He disappeared.

Alex and I stared at each other, contemplating Quin's anger. He never showed so much emotion. I extended my hand. "You better learn how to control your magic before they decide to help you, too."

We landed in the foyer of Dragon Headquarters. I usually used the flashing circles, but wasn't in the mood.

Deva's security waved us through and didn't bother escorting us to her office. As usual, she stood at the windows, watching over the city. "Oh, my. My favorite mental mage. Hello, loves."

Alex jammed his hands in his pockets. "Hey, Deva. How fast can you teach me to block thoughts?"

"I suspect you are close to mastering the skill. But that is not the question, is it?"

"The question?"

"You want to save your sister from herself, even when she does not need saving."

He clenched his jaw to keep from commenting. Smart.

My phone rang, and I pulled it out. "What's up?"

"A group of hybrids blindsided me at the farm." Ann Marie's breathing sounded labored. "A woman I didn't recognize stabbed me several times. A vampire, I think."

I clutched my phone tighter. "Where are you now?"

"Home. Well, at the farm. I could use some healing."

"On my way." I ended the call and swung toward Alex. "They attacked Ann Marie." I texted Ara and raced out the door. As I rounded the corner, I smashed into Tracy.

She held her hands out to steady me. "Holy fates, Jen. Where are you going so fast?"

I darted around her. "I found a couple of runaway hybrids. Ann Marie took custody of them, and someone attacked her."

Alex trailed Deva. "Other hybrids have gone missing. Dale theorized that humans were taking them, and he's trying to convince everyone to relocate to the pocket. We never considered hybrid guardians would sell kids."

I gasped. "They're taking our kids, and no one's doing anything?" My voice came out in a squeak, so I straightened my spine and marched toward the elevator. "Then we'll find them and shut their operation down. Call Dale and see what he found."

Alex looked at me like he wanted to argue. "If you weren't the queen, I'd tell you to piss off with the ordering me around. He already has his people on it."

I chuckled. "You can tell me to piss off. Everyone else close to me does."

"Great. Then piss off."

Drake! Someone attacked Ann Marie, and hybrids are selling children to humans. I'm heading to her farm to heal her.

Jonas has the girls.

Thank you.

My heart pounded as I waited for the elevator. When the doors finally opened, my three companions stepped inside with me. "What are you doing?"

"I'm going to check on my mom," Alex growled.

I couldn't argue with his concern, so I focused on Tracy. "You don't have to go with me."

"Uh-huh. Like I didn't have to go the other hundred times you rushed into danger."

"I'm not rushing into danger." Yet.

"I'm going."

"Don't worry, love. I have no plans to leave my dragons."

"Good." A thought popped into my head. "If dragons spot hybrid children roaming around Allure, will you send them somewhere safe?"

"Of course. Kalth informed me of his adventures, and we were working with the Enforcers on how to approach them when you stepped in. We will house them and work with the hybrid leader until we find a more permanent solution."

Of course, they were on it. Deva loved being included in coalition matters and cared about people more than she'd admit. "Thank you."

We landed inside the hybrid pocket and peered out the gate leading to Ann Marie's original human farm.

"There." Alex pointed down the street. "The agents can't see through Mom's wards."

I hadn't bothered to learn Drake's cloaking magic. So we needed to do something else. "I could flash to the front porch, but I need permission to cross her wards."

"I can give you permission, but I'll need to be the one who flashes," Alex said.

"Okay." I held out a hand. After we landed, I searched for a human doorbell, but didn't see one.

Alex shoved me aside and opened the door. "It's home, so no reason to knock."

Ann Marie's farmhouse and her mansion in Allure were vastly different. The Farmhouse's wooden floors were worn, and the furniture was lived in. The place smelled like lemons and chemicals. A fluffy purple blanket was draped over the back of a sectional, as if tossed there as an afterthought. A half-finished puzzle sat abandoned on a square table in the corner. It was comfortable and happy. I almost envied Lily and Alex for growing up in such warmth. "This is lovely."

"It might not be a palace, but it's the only house we've ever owned that felt like home." Ann Marie's voice came from a human-style kitchen.

We raced in her direction.

She sat slumped on the floor. A spell to contain the pool of blood surrounded her. I held out my hand and waited until she took it before speaking. "It wasn't snark. I love the homey feel." My silver healing magic restored her as I spoke.

She leaned her head against the cupboard and closed her eyes. "Thank you, I guess. Why are you here, Alex?"

"Jen was with me when you called."

"I'm fine. But you have no business hanging out with those two." She released a spell, and the blood disappeared. "They're trouble."

I bristled at the accusation. “What have I ever done to put Alex in danger?”

Ann Marie climbed into a chair. “Seriously?” She brushed her blonde locks away from her face. “Forget I said that. I’m worried. Dale informed me at least fifty children have gone missing, and twice as many adults. Someone broke into their houses and took them.”

My stomach soured. “The Bellicose wanted to enslave the hybrids.”

Her eyes drooped. “It’s not them. We think the government and some rogue hybrids are behind the disappearances.”

Alex shifted from one foot to the other. “I know where the agents are staying.”

“I need some recovery time from the blood loss, so you can go investigate.” Ann Marie handed him a set of keys. “Don’t use magic unless you absolutely need to, Jenella. And if you hurt Alex or lead him into trouble, I will never forgive you.”

Chapter Eight

As we drove into the valley, the air went stale, and my lungs burned. A hazy cloud cover caused the temperature to drop. Unlike the mountains, the valley didn't have snow, so it didn't make sense for the air to be colder. "What is up with the stinky clouds?"

"Inversion," Alex said. "The air becomes trapped and stagnant in the valley. It messes with the temperatures and air quality."

"How do humans breathe?"

"If it bothers them, they stay indoors where the air's a little cleaner."

Sounded like being trapped. I'd much rather live in Allure, where the air wasn't poisoned. I added a filtering bubble to the truck's cab and wondered if our climate mages could clean the air in the valley so no one had to cage themselves.

Tracy turned to face me. "According to Bas, the federal agents were staying in short-term rentals. They checked out of the one in Caldwell, and the other two are closer to downtown." She threw the spell she'd been weaving, and a map appeared. "Here and here."

I leaned closer. "Wouldn't the neighbors say something when they saw people being dragged into a house at all hours?"

Alex made a right and slowed. "Yes, they would. The first address is down here, and you'll need to be my eyes. I'm a fugitive, so I don't want people to recognize me."

"Why don't you just alter their perception?"

"Only as a last resort. I don't like messing with people's heads." Alex pulled to the curb and stopped.

Like me, Alex liked having a lot of power, but also understood the responsibility that came with it. "Is it odd how well you and I understand each other?"

"No. We were both kept in cages as kids and found families who love us. We also have unique abilities we would turn off for a moment of peace."

"I used to wrap my power around myself to hide it. Right after I woke Drake, he gave Tracy and me glamour. For the first time in my life I was truly free. When you learn to block thoughts, you'll have the chance to experience how wonderful it feels."

"I can't wait. Did you say glamour?"

"Yes. We can create a new identity, and the dragons can give you glamour. Be cautious about making deals with them, though. They will take advantage."

"Understood."

A car pulled up to a house down the street. The driver stayed in the car while two men climbed out and scanned the area. Alex pulled away from the curb. "Turn your heads so they can't see your faces."

The men watched the truck for a second and dismissed us as they disappeared into a house. I didn't sense any paranormals on the entire block. "They're not here."

Alex turned onto a main road. "Those agents are sorting through the Bellicose apartments. Let's go to the next one."

The other house was on a quiet street and much bigger than the first. My senses lit up as we drew near. "Several inside. Not all hybrids, and their intentions seem almost bland."

"I'm going to park on the next block."

Tracy dug through her bag. "If we walk by, I can weave a spell to make us uninteresting."

After we parked, Alex slid out, pulled his hood over his head and slid on sunglasses. "I wish Lily were here. She could sneak in and see what's going on without being seen."

"Yeah. Quin does that, too." Tracy wrapped a scarf around her head. "We're three of the most powerful paranormals in the world. I'm sure we can hide ourselves from a few rogues."

I trudged down the icy sidewalk and tried not to gag on the stagnant air. "The air pollution is a problem."

Alex chuckled. "Why do you think we live way out in the boonies?"

"Because you need room to shift?"

"That, too." He sniffed and tilted his head. "Too many thoughts for me to sort through."

"Drake's been watching these houses, but didn't mention the paranormals inside." He might not tell me if he did, since his job was to monitor the valley, and I didn't need every little detail.

"I mean, you could ask him." Tracy's fingers twitched as she wove a spell.

"Let's see what we find first." Drake was close enough to reach us fast. The sense of hypervigilance from him was reserved for times when he thought I was in danger. I sent a little 'I'm fine' signal. "He's aware of what we're doing."

A car whizzed by as we turned onto the street. It pulled into the driveway, and a hybrid and two humans stepped out. The hybrid yanked a teenage boy out and nudged him down the sidewalk.

Alex gasped. "This is the place."

"Yeah." Their intentions said they wanted to drop the kid off fast and move on.

"Excuse me," a weathered voice shouted from behind us.

We paused and shuffled toward an older woman with short white hair. She stood on her porch, wearing loose clothes. Fire lit her eyes as Alex approached. "Yes, ma'am?"

"You don't live in this neighborhood."

"No, we don't. We're taking a walk."

"You can take your walk somewhere else. We don't want trouble." The word 'walk' came out like a curse word.

"The sidewalk is public, and we're not causing trouble."

She fascinated and perplexed me. Her tiny stature didn't match her hateful intentions. Physically, she was so small and weak, without a drop of magic. Yet she talked as if she were a dragon. And she would not let us continue down her street. Amazing.

"Leave now, or I'll call the cops."

I waited for Alex to say something, but he only motioned for us to leave. "Sure. Have a nice day, ma'am." When I didn't follow, he tugged at my arm. "Come on, Jen. Don't mess with her."

"No." I shook my arm loose and brought a trickle of power to the surface. "We will continue our walk. You will go back inside your house and find a hobby other than watching the street. One that erases the hate in your heart. You never saw us."

She turned and slipped back inside.

"Neat trick, but not recommended. Like I said, messing with humans is never a good idea."

"Ruling magic. I don't like using it on anyone, especially humans. But I needed to do something. She'll get herself killed trying to wield power that's not hers to wield."

"Humans aren't designed that way."

My eyebrows slammed together. "Are you telling me they *allow* her to order them around?"

"More like tolerate her. And she's not alone. They're all over."

When he pulled me down the street, I glanced back at the woman's house. "No kidding? Can I find them on the video app?"

Alex's childlike giggle didn't match his calm personality. "Search for Karens when you have a few hours."

The name made me think of Deva's assistant, who betrayed us. "I can't wait."

Another car pulled up, and a human in a cheap suit climbed out. Alex's muscles bunched. "That's the agent who kidnapped us. He's collecting kids," Alex's voice almost sounded like a growl. "They plan to leave the area with them first thing in the morning."

"How do we shut them down without alerting the neighbors?"

"We can put a ward around the house. Kind of like a miniature privacy bubble." Tracy pointed at a tall fence surrounding the backyard. "The back will be difficult."

"Yeah. I could flash us to the four corners to anchor the spell."

Alex shook his head. "No, you can't. It might not look like it, but at least three humans are watching us. And most of these houses have cameras. Keep walking and we'll figure it out over lunch."

The restaurant he chose smelled like smoked meat and cheap perfume. Several heads turned as a woman with tired eyes escorted us to a table. It wasn't unusual for Tracy's beauty to draw attention, so we ignored it.

"This place has passable barbecue," Alex said in a conversational tone as we slid into a booth. "Order anything you want. It's on me."

I didn't recognize most of the dishes on the menu. When a woman set glasses of water on the table, I closed the menu. "Thank you."

"What are you ordering?" Tracy asked.

"I don't know what any of that stuff is," I said in a quiet voice.

She chuckled. "Neither do I. It's fun to pick something new and try it."

Alex took off his fake glasses. "I'll order a family-style meal for you to share. That way, you can try several dishes and decide what you like."

After I tried what seemed like a million dishes, I sat back and rubbed my stomach. Alex wasn't kidding about how good it was. But then, shifters had an unnatural obsession with food. "That was delicious."

"So good," Tracy agreed. "What's our plan?"

I sipped my soda and frowned when I noticed it was almost empty. "Drake and Glacintial are in the area. They could help cloak us."

Alex took another bite of shredded beef. "We'll call them if necessary, but let's hold off. It's best to operate on the assumption that people will call the police over every little disturbance. It will be quieter with just the three of us."

My eyes widened. "Humans are a pain in the ass sometimes. Why would they call the authorities over noise?"

"They might not. But it's a possibility. Especially since we already encountered a nosy neighbor." Alex slipped his glasses on. "We'll find a nearby hiding place, and Tracy can sneak closer to set the wards. But let's wait until dark."

The neighborhood was eerily quiet as we waited in a parking lot a few blocks away. Alex tapped the steering wheel while cars drove by. "Can I ask you a personal question, Jen?"

"Yes."

"After the battle, you'd convinced yourself you were nothing but an enormous ball of rage and pain. Is that why Drake took you to an undisclosed location?"

I shivered as the memories crashed over me. "Yes."

"How did you deal with it?"

The question wasn't for me, but for him. Alex admitted he had a similar childhood. I glanced at Tracy, who pointedly ignored the conversation. "Unlike you and Lily, I never dealt with my childhood trauma. Mat tried for years to convince me to open up about it, but my shame and guilt wouldn't let me. I feared he wouldn't love me anymore if he found out. Jacques said some awful things to me, and part of me believed them." I ran some of his words through my mind. When Alex flinched, I continued. "Mat and Helen kept trying to help, and I avoided their efforts. Eventually, I learned how to pretend I was fine. They weren't fooled, but let it slide. Sort of. After I became a detective, all the repressed pain turned to anger. It all amplified when I lost Mat and thought I'd lost Drake.

"Drake and I can sense each other's emotions, and he uses our bond to help me cope. After Mat's death, I was volatile, grieving, and would have become a tyrant if I didn't deal with all my..." I twirled a hand in a circle. "He saw where I was headed and intervened. It took a while, but I finally opened up. I'm still broken, and probably always will be. But at least I've been able to start gluing the pieces back together."

Alex stared out his window for a while. "My mom has a way of making me deal with things. But I kind of fake it, too. I don't remember a lot of the abuse, but what I do remember haunts me. Anger is the hardest thing to suppress, especially in stressful situations. It's why I became so reasonable." He threw his glasses onto the dashboard. "When my parents first took me in, I wasn't fully functional and didn't trust their love."

"It's hard to learn to trust again after it's been ripped away. I never really knew Mat before he rescued me from Mahri and didn't trust him."

"Yeah. Lily always hovered in the background, watching over me. She never said much, but I saw the same pain and distrust in her eyes. My magic developed early, but her thoughts were still too difficult to read. They slid out of my reach when I tried. One day, she took me for a walk around the farm. She swore to me I was safe with them and if our new parents ever tried to hurt me, she'd take me away. I was skeptical at first, but she made a series of oaths. To this day, I feel safest when she's around."

I had to swim through my turbulent emotions before I could speak. "Yeah. I understand all about that, too."

"She never once broke the promise until now. And I don't know what to do with myself."

"I'm pretty sure she feels the same about you. But she's as broken as the rest of us. Mat once said she hides behind bravado. If so, she's probably convinced taking over Roman's house is the best way to protect you and is too damn proud to admit she screwed up."

"So, the question is, what do we do about it?"

"We'll figure it out."

We walked through the neighborhood, trying to look casual. The sheer number of paranormals in the house made me uneasy. The place was enormous, but crowded. Alex led us behind a tall shrub as we rounded the block.

Tracy latched onto my arm. "Stay here and watch my back. I'll plant privacy spells so humans see a calm, peaceful house, but paranormals can see through it. Four corners, counterclockwise. I'll start on the left corner."

"We won't see you when you reach the back."

"I've got her," Alex said. "Keep your thoughts on the spell because I'll read your mind the entire time."

She blinked. "Um. I mean, that's kind of weird, but okay." Tracy skittered across the street.

We watched in silence as she planted the two spells. She once again amazed me by setting the intricate spell in record time. My heart kicked up a beat as she slipped through the back gate. I kept my senses trained on her while Alex monitored her thoughts, our eyes taking on a soft glow.

Tracy had just placed the last spell when my senses fired with warning. Alex shifted closer to me. "Something spooked her. Her thoughts turned to Quin, so it's probably him."

My phone buzzed, and I kept it low enough so the light didn't alert anyone. After I read the text, I pushed it towards Alex.

Tracy

Quin is with me. We'll go in the back in three minutes. Spells are activating now.

"That vampire is everywhere." He pushed my phone away.

The privacy spell activated with a *whoosh*. "He likes to pop up at odd times. It amuses him and keeps him from becoming bored with life."

"Yeah. And he's almost impossible to read. Ara's worse. I've never gotten a read on her."

"Don't try. Verity once touched Jedediah with her Juror powers, and it threw them both across a field."

He chuckled. "She's a badass."

"Yeah."

One minute before go-time, the front door opened. Three men came out and moved towards the back gate. As they walked, their backs hunched, and their heads became deformed. Two men's arms lengthened, while the other guy's shortened. Their full transformation was hard to see, but even from a distance, they looked awful. As the grotesque creatures skittered through the gate, I scooted forward to get a better look. "Are they like the one who took Lily's fang?"

"Yes."

Their magic was as weak as Lily's half-human friend, Susan. But their signature wasn't like the one we found on that pyramid, or the stuff used against me in the battle. It still seemed familiar, but I couldn't remember where I'd sensed it. "It's not the same."

"Are you saying we have two mystery magics?"

"Maybe. Let's go."

The front door stood open, so it was easy to slip inside. Voices came from every direction, and cigarette smoke clogged my nose. I rubbed it to keep from sneezing and swung towards Alex to see how he was doing. His eyes watered, so I threw one of my boxes around his head.

He sneezed five times in a row, held up a finger, and sneezed again. I changed the box to an air filter, and sucked in the clean air. "Thanks."

No one greeted us, so we moved deeper into the house.

A few men gathered around a television playing video games. They were a mixture of hybrids, humans, and the guys with weak magic. Loud shouts and whoops drowned out the sound of our footsteps as we passed. None of them spared us a glance.

Down the hall, we spotted another group gathered in an office, smoking and drinking. Booming laughter came from inside as clouds of smoke billowed out. A handwritten sign on the door indicated it was the smoking room. I chuckled at Alex's eye roll when he spotted it.

In the kitchen, women gathered around an island, drinking wine and eating a platter of snacks. One glanced in our direction and dismissed us when another woman nudged her and said something. Alex shoved me toward the stairs, and I wasted no time climbing them.

The top floor had six doors, four of which were closed. The first one was locked. I didn't sense any magic behind it, so we moved on. The second one held a hybrid. I reached out to turn the handle, and Alex grabbed my hand. "Adult informant," his whisper was barely audible.

The other rooms were empty, so we crept back down the stairs and through the kitchen. The door to the basement stood open, and I sensed several paranormals, including Tracy and Quin, below. At the bottom, Alex pointed right and disappeared around the corner. My heart hammered as I followed him with a lot less finesse. Damn cat shifters.

When we reached another door, he swung it open, and we peered inside.

Chapter Nine

My breath caught in my throat. Cages lined the wall, stacked three high. Inside, hybrid babies and toddlers screeched, cried, or sat comatose. Flashbacks crashed over me, and I had to take several deep breaths and lock my knees to keep them from buckling. Alex squeezed my hand, not trying to hide his recoil from the scene or his shaking.

Fear and dread flooded my system, so potent that it clogged my lungs. I swallowed several times and gasped for air. "Why does it always have to be cages?" Three human women I hadn't noticed landed on the floor, unconscious or dead. I stared at them, trying to register what had happened.

Drake's internal roar yanked me from my stupor. I tugged Alex back. *Don't come in hot. I'm fine. We found something awful, but this place is crawling with people.*

What did you find?

Alex's shattered blue eyes broke my heart. I'd never seen him look so young and scared. *You'll see when you get here.*

I flashed to our shrub and wrapped Alex in a tight hug. "We're going to get through this."

"It's just...." He stepped back but kept a punishing grip on my arms. "They're black-market babies. The coalition treaty, all those deaths, the bloody battle. It all meant nothing. The assholes are still selling their kids."

I wrenched away from him, leaned over, and puked. After I used one of Tracy's cleaning potions, I stood and allowed anger to wash over me. "Those fucking fuckers." I stabbed a finger toward the house. "The one person in my life who always loved me died for them, and they repay his sacrifice by doing this? It's absolute bullshit. We've been out here fighting our asses off to save them and restore their place in the coalition. I've butted heads with the other leaders, put my friends and family on the front lines, and did everything possible to stop this. And they respond by selling their kids to those....things?" I swung back towards the house. "Not on my watch."

Alex snapped his mouth shut, opened it, and shook his head. "You really care about hybrids, don't you?"

"Would I be here if I didn't?" My words were a little too harsh, so I tried again. "Of course, I care. I'm the damn queen, and every single one of you ungrateful assholes is important to me." Still too harsh, but better.

For some reason, my awkwardness made Alex relax. "You going to be okay going back inside?"

"Yes. You?"

"I'll be fine."

We flashed back.

"It is a wonder you lived to adulthood with such underdeveloped critical thinking skills."

I jumped and slammed into Alex. "Damnit, Quin."

A long, exaggerated sigh. "Must we cover this lesson again?"

"No. These people aren't very observant. And we needed a break. They're keeping kids in cages."

"The security is lax because they believe themselves powerful."

I snorted. "Where's Tracy?"

He motioned towards a door.

We followed him to another room. Inside, Tracy stood talking to two boys. At least fifteen kids of all ages were jammed into the small space. Some looked scared, others defiant as they watched us with skeptical eyes. "At least they're not in chains."

"No," Alex said. "For someone matched with a dragon, you're not too knowledgeable about mental magic."

Because I relied on Drake to spell it out for me. "I'll add it to my list of things to work on."

"The hybrids upstairs adopted most of them. Only a couple realize they've been sold." He frowned. "Not to humans."

"Bellicose?" Quin asked.

Alex shook his head. "They suspect a man they met yesterday was a demon."

"Demon?" I leaned against the doorjamb and gathered my thoughts. "Are they sure?"

"He smelled like sulfur and made their skin crawl."

It was a pretty good deduction. "Demons don't come to this realm by themselves. Someone needs to summon them."

"Yes. We are all aware of semantics." Quin pointed towards a teenage boy. "That boy is under the impression his foster mother is sleeping with a demon."

Alex sniffed. "Smoking with the door open makes much more sense now."

"Yeah." I raised my hand to buy time for my gurgling stomach to settle. "Leave the kids here while we shut down their operation. I want every single person in this house detained and their minds combed through by dragons." I met Alex's eyes. "If demons are involved, I might need Lily's help."

He nodded. "She'll help." He glanced at the stairs. "Glacintial is outside."

"So is Drake."

Tracy patted the shoulder of the kid she was talking to and joined us. "Why is Bastien here?"

"Drake probably called for him when he sensed my reaction to the kids in cages." I took out my phone and texted the hybrid leader. With the magnitude of what we found, I also texted Ann Marie and Jonas. "Clear the house. Avoid killing if you can."

Quin appeared beside Tracy. "I request that the humans be given to us to turn."

I shrugged. "Fine with me, but not until we've squeezed every ounce of information out of them."

He took Tracy's arm, and they disappeared.

Alex dragged me towards the stairs. "Scary Jen is more natural than trying to be kind to everyone, Jen. But I doubt it will win you much support."

He might as well have thrown a bucket of ice over my white-hot anger. "Thanks."

"No problem."

The women in the kitchen were unconscious, so we headed to the smoking room.

The gamers came around the corner, headsets hanging around their necks. One of those guys with the strange magic stepped forward and shifted. His hair turned orange and patchy, and one jagged tooth hung over his bottom lip. He raised a hand as if preparing for an attack. I leaned in to better see his claws. Each one represented a different animal. His buddy behind him formed hooves on his hands and feet, and his face elongated.

I tilted my head. "Are you meant to be a horse shifter?"

He whinnied.

"Should I drop them?" Alex's voice sounded almost too reasonable.

I started to respond when a burning pain shot through my scalp. Someone had yanked me by my hair, I realized as my back slammed into something hard. I sent a knockout spell into the guy, and he screamed. We fell to the floor in a heap. I untangled his limp hand from my hair and jumped to my feet. "Do human men like to pull hair in a fight?"

Alex dropped the two grotesque guys without lifting a finger. "Not in a fight, no."

Footsteps thundered down the stairs.

Regaining my senses, I threw a shield around us and invoked my ruling power. "Stop!" The house went silent. "What are you picking up?"

Alex's head twisted toward me. "The freaks believe themselves to be unstoppable. It's almost as if they can't sense your commanding presence or my danger level."

My head shook in disbelief. "They're supposed to be some kind of shifter, so they should at least sense your power." I gestured at the silenced group of gamers. "And they still obey my commands. Those shackles Morten used transferred my power to him. They used something similar to transfer Deva's power to some kind of demon magic holding spell. What if the humans have something similar, but don't understand how to use it?"

"It's a possibility. But is this really the time to theorize?"

No, it wasn't. I flicked my hand. Every adult in the house, besides my team, hit the floor. When Alex's eyes flashed with alarm, I shrugged. "I once knocked out a whole town by accident. The enforcers still puzzle over how it happened." I picked my way over the unconscious people to reach the back door. "I have much better control now."

Alex trailed behind me. "You're a little scary sometimes."

"Thank you. So are you."

Tracy stood on the back porch, having a mental argument with a cloaked Bastien. Glacintial and Drake shifted and raced toward us.

Drake pulled me into his arms, then thrust me away as he examined me from head to toe. "Are you okay?"

"Physically? Yes." I motioned toward Alex. "Emotionally, we're a little wrecked." I rubbed my stomach. "They have hybrid babies in cages downstairs."

He took my hand. "I take it you disabled everyone responsible?"

"The ones inside the house, yes. The older kids believe they met a demon."

"I haven't sensed demons since the battle."

"Good. I hope they're locked in their own realm." But I doubted it. Especially after the red eyes I spotted in the crowd after Lily imploded the building.

"We took care of the adults outside and upstairs," Tracy said as she joined us. "Quin went to meet Ann Marie and Dale. They don't want to draw attention by driving into the neighborhood."

"Thanks." I stared at the house. "How many more of these places do they have?"

"Several if they're dealing in the black market." Alex slipped his hands into his pockets. "Paranormals who sell kids don't like to stay in one place long."

I flinched, causing Drake to growl. "We'll make them pay."

"Yes, we will." One of the grotesque shifter things stirred, and I marched in his direction. The guy had muscle bulges in the oddest places. One above the knee. Another on his side. His neck looked kinked. Though, unlike the others, he had a thick head of hair. "There are a few of these things inside. Have any of you seen anything like it before?"

Alex leaned over the strange shifter thing. "They're similar to the guy who drugged me and took Lily's fang, but those guys seemed more sadistic."

Bastien appeared beside Drake. "Tracy will not be accompanying you on these little quests anymore."

Tracy crossed her arms. "Not your call. I'll go where I want, when I want."

"You are a dragon princess. This is beneath you."

I whipped my head toward Drake. "Did your cousin just insinuate I'm below him in status?"

His lips twitched. "He did. But it's not our business."

I gestured towards Bastien. "You be nice to her or I'll turn you into a toad."

"Can you turn people into toads?" Alex asked.

"I have no idea. But if the big oaf makes Tracy cry again, we'll find out. At the very least, I can shrink him to butterfly size."

Tracy snorted. "It's okay, Jen. Same ole argument, different day."

"And the same empty threats," Bastien mumbled. "Jen adores me and would never follow through."

I tossed a knockout spell toward the grotesque guy. "If you say so."

Ann Marie appeared in the yard with Dale and two other guys. She marched to an unconscious hybrid and poked him with her toe. "Where's my truck?"

"It's safe," Alex answered.

Two teams of enforcers appeared with Jonas as Dale finished his lap around the yard and approached us. "What's going on here, Jenella?"

Alex, Tracy, and I filled him in. As we spoke, everyone else drifted towards us to listen. When we were done, everyone wore grim expressions. Anger and frustration rolled off Dale in waves. "I'll gather a team to convince hybrids still living in the city to evacuate."

"Great." My stomach churned. "There're kids in cages downstairs. The bigger kids seemed eager to go with the human agents who were trafficking them. They're going to need caretakers who can contain them. Do you have the resources? Or should we take them to Allure?"

"We will care for our people."

I nodded and focused on Glacintial. "Have your people secure the kids. Leave Alex out of it and don't hurt anyone."

His eyes lit with white fire. "Of course."

"Jonas, these guys are some kind of shifter. Have you seen anything like them before?"

"No, but I have a theory I'll share with you once I confirm a few things."

"Great." I started pacing so I could think. "I want every single adult here read by dragons, Bas. Don't leave a single corner of their minds untouched. Once we have every piece of information, turn the humans over to Ara. Kill the rest."

The enforcer colonel flinched. "We are not in the business of killing indiscriminately."

I stopped pacing and met his eyes. "Have you seen the conditions they're keeping those babies in?"

He flinched. "I understand it's a sore spot, but perhaps they can be rehabilitated."

"They're my people, so I'll handle them," Dale said. When we all focused on him, the scary barkeep shrugged. "We've given them many chances, and they not only refuse to comply but have sold us out and abused our kids. We'll assess them and kill them not only because they're traitors, but because Jenella is the queen, and the colonel is not."

"Your enforcer team can investigate the house. Treat the kids with care."

When everyone moved, I kissed Drake's cheek, linked arms with Tracy and Alex, and flashed to Ann Marie's truck. "Are you going to return to Allure with us, or go home?"

Alex opened the door. "Home. I need to shift and think."

I scanned his face and intentions. "Text me if you need anything."

"I'm fine, Jen. Will you help me bring Lily home?"

"Of course. Anything you need."

Tracy watched him drive away. "Never in a million years did I think you'd form a friendship with Alex. I mean, you two are so different."

"Yeah. What's up with you and Bastien?"

"It's the same argument we've had for years. No one ever wins, and I'm trying to end it."

"Okay. Tell me if you'd like to change him into a butterfly. He's wrong about my follow-through. I'll do it in a heartbeat if it makes you happy."

A deviant smile spread across her face. "Oh, don't worry. I will."

Chapter Ten

Sylphira hovered near Charlotte's area, talking in shrill tones as I shuffled towards my office the next day. Razazia rested her elbow on the desk, her lips pursed as if fighting a smile. She wiggled her eyebrows when she spotted me.

Sylphira quit talking and zipped to me. "Hey, Jen."

"Hey."

Razazia smirked. "Hello, Jenella. I have the honor of teaching the lovely young hybrid you rescued about elf magic, so she understands her power when it develops."

"Nice." I needed to stop by and see how the girls were doing. "Have you met her?"

"Not yet. But I've informed Dale I'll take elven hybrids in and give them a safe home." She sighed. "My hybrids would have never faced this fate had Anitta not put me to sleep."

The entire coalition would be much different had my evil mother not interfered with the Firsts. "Yeah."

A shrill buzzing came from Sylphira's wings. "We're not here to discuss the past." She fluttered closer. "We have an idea to win over the humans."

"Who's we?"

Razazia held out her hand for Sylphira. "A group of leaders has discovered something important."

"Oh?"

She leaned forward. "They worship heroes."

I turned to Verity. "What does she mean?"

"That they want to manipulate people. Let's move this little meeting into your office."

Sylphira shot toward the TV remote and stomped on the power button as we settled. "You heard about the humans shooting at our people near pockets, right?"

"Sure." It was an escalating problem, but it wasn't as scary as the various governments searching for us.

"I had some pixies follow them. Guess what we found?"

"Violent humans?"

She grinned. "They want to be heroes."

"How does killing innocent paranormals make them heroes?"

"It doesn't matter. The point is, they believe they're saving people."

"Um. Okay."

"Watch this. Razazia?"

The TV came on and showed a group of weirdos dressed in costumes running through an exploding city. It took a while for me to realize they were saving people. "So, you want us to dress in ridiculous costumes and save people from disasters?"

Sylphira's shrill laugh made my teeth ache. "I'd pay to see you and Tracy in those costumes."

Razazia motioned toward the TV with an amused expression. "I had the same thoughts. It's as preposterous as it is entertaining."

I rarely agreed with Razazia.

"You two fuddy-duddies don't understand. They're *heroes*. And the humans *love* them."

I settled into a chair. "So, you think we need to become their heroes?"

"Yes!"

"I like the creative thinking, but don't understand how it's going to solve our problems."

Razazia raised a hand. "What our little friend means is if we sway the people to our side, most governments will follow suit."

My eyes trailed back to the hero movie. It could work if we didn't need to dress up in costumes. "Give me a list of these movies to study and I'll consider it."

"Done and done." Sylphira did a mid-air loop. "I'm a genius! You'll see."

I grinned at her excitement. "If this works, you'll be *our* hero."

Her laugh reminded me of a cricket mixed with an angry bee. "I wouldn't be a hero among paranormals, even if I saved the entire world, because, unlike humans, we have a real power structure, and it's expected of leaders."

True. Our entire society expected leaders to lead. Aside from the bowing I'd ended, it was our job, and very few glorified us. "Right. Well, I appreciate the innovation."

After they left, I turned to Verity. "What's your opinion on this?"

"I like it." She tapped something on her tablet. "She's right about humans loving their heroes. But the downside is they like to build a person up, place them on a pedestal, then tear them down just to watch the crash. We can't allow them to do that to us."

"Then we can't let them choose a person to put on their pedestal. I'm not sold on becoming superheroes, but if we use her idea, we'll need the Council's support. Then, we'll have to study their problems, find solutions for them, and ensure people see us doing it. All without drawing more shooters to our gates."

"It doesn't matter how we approach it, the solution will be more difficult than Sylphira believes. While y'all wear it like a badge of honor, humans like to pretend they're not violent. It'll take cooperation and more cohesion than the Coalition has had in centuries."

"Yeah." I glanced at the movie. "I'm going to watch these movies and talk to Drake about it. If he agrees, we'll run it by my advisors and the Council. But let's keep listening to fresh ideas. We're a big community, so we can deploy more than one strategy."

Charlotte buzzed in a few hours later, carrying a large tray of popcorn. We were ready to start the third movie and had an entire crowd of staff and palace guards, including some griffins, gathered in my office. The movies were full of action and so funny that my stomach hurt from laughing. "I doubt I can watch another one."

Verity shoved a bowl of popcorn into my hands. "There are a lot more superhero movies. Some are better than others. One more won't hurt."

Drake appeared at his office door and scanned the small crowd. When the staff noticed, they froze like he had caught them doing something wrong. The group shifted as he moved towards me. "No need to end the fun on my behalf."

I winked. "Come watch this with us. You'll love the jokes."

Charlotte slid popcorn to him as he wedged a chair in the gap beside me. "Jen's thinking about making us all superheroes."

His face remained neutral as he settled, but he sent sheer delight through the bond. "Superheroes?"

I nodded. "I think we can pull it off, but we'll never be as funny as the people in the movies."

"They have scripts. Perhaps you can assign the Chimera King the task of writing snarky quips."

The entire room burst out laughing.

I rested my head on his shoulder as the movie started. "Don't give me any ideas."

His shoulder shook with laughter.

"Are you insane?" Tracy wove a spell and wrapped it around a clump of herbs, then lowered it into a boiling pot. "Can you imagine ogres chasing down human gangs without killing them? I mean, they can barely control themselves from destroying the pockets. If they're set loose on humans, there's no telling what those psychos will do." We were in her dad's extensive lab in the basement of his house. Her face held a tranquil expression. Tracy belonged in an alchemy coven.

I tapped my knee. "You're right. It's a logistical nightmare."

"Yep. Not to mention how the leaders will use it to their advantage."

"Some will. But they're coming around." Sort of. "The other suggestions were dull or cruel. Most involved altering minds. We lack the power to do something like that on a mass scale. Even if we did, I wouldn't because it's what Anitta would do."

"There's gotta be something else. Those movies are fun, but meant for entertainment, not a blueprint."

"Yeah. And we'd look dumb in those costumes." For the millionth time, I wished Mat were around to talk to. "I'm having my staff make a list of problems we can solve, like wildfires and crime. We have monetary resources, and some cultures worship money. Maybe we can use it to sway them."

She put the lid on her potion pot and stirred. "What about how vampires are the biggest crime bosses on the planet? They'll take advantage of the situation for sure. And we only have a handful of elementals to help with natural disasters."

I spun an empty potion bottle. "I'm trying to solve a complex problem with a simple solution, which never works. But we need to start somewhere, or the situation will escalate."

"It won't be enough. If you do it, and I'm not saying it's a good idea, you'll need to do it on a massive scale."

Another hole in the plan. Getting the various factions to do anything on a mass scale was almost impossible, and I hadn't worked on my magic in weeks. I thought about what Olwen said about going to Mage Mountain. I'd need to take a couple of days and see if I could reach my grandmother without my memory being wiped. "Did your dad discover how to make healing potions for humans?"

"No. Without magic to activate them, they fail."

"I need to ask the healers if their magic works." Or, I could sneak into one of the human healing centers and test mine. If mine worked, the healers' magic would. "Did you work out your argument with Bastien?"

Tracy growled in frustration. "He's still trying to force me to be more involved with the dragons. I'm not wired into their mind network, so even if I tried to rule them, it would be a disaster. But he refuses to see it."

"Because he loves you."

"And he's a big angry bully."

"And he loves you."

Her eyes brimmed with tears as she moved to the shelves and gathered herbs. "The dragons are his whole life. His identity. He thinks I don't accept them because I won't help him rule."

I flinched. "Yikes."

"Yeah. We'll never agree on the subject, and over the years it's driven a wedge between us. I mean, I love the big brute, but I'll never be what he needs."

My eyes burned. Being isolated for the better part of my life, I sucked at relationships. Without Drake and Tracy, and to an extent, Bastien, being so patient with me, I never would have had friends. "Should I isolate him in a box to give him time to think?"

A ragged laugh escaped her. "Can you imagine the tantrum?"

"Yeah. Deva wouldn't like it." I snapped my fingers. "I could put a barrier around you where he can't touch you until he sees things your way."

She wiped her eyes, and her perfect white teeth peeked out. "You're a good friend, Jen."

"Not as good as you." I sighed. "I have the opposite problem. Drake's so damn patient and reasonable, he's impossible to argue with. He just stands there and sends me calm vibes while I flip out. I want to rip my hair out sometimes."

Her smile turned genuine. "Relationships are hard."

"Yeah." I stood. "I need to go to Mage Mountain for a few days. Want to go with me?"

"Absolutely. When?"

"I need to clear my calendar. Being queen isn't as boring or restrictive as I once imagined." It was downright overwhelming. Especially without Mat taking care of the details.

"As soon as you figure it out, text me. I'll clear my schedule and be there."

Alex waited for me when I landed at the palace. He ran a hand through his thick brown hair. "No one told me you were watching superhero movies. I'm kind of an expert."

Pure glee surged through me. "Really? Because I have soooo many ideas. I'd like to run them by you."

He followed me through the back door. "I want to ask you about something, too."

I stopped next to the breakfast nook. "About Lily?"

"Yes."

I shoved him toward the elevator before Helen could bombard us with food. "Did you think of something to help her?"

"Sort of. I'm having a hard time with it because I'm still pissed." He jerked a thumb toward himself. "I'm the reasonable sibling. Even you, who doesn't need to listen to anyone, listens to me. But she didn't bother. She just dove in."

His description made my heart ache with grief. Mat wasn't always the reasonable one, but he took care of business while I fussed. And, like Alex, he always had to be the one to bend. I missed him so much I could barely breathe sometimes. "If anything happens, you're going to regret not forgiving her."

Alex fell silent. Inside my office, he slumped into a chair. "I'm sorry. I didn't mean to cause you pain."

"It's not your fault. I swing from blubbering mess to denial, to anger, then guilt so fast it's like having whiplash. Drake assures me it's normal."

"No offence, but I'm reminded how lucky I am to have my parents every time I have a conversation with you."

The statement baffled me. "Why?"

"For starters, they taught me how to work through emotions, so I don't have to ask others what's normal."

"Oh. Helen and Mat tried, but it took his death for me to make the effort. Regret hurts more than anything else. I wasted so much time running away instead of savoring every minute I had with him. The last thing I want is for you and Lily to have the same regrets."

"I understand." He eyed the snacks Helen always left for me. "Were you aware that the more you trust someone, the easier it is to get into your head? You should work on it before the wrong person learns your secrets and exploits them."

I smirked. "Not everyone is you, Alex. There are only four paranormals on the planet strong enough to read me. I gave up blocking you when I used your imagination to make the colors inside the pocket. Because I *saw* you. The least I could do is reciprocate."

"You're the queen. No need to reciprocate. And don't tell Lily those colors came from me. She hates them, so it's best we blame Cavil."

"She won't hear it from me. And, if I ever want healthy relationships, I need to make an effort." I pointed at him. "Tracy taught me that. Because

I didn't have friends until she came along." Bastien tried, but we butted heads too much to become close. "At least you and Lily had each other."

"That's sad."

"I like the hybrid pocket's colors."

"Lily hates the color of the house. It's been fun to watch her try to change it."

My forehead crinkled. "Why can't she change it?"

"Because Mom put a barrier around it. It's an old trick to keep Lily's mind occupied, so she doesn't cause trouble."

"That's almost diabolical. And Lily's never figured it out?"

"Oh, she has a few times. But she likes a challenge." He sighed. "Deva and Drake think I'm close to being able to block. I've talked to Rayar and Cavil, and we came up with an idea." He slid his phone towards me. "We can use our land and Cavil's to build houses for her vampires. Then I'll drag her home."

My head shot up. "Cavil's moving in?"

He nodded. "Yeah."

"What does Lily have to say about that?"

"She understands how matches work, so I doubt she'll care. Unlike you, he blocks his thoughts from me."

I laughed and rubbed my hands together. "Oh, I'm going to tease her endlessly."

"Good. She deserves it." He leaned back and closed his eyes. "I'm losing her, Jen. She's always been there and now she has a title and a bunch of responsibilities. It feels like she's leaving me behind."

I was partially responsible for their current situation. And hurting people was never my intention. Especially Lily and Alex. "I'm sorry."

"Oh yes. Let's pretend it is about you."

"*Gah!*" I'd been so focused on Alex, I didn't sense Quin. "Damn it, Quin! This conversation is private."

"Of course." He glided to a chair. "Tell me, have you thought about why you're so attracted to dragons? Or why the Dragon Queen is obsessed with you?"

Alex's muscles bunched. "No."

"Then perhaps you should."

I ran my hands over my face. "Right. Alex has a plan to help Lily."

"Yes, I'm sure she needs others to make decisions for her." Quin squinted when he caught my grin. "Have you considered moving the problematic gates, or are you too busy being a relationship counselor?"

"I can't flash around the country in one day, yet. Besides, the pocket leadership needs to make a request, and I've only had two."

Alex ignored Quin's sarcasm. "I'll go and watch your back if you want."

Chapter Eleven

Drake's emotions scattered, and I gripped my chest as if I could help contain them. *What's wrong? Are you okay?*

He didn't answer right away, and I almost flashed to him.

"Jen?" Alex's voice registered as I concentrated on Drake. "Has she done this before?"

"No," Quin answered.

My eyes snapped open. "Something's wrong with Drake. Hold on for a minute. *Drake!*

Lily found the person responsible for many of our betrayals.

My chair hit the floor when I stood. *Who?*

The vampires that Roman stole from Jedediah. Lily noticed what she calls an echo in her blood bonds. Jedediah is still controlling his people, and they are sabotaging us from their new houses. I will explain more when I return.

I spun toward Quin. "Jedediah's people are sabotaging us."

He appeared right in front of my face. "Explain."

"Lily found something in the bonds and called Drake. Jedediah's vampires are working against us."

"I must warn my love." He vanished.

When I looked at Alex, his eyes glowed amber. Not like a mage, or a shifter, but like a dragon. A deep frown settled on my face. "You can flash, right?"

He blinked, and the glow disappeared. "Yes. Why?"

"Because the glow in your eyes is very dragon-like. They can't flash."

"I'm a hybrid. Everything about me is unique."

"Right. Want to go to Ara's with me?"

Goosebumps popped up on my arms as we arrived in the flashing circle where the chimeras attacked me. I doubted I'd ever trust the circle again, but at least I didn't panic. "What do you know about Jedediah?"

"Not much other than he's an asshole who abused and neglected my sister, then showed up and claimed to love her when it suited him."

"Quin set me up with my first case working for him. I hid my magic back then and wore glamour. The guy was an ass. He left me, Verity, and Colonel Ballard stranded in a human meadow with two mind-controlled dragons."

"That's mild for him."

"Yeah."

The vampires led us toward Ara's kitchen and disappeared. She and Quin stood by a boiling pot with their hands clasped. A strange vampire cowered at the kitchen table, probably from the thick power clogging the room. My skin crawled as we waited a polite distance for them to finish their conversation.

"Hey, Alex. Where's Lily? I want to go home."

My head whipped to the odd vampire.

Alex stepped between us. "You'll return when Ara says it's okay."

I tried to push him out of my field of vision, but it was like moving a boulder, so I peeked around him. "You're one of Lily's new vampires?"

His defiant eyes flipped toward Ara before settling on me. "Who the hell are you?"

Uh boy. "I'm...."

I never got to finish my sentence because his head slammed on the table, and he collapsed. Ara examined the unconscious vampire for a beat. When she was satisfied, she turned her focus to us, and a smile lit her face. "Oh, my. This is a pleasant surprise." Flyby vampires swarmed into the room, removed the new guy, and set four drinks on the table. "Please, sit."

After we settled, she leaned towards me. "Why have the wrong siblings been joined at the hip the last few days?"

A laugh escaped me. "Drake and Deva are tutoring Alex."

"I see. The odd vampire is Pascal. He is Lily's first turn and a bit feral. Her odd magic creates the most interesting creatures."

"Feral?"

"The other two are fine," Alex explained. "Pascal thinks he can defy Lily and return to his human life."

"I see. How much of a risk is he to the Coalition?"

Ara sipped her drink. "As long as we watch him, none. He is improving, but still defiant. I will keep him close until he adjusts."

I glanced at Alex, but his face was a stony mask. It was eerily similar to the one Jonas wore when he was irritated and impatient. "Did Quin explain the situation with Jedediah's vampires?"

"Yes." Her voice was hard as steel. "Your mother had a hand in his deception. It kept me from recognizing the echo when we looked for a traitor. There were seven other elite vampires in House Jedediah. They are being detained as we speak."

Alex leaned forward, a spark of interest in his eyes. "The other masters can't feel the echo?"

"I'm sorry, dear, but no. I believe the magic infused in them by Anitta targeted me." She tapped her chin. "I did not inherit Lilith's powers, but developed my own similar skills. I bond the masters and, through them, monitor their house, so there may be a slight disconnect. It has happened before. Lily has no such restraints, so it's easier for her to sense these things."

"And Anitta was a sneaky, conniving bitch," I added. "I wonder if she knew Lily was your heir."

"No," Alex answered. "If she did, she wouldn't have dumped her at good ole Jed's house."

True. She was all about power and would have used Lily's status to her advantage. The thought of strong, funny, defiant Lily being used by Anitta made me sick. "Drake's taking custody of Lily's traitors."

"I request he bring them here. The holding cells at The Cauldron are acceptable, but my dungeons are better." Her ancient brown eyes landed on me. "And I wish to assist in their punishment. A slow, painful death is the consequence for defying me, and I do not wish to delay it."

I fought not to rub my arms at the deluge of creepy magic rolling off her as I sent the message to Drake. His delight bounced back at me. We were a bunch of violent, bloodthirsty predators. So much so, I began to doubt my plan to turn us into heroes. It suited our skill sets better to take over their governments and use our magic to change their minds.

Alex visibly shivered. "You almost feel like Lily when she's mad."

A predatory grin formed on Ara's face.

We shared a look as we stood, and I filled my mind with thoughts of closed mouths. "Drake's on his way."

Alex's eyes softened. "It's fine, Jen. There's no need for you to shield me."

Drake and two other dragons landed and tossed two vampires at Ara's feet. The other dragons tossed their prisoners and flew away when Drake shifted, his entire focus on Ara. "The Crown is entrusting these prisoners into your care. But make no mistake, they are coalition prisoners. Therefore, Jenella or I will oversee their execution."

Quin's eyes flashed. "You will find no resistance, nor deception from us, First."

"Good. Because it was all I could do to restrain myself from tearing them to pieces."

I rubbed my face. "Um. Can we tone it down?" Everyone stared at me. "Please." The five vampires were unconscious and bloody, and I wondered if Drake or Lily beat them. Not that it mattered.

Ara clenched her fists. "You are right, dear. Please send the Crown Juror to sentence them, so I may begin the punishment."

"Titus will arrive soon," Drake said.

Anger sparked in my gut at his announcement. "Oh? And when, exactly, did I order that?"

His brow furrowed. "You didn't order it. I did."

"I see." Not wanting to start an argument in front of everyone, I scanned the vampires one more time. "Want to help me with those gates since we're not needed here, Alex?"

Drake stomped toward me. *I'm not trying to undermine you.*

It was unlike him to make so many decisions without at least discussing them with me. Half the council already thought he ruled instead of me, and lately, I had to agree. He was doing all kinds of things without bothering to run them by me. *Ordering my juror to a sentencing rubbed me the wrong way. I'm going to go fix a couple of gates and think about it.*

I anticipated your request and fulfilled it. What I didn't do is circumvent your authority.

The explanation sounded exactly like something Drake would do. My insecurities disagreed. "Well, stop doing that until I finish working out my shit."

And when will that be? Because all I've seen you do is wallow in your grief and avoid making hard decisions.

My eyes widened, and I locked my knees to keep from running away. "Do you really believe that?"

"You've deferred everything to the Council, Mathias's assistant, your advisors, and me. So why would this situation be any different?"

I blinked back tears. "That's harsh."

"And true," Quin interjected. "Your hesitancy to lead has caused the humans to become emboldened. Had you acted faster, Lily would not be in her current situation."

My stomach soured. I hadn't acted after the battle. If Mat had been around, he would have cleaned up the mess and tied up every loose end in days. I'd been puzzling over what to do for weeks and had delegated a lot. I scanned their faces and saw sympathy in Ara's eyes. Alex wouldn't look at me. Quin and Drake had their hands loose at their sides, like they were ready for a fight. I dropped my arms. It was painful to realize those closest to me had no faith in my leadership. "When will Titus be here?"

Drake scanned my face. "Soon."

We stood in awkward silence, waiting for him. When he appeared, he held up both hands in the 'stop' gesture. "I don't regulate family disputes."

Everyone's heads turned to me. Impatience oozed through the bond from Drake. I stepped forward. "You're not here for us. You're here to assess these vampires. Drake is charging them with treason. They not only sold us out to the Bellicose, but gave vital information to humans."

"I would like you to evaluate my son, too," Ara added. "Lily believes he has led them astray."

Titus stepped forward and touched them one by one. "They are all guilty of treason and broke a few vampire laws regarding bonds. But that one's not my call." He stepped back. "They are also fiercely loyal to Jedediah and under his command." His hard eyes drilled into Alex. "He's convinced them he loves his daughter and her place is under his control. The bastard cooked up the idea with the second queen." He nudged a woman with his toe. "This one tried to schmooze Lily and manipulate her."

None of it surprised me. I knew damn well my mother was behind every single power play. The question was, how did I fix it? Confusion, guilt and anger swirled through me as I considered all the lives she ruined.

And how, even in death, she still screwed with us. "I sentence them to a slow, painful death to be carried out by The Queen of Umbra. I sentence Jedediah to watch before he meets the same fate. Whether by the hand of the Queen of Umbra, her consort, her heir, or another representative. The Crown Juror will assess all other vampire traitors on an as-needed basis."

Ara's head ticked, and vampires swarmed the traitors while I stared into Drake's eyes, letting the pain and anger from his harsh truth show. When we were done, I laid a hand on Alex's arm and flashed to the first gate we needed to move.

He pushed his mop of hair out of his eyes. "Are you mad at me?"

"No. I'm mad at Drake for not saying something sooner. It wasn't like I was delaying my rulings, so much as I was trying to encourage the other leaders to be more involved. Cohesion takes time and patience. I didn't realize my idea of patience was everyone else's idea of indecisiveness. Including Drake's."

A woman's throat cleared. "Can I help you with something?"

I scanned the area. The pocket was a rural one that housed a few thousand paranormals. It was where Cavil found Lily and Alex after their ordeal. "I'm Queen Jenella, and this is my friend, Alex, son of Jonas the First, and the sorceress Ann Marie. We're here to move your gate to the new location."

Her eyes bounced back and forth between us. "You've heard about the shootings?"

I jerked a thumb at Alex. "He's the mental mage who dropped the shooters a while back."

She beat her fist on her chest twice in a show of respect. "Nice. The gate is currently under human surveillance, and we're stuck inside. We'd like to move it to a secured barn on an elf-owned farm." She activated a hologram and tapped two locations. "From here to here."

I studied the map, then examined the gate. The pocket didn't have a monitoring spell like Allure, and the magic was more pedestrian. "It may take a while."

Her brow furrowed. "Sure. Take your time."

When I created the gates to the hybrid pocket, I used Allure as an example and had a bunch of paranormals on hand to draw from, so the entire experience was new. Not wanting a repeat of when I fixed the crack in Allure, I avoided touching the wards, isolated the gate in a box, and slid it to the right.

A furry head butted my hand, and I jumped. Alex's massive lion paw swiped me back from a cliff. "Thanks." I tightened my ponytail and examined my work. I dissipated the protective barrier and peeked out. The only thing I could see was an abandoned, snow-covered field, so I stepped out.

Alex's growl rattled my bones when he joined me.

"Don't lecture me. I need to be outside the gate to do this and didn't want to get shot." It was more instinct than the truth, but I didn't care. I absorbed the magic and held it in a separate container, like I used to with my healing magic. When the gate separated from the wards, I dug a hand into Alex's fur and flashed to the barn. Dust clouded the air, and I coughed as I sensed for the pocket's wards. They ran along the edge of the rickety barn.

I released the gate and tried to reshape it into a square, but it came out more like an oval. Unsure what to do, I poked it with raw power. The ward's magic pulsed through me and shoved me backwards. Pain shot from my ass and up my back as electric jolts rattled my body. The thing still needed to be anchored, so I ignored the pain as I tied it off, leaving the oval shape. Once completed, I took my time withdrawing my magic.

The jolts stopped, and I held my stomach. A low warning growl brought me out of the trance. "I'm okay." I only stumbled twice as I stood. Alex pushed into my side to steady me. "Thank you." The gate wasn't perfect, but solid. "Okay. Let's test it out." I stepped back through.

A scream ripped from my throat when I plummeted. I flashed to save myself and tilted my head up in time to see Alex leap through and land on the cliff. His roar almost blew my ears out.

I flashed to him. "I forgot about the cliff. No need to throw a fit." I moved the gate back to the checkpoint and poked my head out.

"Did it work?" The gate guard asked, her voice laced with hope.

"Yes. Call my office if you have any problems with it."

Alex shifted and headed for his clothes. "Ready to go?"

"Yes." I flashed us to the gate inside Dale's bar.

Darla peered into the room the moment we landed. "Hey, Alex. Jenella."

"Darla." I pointed at the gate. "I'm moving this. You want it at Maria's warehouse, right?"

"Yes. Thank you."

It only took a few minutes to set the gate up. It was much easier since I created it. I flashed to Alex's house when I sensed Drake heading my way.

Alex led me through the wards. "Look, I can't comprehend what it means to rule, but one thing I understand is that people trust decisive actions. While you were gone, Lily spent every night trolling the city and became frustrated with the progress in the subdivisions we wrecked. When you returned, they moved a hundred times faster. Drake somehow convinced the hybrids to help speed things along. Those are the kinds of actions people notice. Maybe you should have a conversation with him, rather than running away."

I liked Alex. His matter-of-fact demeanor, mixed with his strong confidence, was refreshing. "You're right, but I'm not ready. And I'm aware how good Drake is at getting things done."

He paused in the kitchen. "June and Flintous are hiding in the security office. He gets things done to make you look good. Not for himself."

"Right." I needed to readjust my entire leadership strategy. I wanted everyone to work together for the greater good. But no matter what I tried, it always seemed like I was doing something wrong. And just when I built some confidence, someone would come along and smash it. “So, what’s your plan for the house?”

A goofy grin stretched across his face. “We have some ideas. Let me text Cavil.”

Chapter Twelve

A few days later, we stood outside Lily's house as the god, Cavil, directed Rayar and his team in dismantling his mansion and creating a subdivision stretching from his property to Lily's. Alex's house was large before, but with the changes, it was massive to accommodate Cavil, some vampires, and the extra dragons Deva sent. "Are you sure about this?"

Alex watched the mages put the final touches on a two-story house. "Yes. Deva thinks I'm ready."

"Should I add magic to your bedroom wards so you can sleep?"

"I'm good for now. If I struggle, I'll text you." His eyes trailed toward the road leading to the mansion where Lily was staying. "When do you think they'll be done?"

I spotted Colonel Ballard heading my way and waved. "In less than an hour."

"As soon as everyone's here, I'll get her."

"I'll go with you for support if you need it."

"Thanks, but no. Glacintial wants to help."

I kept having to remind myself that Alex wasn't my little brother. He hadn't complained about my fussing, but he noticed. "Sorry."

"Don't apologize. I'm glad you think of me as family."

I pasted on a smile as Colonel Ballard reached us. He bowed his head. "Alex. Jen. This is quite the project."

I scanned the multiple houses. "Which ones are yours?"

"The ones on the end. I'm not sure why Cavil insists we stay."

"He trusts you," Alex said. "He has a lot of admirers and doesn't want to burden Lily's vampires or the dragons with providing security."

"Huh. I assumed this was a temporary arrangement, but can't say I'm disappointed." He turned his attention to me. "The hybrids are forming an enforcer unit here. They approached me with a job offer."

I eyed the ever-expanding town. "Will you take it?"

"It depends on you. We're still under your protection, and I can't work until you declare me trustworthy."

When he and his family fled Hospa, they requested that I shelter them. Not trusting shifters at the time, I placed them with Cavil and forgot about the agreement. "Verity will send the release to you today."

"Thank you, Jen. For everything."

"You're welcome. I'm glad we could help you and your family."

The flapping of several sets of dragon wings interrupted our conversation. Deva led Drake, Bastien, and a silver dragon as they swept around the pocket and headed toward us. As they landed, she dropped the wyrm dragon with bright green hair from her talon. The same one who protected the girls in Allure. The others transformed into their human forms. I grinned when I spotted Tracy. I shoulder-bumped Drake as I passed and swept her in a hug. "What are you doing here?"

"Deva insisted we come. She's placing two more dragons with Alex. Lily's friends."

"Well, I'm glad you're here. Can you believe this?" I motioned at the completed houses.

"I mean, I still can't believe Lily's leading a house. It's surreal."

"Yeah." It bothered me. And I still wasn't convinced Ara was unaware of Roman's schemes. However much I wanted to interfere, it wasn't my business.

Drake shuffled in my direction. "Jenella."

Tracy's eyes flipped between us. "You two fighting?"

"Not yet." It was inevitable. I had some things to say about how his lack of faith in me hurt. We avoided each other since our little tiff outside Ara's place, but I knew it wouldn't last. The stupid bond ensured it. The whole thing gave me a new perspective on Tracy and Bastien's constant struggles. "How are you guys doing?"

She shrugged. "Fine."

Alex and Glacintial broke away from the other dragons. "I'm going to head out, Jen. Will you make sure everyone's in place?"

"Yep." The growing crowd milled around the yard. The green dragon bent down, dug a hole in the snow, and poked at the curly blue grass. I'd screwed up the colors when I built the pocket, but found them as beautiful and unique as its occupants. "Good luck."

His lips turned up, and his eyes sparkled with hope. "Thanks."

I gathered those close to Lily and asked everyone else to leave. The breakfast nook had been transformed into a cavernous space with a large table. Ara and Quin took seats across from Jonas and Ann Marie. Cavil bent his head to say something to a red dragon, while a purple dragon worked with Drake to conjure food and drinks. Emine sat with her brother, Rayar, as she watched everyone. It was the first time she'd taken part in anything family-related since Mat's death. The sadness in her eyes made my heart ache.

Deva's warm hand landed on my arm. "We will wait in the other room, love. I only wanted to ensure young Alex and his new tutors were situated."

And she was nosy. "Okay."

Tracy gave me a side hug and followed. No doubt they'd eavesdrop on the whole thing.

Bastien stopped beside me. "I hear you are considering setting the masses loose on humans."

"What? No. I'm considering solving some of their problems, so they see us as useful and stop shooting at us."

"I see. May I suggest a few things?"

"Sure. But not today. You can come to the next advisor's meeting with Deva."

"Very well."

It was late by the time I left the gathering and returned to the palace. Lily seemed thrilled at the idea of returning home and didn't even protest when Deva slipped a couple more dragons into her household. Alex was so delighted to have Lily back that he practically glowed. I felt like a cheap substitute, and it would have bothered me if it were anyone else.

As I changed into one of Drake's old shirts, I wondered what it would be like to have a sibling as close as Lily and Alex. Mat and I were close, but we had more of a parent-child relationship for a good portion of my life. We'd only started becoming friends and siblings when he passed.

When my eyes filled with tears, I blinked them away. I refused to be jealous of their relationship. With everything they went through, they deserved to have someone to trust. I sensed Drake in the sitting area and let out a breath.

He lounged on the sofa, his long legs stretched out and crossed at the ankles. I drank in the sight of his rugged greatness and tried to ignore the jolt of excitement. Sure, it hurt how he didn't believe in me, but I couldn't blame him. With all that quiet confidence and patience, it was no wonder he was better at my job than my neurotic, insecure ass. I tiptoed around the coffee table and sat beside him without saying a word.

His arm snaked out and drew me close. "I can feel your hesitancy."

I nestled into his warmth. "No kidding? Because I feel your fatigue."

"It's my own fault. I've flown hundreds of miles in the last couple of weeks."

I missed the feeling of freedom that came with flying. "I can heal your fatigue."

He patted my hip. "If you do, I'll be full of energy and won't sleep."

"It will give you more time to compensate for my shortcomings."

It took him several seconds to answer. "Do you believe that's what I'm doing?"

"Yes." I lifted my head and met his eyes. "It hurt to realize how little faith you have in my leadership. And Alex said you're being decisive to bolster my image."

"He got in my head? Huh. That kid is special."

"Alex is great. It bothers me how much interest Deva has taken in him."

"She's amazed at his mental abilities. It will pass."

"Let's hope it does before Jonas loses his patience with her. Can you imagine those two fighting?"

Drake's chest bounced with laughter. "I would pay money to see it."

I tapped his biceps. "It would be entertaining."

Drake shifted into a more comfortable position. "I'm sorry for hurting you. You impressed many people during the battle. If we had stayed, you could have built on the sentiment. But I whisked you away so you couldn't. Then you were drowning in your grief, and I was hesitant to bring it up. I was only trying to help."

"You also think I'm wasting time trying to build cooperation among the leaders." It wasn't a question.

"I do. Lissa tried for years in a far less hostile environment. I witnessed her attempts fail too many times to count, so I concluded your efforts were pointless. I should have discussed it with you.

"Times were different back then. Paranormals weren't living in pocket realms. She made several entries in her diaries about how they'd be more successful if the factions lived together. I think Anitta got the idea to build the pockets after reading it."

"You're attempting to carry on your grandmother's legacy?"

"No. I'm trying to piece a fractured society back together. No matter how idealistic it seems. But if we don't have at least some cohesion, especially since humans are aware of us and are working with those ugly guys and possibly demons, we won't have a coalition." I caressed his arm. "If I can bring them together and even begin healing the wounds the Bellicose made, I'll consider it a win."

"I apologize for misreading the situation."

"You didn't. It should be me apologizing for not communicating. I gave you the role of my consort, but failed to support you. Part of that's your fault because you're so amazing." I feathered kisses across his jaw. "The rest is on me. I'll try to communicate better from now on."

"Speaking of communication, Bastien said you plan to visit Mage Mountain."

"You were there when Olwen relayed the request."

"I didn't realize you made plans."

"I haven't. Though I asked Tracy if she was interested in going."

He used a finger to make swirls on my back, leaving a trail of fire. "I found some information about Olivia and Tasha this morning."

Fear almost paralyzed me, and I struggled to shake it off. "Good or bad?"

"Their foster parents were with the hybrids who shot up Dale's bar and were killed for it."

My heart pounded. "Did anyone tell them?"

He kissed my forehead. "Ann Marie is working with them."

"She did a great job with Alex and Lily, so they're in excellent hands."

"Yes. The girls won't admit it, but they love her and worship Jonas."

"They're amazing."

"They weren't always. While age has made me more patient, it has humbled them." The swirls turned into a light massage. "Dale is considering sending more displaced shifter children to Jonas and Razazia. He tried to order me to relay a message."

I burst out laughing. "Did you get to use your pointy teeth?"

"I may have flashed them."

Another laugh. "Dale's so cool."

"Cool?"

"Human slang."

"Antiquated human slang, yes. And I agree. The man is brave."

"Stay with me tonight."

His lips met mine, and my entire body burned with need. Drake pulled back and, with a feather-light touch, ran a finger down my cheek. "No pressure, but since I'm here so often, I'd like to move in."

"You can move in any time you're ready. It's a good thing I had the apartment expanded and added a dragon balcony."

"A very good thing."

***

Some days were not worth prying myself away from Drake and showing up. The sea of people gathered inside a throne room talked amongst themselves as they waited for me. I massaged my temples and took a breath. "Why am I here again?"

Verity tucked her hair behind her ear. "Because you care about staying in touch with people and appeasing the Leadership Council."

"I liked the email version of grievances better."

"Of course you did. Being absent is your specialty."

"Cute. Why here?"

"It's your throne room."

"It's always given me the creeps. Too formal."

"I bet Mat let you whine about it, too."

He did, though he gave me a hard look while I whined. As the thought struck, I saw him waiting for me while he drummed his fingers on the arm of the consort's throne. I blinked, and it was gone. The idea of ruling without him made me want to tear my hair out. I squared my shoulders. "Fine. Let's get this over with."

The crowd's murmurings died as I settled on the ornate gold throne with purple cushions. I couldn't have felt more awkward as I crossed my ankles. A group of low-level paranormals stood in the back, while mid-level ones filled the middle. The leaders and high-powered paranormals sat in front. My brow furrowed. "Verity?"

"Yes, Your Grace."

"Why is everyone separated by power level?"

Several higher-powered paranormals flinched at my question.

Her lips quirked. "The council members chose the seating."

"Right." Part of learning how to fight my own battles was choosing them wisely, so I dropped it. "Let's begin. Low-level paranormals first."

An elf stepped forward, dragging a small mage-elf child behind him, and bowed. "Your Grace."

"Good morning."

"I am Melston of the Elves. My match passed away fighting for our freedom in the recent battle. They stripped me of my money and possessions when I matched with her. We worked human jobs, but because of the low pay, we lacked the funds to relocate to the hybrid pocket of Eldritch. I'd like to petition the Crown to return my wealth and possessions so I may build a home for my daughter."

A group of elves in the front row broke out in chatter. I stared them down until they fell silent, then refocused on the adorable little girl and her dad. "Granted. Razazia the First will return Melston's possessions and wealth within forty-eight hours."

The man's eyes filled with tears as he lifted his daughter into his arms. "Thank you, Your Grace." He rushed out, as if I'd change my mind.

When I agreed to reopen grievance day, I thought I'd spend my time listening to the same old arguments. If I could help the hybrids recover and give children a chance, I'd gladly show up every week. "Next."

The doors flew open, and Drake strode in, his eyes hard and jaw clenched. My stomach did a little flip at the sight of him. He sauntered to the throne beside me, lowered his massive body into it, kissed my cheek, and placed his lips near my ear. "I couldn't allow you to suffer alone."

I bit back a smile and tried to tame my aching body. "Next."

A cat shifter I recognized from a case I took in Ferine approached. "Hello, Your Grace. Consort. I am from the Ferine Leopard pack. I am here to request mercy for our alpha."

The alpha in question worked with the shifters to set me up. As a result, we found one of the Bellicose labs and exposed a lot of death and destruction. I tightened my grip to keep my anger and power in check. "Have you asked Jonas for mercy?"

"No, Your Grace. Our alpha was charged with conspiring with the enemy and interfering with a monarch's duties. Your duties, to be exact. It doesn't fall under the First's jurisdiction."

"Oh?" I turned to Titus. "What are the jurisdiction laws surrounding treason?"

"The Queen of Ahl determines the jurisdiction," Titus said without moving a muscle. He was used to my mid-meeting shenanigans.

"Your request will be referred to Jonas the First for evaluation. Next."

Four hours later, I'd worked through the grievances of the regular people. A high-powered Forte mage stepped forward and bowed. He had a rare forte, allowing him to blend into his surroundings. When I sipped his power with too much force, he flinched. "I'm here to request a reevaluation of mage leadership."

It was selfish of me, but I couldn't take the only thing keeping Emine going away from her. "Denied. Next."

"If you would hear me out?"

Drake's hand squeezed my thigh. "You have two minutes." His voice rumbled through my body, and goosebumps broke out on my arms.

"Since Prince Mathias is no longer with us, there is a power vacuum. Princess Emine does not have ruling magic and, therefore, cannot effectively lead the mages. I propose we choose another leader democratically."

His request sounded reasonable if I ignored the glint in his eye and my screaming senses. I rested my arm on the chair. "And I suppose you suggest yourself as her replacement?"

"I would put myself forth as a candidate, yes."

"And whose ruling magic did you inherit?"

His forehead creased. "There is no mage with ruling magic other than you and the hybrid vampire, which is why we must change the process. Princess Emine is distraught without her match and unfit to lead. It is time for a change."

If Drake weren't there to send me calming sensations through the bond, I would have acted on the overwhelming urge to smash him to the ground repeatedly. Instead, I settled for a bitter tone. "I can read intentions. You're not here because it's time for a change. Nor do you care about the best interests of anyone other than yourself. Princess Emine is grieving, but cares about the mages. Request denied. Next."

The other high-powered people were equally petty. I worked through them until the only people left in the room were the Kelpie Queen and the Troll King.

They bowed as their grievances appeared on my tablet. They'd been fighting over bridges and waterways for years. Mat had offered them several solutions. Instead of implementing one or more of them, they doubled down on their rivalry.

"Your Grace," the Kelpie Queen began.

I sipped her magic. "No."

The Troll King cleared his throat. "We would like to address our queen."

I bobbed my head. "I have your written grievances right here."

The Kelpie Queen stomped a foot. "My people need access to all waterways within the pockets. We are becoming too numerous, and our territorial instincts are causing fights. If each Kelpie does not have adequate territory, we won't survive."

The Troll King's roaring laughter rang through the empty room. "Bollocks. She wishes for my people to starve and die because of a harmless prank a hundred years ago."

"Pranks aren't funny unless both parties laugh."

"You wouldn't know what a laugh was if it smacked you in your ugly face."

"Well, I never!"

I let them go on, hoping they'd work it out themselves, but as the insults flew, it became obvious they wouldn't budge. "Enough!" My voice echoed through the room.

They froze.

I leaned forward. "This dispute is hurting both factions and has gone on long enough. Since neither of you intends to compromise, I'll do it for you." I flipped through the solutions Mat provided over the years. "Trolls will occupy all water within fifty feet of their bridges. They may charge standard tolls for passage both under and over them. Kelpies will occupy the remaining portion of the waterway, provided it is deep enough to conceal them. Kelpies may bite any troll who crosses their boundaries. Should children near either faction go missing, a juror will investigate both parties. The guilty party will face execution."

"Preposterous," the Kelpie queen scoffed. "How are we supposed to eat without bridges?"

I let my eyes shine with power. "Perhaps you should have asked yourself that question before repeatedly petitioning the crown with this nonsense." I refocused on my tablet. "As for your constant bickering, I no longer want to hear it. Not at council meetings, on the streets, or here." I tossed the tablet aside. "If I receive so much as one complaint about you two causing suffering, distress, or arguing in public, I'll remove you from your positions on my council and force a vote to replace you."

The Troll King's shoulders slumped. "We can't argue anymore?"

"No."

The Kelpie Queen tapped her chin. "What about silent arguments?"

"No. Not silent or loud. Not a single passive-aggressive action will be tolerated. Nor will you be allowed to do shitty things to each other and claim plausible deniability. Whatever this is between you..." I swirled a finger. "Work it out in private. But everyone else is done with it. Hearings adjourned." I stood and strode out the door without looking back.

Drake took my hand when we reached the elevators. "How long do you think it will take them to break your decree?"

"I give them a couple of hours tops. But they'll never bring it to me again."

The crinkle in the corner of his eyes was becoming permanent because of my impatience. "No, I suppose they won't."

When we reached my office, he spun me around and lowered his mouth to mine. The kiss was so soft and slow, the normal lust didn't crash through me. Instead, it slid inside my core, and a thousand tiny sparks lit. I deepened the kiss as I clutched his T-shirt with both hands.

He pulled back and trailed whisper-soft kisses from my jaw to my ear.

Shivers racked my body, and I moaned.

"Perhaps a room is a more suitable location for affection."

I released Drake and admired the burning desire reflecting in his eyes for a touch too long. "What are you doing here, Quin? Why aren't you watching over Lily?"

"My granddaughter does not need a babysitter."

I pulled my attention from Drake. Quin sat at my desk, his hands folded. Dark circles lined his eyes, and his skin looked too pale. "What happened to you?"

"My love is occupied with Lily's feral creation, and we have many baby vampires. They are most taxing."

"When was the last time you turned someone?"

"Oh, yes. That is the relevant question."

I squeezed Drake's arm and moved further into the room. "Alright. How are the federal agents adjusting?"

His navy eyes flashed red. "They are disciplined and motivated. My love believes they will become elites."

"Nice. They'll also be missed."

"Correct."

I stared out the window and tried not to think of how Mat would handle the situation. "Have you checked on Lily and Alex?"

"Alex is busy working with dragons. And Lily believes her new vampires are boring because of their exceptional self-discipline."

I'd bet anything she cared about them more than she let on. She probably complained while fiercely protecting them. I wished I could see it. "Why did Roman force them on her?"

"An idle vampire is dangerous."

"Except she's not a vampire. Cavil says she's a dark goddess. Like me, only with night magic."

"She is nothing like you. She is assertive and does not doubt her worth."

Ouch. "Right. My point is that she will not be happy running a house. Even if Deva keeps placing her friends there to train Alex."

"Perhaps."

"Also, she'll never have a traditional house. Especially since she declared Cavil her match."

Quin stood. "Jonas believes the god is an acceptable match for Lily."

"Yeah. They're great together. He always hovers around her, and she lets him without being snarky or violent. It's only a matter of time before they have a ceremony." I ignored Quin's flinch. "You should probably check your protective instincts before it happens."

"My instincts are not your business."

"You should have thought about that before you blood-bonded me." Not that I could feel the bond. "I plan to head to Mage Mountain soon. Are you going?"

"Perhaps. I shall check with my love."

I nodded. "Be careful around those agents."

He shot me an exasperated look as he vanished.

Helen rushed into the room a second later. "Jenella! It's the girls. They've gone missing."

Drake's eyes bore into her. "Jonas lost the girls?"

"No. They were waiting for Jonas in the shifter woods with some other kids. When he arrived, they were gone."

"How did someone get through Ann Marie's wards?" My voice was two octaves too high.

"She is unsure. Not even the most sensitive shifter heard a struggle."

"When did this happen?"

"A few minutes ago."

Drake moved towards his office. "I'll do a sweep of the area."

Heart pounding, I expanded my senses. "No! Wait. They're at the checkpoint."

I flashed the three of us to the castle's lobby. Visiting paranormals flinched when we appeared. I raced through the crowd, pushing people aside as I went. Drake transformed into his dragon form the moment he cleared the door.

A man in a black suit and slicked-back blonde hair stood at the checkpoint. A gaggle of shifter kids surrounded him, their eyes glassy.

The mage who manned the gate blasted magic at him. "Stop!"

He smashed her in the face, and she crumpled to the ground.

Helen shifted and darted towards them. Her blood-curdling roar made me shudder.

I threw a box around a few kids, shoved them away, and flashed to them. Drake swooped in and picked up a couple who were not protected by my shield.

The guy pulled the girls close.

I threw anti-Jacques magic at him. It ricocheted, and a chunk of road crashed into the wards.

His cunning smile melted when Helen descended on him. He disappeared with the girls.

"No!" I screamed. Thundering footsteps shook the ground as I stood there with a blank expression on my face, staring at the place where they vanished.

"Jenella?" Gilbert, a manticore and head of the castle guard, raced towards me.

"Did you feel it?"

"No."

I spun towards anyone who would listen. "Did anyone sense a demon on the grounds?"

The guards formed a half-circle around me, shielding me from the gathering crowd. Gilbert pushed one aside. "No. But my centaurs have been spooked for the last hour."

A shadow blocked the sun, and a massive crocodile snout snapped at my face. I caught a flash of green a second before an ear-splitting roar caused guards to cower. The Spinosaurus and Drake tumbled across the road, shredding the bricks as they tumbled into the palace wards.

Zap!

The two massive creatures convulsed and landed in a heap before melting into their human forms.

I stood there with my mouth hanging open, dumbfounded. "Did Jonas just try to bite me?"

Gilbert cleared his throat. "I believe so, Your Grace."

I moved toward the mage whom the demon knocked out and healed her. "Then no healing for him."

I released the kids I'd saved and tapped my chin, as I pointedly ignored the groans from Drake and Jonas as they recovered. The demon wasn't like the ones we'd encountered before. And it unsettled me. Not only because he could hide from us. Helen's call echoed across the palace grounds. It was the one she used when she wanted her family close, only much more mournful.

Drake drew enough strength from me to climb to his feet and push through the crowd, anger radiating from him. "Did anyone see the demon enter the shifter compound?"

Gilbert shook his head. "No. Nor did any of the patrolling shifters spot him."

"He made it through Ann Marie's wards and deflected my magic," I added.

Jonas limped towards us, his head hanging. "Sorry about that, Jenella. My predatory instincts got out of hand."

"Don't let it happen again, or I will kill you," Drake growled.

I sighed. "He took three kids. It could have been much worse. I'm going to research more about my ruling powers. Jonas, work with the other leaders. They're brainstorming ideas to integrate with humans. Have some of them devise a plan to bring our kids home."

He nodded and stomped towards the shifter woods.

Chapter Thirteen

THE LAST TIME I went to Mage Mountain, I was running away from a whopper of a lie. Mat and Drake tracked me down, and I got my magic restored, my memory wiped, and in a sloppy battle with the Bellicose. This time, I hoped to have a couple of meetings, talk to my grandmother while keeping my memories, and maybe master my magic. No running this time.

I pulled on a winter coat as we waited for Tracy and Bastien. Quin stood by the open door, not even bothering to pretend he wasn't listening to my staff as they went about their business. Lily strode in, considered him for a second, then strutted to me. "Whazzup?"

"Hey." I glanced toward Drake's office. "We're getting ready to leave."

"You're going to some freaky place to dig up our grandmother. I'm going with you."

"Who told you?" My eyes trailed to Quin, who hadn't moved a muscle. "Never mind. What about your house?"

Lily's nose scrunched in disgust. "Other than the vampires I turned, they're a bunch of rule followers. I'm having them convert Roman's mansion into a hotel. In their free time, they're helping to relocate some hybrids, so they'll be busy for a while." She zipped toward the window. "Dad said he tried to bite your head off, and now Drake hates him."

"Hate is a strong word," Drake explained. "A demon broke onto shifter grounds and took some kids. Jonas was running on instinct, and now I am, too." He leaned towards her. "Would you like a sample?"

I shivered at his icy tone, but Lily didn't even flinch. "Nope. Why would a demon want shifter kids?"

"He went through wards like they weren't there, and no one sensed him. This isn't like the other demons we've come across. He stole the kids right out from under Jonas's nose. I don't blame him for his anger."

"I do," Drake said as he glamoured some thick boots onto his feet.

"No shit? So, we're not only dealing with the government, but now we need to watch out for sneaky demons, too?"

I shut my eyes. "I'm heading to Mage Mountain to see if our grandmother will help me learn my magic better. Your parents are already working on recovering the kids. If demons are messing with the humans, we need to double our efforts."

"Nice. Don't let Dale give you shit about helping the hybrid kids. He's trying to see how far he can push you."

Tracy stomped in from Drake's office. "Sorry we're late. I had to finish a potion."

Bastien appeared behind her, wearing sweats and a black T-shirt. His feet were bare.

I eyed them. "What is it with you and Deva not glamouring shoes?"

His intense black eyes bore into me. "What is it with you asking about things that are not your business?"

"Fine. Gather around."

Cavil's magnetic presence preceded him as he swept in and shoved coffee into Lily's hand. "Hello, Jenella. If you are going to learn more about your magic, I wish to attend."

He wore jeans, an electric blue T-shirt, and a bright yellow coat. The guy would stand out in the frozen pocket. "Sure. But we'll need to tone down your wardrobe so you're not a target."

"They will feel your presence, so my attire won't matter."

I raised a hand. "They might not. The magic there is odd and fluctuates. The locals learn to ignore it, so they might ignore mine."

"Doubtful," Quin said as he glided to Lily's side.

I held out my arms, made sure everyone touched me, and flashed.

Pelting snow slashed my cheeks, and icy wind cut through my coat when we landed outside the wards of my cabin near the outskirts of the town of Brumal. I grinned at the multicolored magic rolling off the mountain as I pulled everyone through. Inside, Drake ignited a fire and moved to the kitchen to check the magichef. It had been quite a while since I'd been there, but it still felt like home. Odd, considering I'd never lived there.

After we settled around the fire, I considered everything I needed to accomplish. Olwen wanted me to visit the sasquatch leadership and the rübezahl. I planned to take care of those errands first and convince my grandmother to help the next day. We needed to hurry. I cracked my eyes open as Lily plopped next to me. "If I bring this many people to the mountain, she might not meet with me. I think Lily, Drake, and I should go alone."

Bastien somehow added an admonishment to his loud sigh. "No. The Bellicose might not be crawling out of every crack, but they're still around. You need us."

I wrung my hands. "Quin can hide, I suppose."

"Yes. Let's pretend Lissa can't sense me." Quin stood. "If this is her resting place, she already knows we're here, so you will not sneak up on her."

"We're not leaving you," Tracy said.

"Fine. Let's take care of business today, and we'll try to see her tomorrow." I texted Olwen.

After a short time, the wards pinged. Olwen stood two inches taller than his companions, his silver-white hair free and flowing with the wind. The fluffy snowflakes soaked me to the bone, but curled around the elves as if afraid to touch them. After I pulled them through the wards, Olwen motioned to his companions. "Your Grace. These are my most trusted elves, Elson and Volat."

"Pleased to meet you."

Neither spoke as I led them into the house. Olwen's eyes landed on Cavil. "What is the sun god doing here?"

A blinding smile lit Cavil's face. "I am a god. I can restrain my magic if I wish to. Therefore, unless a situation requires shields, I'll refrain. I am here to support Lily."

"He's my sister's match," I explained. "What do the sasquatch leaders want?"

"They wish to help with the human issue."

"Right. But how?"

"They didn't say."

Great. I'd need to slip into my detective persona and hope they wouldn't waste my time. Especially after what happened the last time they pretended to help. "Who's going with me?"

We landed a half mile outside of the Rübezahl village. Olwen and his elves showed us the path to the sasquatch camp and went to inform them we were on our way.

When I worked as a detective, the Rübezahl were always finding excuses to bring me to Mage Mountain. I glanced toward the mountain as a colorful magic plume erupted and trickled to the ground. "Mind your manners here, Lily. The people in this village are part spirit, territorial, and dangerous. They'll attack for one snarky comment."

"Gotcha." She scanned the surrounding buildings. "No one will even know I'm here."

We stopped outside the general store, and I motioned for my group to stay outside.

The man I normally met with stood behind the counter. "You have brought an army to my village."

I sipped his magic and coughed and sputtered as I fought to expel it. The stuff was slimy and wrong. As if it had no business in any realm. "Hello, Johan. It's part of being the queen."

His chilly gaze settled on me. "No gifts?"

"We've already established a rapport. King Olwen of the Snow Elves said you wanted to speak with me."

A small smile ghosted across his face. "You are different."

My throat tightened from the putrid aftertaste of his magic, and I had to swallow before I could answer. "Yes."

He scanned me one more time and walked right through the counter. "There was an attempt to breach the pocket about a week ago."

My mind spun. Mage Mountain's gate was so remote, it was the last place I expected a breach. "Humans?"

"Yes. They were coated in odd magic, and clearly not the downtrodden. The sasquatches reached them before we could defend our mountain and would not turn them over."

I rubbed my chin. "There was a similar incident in another pocket. They shot up the transport station. Did the sasquatches kill them?"

"Unfortunately, no." He glanced toward the door. "Have you awoken Lilith?"

"No. That's her heir and my sister." There was no point in lying to the Rübezahl because they'd see right through it. "Is everything else okay here?"

His eyes gleamed with curiosity. "Lilith was not only the vampire First, but ours. She discarded us by giving us a mission. Can her replacement alter it?"

My eyes narrowed. "Alter it how?"

"I wish to leave the mountain occasionally." The predatory glint in his eye told me it wouldn't be a good idea to set him loose on the world.

"No, she can't. She isn't the same as Lilith."

His shoulders slumped in defeat. "I suppose we will find another way. The sasquatches still hold the prisoners."

An icy chill ran down my spine at his determination to leave, but I didn't dare ask. "Thank you, Guardian. I appreciate your diligence in notifying me." I turned to leave.

He blocked the door. "One more thing."

When Drake moved closer, I sent 'no' vibes through the bond. "Yes?"

"You are a good queen. I have heard rumors about how you willingly sacrifice your people to the spirit realm for the greater good. You are not above inserting yourself into fights. I shall contact you through King Olwen should more strange incidents occur or I need assistance with my plans."

"Erm. Sure. Thank you." I tried to keep a steady pace as I left. The Rübezahl leader always unsettled me, but it was worse that day, as if he were testing me. The minute we cleared the edge of town, I allowed myself to shudder. "That guy is creepy."

"What did he say?" Bastien asked as he scanned the forest.

"Humans breached this pocket last week. The sasquatches stopped them."

"Why is the government sending people to their deaths?" Lily asked. "Especially since the ones they sent to attack Domerage didn't return."

Bastien shrugged. "Humans have a long history of killing their own for no reason."

Tracy stumbled and grabbed his arm to catch herself. "Bastien's right. But there's more to it. When witches practice spells or potions, we test them until they work, even if we lose someone. I mean, maybe they're trying to perfect their formula."

Drake scanned the trees. "Or they suspected this pocket isn't as populated and hoped their people could infiltrate without notice."

I shook off the residual creeps. "What's your theory, Quin?"

"Speculation without facts is unproductive."

The guy was extra grumpy since he turned those federal agents. My foot skidded on the snow, and I laid a hand on Drake's back to steady myself. The heat rolling off him felt so good that I left it there. "There isn't a single unguarded gate, no matter how remote the pocket. I've only managed to move two of them, and the first one would have failed without Alex's help. I need to move faster."

"Hang on." Lily lifted a hand. "Alex's help?"

"He helped me with a few things while training with Deva. He was never in danger." Much.

"So while I was wallowing in guilt for abandoning him, he was jet-setting around the country with you?"

"Only once. The rest of the time, we kept our efforts local."

It was almost like a lightbulb went off in her head. "You and Alex saved those kids. Without me."

"Well, you were busy, and Tracy was with us." I didn't meet her eyes.

"That little shit never said a word about it."

"Sorry."

We fell silent and concentrated on the trail. The path ended in a small clearing with a half-frozen stream running through. Shelters made of foliage and animal hides took up the entire area. Massive hairy creatures gathered around raging bonfires. Some sat on stumps, while others stood. One carried a log on her shoulders and dumped it near a group. Smaller creatures played in the snow and trees under the watchful eyes of the community.

The sour smell of body odor and skunk slapped me in the face as we moved closer, and I pulled my spelled scarf over my nose. When Lily gagged, I chuckled and created a scarf for her.

Olwen and his two elves stood near an A-frame structure covered in leaves and sticks. A log stuck out of it, one end burning inside the shelter. The sasquatch we ran into once before stood near him.

Kids were yanked away, and the fireside chats cut off as we approached. I sipped magic from the ones who puffed up and tried to look threatening.

Cavil crowded closer to Lily. "These are creatures of the night. Olwen was correct that I should not be here."

"You're here as my guest, so they'll have to deal with it." I magically shoved a couple of big guys out of our path.

Lily took his hand. "We can take them."

"We have already done so." Drake stayed focused on the leader. "Without Jenella's magic or your fighting prowess." He failed to mention how Deva and Ara made the difference.

I gave him a nod of agreement. "We'll be fine."

Drake pulled me closer. "Spread out around us."

Quin stayed close to me, but the others complied.

Olwen bowed his head. "Your Grace. This is Bronduk, the leader of this clan of sasquatches."

"We've met." I couldn't keep the bitterness from my voice. "Where are the humans?"

A low growl came from his throat. "The humans are ours to do with as we please."

I scanned the gathering crowd. Behind me, my friends stiffened. "No, they're not."

"They are the spoils of war."

"We're not at war with the humans." Yet.

"You are blind."

"No, I'm not. I prefer a different solution."

"Explain this solution to me."

Olwen's magic flared, and the surrounding air froze, then thawed. "The queen owes you no explanation."

"The humans are ours." The sasquatch made up for his lack of critical thinking skills with bravery.

Quin eased behind me. A second later, I sensed him and Cavil disappear. They reappeared, toting five humans. Tracy touched one. "It's not witch magic."

I could sense it. It wasn't the same as the freaks we encountered, but more in line with the magic we found on the pyramid in Pyron. "Drake?"

"They were attempting to find something called Bigfoot when a scientist approached them and offered to help. The man worked with them under the name Russell Millworth." He pointed at a middle-aged man who looked to be in decent shape. "That man is their leader. He didn't believe the scientist worked in the best interest of the research organization they volunteered with, but agreed to try his experiments. These humans are not hostile but entranced by the sasquatches. They have been treated well by Bronduk's clan."

I concentrated on the leader, who visibly shook under Drake's assessing stare. "Explain."

He swallowed so hard I heard it. "I founded a research organization to prove the existence of sasquatches. We've spotted the creatures many times and have even collected some evidence. The scientist said he could get us closer. When we were out hunting, he and his team pushed us off a cliff, and we landed here. We didn't intend to enter this...place."

I glanced toward the gate. "How did he coat you with magic?"

"I don't know anything about magic."

I glanced toward Bronduk. "Would you like to stay with this clan? Or return to your life?"

"Three of us wish to return and two want to stay." He motioned toward a couple who clung to each other.

"If you return, we will wipe your memories," Bastien explained. "If you stay and your magic coating wears off, it may be painful."

"Doubtful." When our heads swung toward Lily, she shrugged. "My friend's daughter is three-quarters human and lives with us. She's fine."

I frowned. If a young girl could live in the hybrid pocket, then once inside, other humans could. It bothered me. "Can you monitor them, Bronduk?"

"We can, though this climate is not ideal for such fragile beings."

Not to mention the sasquatches' nomadic tendencies. If another clan moved too close, they'd take off and drag the humans with them. "How long have you held this area?"

"Ten years."

"These humans won't live long with your lifestyle. They need heat, healers, and healthy food. None of them can keep up with you if you need to run."

The sasquatch shook his head. "We did not plan to keep them here, but place them in Brumal under the watchful eye of the mages. You must admit they are safer with us than their kind, who will dissect them to gather information about us."

"How do you know what they will do?" Drake's voice sounded too calm.

"We have been studying the scientist. He, along with a group of mutant shifters, awaits their return. It is quite disturbing."

I eyed the humans. "Did you notice anything strange about this scientist and his team?"

The lone woman shifted her weight. "They made me nervous, but these guys thought it was my imagination."

"Human women have developed a strong sense of self-preservation when dealing with men," Lily said.

I knew there was a power imbalance, but I never considered how they coped. We might help them with it, should we go the route of heroes. "You understand if you return, they will torture you for information, right?"

His face paled. "We're just here to prove sasquatches exist."

"Looks like you got your answer," Lily murmured, as she poked at a clan member who'd gathered around us to listen. "You can't let those mutant freaks live unless you want more humans in the pockets."

Drake and Bastien had me pinned between them, so I stared at the ground to think. If our goal was to endear ourselves to humans, we couldn't dispose of the non-violent ones. Drake was right about how indecisive I'd been. I was so worried about getting more people killed that my decision-making lagged. "I agree with Bronduk. These humans must be protected. How powerful are the mutants?"

"Not very," Olwen answered. "The leader is mid-level at best. He is also overconfident."

I met Bronduk's eyes. "Can you eliminate them?"

A wall of brown teeth greeted me. I guessed it was his smile. "We rarely kill humans, but won't hesitate to eliminate those who wish to harm us."

"Great. Then I give you my permission." I motioned towards a man. "You're injured. Let me try to heal you." It would make their trek to Brumal easier, and I'd see if my healing magic worked on humans.

The guy cradled his fractured arm close to his body. "I'm fine."

"No, you're not. Let the lady help," the leader said.

The guy shuffled forward. I touched him with my silvery magic. Once it coated him, it sank into his skin, and his arm made a horrific cracking sound. I flinched. "Sorry. The bone resetting is always the worst part." His companions watched with open mouths as the guy's body healed and his appearance changed to one of a much younger man. "Better?"

He tested his previously broken arm and clenched and unclenched his hand. "What did you do?"

I ignored the question as I turned to Bronduk. "We're considering a plan to make humans see us as heroes. Will you help?" It was a long shot. From what I understood, the sasquatches liked to scare humans, rather than help. But they'd also saved some over the years.

More brown teeth. "It would be our pleasure to eliminate the mutants and assist the humans. Do you wish us to show ourselves?"

"Not yet. Olwen will inform you when we're ready to help them. Cavil, please return the humans to their shelter." After they disappeared, I refocused on Bronduk. "Set them up in Brumal soon, or they'll get sick. Have a healer check them over, and make sure the Rübezahl don't get their hands on them."

The sasquatch clan watched us in awed silence as we exited their camp. It was a small win in building trust, but I'd take it.

Chapter Fourteen

Misty breath trailed me as I glided down the trail on cross-country skis. As always, I struggled to pay attention because I was in awe of Mage Mountain's beauty. The cold sun peeked over the horizon, casting pale light across the trail. Ahead of us, a waterfall of magic containing every color imaginable slid down the mountain, allowing the sun to dance off the surface and light it up in fluorescent hues.

Cavil caught up to me, his blue eyes sparkling with excitement. "This is a fun mode of transportation."

"It's ridiculous," Lily grumbled. "Especially when we can flash."

"Complaining often ruins the enjoyment of new experiences," Quin said from trees, where he somehow kept up without skis. Drake was somewhere in the trees in his snuffy form, too. I couldn't see him, but his frustration over our slow progress mirrored Lily's.

"If it's our grandmother, I want her to sense us coming."

"Do you really believe Lissa would miss such a group inside her domain?" Bastien asked.

I didn't bother responding. "How are you doing, Tracy?"

"I'm having fun. We should do this more often." Defiance laced her voice.

"We really should. Let's make it a girls' retreat. No grumpy dragons or crotchety vampires allowed."

"Hey!" Lily protested. "Never mind. Hanging out with a bunch of chittering women is not my idea of fun."

"I can't wait to tell Ara you think she's a chittering woman." I glanced toward where I felt Drake stop.

"You sound like Alex."

"Thank you."

We grew silent as we neared the cave where Drake, Mat, and I lost our memories. I ignored the pang of grief as I removed my skis. When my ski boots touched the snow, they transformed into waterproof snow boots. "Maybe everyone should stand back."

"No way," Lily said as she shook her skis loose. "Even if this is a dumb idea."

"It is quite normal for Jen."

I ignored Quin's sarcasm and shuffled forward. My stomach fell when the entire group followed me. I couldn't bear losing anyone else and hated how they were all willing to dive into danger with me. Drake looped his arm around my shoulders as we neared the boulder covering the cave's entrance. I stretched out a trembling hand and placed it on the rock. My magic swirled around the creases and met the colorful mage mountain magic. They mixed and danced as if testing each other, then retreated.

When there was no response, I stepped back. "Look. I understand if you don't want to be bothered. Maybe you're even trying to sleep, but I need help and don't have anyone else."

Lily moved to my side. "I have a few things to say, too." She paused when a puff of a thousand colors spewed from the tiny crack around the opening. It seemed like a warning, but it didn't deter Lily. "Like how you left and allowed your daughter to abuse her kids and tear the coalition apart. Twice. About how you didn't step in and take some damn responsibility when you clearly saw how bad she sucked at being queen. She summoned demons and used mind control for fuck's sake. And instead of mentoring Jen when she came to you for help, you screwed with her magic and stole her memories."

Cavil attempted to pull her away as he whispered something in her ear. Quin wedged himself between us. Tracy and Bastien crowded close behind.

The concern seemed to piss her off more. "You failed as a creator, a leader, and a parent. And you failed as a grandparent. Now you won't even talk to us. You fucking coward."

I had never seen Lily look so traumatized, and I had to recover from the shock. "Lily's right. You suck. Anitta's been out here abusing your family, your people, and your friends. And all you do is sit inside this mountain. We needed you!" I motioned toward Drake. "The Firsts needed you. And you hid like a coward while Anitta tore everything apart." I shook myself loose from Drake and Quin and turned to storm away. My face smashed into Bastien's chest, so it wasn't as dramatic as I intended.

Drake tugged me to his side as I rubbed my sore nose. "Look."

When I turned to look, my knees went weak. I grasped Drake as the boulder rolled toward us. Together, we shuffled backwards. It stopped, and an explosion of color whipped out and wrapped around us. Like the last time, it lifted me off my feet. Except it didn't spin me around, nor did a wedge slam into my chest. Instead, the mass of colors propelled me into the cave. A grinding sound behind us indicated the stone had moved back into place.

Lily cursed.

Bastien roared.

No one else made a sound as we floated through the passage, clinging to each other, the magic so thick I couldn't see where we were going. I tried to sip it, but nothing happened, so I lifted a hand and poked it. The stuff didn't give away a single secret. My mind went fuzzy, and an overwhelming urge to sleep washed over me. When I pried my droopy eyes open, I was on my back on a plush rug, cocooned in a pillow of color. "Drake?" I pushed myself to a sitting position.

A man with auburn hair and a boxy face sat in an old-fashioned wooden chair. His caramel-colored eyes sparkled with delight. The bank of windows behind him allowed bright sunshine in and made the room too bright. I tried and failed to create a shield around myself. "Who are you?"

"My, my, my, Belnaught. What beautiful babies our Anitta made!" The first queen of Ahl, my grandmother, marched into the room. The paintings I'd seen didn't do her justice. Her waist-length golden hair spilled over her shoulders, the fat curls bouncing as she walked. Her golden eyes were so pale, they were almost transparent. She floated to me, a pleasant smile on her striking face. The scent of lilacs and earth engulfed me as she leaned over. "You look so much like her, yet so much like me. It's uncanny." Sadness laced her voice, although her facial expression didn't change.

"You're awake? All this time, we've been fighting to save the coalition, and you sit up here in your mountain and do nothing?"

She threw her head back and laughed. "I'd hardly say I did nothing. I've been a guiding hand to Mathias for years and have given you the tools you need to thrive. Welcome to our home."

Fiery anger lit inside me. The woman didn't understand the first thing about my brother. I tamped it down so she didn't throw me out before she answered some questions. "This place has always called to me." I ran my hand over the cold stone floor to clear my mind. "Why didn't you talk to me when you fixed my magic?"

"Oh, my sweet girl." Sympathy and disappointment laced her voice. "This is our resting place and has been for hundreds of years."

When she didn't continue, I climbed to my feet and took in the room. The wooden furniture was old but not worn. The chairs had cream-colored padding with a pink and red floral pattern. Asymmetrical windows extended from the floor to the ceiling. They molded to the shape of the stone walls, following the contour of the mountain and offered a breathtaking view of the entire pocket. The room has solid, smooth stone floors and walls. "It's lovely."

My grandmother preened. "Thank you. Now, please take a seat. We have much to discuss." She pointed to a sofa. "You, too, Liliana."

My head swung toward my friends. Cavil was on his knees, his entire body lit like a beacon. Lily sat in front of him, speaking in low tones. Tracy, Bastien, and Quin lay on the floor, still cocooned in bright magic. Drake stood in the far corner, spine straight, his feet shoulder-width apart, and his hands behind his back like a human soldier. I frowned. "Let my friends go."

She gestured in their direction with an exasperated sigh. "You trust too easily, Jenella. Tarquin has always been less than reliable. However, you chose well to befriend the Dragon Heir. Tell me, how is my old friend, Devarkalara?"

"She goes by Deva now, and is one of my dearest friends, an advisor, and sits on the leadership council." I motioned toward Quin. "As is Tarquin. He and Tracy are my closest friends and have saved my life more than once."

"Cavil is new to this realm, sent here by The Deity to find his soulmate," Lily said. She took his hand and the glowing faded. "He's been helping Jen learn her magic."

My grandmother's intelligent eyes assessed my friends. A sofa appeared behind them, and the colorful magic shoved them into it. She pointed at the longer one near the redheaded man. You may bring your match, Liliana. I have no animosity toward the third district gods.

"It's Lily."

I perched on the far end of the long sofa as Lily and Cavil took the other end.

My grandmother jammed a hand on her hip. "Don't just stand there, Deslaurian. Sit with your lovely mate."

Drake's unfocused stare remained straight ahead. Even our bond seemed devoid of emotion. "I cannot, Your Grace. The old agreements are still in place."

"Pishaw. I absolve you of any agreements and consider your contracts fulfilled to my satisfaction. And I haven't been the queen in a long time, so drop the title. It now belongs to Jenella."

Drake, or Deslaurian, visibly relaxed as he marched toward her. He took her hands in his and smiled warmly. "It's good to see you again, Lissa."

"You, as well. I was thrilled to learn you still lived the first time you came to my mountain with Jenella."

I arched an eyebrow as he released her and took the seat between me and Cavil. "Deslaurian?"

"My birth name. I have not used it in thousands of years. Lissa knows this but refuses to call me Drake."

My grandmother took the chair next to the man whom I assumed was my grandfather. "Now, Jenella, why have you been resisting my call?"

"Call?"

"Oh, my. I see. Your mother lost her power before she taught you. Have you not read my diaries?"

My eyes darted towards Tracy. "I have."

"Then you saw I handed your mother a thriving coalition before I retired. In hindsight, I should have never given her the power to rule. It was a mistake I realized too late and tried to fix. When I transferred the ruling powers to you, she anchored my mountain here and ensured the climate in this pocket was undesirable. She used her ill-suited match to merge with three different beings and conceive children. Mathias is the son of a Mage god hybrid who is no longer in this realm, and Liliana is the daughter of the natural born vampire, Jedediah."

"Ara had heritage mages test us when we found Lily."

"I see." She cocked her head. "Liliana was Anitta's chosen heir. She disregarded several magical rules by making the proclamation, especially since I'd already transferred some of her ruling magic to you." Her golden curls bounced as if they were alive when she moved her head. "Anitta knew magic had already chosen her third born. I didn't learn of Liliana's existence until Anitta discarded her, and Ann Marie took her in." Her eyes met Lily's. "For that, I apologize. Belnaught and I cannot see everything, and Anitta was sneakier than most."

Lily's jaw clinched. "Then why turn the coalition over to her?"

"It wasn't by choice, I assure you." She stared Cavil down before refocusing on me. "It took me time to learn how to monitor my family after we confined ourselves to this mountain. Even then, I found my influence less effective than I'd like. When I learned how she treated her kids, I acted."

I leaned forward. "Acted, how?"

A door at the opposite end of the room opened. "Let me show you." When we all stood, she shoved everyone back down. "Jenella and Liliana only."

I was in awe at her sheer audacity as I squeezed Drake's arm. "We'll be fine." I couldn't read her intentions, but didn't think she meant us harm. Her power was so immense that if she wanted, she could have crushed us before we entered her home.

The door led to a spiral staircase. As we ascended, the colorful magic became so thick that I struggled to see. The clean scent of the house gave way to a sweet, citrusy scent. Lily tugged my coat twice in what I assumed was some kind of signal, but I didn't understand it. The magic cleared when we reached the top, revealing a modern leather reclining chair. Lissa motioned us towards it. "One of you can use this chair."

Lily appeared in the seat before I could open my mouth to volunteer. "I'll go first."

Lissa's boisterous laughter sounded forced. "I should have guessed, considering your protective nature." Two identical chairs rose from the stone floor, and she settled into the center one.

When I didn't move to take the last one, the magic shoved me from behind. I careened towards it too fast and lost my footing. My feet got swept out from under me, and I found myself in the chair.

Lissa nodded, then turned towards Lily. "Even with your vampire immunity, this will sting, so brace yourselves."

"It's fine." Lily's voice was as hard as dragon glass.

The sensation started as millions of tickles, and I clenched my jaw. Just when I thought I'd burst, the tickles turned to itches. I clenched my fists. Tiny needles stabbed into my body, and all the sensation faded. My eyes snapped open to a great white abyss.

"Over here, ladies."

I tried to fly to Lissa's voice but couldn't, so I pretended to walk. She came into view, wearing an ancient white robe with golden accents. Her hair was in an intricate hairstyle and piled on her head. Beyond her, Lily wore solid black with gold accents. Her one gold and one red streak were the only pieces of hair hanging out of an intricate up-do. I looked down to find myself in a golden robe. "What's this?"

"This is the pinnacle of power. I tapped into it shortly after we became stranded here and, until today, never told a soul. It is a volatile place and does not appreciate visitors, so stay close."

I scooted closer to her. "You control the realm's magic?"

"Such an absurd question. No one can control magic. It does as it pleases. We only have the most basic understanding of its rules and we cannot...No, we must not reach for more." Lissa motioned to an opening in the mist. "We must follow the path."

We padded down the path, staying side by side. After what felt like hours, the trail dumped us into a round, orb-like transparent room hovering above the palace. A griffin launched from the wall and swooped low over the checkpoint where a group of tourists checked in. "Is this in real time?"

"Yes. A slice of my magic can make it through. I once held more influence, but The Deity has limited my efforts."

"There's my dad." Lily leaned forward for a better view. "How did you influence us?"

"When I observed Jenella's treatment, it broke my heart. So I transferred a great deal of Anitta's power to rule to Jenella and cut my daughter off from using it. After she ordered Jenella's death, I compelled Mathias to bring her to Allure so my allies could watch over them. Anitta spent the rest of her days focused on vengeance. The mists wouldn't show me her plans. By the time they allowed me a vision, she had already blackmailed Mathias. When Jenella proved herself a suitable heir, I granted her a great deal more power." She turned to me. "I believe Deslaurian helped you through the adjustment."

"How could I forget?" She didn't give me any warning, and I blew up our magichef. Drake used my summoning room to isolate me until it settled. My mind spun at how much power and influence she had over our lives. It made the ever-present anger inside me grow. "If you have all this power and control, why aren't you still ruling?"

Lily tore her eyes from the shifter woods. "Because she can't."

Lissa nodded in agreement. "The Deity visited me and insisted I retire. I hoped your mother would grow into the position, but she fell in love with power. I requested permission to intervene when I learned she'd hunted down and eliminated the other Firsts and the Deity agreed. But I can only nudge you in a direction. If you choose not to go, there is nothing I can do. In addition, I'm allowed to grant and take away the power of my direct descendants."

"What about me? Can I grant someone ruling magic?"

"Perhaps. It depends on how worthy the person you bestow it on is, and your reasoning."

It didn't seem right to discuss transferring ruling magic to Emine with Lily present, so I nodded.

The vision disappeared, and we found ourselves on our backs in chairs, wearing our normal clothes.

After we made it back downstairs, she continued the conversation as if we hadn't been ripped from one reality to the next. "Anitta could never get to Jonas. Deslaurian almost escaped and would have if one of his own did not betray him." She paused. "I'm thrilled that you saw the injustice and woke the Firsts. Tell me, will you wake Celia?"

I blinked at the question, still trying to process everything. "Maybe. Right now, we're dealing with humans. We suspect some demons are still around."

"I suggest you consider waking Celia before you merge societies. She can be quite useful."

I didn't plan to merge societies. Paranormals enjoyed having space to be themselves without worrying about being hunted or gawked at by humans. "Are we not going to talk about the vision we just had?"

A knowing smile formed on her face. "No, we are not. You chose such an honorable man to match with."

I took Drake's hand automatically. He squeezed it back so hard I thought it would break. My grandmother made him nervous.

Lissa clapped her hands. "Now, to the problem at hand. You are quite misguided about how your magic works."

"Misguided is a funny way to say it," Lily mumbled.

"Lily has a unique blend of Lilith's power and ours." She pointed at the silent man. "We can only somewhat help you sort it out." Her amused eyes focused intently on me. "And you are keeping many of your abilities suppressed."

"Cavil has taught me well. But I still can't use the magic I've absorbed and don't understand the extent of my ruling power. I hoped you would help me with it."

"Cavilourianabalvivelario is from the third district. Their magic differs from the first district."

The man, my grandfather, leaned forward in his chair. "Jenella has strong healing magic, where Liliana does not, though her self-healing is much stronger than Lilith's."

"Yes," my grandmother agreed.

"I generally throat-punch people who use my full name and don't want to cause an incident, so call me Lily."

"My apologies, Lily. I will use your chosen name." The man shifted in his seat. "Will your companions be staying for your training, Jenella?"

I scanned my friends. Quin watched the exchange with an interest I rarely saw from him. Bastien had Tracy tucked under his arm as if he could hide her. She didn't look pleased. "Tracy, would you like to stay or wait for us at the cabin?"

"We will wait for you at your cabin," Bastien answered for her.

She elbowed him. "Bas needs to get back, but I'm staying."

"As am I," Quin said.

Bastien sighed. "Very well, we will stay."

Lissa clasped her hands. "Wonderful. Please take care to follow my rules." She directed the comment at Quin.

"Of course."

I examined the man. He had the same square jaw as Mat. His auburn hair seemed almost otherworldly, and the feeling emanating from him was that of a healer. "I thought the power of Ahl overwhelmed other magics?"

My grandmother nodded. "It does. When ruling magic is transferred, we can choose what we give to our heirs. Your mother received very little, while you, with your soft heart and excellent choice in men, received three doses of my power and two doses of your grandfather's. Or did you not notice it stab you in the chest during your last visit?"

"Oh, I noticed. I thought it was part of fixing my magic."

"Your magic was not broken but blocked."

"Blocked by who?" Drake asked.

"By Jenella. She wished to hide her power, so it complied. She didn't fully wish to reveal it, not even when she arrived here for help, so it stayed hidden. Our magic is quite malleable and fueled by our true intentions. I helped her remove the block, and we will work on intentions. Cavilourianabalvivelario is correct about your ability to mimic the magic of others." She tapped her chin. "You mirrored Mathias's magic most of your life. Accessing the others should not be difficult."

"I've managed it a few times, but I'm not proficient."

"Show me what you've absorbed."

I conjured a ball of magic. It had been a while since I looked, and I'd absorbed a lot since then. Several colors were almost as bright as those shooting from Mage Mountain.

"Very good. Lily?"

"You don't want me to access my magic here. It will blow up your mountain."

"Oh, I doubt it. Lilith tried many times, and it still stands, so I doubt yours will succeed."

Lily's eyes bounced toward Quin, then settled on her hand. A black ball of magic with every color of red imaginable in it formed. Before she could dissipate it, the thing bounced into the air.

Dragon scales blocked my vision, and pain shot up my side when I hit the stone floor. Bright light flashed, and voices rose.

When Lissa's laughter bounced off the walls, Drake helped me up and lowered me back to the sofa. "Careful, Lissandra. Lily's magic is deadly."

"You still have so little faith in me, Deslaurian."

The ball of Lily's magic hung in the air in a box resembling the one I'd put the Ogre Queens and Gorman in. Except that the magic radiating from it was much more powerful. "Can I control her magic?"

"Of course. Your power rivals my own. It is the execution you struggle with. I suspect it comes from your years of suppression. You had excellent reasons, but it's time to learn to use it properly." The box, along with Lily's magic, dissipated. "You are quite unique, Lily. It will be fun to teach you control."

A small part of me still hoped she'd return and take the throne so I could be free, but my rational side understood it would never happen. "How will you teach us? Will you come to the palace?"

"I wouldn't set foot in another castle for all twelve worlds." She slid off her chair and lowered herself to her knees. "I left your mother with a peaceful kingdom, and she tore it apart in her quest for power. I knew her nature and didn't trust her. She only cared about herself and not her people, so magic itself removed her from the throne. Like me, it chose you over her. She tried to kill you out of jealousy, hoping the power would transfer to her unborn child. She would have succeeded had Mathias and Tarquin not ensured your escape."

"Wait. What?" My head was fuzzy with information overload. "Quin wasn't there when we escaped."

"The lack of willingness to use your senses is astounding," Quin said. "We raised Mathias and have always watched over you. I did not choose to become your mentor simply because Tracy suggested it."

My head spun. "What? You were hesitant."

"Correct."

"The vampires did a wonderful job of raising Mathias. And Ara thinks of you as her own," Lissa interjected.

"You talk to Ara?" I asked.

She shrugged. "I keep in touch with a few friends. Now. Deslaurian, you must stop using your bond to help Jenella cope. She is using it as a crutch."

"No." Drake drew me closer. "She is not using it as a crutch, but to deal with trauma from abuse you allowed her to suffer. I will not leave my mate to deal with it alone, any more than I will allow her to face you alone."

"Dragons are so fun." She ignored Bastien's growl. "I did not allow anything, my friend. As I demonstrated to my heirs, my reach is limited, and I did my best. I've called Jenella since she first set foot in my domain, but she ignored me."

"I didn't realize it was you." If I had, it would have saved time and maybe some lives. Maybe Mat would still be there if I hadn't been so reluctant.

Her smile melted. "You ignored me because you did not wish to rule, Jenella. But you must. I can sometimes manipulate events from afar, but cannot go against The Deity and resume my position among the paranormals in this realm."

"The Deity speaks to you?" Cavil asked.

"Occasionally, yes. I believe it keeps track of all gods, especially those who live in foreign realms."

He nodded. "I also speak to it."

"Then you understand." She stood. "Now, let's move to the training room." Our grandmother turned and marched toward a curved doorway without looking back. The man's tranquil expression never changed as he followed.

Chapter Fifteen

"Every time you step foot into my life, something bad happens," Lily grumbled as we limped into the suite reserved for us after several long hours of magic training.

"You barged in and announced you were coming with me."

"Don't try to reason with me right now." She rubbed her shoulder. "That woman packs a punch."

"At least she's willing to help." My voice lacked enthusiasm. Our grandmother was a thorough and tough teacher. I spent almost an hour practicing making a perfect circle using creation magic. It took away valuable time I needed to spend learning how to use what I absorbed from other factions.

"Psh. Help smelp. We'll be here a year at this pace."

True. I sank into a chair. "I'd argue, but I'm exhausted."

Drake and Cavil strolled in, platters in their hands. Drake set one on the table. "Lissandra insisted I restock her magichef."

My stomach growled when the scent of roast chicken filled the room. "I don't blame her. Your food is the best."

Quin appeared across from me. "Lissandra will not allow me to use shadows or move too fast. Each time I try, her magic envelops me and slows my progress."

"Found someone who can best you, eh?" Lily took the plate that Cavil offered.

"There are many who are capable, but few try. You may consider the lesson when building your reputation."

I wondered if Lily and I could beat him if we worked together. Probably not. "How are you holding up, Bas?"

"I dislike having my wings clipped. There is no reason for us to stay and watch you train."

Tracy rolled her eyes. "Being a supportive friend and cousin is a valid reason."

He shrugged. "I suppose."

As we ate, I tried to process everything I'd learned. I had suspected my grandmother wasn't dormant after she fixed my magic, but seeing them living in domestic bliss while The Coalition fell apart was jarring. I wished I could ask what Mat thought about them. And Lily was right about how we didn't have much time. We had kids to rescue and humans to deal with.

A plume of colorful magic outside the window dragged me from my thoughts. It shot straight up and swirled around before disappearing in a puff of mist. I recognized some colors, or at least, what they represented. But others were foreign. "Lily's right. We need a crash course instead of the slow version. We have too many responsibilities to stay too long."

Drake motioned toward my uneaten food. "Lissa and Belnaught can combine their powers to manipulate time. Perhaps they'll help."

"Maybe." I shoved a bite of chicken in my mouth. "Do you think she'll wipe our memories this time?"

"No."

Cavil set his plate down. "The chosen from the first district take care of their own. She will not abandon you."

"Our mother sure as hell didn't have a problem with it," Lily grumbled.

"She was not raised in our realm. Lissandra was the heir when the Deity chose her to move here. There's a stark difference."

I picked at the perfectly roasted chicken. "It doesn't matter. We're here, so let's give them a chance. Stay alert, though."

Quin's eyes snapped into focus. "Perhaps you should take your own advice."

I chuckled. "Perhaps."

"At least Belnaught regrew my fang." Lily tapped her shiny new tooth. "Maybe he can teach you, so if it happens again, I don't have to do the hiss of shame when I'm mad."

"Hiss of shame?" I asked, half laughing.

"It's hard to look intimidating with a fang missing."

Lily and I stood back-to-back in a cavernous room deep inside the mountain. Drake leaned against the stone wall with his arms and ankles crossed. Cavil sat on a stone bench beside him, his eyes glued to Lily. Tracy and Bastien stood nearby, having another mental argument. Quin stood on Tracy's other side, watching Lily.

Our grandmother tugged the sleeves of her billowing blouse as she considered us. "Now, ladies, we will divide the room in half. Liliana, turn your half dark as night and set traps. Ensure they do not detonate without the trigger being activated. Try not to collapse my training room."

"Uh, huh."

"Jenella will use the magic of five or more factions. Should you need containers to hold the magic, you will create them. Practice with care and be precise. Do not use witch, mage, or multidrakelandarnarian magic. Should you veer off course, start from the beginning."

"Sure."

I started with pixie magic since it was one of the stronger colors. Pixies always hovered around since I befriended their queen, so I had many opportunities to absorb their power. They used their wings and legs to create dust and aim. I didn't have wings, so I needed to improvise. I formed a table and made five small boxes before I brought the pinkish color forward.

"No!"

I jumped and my head whipped to Lissa. But she wasn't yelling at me.

Lily looked more defiant than upset. "What now?"

"Think of your magic as a water faucet where you can turn down the pressure. Right now, you work on full blast." She leaned down to examine a wide black streak of sheer power. "I bet Jonas adores the intensity. It is handy when using your physical skills, but not magic. Turn it down to a trickle so it is easier to control."

Lily nodded. "Yeah. I lived in the human world, and using my magic had consequences, so I rely more on my physical abilities. When I went to Allure to release my magic, I did it fast to avoid being there longer than necessary."

"You must break the habit if you want to stop killing everyone in your path."

I refocused on the pixie dust. It didn't take long to realize filling five containers was overly optimistic. I made two colors, pink and orange. The pink was supposed to heal, and the orange mimic Sylphira's ward breaker trick. It wasn't right, so I tried again. After nine failures, it worked. Lissa approved, so I moved on to elf magic.

Most elves had plant-based magic, except for the snow elves, who could manipulate ice and snow. I'd absorbed them all, thanks to their help in our battles. For my first try, I chose forest elf magic to grow a fern. It wasn't like creating one. I had to create and coax the seed to grow without injecting more creation magic into the mix. It took more concentration and time than I planned, but eventually I grew a thick green fern in a peach planter.

Unable to decide on a third magic, I sat on the floor to think.

"Jenella. What are you doing?"

"Thinking about what magic to use next."

"Your shifter magic is rather strong. As is your vampire magic. Try those."

"How? Both are embedded in their blood. And I don't have shifter or vampire blood."

Lissa morphed into a massive golden wolf, trotted around, and shifted back, not losing her stylish, yet loose-fitting clothes. "You are correct. It is a different skillset. You must infuse the absorbed magic into your blood. Try it."

I glanced toward Drake, but he wasn't watching me. His eyes crinkled in the corner as Cavil pointed at something Lily worked on. All my friends were watching her with amused or intense expressions. I wondered what she was cooking up. With a sigh, I stood and brought shifter magic forward.

"Don't use it on a surface level. Let it sink into your blood," my grandmother coaxed. "Let it engulf you."

I clenched my jaw and sank deeper. And pulled back when my bones creaked. Before she could say anything, I raised a hand. "Let me brace myself." Once I was steady enough, I sank into the feeling and ignored the pain. When my eyes opened, my vision was off. The floor was too far away, and the ceiling too close. I took a step and flinched when the floor shook.

My heart raced as I searched for Lissa. She stood next to Cavil, a smirk on her face. I tried to lean back, lost my balance, and crashed to the floor in my regular form. When the cool air tickled my skin, I realized I was naked.

"What in the hell was that?" Lily screeched.

"Uh." I created a baggy T-shirt and yoga pants and slipped them on. "Something tall?"

Everyone except Lily laughed.

"It was a dinosaur. Only much uglier than my dad."

My stomach fell. "Please tell me I didn't mimic Morten."

"You looked similar to Morten," Drake used a conversational tone, but humor laced his voice.

My head spun, and I sat down to keep from passing out. "It's not funny. That asshole almost killed you and succeeded in killing Mat. I don't want his magic."

"It wasn't an exact match, but a mixture between him and Jonas."

Tears flooded my eyes, but I refused to let them fall. "I don't care. I'm not doing it again."

He was across the floor in a split second. "I'm sorry." He wrapped his arms around me. Not a drop of amusement came from the bond. "Then don't." He rested his cheek on top of my head. "Try to become Travis's wolf. You can use it to get back at him for pretending to be a friend."

"I like that idea much better." I took a shaky breath, stepped back, and faced my grandmother.

Her gaze held too much understanding. "Intent is everything. Try again with more focus."

"Right."

She shuffled forward, looking regal and in charge. "Stop gawking at your sister, Lily. You've only created one trap. You girls are such slow learners. We will accommodate you for a few years, but the coalition may not survive."

I appreciated her lack of sympathy. As I moved away from Drake, a thought struck. "Can't you manipulate time?"

"When Belnaught and I combine our power, we can manipulate a few minutes." She assessed Drake. "Though the Firsts often believed the ability was much more expansive. I learned early on to use every tiny anomaly to my advantage when ruling, so I never corrected them."

"Then we need to wrap this up. We've already been gone too long."

"Excellent idea."

I thought about Travis's wolf form, only in the bright pink color of Cavil's shirt, and gave myself over to the shifter magic.

Drake's deep laughter made my sensitive ears ache. I trotted to Bastien and tried to lick his cheek, but he shoved me away. Tracy hooted with laughter, so I nuzzled her and charged Cavil. He laughed as he let me tackle him. When Drake pulled me away, I shifted back. "I did the coloring on purpose."

The last magics I tried was Ogre, which ran off anger, making it easier to access. And troll magic, which made them invisible unless they revealed themselves. Because it only worked when they were near water, I had to create a pool and a bridge to stand on. When I was done, I wiped the sweat off my forehead and took the bottle of water Drake handed me. "I think I've got it."

"Execution was never your problem."

I moved closer to the hair-raising magic emanating from Lily's side of the room. Pools of darkness swirled in sync, giving a tiny slice of hope that light could peek through before sealing itself. A brilliant form of torture. The light from my side reflected on her skin as she stood on one hand and whirled her other one around. I squinted to see what she was doing, but couldn't quite make it out.

Nearby, our grandmother crouched low, her eyes glued to the project and beaming with pride. "Very good. Now back out without triggering it."

Lily disappeared, then reappeared beside her. "My speed and agility make it easy not to trigger traps."

Lissa's white teeth gleamed as she smiled. "You are so much more than Lilith ever was. I could not be prouder."

"Sure." Lily didn't hide her skepticism. "So, can I go home now? My uncle Roman tricked me into taking over a house, and they need guidance."

"Soon." Lissa skirted around the pool of darkness to address me. "Tomorrow, you learn how to rule. Tarquin, do you wish to navigate Lily's maze?"

"I have been to war with her. Even if I had not, I have no desire to be caught in Lilith's traps again." There wasn't a drop of sarcasm in his tone.

"My apologies. My memory sometimes fails me." She clasped her hands. "Cavil, you will go inside the darkness with Deslaurian and test the traps."

"*No!*"

"Not a chance."

Lily and I protested in unison.

Cavil's chest puffed out. "I would be honored to support my soulmate."

Drake patted my hip. "It's okay. If you haven't noticed, I have scales."

"How effective were those during the beanbag incident?"

He laughed and kissed my temple. "Should my scales fail, I have you to heal me."

I rubbed the line where I cut off my hand. "Fine. But don't come whining to me when you turn into a pile of goo."

His laughter made my stomach flip. He joined Cavil near the boiling darkness. I knew from experience Cavil could dissipate most magic, and his sunny power naturally countered Lily's, so they'd be okay. It didn't mean I wouldn't watch them like a hawk.

Lily must have had the same thought. She leaned forward, her eyes glowing an eerie golden red. "I don't like this."

Lissa stepped between us. "Don't worry. I wouldn't have sent them in if they couldn't handle it. Your work is exquisite and will provide them with a rare challenge. If I remember correctly, Deslaurian likes a fun challenge."

"*Drake* is adventurous, yes," I emphasized his name. Her intimate use of his birth name irritated me.

"Cavil isn't exactly a risk-taker," Lily said. "But he does like solving problems."

"Good. It will keep them busy while we chat."

"Chat?" I asked.

She motioned toward Tracy and Bastien. "Do you mind if your friends hear this conversation?"

"No. Tracy and I share everything."

"Very well. Let's discuss your lack of confidence." She pointed at Lily. "And your lack of pride."

"Sorry. My mother beat the pride out of me." Lily's eyes stayed on Cavil. "And I don't talk about feelings with strangers."

"She did the same to my confidence. Only she used Jacques to do her dirty work. If only you were around to help."

Sadness washed over Lissa, and her eyes filled with regret. "It is true I could have done things differently. I commend you both for working so hard to cope. However, you should not overcome your weaknesses, but embrace them."

My focus turned to her.

"Don't look at me that way." She gestured toward Cavil, who cursed as something swept his legs from under him. "The strongest people are always those who work through life's obstacles and fight to heal from their wounds. Your lack of confidence allows you to listen to the opinions of others with an open mind—a difficult skill for more confident people like me. But you do it with such grace. And Lily's lack of pride keeps her from being seduced by the darkness inside her. Lilith never understood the perils of her darkness. But you do. And you need to remember them."

"Meemaw said something similar."

"You're both doing much better than those around you will admit. They can't see it because many have never faced the pain you've endured, or don't remember how it felt." She leaned forward. "It's why I requested Tarquin attempt your maze." When we didn't react, she continued. "As a reminder of being young and helpless. I advise you to work through your perceived weaknesses on your terms. Use your emotions to your advantage when appropriate, but never forget their impact on you."

I swallowed the lump in my throat and nodded.

Lily's face turned thoughtful.

Light pierced the dark a second before a snapping sound echoed through the room. The two men groaned, and a series of thuds followed.

Lily beamed with pride, which she supposedly didn't have. "Proximity sensor with ankle spikes."

Chapter Sixteen

Verity's face screwed up in confusion when she met us outside the family flashing circle.

I paused before moving in her direction. "Sorry for being gone so long."

"You said it might be a few weeks."

"Yes, but I hoped it wouldn't."

"Lissa can manipulate time but only by minutes," Drake said.

"Oh. Is time manipulation a trick you inherited?" Verity asked.

"No. She and my grandfather do it with their combined magic."

When Lissa released us, Cavil took Lily home at her insistence. Bastien flew off with Tracy when we landed in Allure, and Quin vanished. I'd miss seeing them every day.

Lissa taught me finesse and how to hide my magic so it wouldn't be noticed. I only needed to control the message my magic sent to other paranormals, rather than wrapping the power around myself. I needed to lace it with the intent of invisibility, so others wouldn't notice me. Though she cautioned me to use it sparingly.

"Well, I'm going home. You can fill me in on your training tomorrow."

"Sure. Have a nice night." I slipped my arm through Drake's as we strolled toward the family entrance. "So, have you thought more about our match ceremony?"

He smiled. "Are you trying to push the planning off on me?"

"Absolutely." I let out a dramatic sigh. "It's too bad my match is too smart to be manipulated."

"And too mean to play along."

I chuckled. "Yes. It would be much easier if you were less strong-willed and did what I said."

He stopped and pressed his lips to my ear. "Is that so? Because I have a few ideas." He feathered kisses from my ear to my mouth.

I shivered and stepped back. "I like your ideas."

He ran the back of his knuckles down my side. "You'd tire of me within a week if I allowed you to manipulate me." He took my hand and guided me toward the elevator.

And I'd never forgive myself for it. Drake was too damn honorable. "We'll need to start planning soon."

"If you're serious, we should talk to Helen first."

My forehead crinkled. "You don't believe I'm serious?"

"I often find myself baffled as to why you keep choosing me, yes."

"So we're both insecure for no reason."

He tugged me to a stop outside my, or our, apartment. "Perhaps."

"Then let's work on it so Helen can start planning."

The mixed reactions to Sylphira's hero idea didn't surprise me. What I didn't expect was for a few advisors to agree so fast. Deva leaned back, and considered it. Ara and Quin whispered to each other. Jonas and Ann Marie huddled with Razazia. Tracy talked animatedly with Olwen and Cavil. I stayed silent and waited for them to finish.

When the chatter died, Deva squared her shoulders. "Becoming heroes to humans is a dangerous game, love."

"I've heard how they build people up, only to tear them down. What do you suggest?"

"I believe we can solve some of their problems. But we should approach it as if we're humanitarians."

"Yes. Vampires and dragons make excellent humanitarians." Quin's voice dripped with his usual sarcasm.

Ara patted his hand. "It is not a terrible idea, but it will be difficult to navigate."

"Correct," Drake said. "It will require cooperation and precision. Paranormals must maintain strict control over their predatory instincts. Humans will need to testify to how magic helped them. In addition, many of our established businesses have paranormal employees. If they include humans, the authorities will put them under surveillance."

"Drake is right about exposing our entrepreneurs to the authorities." Ara tapped the table. "Most businesses on human soil are vampire-owned. They will not be pleased if the government investigates their business practices."

"Ah, so we're calling them entrepreneurs now? How creative." Razazia folded her hands. "Perhaps they should reconsider their illegal dealings. Unless we only use the more legitimate businesses to employ humans."

"My vampires follow the law, dear. Still, some are more creative about how they do it than others."

I wanted to bang my head on the table. "Ara can choose which businesses are involved. How do we win people over?"

A little of Emine's crazy returned to her eyes. "Social media is a splendid weapon. Start accounts and have our most beautiful people make videos about our efforts. Humans love a good rescue story."

"Verity said social media is manipulative and disingenuous."

"I mean, people understand it's not always real." Tracy set her phone down. "And it's not disingenuous if we're really helping people."

"Correct," Bastien agreed. "The trick is to ensure those we send out are self-disciplined."

Ann Marie shook her head. "You'll get more attention if you rescue animals."

It blew my mind that they were even considering it. "If people care about animals, we'll help them, too. We have enough paranormals to form several committees." And, if I could convince everyone to cooperate, it might solve a few of our problems. "What type of personalities do well on social media?"

"Charismatic ones who are also pleasant to look at," Ann Marie answered.

"And attention seekers," Verity added from my desk. "Extraverts who love to be the center of attention do very well."

An idea formed. "I know exactly who to put front and center."

Jonas leaned forward. "Oh? And who is that?"

"Travis. He's good-looking, charismatic, and loves to feel important."

He rubbed his chin. "It will give the shifters a renewed sense of belonging. Something they are missing after their leaders betrayed them."

How it would look to the shifters hadn't even crossed my mind. "Yes."

Verity made a note. "And the ladies love a strong shifter. He'll drive us all crazy, but he'd be very good."

"I'll handle his ego," Jonas said.

"Great." I motioned to Cavil. "How do other realms work these things out?"

"This is the only realm where paranormals hold themselves apart from the indigenous population. Though there are a few who subjugate the non-magical."

"We want to co-exist, not enslave people."

"I am aware. Which is why comparing yourselves to other realms is useless."

"I agree with the god." Quin barely ground the words out. "We are unique. Therefore, we need unique goals. It will take strong leadership to meld our societies. The question is, are you up to the task?"

"Yes," I answered without hesitation. When everyone's faces showed a mixture of disbelief and skepticism, I shrugged. "I care about people. Right now, we're divided. And I'm not convinced we've taken care of all the Bellicose leaders. We need to unite, stop the guys with the odd magic, figure out why demons are still here, and work out a cooperation deal with multiple human governments. It might take years, but maybe we can build a better world for everyone."

"How idealistic," Razazia drawled.

"It is a bit naïve," Ann Marie agreed. "But it may work."

"Hope is a dangerous emotion."

My head whipped toward Drake. "Oh?"

"It's not a criticism, Jenella, but a truth based on experience."

I supposed with the rejection he'd endured, it was his truth. Still, it seemed like a rather bleak view. "We have a council meeting tomorrow. If this won't work, give me a better idea."

No one had a better idea. We discussed violence, war, mind manipulation, and a bunch of other strategies I wasn't willing to consider. As it dragged on, my self-doubt crept in. I dragged my feet toward my office, barely noticing the palace guards, who no longer bowed. "Am I an idiot for considering this?"

"No." Drake placed a hand on the small of my back. "But it's a big step. Taking the time to think about the effects is wise. When the dust settles, we will all need to suffer the consequences. Hearing opposing views helps you think critically and make better decisions."

We had plenty of opposing views. "If we don't act soon, the humans will."

"Perhaps. Or they might find another shiny object to chase."

"Directing them away from us is a great idea. Why didn't you bring it up in the meeting?"

"Because it's a big gamble and does not bring us closer to finding the kids or banishing what remains of the demons."

"So, we suggest it to the council as an alternative. It might make our humanitarian campaign more appealing."

"Sure, if you want to manipulate them into agreeing with you."

"Sometimes it's necessary."

"And sometimes it's not."

"Then I won't use it unless it's necessary."

He kissed my cheek. "Sure, you won't."

"I'll try not to, but yeah. I'll probably end up leading with it."

The Council buzzed with activity when I sauntered in and took my seat. Drake stayed cloaked, and I didn't bother asking why. I scanned everyone's intentions as they settled around the gigantic circle. They had turned the seating into a fun game. I had to fight off a smug smile.

Deva's overwhelming presence moved behind me, and she settled to my left. Bastien's sharp eyes had a knowing gleam as he studied the blank space where Drake sat.

I pressed my lips together so I didn't laugh. "Hello, Deva. Where's Tracy?"

"She's angry," Bastien answered. "And is staying at her dad's house for a few days."

I leaned around Deva to see him better, but his expression gave nothing away. "And why do you suppose she's mad?"

"Don't try to run my life, Jen."

"You mean like how you try to run Tracy's? Not a chance."

Smoke billowed from his nose. "Not your business."

"Temper, temper. Honestly, Bas. If you didn't share a bond, I'd encourage her to dump you and your controlling ass."

Deva's sultry laugh was barely audible. "Perhaps now isn't the time."

Bastien's pained eyes met mine. "It is not."

The look was intentional and made me pause. I'd need to track Tracy down after the meeting so she could vent. When everyone settled, I signaled for Verity to project holograms of the gates humans attacked, followed by the footage Alex and Elsie took inside their prison.

"Is that the building the hybrid imploded?" Someone asked when it finished playing.

"Yes. Lily collapsed the building as they fled from their abductors. We had paranormals on the ground and safeguards in place, so no humans were killed."

The Council chattered among themselves.

When it died down, I continued. "I've moved the affected gates, and the witches have been working with the tech mages to better protect our transports. The traitor who leaked the information is in our custody. In addition, the God Cavil has rescued several paranormals from human dungeons." I rested my forearms on the table. "The First Razazia and Queen Sylphira have presented an interesting idea."

I explained it, only instead of heroes, I used the term humanitarians. After I finished, the First Gorman stood. "With all due respect, humans have always hated us. It is a terrible idea to intermingle with them."

"Hated you, you mean." Razazia stood. "Although I'd like to deny it, the First Gorman makes a good point. It will be a difficult task, but with the right finesse, we can accomplish it."

Several leaders nodded in agreement as the Minotaur King stood. "They have been hunting hybrids and shooting at us. It may not be possible to repair the damage."

"I agree." I tapped the desk, since I couldn't pace. "The question isn't whether it will work, but whether it's worth trying."

The Queen of Giants, who rarely spoke in meetings, stood. "If I may, Your Grace?"

"Of course."

"I am pleased we are considering reintroducing ourselves to humans. Perhaps I could suggest a series of committees to implement multiple humanitarian efforts? If we diversify and help them in multiple ways, our chances of winning them over will increase."

"Absolutely. What are your thoughts?"

By the time we closed the meeting, we'd divided the leaders into several committees to develop solutions for different countries. I gave them a week and was pleased to see everyone working together.

Until the Chimera King stood. "I wish to discuss a more personal matter."

I kept my face neutral. "A personal matter?"

"I understand you and Drake the First are close, but I do not believe the Dragon First is the right choice to become your official consort."

The ball of anger inside me ignited, and I tamped it down. I wanted to see what he had to say when he thought Drake wasn't in the room. "On what grounds do you base your opinion?"

He blinked in disbelief, probably because he expected a fight. "Because he cannot even show up for important meetings and has, on more than one occasion, bullied council members. In addition, he often issues rulings without you."

Drake never mentioned what he did to intimidate the Chimera King, but the pride blasting from him told me it was a doozie. As far as making decisions without consulting me, I agreed. But he did what was best for the coalition, so I let it slide. "Explain."

"He hovers over my territory and watches us. It's disconcerting. He has also had my people removed from palace grounds more than once, stating we are a security risk."

"Did Consort Drake give you a reason for this behavior?"

"He insists on holding me responsible for the sins of my people."

I had to pause to keep from bursting out into evil laughter. The chimeras attacked and kidnapped me before I knew we bonded, and Drake wasn't one to let something like that go. I yearned to ask him about it, but it could wait until we were alone, so I could thank him properly. "Anyone else share this opinion?"

Several people stood, including a few I counted as allies. The anger inside me slammed against its cage, begging for release. I was sick of them criticizing my age, competence, power level, and decision-making skills. But their reluctance to accept Drake flat out pissed me off. Especially since he was the most amazing man I'd ever met. He was patient, loyal, and thoughtful. He was nearly killed fighting for a coalition that had rejected him for centuries. And now they wanted to reject him again. They were idiots if they didn't see how lucky we were to have him.

I sent my senses around the room while I tamped down my anger. Drake didn't help. Because we understood each other, and he knew it wasn't what I needed. Our compatibility terrified me sometimes. We even had a similar sense of humor. And he wasn't afraid to call me on my shit in the most amusing and respectful ways. Not to mention, he was also the only other paranormal who could match my power. And I wouldn't let them treat him like he wasn't good enough.

"Sit down." Their buts hit their seats at my command. Realizing what I'd done caused me to look inside myself. I truly felt powerful. Not magically, but with an inner strength that forged into steel from trauma and self-doubt. As if it were there the whole time, just waiting for me to notice. The strength was like an adrenaline rush that eased my inner pain and extinguished the anger. I finally recognized what my friends had been trying to tell me. No one had power over me unless I gave it to them. And I wouldn't stand by and allow them to insult my match.

I projected my newly found confidence. "You have accused me of many things. But none of them were as insulting as pretending Drake wasn't instrumental in our defeat of the Bellicose. Many of you wouldn't be alive right now without him. And have you forgotten how he nearly died fighting for the coalition?" I paused. "You can share your opinions here, and I'll listen to them. But my consort is not up for debate." I indicated the Chimera King. "You are not the Queen of Ahl. I am. Which means I decide who is worthy to walk by my side." I allowed power to fill my eyes. "If I hear one insult lobbed in his direction, I will unleash a hell like this council has never seen."

Many of the council members paled. I couldn't tell if it was from my power display or my words. I didn't care. Drake was mine, and I was his.

Sylphira rose from her seat. "Um, may I ask when the matching ceremony will be?"

The Pixie Queen never missed an opportunity to make herself relevant. "It's yet to be determined."

The Chimera King scoffed. "If the First is so great, why isn't he here at this monumental meeting?"

Drake uncloaked himself, his face hard as stone, even as pure love and joy wrapped around me.

"Don't tell me you forgot dragons can cloak themselves."

The Chimera King sputtered as he tried to form a response.

"It is common knowledge," Deva said with too much enthusiasm. "And my nephew is better at it than most."

"Correct. However, there isn't a human alive who could detect even the weakest dragon," Drake explained as if the exchange about his competence didn't happen. "Vampires can lurk in the shadows. Mages can flash. And trolls are undetectable when near water. I suggest you think about how to use the skills of each faction during your committee meetings."

I scanned the stunned leaders one more time. "Meeting adjourned."

Chapter Seventeen

My newfound confidence stuck with me as I landed near the alchemy village where Tracy's dad lived. Silhouettes of witches reflected in greenhouses as they worked to maintain the herbs used in their potions against the harsh winter. A few stood on their porches or the street, mingling. Some stopped and stared as I approached Calvin Cordalia's cottage.

The village always amazed me. Calvin and his coven had carved out a space near the gates, where no one would bother them. In the summer, the landscape looked more like a dreamscape. The colorful cottages popped out of the snow in the winter, making them look like scattered candies.

Tracy sat on the front porch, a steaming mug in one hand, her phone in the other. Her head lifted, and she set her things down to pull me through the wards. "Hey, Jen."

"Hey." I settled beside her and threw a warm bubble around us. "Bastien said you're staying here for a while, and I thought you might need a friend."

"He's lucky to be alive after what he said."

"Yeah?"

"Do you remember the day I showed up in his office all beat up and agreed to guard you?"

"Sure." It was the best day of my life. Not only did I wake Drake, but I found my best friend.

"We've lived apart throughout our entire relationship. I did my thing, and he did his. We didn't interfere in each other's business. Occasionally, he'd insist I stay with him. Or he'd show up to check on me and stay for a while, and I did the same. Then we had that battle at the palace." She took a sip of her drink. "I went after that sorry excuse of a grandmother with a vengeance that night."

"I remember."

"What I never told you is that he stole my kill. I was less than a second away from revenge, and he stole it from me. When I threw a fit, he said vengeance never feels like you expect it to. I mean, I understand what he's saying, but I would have liked to find out for myself."

I picked at my coat. "I understand vengeance, yes."

"Oh, I didn't mean you didn't." She shut her eyes. "To be honest, I hesitated to kill her. Where you stepped up and got your vengeance, I failed. And Bas decided he needed to take matters into his own hands. It made me feel like an inferior coward."

"I didn't kill my mother. Mat did."

"Oh. Everyone said it was you."

"I had a hand in it. She screwed him up much worse than me, so he needed to confront her."

"See, I would have done the same for my dad. But it irritates me how Bas took charge and killed her before my brain overruled my emotions."

"Yeah."

"Now, he wants to keep me close all the time to protect me. I don't need his protection, Jen. I enjoy working with my dad to develop the next great potion to sell to my clients. Or reading some ancient tome to create a new spell. It gives me flexibility, so if you need help, I can be there. He doesn't like how I drop everything for you. Even though you have a lot more going on, you still make time for me."

"I can back off if you want."

"No way. I can't rule dragons, and I like it when you involve me in your plans."

We were quiet for a few minutes before a thought hit me. "Holy hell, Tracy. We've come full circle."

Her brow creased. "How so?"

"Now you're the one who doesn't want to rule and trying to gain her freedom, and I'm the well-adjusted one who's comfortable in her place."

"And when did you become comfortable in your place?"

"It's growing on me."

"And what freedom?"

"Are you kidding? I can flash anywhere in the world in the blink of an eye and fly with a dragon. That's about as free as it gets."

"Sure."

"I mean it." I clasped my hands. "At my coronation, I thought my life was over and I'd be locked in a cage of decorum and responsibility for the rest of my days. And in a way, it's true. But you taught me a lot about independence, and Drake taught me the power of perspective. Even Quin helped me with his sarcastic comments about my leadership skills. It sounds strange, but I finally feel free even with my obligations to the crown."

"That's good."

And it didn't help. Because the situation wasn't about me. My heart went out to her, and I wanted to help. But I still sucked at setting my selfishness aside and being a good friend. "To put it another way, you can be both free and responsible."

"You're missing the point. Bas wants me to give up everything I love and focus on the dragons."

"Are you sure?" I couldn't imagine someone with a dragon bond being capable of stealing their partner's happiness.

"No. Yes." She flung her hands in the air. "I mean, he's pushing me in the direction he wants me to go, and I don't like it."

"Understood. What compromise have you suggested?"

"He tells me what he expects, and I tell him to piss off. That's pretty much our way of compromising."

"Yet you've always been so patient with my bullshit."

"It's different. You've always respected my boundaries."

True. I squeezed her arm. "Should I help you come up with solutions, or do we ride at dawn?"

"Please tell me you haven't been studying human cliches."

"Drake likes them."

The smile on Tracy's face melted. "I'm half the problem because I won't give up the life I've built without him."

"So, don't. Our house is still empty, and yours if you want it. Tell him you'd be glad to live with him there. Have Rayar set up a lab. Bas knows how happy running your business and practicing your craft makes you. And it's close enough to downtown that he can fly to Dragon Headquarters in a few seconds."

"He'll never leave the dragons."

"Are you sure? Because we're talking about the guy who practiced alchemy with your dad to win your heart. Maybe he'd be open to trying if it helps heal your relationship."

She considered it. "Maybe."

I stood. "I need to meet with Travis"

Her face puckered. "I'd rather argue with Bas for a hundred days straight than talk to that guy for one minute."

"Yeah. But he'll make a great front man."

"Call me when he frays your last nerve."

The brownie who worked as my former friend's assistant stood on her chair as I breezed by. "You can't go in there, Your Grace."

I ignored her plea and threw the door open. And stopped in my tracks.

Travis stood behind his desk with a woman. Her legs were wrapped around him, and his hands squeezed her ass. My face burned with embarrassment, and I took two steps back. "Ew. Gross. Ick. This is a workplace!"

Travis set the woman down, and the two brushed their clothes to straighten them. "Er. Ah, Jenella. Didn't my assistant stop you?"

"She tried." I forced myself to step forward. The woman stirred and drew my attention. "Ha! You're the hybrid who tried to sell her people to the Bellicose."

"I'm Sheila. And I did no such thing."

"I talked her out of it," Travis said. "Do you need me for something?"

My power rose at his superior tone.

Sheila skirted around his desk. "I'll let you two talk."

"No. Since you two are...close, you can stay."

She shuffled sideways and perched on the edge of a chair.

Travis smoothed his messy hair. "What's up, Jenella?"

I explained our plan to win the humans over. "I'd like you to be our face on social media, if you're interested."

Sheila eyed me like a lab experiment. "I heard you weren't very smart."

It was all I could do not to slam her to the ground with my magic. "And I heard you screwed random wolves in offices." I dug into my pocket and set a cleaning potion on the desk. "To sterilize the place."

"I see you haven't matured." Travis tapped his desk. "If I do this, what's in it for me?"

"Just because I prefer not to see you screw someone in your office doesn't mean I'm immature." I swung toward Sheila. "Honestly, what do you see in him? Because he is only concerned about the payoff, rather than the greater good."

Sheila suppressed a laugh. "Holy hell. You're like a less crude version of Lily First."

"Oh, I'm not nearly as funny as her, but thank you. I adore my sister." I focused on Travis. "Want to become the face of the coalition on human social media?"

His eyes sparked with interest. "Why?"

"We plan to begin humanitarian efforts and need someone to document it. Which means you'll represent me and my administration. The pay is good, and Jonas believes you're a good choice to represent how the shifters are atoning for their betrayal. It will also prove I don't consider all members of your family traitors."

His jaw clenched, and it took him a minute to answer. "Can I think about it?"

"Sure. You have one day. Call my office by noon tomorrow. If we don't hear from you, consider the offer revoked." I stood.

"Do you understand social media enough to pull this off?" Sheila asked.

"No, but the tech mages do. And so do many other paranormals. If you're interested in becoming a consultant, call my office and talk to my assistant. You'll need to have your mind read by dragons and your crimes assessed by a Juror."

"I would love to help. I've tried to gain traction on social media for years."

"If Travis accepts the offer and you pass the screening, you can work together on the project." They were both good-looking and self-centered enough, though I wasn't sure what the council would think about a hybrid representing us.

"I'll do it," Travis said. "But only if you promote my Deputy Director. She's been a detective almost as long as Tarquin and overlooked for promotion too many times."

No doubt Travis weaseled his way into the position ahead of her. "I'll screen her, sure. But no promises."

Sheila stood. "And I will call your office to discuss the opportunity. That is, if Travis is okay with a tag-team."

The way she said the last sentence sounded so suggestive, I shuddered. "Sure." I left before they made me puke. In a way, they deserved each other. But I wasn't spending the next few years listening to their innuendos. My stomach couldn't handle it.

The area around Alex and Lily's personal village buzzed with activity as vampires zipped from one house to the other. A few dragons stood near the front, huddled around a woman who registered as mostly human and a girl who had the potential to become a strong air elemental. I paused as I examined them. They had to be Lily's friend, Susan, and her daughter. But Lily said the daughter was human. A simple mistake, since the girl's powers hadn't come in yet. Elementals were rare, and their powers never developed before their mid-twenties.

A vampire materialized. "Good afternoon, Your Grace. How may we help you?"

"Is Lily around?"

"She isn't. Mistress Lily has gone to see the hybrid leader."

"You can just say she went to the bar. I don't mind."

His bland expression didn't change. "Of course."

I landed at the gate closest to Dale's bar. A new bar with a hologram above it that read 'Hooves' had been built inside the gate. I sensed Lily inside, so I made my way to the entrance.

Glasses clinked, and the smell of ozone from spent spells lingered. Dale's muscles bunched when he spotted me. Other than his obvious disdain and the silence that swept through the place when the patrons spotted me, it was welcoming and had a lot more space than the pub. In the corner, Lily glared at me from her spot between Alex and Elsie. Three dragons swung their heads toward me.

I pasted on a pleasant smile and pretended not to notice the silence as I approached her table. "This bar is great." I formed a chair and sat. "How long has it been here?"

"Not long," the purple dragon, June, answered.

"What have you come to drag me into this time?" Lily's voice sounded bitter.

"Nothing. I needed to check the progress of the kids we recovered and thought I'd say hi."

She raised her glass in my direction. "I don't believe you. Not once since we met have you shown up without an agenda."

"Yikes," the red dragon, Flintous, mumbled.

I'd done a terrible job building a relationship with Lily. And was right about how I only showed up when I wanted something from her. "I don't want anything. I swear."

"What in the fates brings you to my bar?"

I turned to Dale. "I wanted to enjoy a drink with Lily and check on the kids we rescued."

"They're fine. Maria set up a group home while we find parents who won't sell them. But what is the real reason you're here?"

"Fine. I wanted to share some news. Have you heard anything about the disappearances or the demons?"

"We're still working on the disappearances, and about a quarter of hybrids won't move to the pocket. The enforcers have all the info you need." He slid a drink in front of me. "Keep me out of the rest and don't fuck up my bar." Dale clomped away.

I took a sip. "How does he always figure out what to serve?"

"He's been running a bar for a long time," Alex said.

Lily eyed her beer. "He gives me different beers every time because I hate it."

"Oh, please. Like you couldn't end it in a second." I took another sip and frowned. "My healing magic refuses to let me get drunk."

Glacintial, one of my favorite dragons and a general who led a division of my army, leaned forward. "That is not necessarily a bad thing."

I set the drink down with a scowl. "Says you."

"You said you have news?" Lily's voice sounded exasperated.

"I have some good news and some funny news. Which do you want first?"

She face-palmed. "Good for you or me?"

"You."

When I didn't continue, she kicked me. "You're ruining our party."

"That's harsh." She didn't react, so I continued. "Fine. The funny news is I caught Sheila and a former friend of mine making out in his office today." My shoulders slumped when everyone continued to stare with various levels of hostility. The news was hilarious if you knew Travis. But no one at the table did. "The good news is I discovered how to transfer ruling magic."

Her stern expression melted away. "How is that good news for me?"

"Because I can appoint anyone my heir and pass my power to them."

"Does that mean people will stop calling me princess?"

"No. The title is your birthright. But it does mean you're no longer my heir. I've released you from all obligations to the throne of Ahl."

The three dragons gawked. Elsie tried to look anywhere but at us. Alex stared at me with a thoughtful expression.

Lily looked like a constipated troll. As if she couldn't fathom it. "Why?"

"Because I'm pretty sure Mat added you as a joke. And I understand what it feels like to be forced into a position you never wanted. No one will confirm it, but I suspect Roman already trapped you. There's no reason for me to pile on." I downed my drink. "The difference is, I've always known I'd one day be queen. It's not fair to expect you to be my heir after Anitta's bullshit. I plan to make Emine my heir until Drake and I have kids."

She tapped her beer bottle. "How is Emine doing?"

"Emine's a fighter." It was all I was willing to say. In truth, she fought to keep going every day.

"Yeah. Thanks, I guess."

I didn't expect her to jump for joy, but hoped to at least ease her burden. "You're not happy about it."

"Because that's not how magic works."

True. I leaned back. "I'm trying here, Lily. There's only so much I can do to compensate for all the shitty things our family did to you, including me."

"I don't need you to compensate."

"Then what? How can I make you see I don't want to use or abuse you?"

"Stop putting pockets in my yard and showing up unannounced. I just want to be left alone to live my life."

Pain and anger flared as I stood. I hoped removing her as my heir would help build a stronger relationship. When we were inside Mage Mountain, I even thought we'd become friends. But she only wanted me around on her terms. And if Tracy taught me anything, it was that real friendships don't work that way.

"Consider it done." I stood and tried to leave, but the pain of losing another sibling to something so stupid gnawed at me, so I planted my feet and clenched my fists. "In fact, I'll leave you completely alone to wallow in your self-righteous pity." I leaned forward. "You're drowning, and I'm trying to extend an olive branch. But you keep slapping it away. You're not the only one thrust into an ocean of extra responsibilities. The difference is, I'm fighting against the current, and you've chosen to drown." When I met Alex's eyes, the disappointment in them almost ripped me apart. We'd become close since he made me a Lily substitute, and I would miss him. "Have a great life." When I flashed away, I found myself on Tracy's doorstep.

"I mean, you could have handled it better," Tracy said after I explained what happened.

"I could handle so many things better. But you didn't see her face. She hates me and doesn't want me in her life."

"She'll come around."

"Will she? Because she seems to have built herself a pretty good life and all I do is screw it up. She's funny, tough, confident, and everything I'm not. And I only wanted to build a healthy relationship with her. But instead, I made her hate me. There's no room in my life for more people who hate me."

Tracy didn't respond. She didn't need to. We both knew I sucked at connecting with people. She shifted her weight. "Fine. I'll see if Bastien will move into the house with me. But only if you sign it over, so it's in my name."

A harsh laugh escaped at the subject change. "Consider it done."

Chapter Eighteen

Footprints in the snow zigzagged around trees and led to a bridge over a frozen stream in the woods behind the palace. Despite the frigid temperatures, a trickle of water weaved around the ice and kept pushing downstream. It was resilient and determined not to let the frozen temperatures stop it from reaching its destination. If I wanted to be successful, I'd need to become water. "The worst part about learning my magic is you can't jump scare me anymore."

Quin appeared beside me. "My sudden appearances were an attempt to help you with an important skill. You missed the entire point."

"No, I didn't."

"You disowned Lily. Why?"

"She doesn't want me in her life."

"It is her birthright."

"Yes. One she hates. Or did you forget I can read intentions?"

"I rarely forget."

"That's too bad, considering your past."

"Correct. Then why?"

"Every time I show up, her first instinct is to become defensive. She doesn't like or trust me, and I can't change it."

"It is wise to be skeptical of your power."

"Sure. Let's pretend she hates my power, when she never hesitates to flip off Drake and order him around."

Quin leaned against the railing. "Perhaps she needs time."

"Time will dull the damage Anitta did to her, but like you, she won't forget. She also won't forget how we took over her life and forced her to take on responsibilities she didn't want."

"It is her destiny."

"Which she should have a say in. Roman's clever little trap and my insistence on planting that pocket on her property took away her choice."

"Perhaps. But you did not need to remove yourself from her life."

I swung toward him. "The mood in that bar went from festive to flat the second they spotted me. Before I even said a word. Lily and Alex see me as a killjoy who ruins their lives when I show up. So, yes. I needed to remove myself from her life. Not only to give her a break, but because I refuse to stay where I'm clearly not wanted." I stepped off the bridge and started back down the trail. "If she changes her mind, she knows where to find me."

Quin caught up. "Roman meant well. According to him, he created the house as a gift for his favorite niece. Her challenging him and winning was always his plan."

"It doesn't matter. Trapping her was not the way to go about it."

"I agree. We wish for Lily to thrive."

"Me too. Which is why I cut her loose. Now she doesn't have to worry about me popping in and ruining her day."

Quin was silent as we trudged through the forest and down the walkway leading toward the palace. My eyes drifted to the sky, where I felt Drake, but I didn't see him. "I'm going to conscript your division of the army when the Leadership Council gives me their proposal. I'd use Glacintial's, but the hybrids still aren't happy about being part of the coalition."

"Perhaps use Olwen's division as well. He has soldiers with unique insight into humans."

"He does?"

"Razazia placed the recovery teams under his leadership."

"Of course she did." We reached the family entrance. "Do you think I'm too slow at making decisions?"

"Yes. Caution is warranted in many situations, but not this one." He vanished.

The council was determined and happy as they took their seats. The Kelpie Queen settled into the seat beside me. "Good morning, Your Grace."

I blinked at her polite tone. "Good morning."

"Is the consort cloaked again, or has he finally come to his senses and released your bond?"

There it was. "Neither." I went back to paranormal watching.

"It is odd how he does not come with you."

"No, it's not."

"If you keep arriving at different times, people will talk."

"I don't care. We don't owe you, or anyone else, an explanation."

Drake entered through the side door with the Firsts. Jonas said something that made him smile, and Razazia patted him on the arm. Gorman threw his hands out and talked animatedly. The Firsts no longer viewed Drake as an outcast. I pried my eyes away as Dale, the hybrid leader, came through the opposite door. He spoke to the Fairy Queen before taking the chair beside her.

"Why do you feel like defeat and defiance?" Drake asked as he settled into his seat.

"No reason. I see you're getting along well with the other Firsts."

"Yes. I seem to recall you mentioning how everyone would kiss my ass if I were bonded to you. It proves your theory true."

I chuckled as I twisted toward him. "People do like to suck up to power."

"I don't," the Kelpie Queen said. "It is a waste of time and energy."

For the first time ever, I agreed with her. "And it's annoying."

"Yes."

Drake laid a hand on my thigh. "What is your strategy for this meeting?"

"To listen and decide accordingly."

Turns out, some leaders had great ideas. The vampires, who owned several human businesses, planned to open similar operations to employ the homeless. It would provide more jobs and keep their current ones from being investigated by the human governments.

The dwarves agreed to buy abandoned buildings and turn them into affordable housing. Elves would help farmers and ranchers to bolster their crops and create community gardens. Several factions agreed to work together to patrol the streets of their local communities and stop crimes.

Dragons agreed to feed people and assist with fires. The aquatic factions would watch out for sailors. Mages and witches planned to use spells to help the poorest communities. Shifters were going to fight crime and protect vulnerable populations. Those who couldn't look human would work behind the scenes to strengthen small businesses, flood animal rescues with cash, and fight hunger.

Sylphira and the Fairy Queen created little paper calling cards with a symbol representing the coalition. We agreed to use it as our social media logo. By the time the meeting ended, I had a restored sense of hope and optimism about the plan. We wouldn't be superheroes, but we were going to save people and bring our own community closer together, which was much better than going to war.

"After we win over the people, the world governments will reach out and want to meet with you," Ann Marie said.

"That's the goal."

"What are our terms?" The Gargoyle King asked.

"Excellent question. I want our factions to unite and our communities to live peacefully. Whether it is among humans or inside the pockets."

"Each country and its leaders will demand different things. We will decide on specific terms when the time comes," Drake added.

I gave a nod of agreement. "We already have a committee studying the various human governments, they can shift their focus to develop an outline of logical terms. If it's too early to guess, we'll work it out as we go."

Several leaders stayed and mingled after the meeting. They pulled me into conversations before I could make my escape. Drake waited outside and took my hand as I joined him. "You're bringing them together."

It sure seemed like it. "Didn't you say hope is a dangerous emotion?"

"Yes. But it's also an effective one. Your gamble in hope is paying off."

"For now. Our strategy is extremely optimistic. Not everything is going to work out the way we hope. It will be interesting to see how well we stick together through the struggles."

"You sound like a queen."

"Crazy, right? Especially considering how reluctant I was to take the job."

"I never doubted you."

"Liar."

His deep rumble of laughter made me quiver. "Not a lie. You must admit, your methods are unconventional."

"Thank the fates. Can you imagine what would have happened with the Bellicose if I were all about decorum and rules?"

He shuddered. "I won't even entertain the thought. We did not address the strange magic or demons during the meeting."

No, we hadn't. "Cavil thinks the strange magic might be from a warring faction from another realm. And we haven't confirmed that the being who took the girls is a demon. What if we're being invaded?"

"Gartolians aren't subtle when they attack. And after examining the weak shifters we imprisoned, Cavil believes the magic is native to this realm."

"I have two theories. The humans might have learned how to circumvent their immunity."

"Yes. But it doesn't account for the advanced magic we found. It takes precision and time to master such intricate spells."

"Which is why I think someone powerful is manipulating the others. The grotesque guys may be failed experiments. Lily said their egos are bigger than yours. And the ones we captured had too much confidence for their power level. It sounds like someone is giving them minimal power and telling them they're unstoppable."

Another sexy laugh. "Your sister does like making fun of me."

My heart ached at the mention of Lily's snark. I'd miss it. "She does."

"What happened between you two?"

"I'm not talking about it here."

"Very well. Who do you think took the kids?"

I paused while I gathered my thoughts. "For the first time in all the cases I've solved, I don't have a theory. And I'm not wasting resources on finding out because if there's one thing I've learned about the bad guys, it's how they love to reveal themselves."

"Who benefits from the chaos?"

"I see where you're going. But I've never sensed demon magic so clean, so I'm not sure they're the ones behind the disappearances."

"Nor have I. But there are many factions of demons."

Chapter Nineteen

WIND RUFFLED MY HOOD as Drake swooped low over a lake. A sasquatch dodged trees and brush as she ran through the forest, an injured human in her arms. She stopped, cocked her head, and readjusted her direction. As she drew near a line of rescue workers, she carefully placed the man on the ground, handed him our calling card, and melted into the woods far enough to hide while she waited for them to discover the injured hiker.

It had been two months since we implemented our plan to help humans, and our efforts were paying off. The internet buzzed with stories about how someone with magic or special abilities helped them out of a tricky situation. Governments were touting lower unemployment and crime rates. Thanks to our housing efforts, homeless camps were disappearing, and fewer people were starving.

Even so, some humans still hunted us. I had to move three more gates, though only one was because of violence. The others became inconvenient as cities expanded, and they were no longer hidden.

While some governments praised us, others were less happy about our efforts. The government hadn't given up trying to capture us and still lingered in the area. As a result, another transport was destroyed. Luckily, it was in a remote area near a gate, so we eliminated the evidence and evacuated everyone before they showed up.

Another successful rescue. Drake banked right, heading towards Allure.

It feels good to help people.

Yes. It might be worth continuing our efforts indefinitely.

I find it strange how they don't take better care of their people. Poverty didn't exist in our communities. We based our classes on power level, rather than money. And the leaders went to great lengths to ensure their people were employed, housed, and fed. Right down to the least powerful. If they couldn't, then the Crown offered resources. Taking care of each other was ingrained in our society. Which is why hybrid discrimination never sat well with me. It went against everything we were supposed to stand for. *Let's swing by Eldritch and see if they need anything.*

They don't. Deva and Emine have worked together to ensure they thrive.

I still want to see it.

You want to check on Lily.

He knew me so well. I kept my promise to leave her alone. And, according to Cavil, she was content running her house and convincing hybrids to move into the pocket. She even turned Roman's house into a hotel so she could employ her vampires and give hybrids a place to stay while they transitioned. Alex texted me occasionally, but not Lily. She didn't want me in her life and was probably thrilled I'd removed myself from it. *I can't help it, even though she doesn't want anything to do with me.*

She never said she didn't want to have a relationship. You decided for her.

Yeah. Because I sensed her intentions.

Communication is key to any relationship. You should have talked to her before cutting her off, and spying on her won't help.

I hated how Drake was always right. My decision was a little abrupt, but something about her and her friends reacting like a group of palace guards when I entered the room bothered me. She shouldn't need to be guarded around her sister. *Fine. Then let's go home.*

Our staff was growing. As a result, conversations buzzed around me as I passed the outer offices. With the influx of staff, the castle hummed with energy. It was like a mixture of hope and purpose. Paranormals were thriving.

Gilbert, the castle guard leader, stood near the waiting area outside my office, so I waved him in as I passed. He'd been around since we first came to Allure, and Mat trusted him. My chest ached as I took the plush chair behind my desk. "Thanks for coming in. Please have a seat."

His brown eyes hardened. "I prefer to stand." He was a big man who would be beautiful if not for the permanent scowl etched on his face.

"We need someone to run operations and oversee security. Would you be interested?"

Gilbert was slow to answer as he scanned every corner. He knew Quin often hid in my office, though it had become less frequent since Lily crashed into our lives. "Are you asking me to take over Prince Mathias's duties?"

I swallowed the lump in my throat. "Not all of them, no. Only those pertaining to security and logistics. It's my understanding you're already doing most of the work. I'd like to make it official."

He stared intently for too long. "Will I be required to take Regent Mathias's office?"

"No. Pablo and I cleared it out, and you can make it your own if you want to." I failed to keep the pain out of my voice.

"I'm honored to assume the duties, but prefer not to work from his office. It's too...."

When he didn't finish, I took a deep breath. "Yeah. It's up to you."

"I accept this new position. What will my new title be?" Unlike me, the guy thrived on protocol.

"Chief of Logistics."

He bowed. "Thank you for trusting me, Your Grace. I swear I will not let you down."

"Thank you for holding everything together the last few months."

He bowed again and strolled out the door.

As soon as he left, I swung toward the back corner. "What's up, Lily?"

"Dang it! You weren't supposed to notice me."

"I sensed you. And so did Gilbert, but he thought you were Quin."

She melted out of the shadows and plopped onto a sofa. "Back to the drawing board."

Hope bubbled inside me, and I couldn't resist smiling. "I'm the worst person to try to hide from."

"True. But I figured if Gramps could hide from you, I'd try it."

"Logical."

She rubbed her eyes. "I'm exhausted."

I felt it radiating from her. "Need a place to hide while you sleep?"

"No. I'm staying at Cavil's place. I love the house, and he keeps saying it's ours, but it doesn't feel like home."

I turned on my tablet. "He wouldn't protest if you made it your own."

"The bright colors he added make him so happy that I refuse to change a thing." She lifted her hand in a half-wave. "It's complicated."

"Uh, huh. So, you came here to avoid color?"

"I wanted to argue with you about how you dumped me like a cheating boyfriend, but I'm too tired."

I laughed as pure joy filled my heart. "I didn't dump you, so much as give you space."

"Bullshit. You removed yourself from my life because you were slightly inconvenienced."

"Shows how much you know."

Her eye cracked open. "Alex told me all about how horrified you were when you figured out how Roman framed me. What he didn't tell you is that I figured it out before I even showed up to fight him."

"I removed myself because when I pop in, it ruins your day, and you can't wait for me to leave." I patted my chest. "I can feel intentions."

"We're having two different arguments here."

"And it wasn't only Roman's actions that horrified me. Mat's and my actions were inconsiderate, too. So, I removed the burden."

"I still call bullshit. You ran away because my friends and I made you feel uncomfortable."

"Yeah. Running away from my emotions is my specialty. I'm working on it. But in this case, I set you free."

"Except I didn't ask you to."

"No, you didn't. But you also didn't put up a fight."

"Because you blindsided me. I like you when you respect my boundaries. And it's not you, but politics I don't want in my life."

I rested my chin on my hand. "I'm the queen."

"What is that supposed to mean?"

"You can't have a relationship with me and not be involved in politics. And I removed you from the line of succession to respect your boundaries. It's not much, but the best I could do given you're my sister and magic thrives off birthright." I drew a deep breath. "I would have moved the gate from behind your house, too, but you and Alex like having access to your human property."

"You're unbelievable."

Verity stomped in and headed toward the conference table. "Did you see the news?"

"No." I stood. "Did something happen?"

She flipped on the TV and pointed. "They're trying to turn the public against us."

A man stood at a podium, wearing a dark suit. "These creatures only care about preying on us. Be cautious when accepting help from them, especially if they request money." He pointed at someone off-camera.

A woman with dark hair and a light blue suit held a microphone. "The supernaturals have reduced crime, saved farms, and provided housing. How is that dangerous?"

"Those acts alone aren't dangerous, but I assure you, they have an ulterior motive. Beware of things that are too good to be true."

"Is it true they've lived among us for thousands of years?" Someone shouted.

"The matter is being studied. But so far, we've concluded they've been here for the last five years."

The answer irritated me. "He's lying. The guy knows we've always been around."

Lily appeared in a chair at the conference table. "Yeah. You're stealing his power. Since they acknowledged your efforts, it's time to turn up the pressure."

"You're right." I lowered myself into the seat beside her. "Let's see what they're saying on social media."

The narrative from the human media didn't match what the people posted online. They loved us. There were thousands of testimonials from people we helped or were in the process of helping. Fan groups were popping up, and it became a game to spot us. The disconnect baffled me. "Why are they so different?"

Verity turned down the TV. "Because the media sticks with the official narrative."

"We can't believe them?"

"No."

Lily held up my tablet and pointed at a heart. "People jump on the latest trends to increase their likes and follows. I suspect the truth is somewhere in the middle."

"It doesn't matter." I stood. "We forced them to acknowledge us, and people are noticing our efforts. Contact Travis and tell him to disprove the politician's comments. Maybe act insulted and hurt. I want his and Sheila's faces front and center, showing our efforts. Email the council and tell them to branch out into other areas if they can." I picked up my phone. "My healing magic works on humans, so maybe our healers can help sick kids."

"Saving kids and animals is a great way to draw attention on the internet, but this is people's lives we're talking about. You can't abandon them when you get what you want." Lily stood.

"We won't. If we reach a co-existence agreement, we're in it for the long haul. If not, we might have no choice unless we're sneaky about offering help."

"Great. I'm heading back to Cavil's for a sleep period, but we're not done with our argument."

"Of course not."

"This is nuts." Emine tugged at her suit jacket.

"No, it's not. You just don't like your clothes." I motioned for the healers we brought to go ahead of us.

"Yeah. It's not my style. What are we doing again?"

"Healing sick kids."

"The children's wards have extra security measures."

"We have dragons." I pointed to the three dragons trailing behind us. "And I can disable their cameras."

"And turn off medical equipment in the process."

"Not going to happen."

"Sure thing, Chickee."

We took an elevator to the children's ward, and I disabled the cameras as we went. The healers' faces lit up when they spotted some children gathered around a woman reading a book. Some of them looked pale, others were bald. Some kids seemed fine, but the overpowering smell of antiseptic couldn't mask the scent of death. Three healers and a sandy-colored dragon moved in their direction.

Two healers and a gray dragon split off and disappeared down the hall on the right.

I tugged Emine away to the left. "Our spy said the sickest ones are down here."

She jerked her arm from my grip. "You can say Lily's name. And why am I even here?"

"You're my security."

"You have fucking dragons."

"Okay. Then you're my personal guard. I trust you to have my back."

Emine quit arguing as we slipped through a set of double doors and into an area clouded with panic and desperation.

The yellow dragon who followed us scratched his nose. "The nurses will ignore you. I suggest you speak to the parents if you want credit for your efforts."

I turned to face him. "What is your name?"

"Mendalo. I often guard the entrance to the hotel."

"Right. You're one of my sister's friends."

"Lily is quite unique."

I peeked into the first room. A small lump covered in blankets lay on the bed. A man and a woman huddled together beside it. The woman dabbed tears from her eyes, while the man's shattered face focused on the monitors.

"Good morning." I tried to sound quiet and respectful as I stepped inside.

The dad's spine straightened. "Who are you?"

"Someone who might be able to help." I shuffled forward. "Mind if I try?"

The woman's mouth dropped open. "You're one of them. The magical people."

"Yes. If you choose not to let us heal her, then I'll leave."

They shared a look, and the man stood. "We're desperate enough to allow it, but you harm one hair on her head, I'll kill you."

I admired his protective instincts. "Understood." I moved close enough to touch the child. The illness inside her was widespread and winning. She wouldn't have lived more than a day or two if I hadn't shown up. It took half as much magic to cure her as it did to heal a paranormal. One little zap and the tumors disappeared. Her failing organs healed, and her color returned. I stepped back as the child's eyes fluttered. "All done. She's healthy now."

"Will it come back?" The mom barely choked the words out.

I handed her one of our calling cards. "If it does, contact us through this website and we'll heal her again."

We moved on. Some kids didn't have parents with them, but most did. Only one refused our help. A woman with hatred in her eyes screeched at us. Mendalo stepped in and removed us from her memory as Emine and I raced away.

The other healers were pale, and their magic was depleted when we met beside the elevators. No one was around, so I flashed back to the healing center in Allure, and Emine and I headed toward the main flashing circle.

As we joined the line, Emine scanned the crowd. "You don't need my help when you're healing."

"Nope. But you needed the distraction."

"No, I didn't. I'm busy trying to coordinate the various Forte mages and transfer my enforcer duties to the centaur you hired to replace me."

I snapped my fingers. "That reminds me." My magic stirred as I latched onto her hand. With a zap, I transferred a small portion of my ruling magic to her. "Now, no one can dispute your fitness to rule the mages."

She stared at her hand with wide eyes. "What kind of bullshit did you concoct this time?"

"It's not bullshit. My grandmother tutored me, so I understand how my ruling powers work now. I transferred a piece of ruling magic to you."

Chapter Twenty

My eyes stayed on my phone as I stretched and turned onto my side. Video after video of humans expressing their opinions, having fun, or making funny skits with their pets played on my new app. I'd been there for over an hour and couldn't drag myself away.

"What has you so entranced?"

Butterflies exploded in my stomach when Drake's voice registered. I hadn't bothered to sense for him. "Studying."

"Really? Because it looks like you've fallen into the human social media trap."

I peered over the tablet. "It's fascinating."

"Yes. And addictive." He lifted my legs and rested them on his lap. "I heard you're healing children."

"Yep. And rescuing animals. My team of volunteers has saved nearly a hundred kids and even more cats and dogs. Healers all over the world have been working on it." I jiggled my tablet. "Which is why I picked this up. Humans are resilient and amazing. I wanted to learn more."

"You understand people will flock to you begging to be saved now. They don't heal like us and are vulnerable. Many are desperate."

“Sounds reasonable.”

“Until they mob you.”

“They can’t get past my barriers. Besides, I don’t mind healing them if they approach me. It takes a minuscule amount of energy.” I flipped to another video. “Maybe we should set up healing centers where they can go if they’re desperate.”

“The governments will shut them down. They’re already deploying police to stop your healers.”

“Why wouldn’t they want us to heal kids?”

“They’re claiming it’s unsanitary.”

“Oh, puh-lease. It’s safer than most of their methods.” I tapped out an email to the healing committee to set up inconspicuous healing centers. “What have you been up to?”

“Extinguishing house fires and stopping crimes.”

“Fun.”

Drake pulled my foot closer. “Not really. I preferred rooting out the Bellicose.”

I groaned when he began a slow massage on my foot. “You could always help feed people.”

“Perhaps I’ll try it next. Have you decided how long we will continue these efforts?”

“Indefinitely. I find it odd how so many people are suffering, and their leaders don’t care enough to help.”

“It’s not cruelty, nor is it all governments. Though I agree their efforts don’t meet our societal standards. Keep in mind, you hear more about the bad than the good on the internet. I’ve seen people living under the cruelest regimes in the worst conditions sacrifice themselves to care for their neighbors.”

“Seems both endearing and illogical.”

He switched to my other foot. “We also struggle to balance cruelty with kindness, so judging them is pointless.”

"True." I didn't want to waste any more mental energy on the puzzle. "What if I did one of those speech thingies like their politicians? Will they meet with us if I request it?"

"A press conference?"

"Is that what they're called?"

"I suggest you have Travis field the questions. He's very good at it."

"So is Sheila. That woman can manipulate any narrative to her advantage."

"Yes. It's too bad their personalities make it hard to tolerate them."

"Yeah." Picking Travis to field the human press was a big gamble, but he thrived in the spotlight. And Sheila had questionable morals, but people online loved her. "They're perfect for the position. I got lucky the day I walked in on them making out."

Drake's laugh rumbled through the room.

My entire staff bunched around the TV as Travis stepped onto the stage. Behind him, an unassuming Jonas stood beside vampires, dragons, mages, and witches. Their placement made them look like his employees or friends. The thought of Jonas answering to anyone amused me. Travis made a smooth and convincing speech as pictures of our efforts flashed behind him. His polished, professional demeanor and chameleon personality made him seem like an ordinary, good-looking human. Beside him, Sheila swooned at his every word. When he flashed his predatory smile, a few human reporters gushed.

"That guy grates on my last nerve," Verity said.

"Yeah. Mine, too."

Drake's hand rested on my back. "He is as competent as he is annoying."

I snuggled into his warmth. "He's perfect for this."

When the speech concluded, reporters shouted questions. Travis half-winked as he pointed toward one of the moon-eyed women. She batted her eyelashes. "If your people could do all these helpful things, why didn't you do it sooner?"

"Because we cherish freedom. Our leaders believed you could govern yourselves without our help or interference. The various problems humans face have only recently come to our attention. We debated whether to involve ourselves after seeing how little your government cares for its people. Some of our leaders believe humans like to suffer."

Reporters shouted more questions. It allowed him to pick which ones he answered. "We are many factions that formed a coalition. Our people have different forms of government, all under the umbrella of a monarch." He moved to the next. "As I said, we value freedom, so we don't plan to take over your society, but coexist in a way that benefits everyone. Our leaders are open to negotiation with the various governments, should they wish to engage."

The questions went on. When Travis was confident he'd relayed our message, he left the stage, his entourage trailing behind him.

Verity clicked the TV off. "That went well."

"He did great. Now we wait."

Over the next few days, the leadership committees stepped up their efforts. Not because I asked them to, but because we'd all become invested in making the world a better place. The press conference resulted in mixed reactions from around the world. I found them predictable, so it didn't take me long to lose interest. Humans were flocking to us for help. The tech mages created an app where they could submit a request. It helped us better organize our efforts. People on social media were singing our praises, and even a few politicians said some nice things about us. Our plan was working.

Tracy sat in what used to be our kitchen, a small smirk on her face. "We did it." She flicked the vial of clear liquid. "Or at least the tests went well."

I rubbed my eyes. "You can't randomly test potions on sick humans."

"Sure, I can. As long as they understand it's an experiment and agree to take it. I mean, they were dying and desperate for help, but still." She shrugged. "It's not like we don't test them on paranormals all the time. Wasn't it you who shoved that potion down the sasquatch's throat?"

"We aren't nearly as fragile as humans."

"Meh. They're tougher than you think. Plus, I got to meet the nicest people. This potion only works on injuries. We're still studying diseases. Learning about them will take a while. This way, witches can focus their energy on something more productive than avenging the death of their former president, and it will give the healers a break."

I picked up a vial and examined it. "How fast did it work?"

"So fast, my dad sent some with the traffic control team. If they can't prevent accidents, they can use them to save lives. I'm thinking about giving a batch to the hybrids, too. They have human friends who might need them."

"Good idea. Do you need a ride to their pocket?"

"I thought you'd never ask."

We landed outside the distribution facility inside Eldritch. The blue grass was beginning to uncurl from winter, and several blades stood straight up. I chuckled at how awkward it looked. Over the winter, hybrids moving to the pocket lined up waiting to receive supplies. Drake teamed up with Lily's vampires to speed the process up. According to Alex, most of the holdouts in the valley were considering moving to Eldritch, though he thought Lily's relentless hounding had more to do with it than the improvements we'd made.

The warehouse was much larger than the one used for hybrid rescues in the human world. It also had a lot more supplies, including furniture and potions with the Cordalia logo on them. Tracy's dad was as amazing as she was.

Maria, the boggart who ran the place, stepped out of an aisle, a deep frown on her face. "What can I do for you, Your Grace?"

"Nothing. I'm playing taxi."

Tracy hefted a crate full of hundreds of vials. "I have potions to heal human wounds. Do I drop them off here, or does Dale need to approve them?"

She motioned toward a table with a mountain of unsorted supplies. "We don't have the time to do targeted distributions. Dale is aware of who needs such things."

Tracy nodded. "Thanks."

"Wait!" Maria skirted around a pile of shoes. "Why are the purebloods helping humans?"

"Because we want to establish diplomatic relations. If we win the people over, they'll have no choice but to negotiate. I hope to coexist. We're showing the value we can bring to their society."

Her eyes twinkled. "It won't work. They'll try to tax you until you're broke and push you out."

"If so, we'll use our centuries of experience to work around them. If they tax us, I'll tax them back." I winked.

Maria's laugh followed us out onto the street.

Aside from an occasional shifter, the hybrids going about their business stayed in their human forms. I hoped one day they'd use their magic freely. We turned right and headed towards the bar.

Hooves buzzed with activity, and I tested my new cloaking ability so hardly anyone noticed us as we headed to a couple of empty barstools at the end. Tracy hefted her potions onto it and scanned the place. "This is nice."

"Yeah. It's where Lily and her friends hang out."

Dale's face hardened as he flipped a towel over his shoulder. "Your Grace. Tracy. What brings you here?"

Tracy shoved the crate of potions toward him. "Healing potions for humans. They only work on injuries. Maria said it would be best if you handed them out."

He peered into the crate. "No shit?"

"My dad and I are good at potions."

I rested my arms on the bar. "They're geniuses. And they even tested them for us."

"Huh." He picked up the crate and moved it to a back shelf. "What can I get you?"

Tracy pointed toward another patron's drink. "We'll have one of those."

Dale shook his head. "Those are made for the heartier factions. But I have something similar." He moved down the bar.

"Why did you order a drink?" I asked.

"Because neither of us ever stops to relax. This place looks fun."

Three dragons burst through the door. The red one spotted us right away and veered in our direction. "Your Grace. What brings you here?"

"Why does everyone always ask me that?"

A laugh rumbled out of him. "Because you're the queen."

"I am aware." I motioned toward his buddies, who settled at a table. "What about you?"

Our drinks landed in front of us, and he swiped them off the bar. "Come sit with us."

I hesitated, but Tracy hopped off her stool. "Great idea."

"It is?" I asked as I trailed behind her.

"Yeah. I mean, they know I'm mated to Bastien, and didn't even acknowledge me because they were so laser-focused on you. Which means they want something."

The eight-person table seemed too small as we settled across from the three massive dragons. The purple one, June, leaned toward Tracy. "What in the ever-loving hell are you doing hanging out in a hybrid bar, Tracy?"

"Jen and I had some business with Dale and decided to have a drink."

"I see." She gestured towards me. "The hybrids hate you. Your efforts with the humans are making it worse."

I took a sip of my drink as I considered my response. But the only one I could come up with was the truth. "I don't care."

Her face gave nothing away. "You should."

"I should do a lot of things." I tapped the table, trying to decide if I should say the next part. "But I've gone out of my way to atone for their treatment. And let me tell you, changing the minds of most leaders wasn't easy, and I still struggle to eliminate the sentiment. But we came together and built the hybrids a pocket where they could be themselves. I almost died trying to save them from slavery. My brother, along with many other paranormals, did die. Recently, I rescued several of their children from the black market. And how did they repay us?"

I leaned forward to meet her eyes. "The hybrids refused to lift a finger to help when our architect mages came to help rebuild their homes and harassed them the entire time. The ones in the pocket treated the paranormals who Drake sent here to improve their lives like they were intruders. If hybrids still resent me after everything I've done to help them, then they are simply hateful beings who can fuck right off." I stood. "Have a great night."

Tracy put a hand over her mouth to hide a smirk as she joined me.

The bar had gone silent during my rant, so she didn't comment as I flashed to the mixed magic neighborhood behind what was now her house. When we landed, I bent over and put my hands on my knees to catch my breath. "I shouldn't have lost my temper. They're going to revolt."

She burst out laughing. "I disagree. They *are* ungrateful haters who needed a reality check. And you *have* done more for them than any other faction."

I straightened. "You're right. There are other factions who could use my support." I flung my hands in the air. "Hell, even my sister can't stand to be around me, so why keep trying? Maybe it's time to let them figure it out for themselves." Except for finding the kids. I wanted to make sure they had a good life.

"That's a little extreme. I mean, Lily likes you. And she's the only hybrid who has a reason not to."

Her words made me pause. "You're right. The problem isn't my efforts, but I have meddled with them more than I should." I focused on the other end of the alley, where I sensed Drake and Bastien. "We'll pull our support back to the same levels other factions receive."

"If you say so. Brace yourself for trouble when you do."

I nodded. "Thanks for helping with the potions. I hope one day we can enjoy a drink at Hooves."

"Oh, we will."

Drake uncloaked himself and morphed into his human form a second before Bastien. Tracy patted my arm and disappeared into her privacy spell. Bastien followed her without acknowledging me.

"Are they getting along better?" I asked.

"My cousin rarely discusses his bond with me." Drake leaned down and brushed his lips against mine. "I fed hungry people today."

"Nice. Did you like it?"

"It suits me better than fire patrol."

"Good. I chewed out an entire bar full of hybrids."

His eyes filled with admiration as he laced his fingers with mine. "Sounds fun. I talked to Deva about deploying dragons with culinary skills to less developed countries. She agreed."

"Great idea. The fewer hungry people, the better. After I chewed them out, I had a panic attack over it and decided to scale back our support."

"Do you think it's wise?" He tugged me down the alley.

"Don't go all ancient on me. We've provided them with more resources than all other factions combined, and it hasn't changed a thing. They still hate us."

"Old resentments die hard. Would you like to join me for dinner at the deli?"

I flipped a curl out of my face. "I'd love to. It's not like I expected their attitude to turn around overnight, but we've worked hard on their behalf and don't deserve the hate."

"We don't. But life isn't fair, and you're an easy target because of your title." He motioned down a side street. "Providing aid with expectations attached is a business transaction, not charity. What you need to ask yourself is why you expect their unwavering support."

"All I want is a little less hostility." I fell silent while I pondered it. "My responsibility is to all the people of the coalition, not just the hybrids. I haven't provided as much aid to other factions. It might be time to shift focus."

"You mean, besides removing corrupt leaders and returning their Firsts?"

"That doesn't count."

"I disagree. What did you have in mind?"

"The smaller factions have formed a commune. I could send them help."

"They are thriving on their own. And if the factions other than the hybrids need help, they can petition you. Everyone understands how it works."

"Your practicality is showing again." I squeezed his hand, so he understood I was teasing. Drake's thoughts were almost always welcome.

"I don't know how to be any other way."

“No, I suppose you don’t. I’ll think about the hybrid situation more before I act.”

“Wise. What kind of sandwich do you want?”

Chapter Twenty-One

After a nice, long evening with Drake, where we not only went to dinner but also flew high above Allure and spent the night in each other's arms, my heart was so full, it felt like it would burst. And, despite our many problems, I glowed as I headed to my office the following morning. I waved at the palace guards, said good morning to griffins and other staff as we passed, and smiled at anyone who glanced in my direction.

"Jenella, do you have a minute?"

My little bubble of happiness deflated at the arrogant voice. "Sure."

Travis shoved his phone in my face. "We made contact."

I read over the email submitted on our website. "The Irish government wants to meet?"

"Correct. It doesn't surprise me, because they have always known about us. Many of their legends stem from our people."

"Several countries have legends that stem from us. It could give us a slight advantage."

Travis nodded. "What's our next move?"

His focus on the assignment almost completely hid his self-serving nature. "Set up a video meeting with them to test the waters. Have Sheila sit with you, but no one else. See what they have to say, but don't give them additional information about us beyond what we've already put out there."

"Will do." He took two steps away and paused. "And thank you for giving me a chance to redeem my family name."

Coming from Travis, the statement struck me as odd. "Sure."

I motioned for Verity to follow me to my office and filled her in. "Have we made any progress in finding the missing kids?"

"We're working on it. The Enforcers have several leads. They're investigating the group who kidnapped Lily and suspect they're being kept in the Washington D.C. area, but so far, they haven't been able to pinpoint an exact location."

"If they have some of those magic sucking cuffs, those kids don't stand a chance."

"According to Deva, Mat destroyed the key to save you, so even if they had cuffs, they wouldn't work."

My eyes burned with tears, and I blinked them back. "So why do they want a bunch of hybrid kids?"

"Unknown. The magical shifter-like guys we detained are so weak, I doubt they can hold the mage hybrid kids once their magic emerges."

"Weak magically, or physically?"

"Both. Their magic is erratic, and the healers visit them twice per week just to keep them alive."

"What about the demons? Has anyone spotted them?"

"No. But a few vampires have reported feeling dread in a specific area. Drake is deploying a team to check it out. Are you sure it was a demon you saw and not someone from another realm?"

"No. But my senses registered it as a demon. After he left, I started doubting it because his magic felt so clean."

"Right. Then let's hope they're gathering kids for humans."

I rubbed my temples. "The kids inside the house we raided were sure they saw a demon. How would it benefit them to infiltrate the government?"

Verity shrugged. "It would be a feast for them. But it's all speculation. We're still working out what they're doing."

"You're right. How can we move faster?"

"We're moving as fast as we can. Wanna tell me why you and Lily aren't talking?"

"No." We were talking. Sort of. At least we had the one stilted conversation. "We're both busy."

"Sure. Find me if you want a shoulder."

"Thanks, Verity." I moved to the window. A griffin swooped over the guards on the wall, distributing food and drinks. Several other guards milled around the side yard, warming up for a training exercise. Visitors lined up, waiting for the palace to open for tours. Beyond the grounds, flying paranormals drifted across the sky. Everyone seemed more content since we eliminated a good chunk of the Bellicose. I hoped to deliver the peace and happiness they believed they already had.

My buzzing phone pulled me out of my thoughts. When I saw it was Travis, I answered. "Yes."

"A representative from the Irish government wishes to meet with us next week."

"Where?"

"They suggested a few locations in Ireland."

"Tell them we'll be there. Release a video praising them for their efforts and drop a subtle hint about our willingness to meet other governments."

"Will I be going with you?"

There was the smug Travis I knew. Complete with a hint about how he wanted to be seen by my side. "No. You and Sheila will stay here. Keep reporting on our efforts."

"Okay. I'll set it up."

"Thank you."

I stood on the beach and stared at the palace where I was born. The sea breeze and the smell of the salty air swirled around me. I brushed my hair back and swallowed emotions I recognized as grief and anger. Jonas patted my head as he passed, then picked up his pace. I stayed focused on Castle Mahri when Drake put his arm around me.

He kissed my temple. "If you need a few minutes, I'll cover for you."

"I'm fine. When Mat dragged me here for my coronation, I was a different person, I think. Naïve, foolish, with a ton of repressed anger and resentment. I released it by throwing a fit and tore up my childhood bedroom because of a painting depicting me as happy." I tugged him towards the front door. "Mat blamed himself. Emine gave me the most colorful lecture. For the first time, I started learning how to deal with my trauma. As hard as it was, I'm glad Mat made me face my fears. I'm equally glad you found me in that hallway fighting my internal war."

"It was where our bond formed," Drake said the words carefully, as if testing them. "Your emotions were turbulent and it rattled something inside me, so I gave in to your delicious magic."

I flinched. "Sorry about that. I had no idea."

"I am aware. And don't be sorry. It's the best thing that ever happened to me. Not only did I gain a purpose, but I also began my healing journey."

"The day we truly set each other free."

"In a way, yes."

I passed through the oversized front doors and admired the old-world charm of the place. "I don't hate, nor fear, the castle anymore."

"Because you've healed."

"And because Mat changed the whole thing to make me more comfortable."

Helen stepped out of one of the many halls. "Hello, Jenella. Do you want the same room or the royal suites?"

"Hey, Helen. The same room, please." I was better at dealing with my emotions, but I wasn't ready to sleep in my parents' room.

We settled in, and I dragged Drake through the corridors, exploring. "I've never been to some parts of this castle. At least I don't remember it. When we stayed here last time, Mat arranged afternoon tea in this room."

Drake stood in front of a painting of his aunt perched on a cliff, the sunshine lighting her bronze scales. "I don't remember Deva perching on the cliffs of Mahri."

"The paintings are lies."

"I don't believe it's a lie."

"Why not?"

"Because there was a time when I stayed at my horde for months at a time to avoid the other Firsts. My aunt and I weren't as close as we are now."

"Huh."

Jonas came in and scanned the portraits. "Why isn't there a current one of you?"

"I suppose we should hire an art mage and have one done," I said, even though I didn't plan to be enshrined in the portrait room.

"No need to lie." He drifted to a portrait of himself in his spinosaurus form, with Ann Marie standing on his foot, her arms crossed, and her hair blowing in the wind. "The others are on the way."

I'd chosen Jonas, Tracy, Verity, Titus, and Cavil for our first meeting. Meeting with humans made me nervous, so I wanted people with level heads. I'd asked Ann Marie to join us, but she was busy working with the witches to develop spells.

Verity's eyes swept the portraits as she and Titus joined us. She stopped in front of one showing Mat and Jacques laughing as toddler me twirled between them. "Wow. This is surreal."

Tracy pushed past her. "I mean, it's kind of creepy to have refreshments in a room where so many eyes watch."

Bastien, whom I didn't invite, grunted.

Commotion in the hallway preceded Cavil's arrival. He glided in and stopped. "This Castle is full of character."

"It is," Drake answered when I didn't acknowledge him.

I was too busy glaring at the two people hovering in the hall. "You brought Lily and Alex?"

"They insisted."

Lily dragged a reluctant Alex into the room. "So, this is where Anitta hatched her evil plans, eh?"

"Sort of. Mat renovated the castle, so it's much different now."

"What are you two doing here?" Jonas asked in a mild voice.

Alex flinched. "Lily thinks the meeting's a trap."

"It might be," Drake agreed. "But I doubt it. We've had dragons watching. They report the Irish government is excited to meet us."

Verity activated a hologram. "This is a list of everything we've helped their people with."

I'd memorized the list, so I turned to Lily as she settled beside me. "Why are you here?"

"Because I heard my sister was going to a risky meeting on someone else's terms."

My eyes didn't roll, but they wanted to. "Uh, huh."

Alex elbowed her. "We can't go to the meeting with you because the humans consider us fugitives. But we can help in other ways."

"I'm sure you can. But why come all the way to Mahri?"

"Fine." Lily waved a hand. "We were worried. When Cavil said he had to attend a meeting with a human government, we begged him to bring us."

My lips twitched. "I call bullshit."

"It's true."

"She's not lying. They were also worried about Cavil and their dad." Drake feigned disappointment. "I'm heartbroken they didn't include me."

"Keep teasing me, you big oaf, and see what happens," Lily said.

"I'm terrified."

I burst out laughing. When everyone paused and looked my way, I stopped. "Sorry." I waited for Verity to continue before pressing my lips to Drake's ear. "Wanna switch seats so you can terrorize Lily?"

She kicked my leg. "I heard that."

"Will you two stop fighting like children?" When Verity had our attention, she tapped the board. "This is important." After we apologized, she continued. "They've scheduled the meeting here."

"A hotel?" Bastien asked.

"Correct. The officials rented a large conference room and are having it catered." Titus crossed his arms. "It's a security nightmare."

I studied the map. "We can work with it since people we didn't invite keep showing up, and there's a large cave system full of dragons here. Will you contact them, Bastien?"

"They already planned to help. My mother is there now coordinating their efforts."

So, Deva also encroached on the meeting. "Great. Keep me posted. Lily and Alex can work with Quin and Ara. I suspect human security will be tight, so let's have them pose as hotel guests."

Lily's spine straightened. "Meemaw and Gramps are here?"

"Not yet, but my chief of logistics said they hopped on a transport an hour ago."

"I find it interesting how easily you've stepped into Mathias's role," Jonas said.

For some reason, his statement sounded like an insult. "I've been training with my brother my whole life. Contrary to popular opinion, I pay attention and take my lessons seriously."

"I didn't mean to get your dander up. You've adjusted well, is all."

My glare stayed on him as I continued. "Make reservations for Lily and Alex at the hotel. Quin and Ara will sneak in, no matter the level of security." I tore my eyes away from Jonas. "Drake, can you give Alex glamour?"

"Of course."

"What about me?" Lily asked.

Drake smirked. "Glamour won't work on you, but I could rearrange your face."

"Har har."

"Helen can do your hair and makeup, so no one will recognize you. But I doubt they'll be looking for you here, since your supposed crime took place in another country."

"Don't count on it. I'd appreciate Helen's help."

Verity wiggled her phone. "Reservations made. The tech mages will deliver your fake IDs tonight."

The hotel security blocked off a side door and directed our human vehicles towards it. Jonas and Tracy rode in the first car, and Cavil rode in the third with Verity and Titus. Drake and I rode alone except for our driver, a peach-colored dragon.

I wiped my sweaty hands on my dress pants as I watched Jonas step out and offer Tracy a hand before straightening his suit jacket. "Are you sure he's not a chameleon shifter?" The unassuming, average-looking First had transformed for the meeting. I'd never seen Jonas with so much confidence and poise. Power oozed from him in a way I'd never witnessed.

"Tracy is equally impressive."

My best friend wore her glamour earrings to tone down her appearance. Her inky hair was swept back into a professional style that cascaded down her back, and she wore a tailored navy suit. "Yeah. She looks downright regal."

Cavil led Titus and Verity toward them, and the group waited near our car.

"Time to put on a show." Drake stepped out and offered me a hand.

I threw an opaque shield around us so the human cameras couldn't take pictures. We'd debated whether to let them, but I wanted Travis and Sheila to be our faces for a while longer. The moment the humans found out I was queen, they'd transfer their gratitude or ire to me.

A man with light brown hair stepped forward and smiled at Drake. "Hello." He introduced himself and shook Drake's hand before turning to me. "I take it this is your wife."

"I'm Jenella." It wasn't until then that I realized the people waiting for an introduction were mostly men. *Let them think you're the one in charge. I want to see where this goes.*

Drake sent frustration through the bond, but didn't argue.

They led us to a conference room big enough for a group twice our size. I sensed Lily and Quin in the hallway and Ara inside the room behind a plant. Our group sat facing it, so I glanced in her direction but couldn't see her.

The man who greeted us motioned toward the catering. "Please help yourselves." A deep frown formed on his face when we didn't reach for the refreshments. "I assure you, we would never try to poison the fair folk."

"We're fine. Thank you," I said.

He examined me with renewed interest. "I see. Very well, on to business. We do not have the same issues as many other countries, yet you've sent your people to help us. For that, we are grateful."

Drake rested his hand on the table. "You wonder what we want in return."

"Our whole lives, people have warned us not to make deals with you, so yes. Why did you come back after all these years?"

"We never left," Jonas said. "You wanted us out of your world so you could live in peace without worrying about magic. We simply granted your wish and retreated to our pocket realms."

"Yes. About your pocket realms. If you give us the locations, we'll be happy to avoid the area."

"No," I added power to my voice. "If you'd like to discuss a treaty, we're open to it. But we will not compromise the safety of our people."

The man's eyes narrowed. "Which one of you is in charge?"

No one answered.

"I see. Very well. The people of Ireland have always had a special relationship with you and would like to negotiate. We do not wish you harm."

Chapter Twenty-Two

My eyes were heavy as we returned to Castle Mahri. I gave the former dungeon door a dirty look as I led the group to the breakfast room and collapsed in a chair. "That went well, right?"

Tracy rested her head on her arms. "It went better than well, I think."

Ara appeared next to the snacks. "I believe it was a productive meeting, yes. I suspect other governments will be more resistant."

"Yeah." I pulled up the schedule for the next two weeks. "There's an invitation to meet with some officials from the European Union. Does anyone understand their structure?"

"I have some notes. If we have questions, we'll look it up on the internet." Verity tapped her tablet.

"What does the attendance roster tell us?" Drake asked.

"They're serious about negotiations." Deva sauntered into the room and patted Drake on the back like he was a kid. "We've been monitoring them closely. The EU supports our mission to help their citizens and is open to negotiations, but they're also skeptical."

I massaged my temples. "The meeting today was a test."

"Of course it was a test, love."

Our discussion went well into the night. When we finally stumbled to bed, I was convinced meeting with humans was a big pain in the ass game we couldn't afford to lose. Especially since they had confirmed our existence. I was grateful for the friends and family who followed me to Mahri. The information they provided was valuable.

Two days later, I sat inside a well-maintained stone building and fought not to fall asleep as we hammered out details of another agreement. The EU delegation was a diverse group who were concerned about the safety and well-being of their people. They were also very direct. Most weren't afraid to express their fears about the harm we could inflict on them. It was a challenging discussion, since many of their fears were justified. So we steered the conversation to our plans to help them while maintaining our status as a sovereign society. Afterwards, they were less skeptical but still guarded. Overall, I liked the direction the discussions were going, even if we didn't reach an agreement.

After the meeting, I needed some fresh air, so I went to the beach and watched a mermaid as she guided a group of children through the strong currents where a merman waited for them.

"What are they doing?" Lily approached at a human pace.

"Training their kids to swim against the currents."

"Huh. Anitta never taught me about the sea creatures."

"Because they couldn't help her with her plans."

"Sounds about right. The bitch."

The crashing waves drowned out my laugh. "Thanks for helping this week. You really didn't need to come."

"Holy hell. You're as hardheaded as I am."

"We are sisters, whether you like it or not."

"I never said I didn't like it. You did."

"Actions speak louder than words."

"Psh. And look. Here I am."

I suppressed a smile. "Yeah. Here you are." The first child made it to her dad, and they celebrated by flipping their tails in the air and splashing around. "To be honest, I don't know what to do with you."

"Very few people do." Her words were so honest, they made my heart ache.

"What I mean is I can feel intentions. And you always intend to get rid of me as fast as possible."

Lily raised a fist and whooped when the smallest one made it to his dad. "Sorry. But that looked impossible for the little one."

"Yeah. They're tough creatures."

"I can't help feeling like you always want something from me."

"It's a common misconception based on my title and manipulative tendencies."

"Your manipulative tendencies will serve your title well."

"They already do. I only hope I don't become Anitta."

"You won't." She kicked at a discarded shell. "Thank you for taking me off the list of succession. I would make an awful queen."

"No, you wouldn't." I met her eyes. "I understand trauma responses. You want nothing to do with me or my office because our bitch of a mother tried to force it on you. It's the main reason I set you free. Because we both carry enough of her baggage."

She fell silent for a full minute. "I had to call my dad to ground me when Verity dragged me to the palace."

"I heard."

"Being your heir was a joke until then. But sitting in your office made it real, and I freaked out."

"I don't blame you. I've been freaking out every day for years. The only people I had to turn to were Mat, who repeatedly told me to get over myself and deal with it, and Bastien, who thought my insecurities were ridiculous."

"Shit."

"Yeah. The worst part was when I realized they were right. It didn't click until I met Drake and started to heal."

"I have no words."

"You don't have to say anything and I'm not manipulating you. I suck at relating to people on a personal level. It comes from the abuse I suffered, followed by being isolated and told I was the only paranormal who could save the coalition since I was seven. Removing myself from your life was my way of protecting you."

Her eyebrows slammed together. "From what?"

"The crown. My life. Everything. You didn't deserve the crap we've thrown at you and needed time and freedom to adjust. I was trying to give it to you."

"You're right. You *do* suck at people. Did it ever occur to you to ask me what I wanted?"

"I sensed it."

"Well, you sensed wrong. Because I want to know you. What I don't want is you making all the decisions."

My face flushed. "Oh."

"Yeah. Oh." She glanced toward the castle. "Alex said you two hung out while we weren't talking."

"We did. He's amazing."

"He is. No offense, but I can't imagine you two as friends."

"He and I had similar childhoods, so we understand each other. And I think he used me as a substitute Lily. I adore him, so I didn't mind."

"Yeah. He's great, but don't mention I said so. He'd never let me live it down."

"So are you."

She snorted. "I'm a snarky bitch and we both know it."

"I like your snarky bitch mode. Plus, your bravado amuses Drake. And I like anything that makes him happy."

"That's good. Because I have tons of snark and bravado to share."

I peeked around the bush and checked on the right. "Let's go."

"It's not some big secret. I mean, it's not like Drake and Bas are clueless." Tracy still raced from the bush to the hovercraft with me.

I hopped into the driver's seat and twisted in her direction, a big grin on my face. "We did it."

"Yeah. Because no one cares."

Mat used to care. If he were around, I would have spent the last hour in a lecture about my safety. And I'd hate every minute of it. A pang of regret reverberated through my chest. It's funny how the things that bother you the most about loved ones are the same ones you miss the most when they're gone. "Yeah. No one cares."

Tracy rested her hand on mine. "I didn't mean it that way."

"Don't worry about it. It's a strange grief thing."

The back doors opened, and Alex landed in a seat, followed by Lily. "Where are we going?"

I made eye contact with Tracy. "To find another First."

"Please don't tell me we need to camp in the jungle again." Lily slammed the door.

"No camping this time. We're only going for a drive."

"Which is much worse." Tracy twisted in her seat. "You might want to hold on."

I tore out of the parking spot and careened down the long driveway onto a narrow road leading to town. A cart heading in the opposite direction approached. I pulled the steering spell back, climbed to the treetops, and pushed it forward so the nose pointed down.

Someone screamed as we plummeted.

I pulled up and continued down the road.

"Nice driving." Amusement laced Lily's voice.

"Thanks. It scares Tracy."

"You should never be allowed to drive. You're too reckless. I'm taking over at the next stop."

"See what I mean? She acts like I couldn't catch us with magic should we fall."

"I don't care if you create big fluffy pillows over a bed of marshmallows to catch me. There's no reason to drive like that."

"I agree," Alex said in a too-reasonable tone.

Because I risked losing my friends, I slowed down.

A large disc-shaped rock jutted from the ground inside a meadow of seagrass and sand. The salt-scented sea breeze blew my hair into my face, and I brushed it away as we approached a landmark mentioned in my mother's diaries.

"Wow." Alex moved toward the disc. "I'm not picking up any brainwaves."

I swept the clearing with my senses. "Because she's not here. Let's head to the sea. If the First Brogan is still around, maybe he knows something."

When Tracy and Alex ran toward the cart to fight over the driver's seat, I scoffed. "Those two have no faith in me."

Lily glanced at the rock. "Alex is no fun, but I had hopes for Tracy."

Alex stumbled and twisted in a cat-like move to catch himself when Tracy tossed a tripping spell in his path. She raised her fist in triumph. "Ha! I'm tons of fun. But I prefer not to die in a freak accident."

"We need to get to the sea before dark," I teased.

"It's ten o'clock in the morning and the sea is three miles away," Tracy hip-checked Alex and climbed into the driver's side.

I took Alex's spot in the back without an argument. "Did Anitta ever mention Brogan or Celia?"

Lily's expression grew dark as she climbed in beside me. "Not really, other than to teach me about what she called the meddling Firsts."

"She didn't complain about Brogan being slippery or anything?"

"Not that I remember, no."

My heart sank. If Celia were nearby, I'd sense her like Razazia and Gorman. But I didn't, and we'd been all over the pocket. The disc was our only clue. Trying to reach Brogan, who might not even be around, was a last resort.

When Tracy pulled the cart into a parking spot a respectable distance from the Castle Mahri, I hopped out and followed the trail to the ocean without looking back. At the shore, I crouched down and paused. "Here goes nothing."

Lily crouched beside me and grabbed my arm. When I gave her a puzzled look, she shook her head. "I've seen too many movies where tentacles crawl on shore and pull people under. If there are two of us, we have a better chance."

"We don't have time for that nonsense." I extended my other hand, touched the water, and sent what I hoped was a signal for Brogan.

When there was nothing but silence, I stood, pulling Lily with me. "Nothing. Not even an acknowledgement from the merpeople we saw in the bay."

Lily dropped her hand. "Well, that blows. What's next?"

"I need to give up and go home. We have too much going on to waste more time."

Chapter Twenty-Three

Several other governments had reached out when we returned to Allure, and I couldn't meet with them all. I requested other leaders to volunteer and spent an entire day briefing them. Canada requested a video conference, so I attended it in between briefings. It was productive, and we scheduled a future in-person meeting. Just after I logged off, Travis and Sheila burst in.

Travis stomped to the remote and turned on the TV. "You need to see this."

Sheila clasped her hands. "Ignore the lies and watch the crowd."

A man wearing a suit identified himself and stated he didn't understand why other countries were so impressed. I followed Sheila's advice and tried to focus on the blurry faces behind him. When I spotted it, I stood. "It's the guy who stole the kids." There was no mistaking the arrogant smirk or the spark of greedy red in his eyes. "So, demons are working with or influencing humans."

"Not necessarily," Travis said as he muted the TV. "But it's suspicious."

"I'll have someone gather more information about the human. Maybe there's a trail." I tapped my chin. "We need to counter the fraud claim right away. How about one of those things where people can type at you?"

Sheila frowned. "You mean, go live?"

"Yes. Invite me on. I'll bring Drake, and you can ask us about our other meetings."

"Then drop this on you, hoping you're unprepared, like the human news does?"

"Sure, if it gets more views. But don't be hostile. Act like you truly want the answer."

Travis scanned my office. "You need an appropriate background, so we don't look like fools."

Drake appeared in the doorway. "Should we look formal and regal, or casual and relatable?"

"Relatable," Sheila answered. "Dress nice, yet casual, and don't be afraid to be funny." Her face paled at the lack of reaction. "If you have it in you."

Travis nodded. "The backdrop should show your status."

Over the next couple of hours, we chose a background and settled on a family crest. Shiela wanted to use paintings of Lissa and Anitta, but I refused. My mother had no business being included, and my grandmother was in the painting of the Firsts we chose.

Verity and Charlotte hung them in an unused storage room and set lighting spells to make us look good on camera. Drake glamoured himself in a deep green T-shirt that showed off his muscles, and I wore a stylish dark orange blouse that made my golden eyes look amazing and boosted my cleavage. Helen even plastered human makeup on my face.

When we were up to TV standards, Travis had his crew set up an expensive camera and microphones and handed us headphones to wear. "We won't turn on your microphones until you're introduced."

The nerves didn't set in until Travis and Sheila popped on the screen with a similar setup. Travis flashed a too-good-looking smile. "Hello, believers. And welcome to a special edition of The Real Magic podcast. I see there are a lot of new people here, so let me introduce myself. I'm Travis, a wolf shifter, and my lovely companion is Sheila."

Sheila's face lit with false excitement. "I'm both a witch and a mage." She created a ball of raw magic.

"You're so much more," Travis said with a flirtatious grin.

"Why, thank you."

His face grew serious, and his eyes took on an amber hue. "If you've followed our social media, you've heard our royals have met with a few governments. Until recently, we minded our own business. But too many people were suffering, and it broke our hearts." He tapped his chest. "Our leaders wanted to help regular folks with small things. As many of you have witnessed, our little things turned into big things when we learned how many good people were suffering."

Sheila nodded a little too enthusiastically. "The royals have met with governments worldwide to form a partnership. Many have been receptive and even supportive of our efforts."

"That's right." Travis winked at the camera.

"Until today." Sheila's tone was filled with disappointment. "Should we show it Travvy?"

"Travvy?" Drake's mind voice sounded amused.

I grinned. *"They were a good choice for this."*

"They are. But Travvy?"

The video of the government official played. When it ended, the two came back on camera, shaking their heads in disbelief. Sheila sighed. "It's slanderous."

"After everything we've done for people, this is how they thank us? By lying and calling us weak?" Travis leaned into the camera. "I can assure you that if that man met our royals, he would never describe them in such flippant terms."

"Yes. But then, we don't need to lie to maintain our power."

"True. Let's answer some questions, and then we have a surprise for you."

We watched in awe as the two interacted with their audience in a familiar and entertaining way. When they introduced us, they did it like talking to us was a rare privilege. Or we were rewarding the audience with our presence. No way could I match the energy, so I didn't try.

When our faces showed on the screen, I blinked at how pretty and polished we looked. I used my most genuine smile. "Hello, Travis. Sheila. You've built an amazing community."

"They're fantastic," Sheila's eyes flashed a warning.

"We said we had mystery guests. Please introduce yourselves."

"Sure. I'm Jenella, and this is my..." I glanced at Drake as if I needed help.

"Fiancé," he said in his smooth, deep voice. "My name is Drake."

"Thanks for agreeing to talk to us." Travis puffed out his chest.

"Thanks for having us," Drake said.

I leaned forward. "I absolutely love your dress, Sheila."

She blushed on cue. "Thank you. You look lovely, too."

A playful grin formed on Drake's rugged face, and I could imagine the women watching on the internet drooling over him. The bitches. He feathered kisses across my knuckles. "We're here to set the record straight."

Travis nodded. "Yes. It was our understanding that you hadn't met with them, but this man claims you have. Are his claims true?"

"No," I said. "When we saw the video, we were confused. The only entanglement we've had with them was when they kidnapped and tortured my sister."

Sheila leaned forward. "I've known your sister since she was a babe. It was a tragedy how they picked her up on bogus charges. I'm so glad she and her companions escaped."

"Me, too. But it forced us to intervene and save the lives of the innocent when she finally lost her temper with them." I tapped the desk. "We prefer to help people, rather than use our power to destroy."

Drake nodded. "Yes. We have helped many and will continue to do so. It's unfortunate they thank us by kidnapping our family members, stealing our children, and lying about us."

Travis swallowed. "Stealing our children? Is there proof of this?"

"Yes. We have several federal agents in custody who we found in a rented home. They were guarding paranormal children who were being kept in terrible conditions. Some were only babies."

"It broke my heart. And those incidents are only a small sample of the reasons we've hesitated to set up a meeting. However, we're surprised how they lied to the people they represent."

The chat went wild, and people even donated money. Travis took advantage and started asking us questions from the audience.

After what seemed like an eternity, our camera turned off. I tossed the headphones on the table. "How do people do that every day?"

Drake stood and dragged me with him. "It suits them better than it does you."

"That's an understatement. I'd much rather solve problems."

"I'd rather fly. Care to join me?"

We flew low and at a leisurely pace over witch territory. Below, several witches milled around. I sent my senses out and found a complete lack of hostility. Tracy's dad was making progress. Though it would be a long time before I fully trusted them.

When we banked left, I spotted several dots on the horizon and squinted. A rainbow of dragons hovered over downtown. *What is going on?*

Someone is fighting with Bastien. He zipped toward the action and hovered over a ruined park near dragon headquarters.

The one-eyed ogre queen raced toward Bastien at full speed, an oversized warhammer in her hand. "I will break your neck and drain your blood one drop at a time!"

The two-eyed queen moved to flank him. "Our enemies will cower when they hear the names of the great dragon slayers."

Bastien flicked a toe and wagged his tail, sending both queens flying. *You couldn't slay a fly if it landed on your ugly hammer.*

The queens didn't stay down. Instead, they threw what I recognized as a curse at him.

"They're cursing Bastien?" I prepared to flash to the street.

Wait. Look.

Tracy stepped out from under Bastien and threw a tightly woven spell. The curse crashed against it, and the two exploded in a shower of sparks. She stuck her hand in them as they fell. "Nope. We're close, but not quite there yet."

The Ogre Queens stopped, and the one-eyed queen tapped her hairy chin. "We are better at breaking curses than creating them. If you cannot break this weak curse, you don't stand a chance against a stronger one."

When Bastien shifted and joined the group, I tapped Drake's back and flashed to them. "Are you guys sparring?"

Tracy ignored me, but the Ogre Queens took a step back.

"We find the dragon prince and the witch formidable and entertaining foes," the two-eyed queen said.

The one-eyed queen nodded. "We have yet to slay the dragon and curse his match. We will rejoice in blood when we do."

I arched a brow.

"It will be a hot day in Mage Mountain before they defeat me." Mischief danced in Bastien's eyes. "They're too puny and weak."

"How dare you!" The queens stomped around and protested, but they were all having fun.

"Right." I turned to Tracy. "You good here?"

She bit her bottom lip to keep from laughing. "Great. The queens have been good sports, letting me practice spells on them and sparring with Bas."

It was such an odd alliance. "Okay. Well, we'll try not to be nosey next time."

Tracy's shoulders shook with laughter. "It's so much fun. And useful. They say the funniest things when they fight."

"Yet, the fighting itself is barely a challenge," Bastien added.

I flashed to Drake's back before I had to hear them argue.

Drake zipped toward the mountains. *You were the one who called for unity.*

Yeah. But I didn't expect it to look like insanity.

By the time we finished our flight, followed by a spring picnic, there were several response videos to my interview. Most of them were regular people looking for clicks and views. Others were reporters shoving microphones into the faces of government officials and asking about kidnapping and torturing kids, which wasn't what I said, but close enough.

My phone lit up with texts from Lily, both cussing me out and praising my efforts. I texted her back to apologize for using her incident to prove our strength. It was a gamble because some politicians would try to use my statement to fear-monger. Hopefully, our humanitarian efforts were enough to counterbalance it. If we couldn't reach an agreement, we'd need to withdraw from their country.

Verity came in and shoved her tablet in front of my face. "We got them."

"Excellent." As I read the message, my hope drained. They would only meet with us if we made concessions. I read down the list. "They want a tour of our realm and our security plans?"

"It's a negotiation. They don't expect you to do most of it."

"So, they're playing games."

"Sort of." She moved a chair around my desk to sit next to me. "But like I said, you can negotiate with them."

"They want us chained and blindfolded."

"Okay, that's weird."

"And they want me to place the coalition under their rule." I tossed the tablet. "That's ridiculous."

"It is a little extreme."

"So, should we send a list of counter demands and play their game? Or should I release clips of video we took of the kids in cages?"

"Releasing the video isn't a good idea."

"Why not? It's the truth."

"Most people can't stomach seeing stuff like that."

"I'm one of them. It's still the truth."

She scratched her head. "The government likes to sweep its violent tendencies under the rug. So, it might be effective, but don't show the kids. If you go that route, be careful."

"Sure. Have the tech mages consult with Travis and make the video. I want my advisors to approve it before it's released. We'll leave it out there for a couple of days before we counter their demands."

"And what will you counter with?"

"See if Lily and Emine will work on a response. They're snarky and will come up with something good."

"What if we tack their demands and our response at the end?"

"Will it be as effective?"

"I believe it will."

"Then do it."

Chapter Twenty-Four

Laughter filled the conference room. Deva swiped her sleeve across her eyes. "It's hard to decide who has the most ridiculous demands."

"I like the changeling demand." Razazia blew her nose. "Can you imagine trying to raise fragile human babies?"

She referred to our fake demand where they either returned the kids they stole or presented us with human kids of a similar age. Lily pulled it from some old fae legend. She even explained how their kids would be better off with us. It was damn funny, but also stressed how serious we were about it.

Tracy swiped through our list of demands. "My favorite is the insistence of a Pentagon tour, complete with their national security plan."

Emine shrugged. "They made the demand first. We only parroted them. Which is seriously fucked up to begin with. Who in the hell do they think they are?"

"They think their small amount of magical power gives them the upper hand," Jonas said. "I doubt they'd treat us justly, even if we negotiate in good faith."

"The question is, do we post the video or not?"

"Show of hands for yes," Verity said.

Everyone except me raised their hand. I leaned an elbow on the table. "Are you sure it's not too cheesy?"

"It's funny, dear." Ara folded her arms. "And it highlights their cruelty."

"Alright. Let's post it."

It only took two days for them to contact us through our website without demands. They wanted to meet in Washington, D.C.

Drake threw the invite on my desk. "Your thoughts?"

"It's a trap."

"Or damage control."

"Maybe. If we meet with them, we'll need some safeguards."

"We can surround the entire place with dragons. Vampires can hide in every corner, and both you and Cavil can flash everyone to safety. What more do we need?"

I stood. "Let's talk to Deva about it."

He slid an arm around me. "Very well. Let's go see my aunt."

Deva stared down her nose at me. "You want to bring a bunch of human officials here?"

"They called us weak."

"It's a bogus meeting," Drake said. "They don't want to meet with us so much as arrest us for the building collapse."

"Oh, please. As if they could." She stood. "I suppose it is one way to dispel their misguided beliefs."

"Yes." The wind whipped my clothes sideways when I followed her to the open balcony. "Maybe they'll stop with the power plays and negotiate."

"It's too risky. Humans are fragile. You would need to give them ample warning about the pain, or some may die from it."

My shoulders slumped. "Then what's your suggestion?"

"Send a message. We will meet with them when they return our kids."

Deva's dragon wasn't the largest, but the power radiating off her when she shifted made it clear she was in charge. She launched herself off the balcony and swept around the downtown area.

Travis released a video showing us shaking hands with other dignitaries and the new facilities we'd installed to help people in the countries we'd reached agreements with. The last frame was the latest insult lobbed at us from the government, followed by a woman with an exaggerated shrug. My former friend made an excellent internet troll.

Many humans were horrified by the video we released, showing a watered-down version of what we found in the house. Some even began actively looking for our kids. I read through the forum where they posted their investigative efforts. "They're good at this."

"They see it as a challenge." Emine jabbed a finger at the screen. "This one is credible."

Because of their efforts, we had five locations where they may have taken our kids. Drake deployed a small crew from Olwen's army division to investigate. I wanted to go, but everyone insisted I delegate until we had a solid lead. Sitting back and doing nothing was hard when we were so close to finding them.

Travis's snarky quips and grateful responses to those helping were on point. So on point, the government tried to ban the account. The tech mages had to add magic to protect it.

Emine held up her phone. "Are you kidding me with this shit?"

"Somewhat. Travis tries to use my more insulting thoughts in creative ways."

"Mat's rolling in his grave."

"He's probably searching for a death mage so he can warn me about slippery slopes."

We burst out laughing and it felt good to laugh together. Emine shook her head. "Dontcha think you're taking it a little too far?"

"All the time. But being rude to other internet people is kind of fun."

"And all the negativity you're casting into the world will eventually come back and slap you in the face," Verity said from my other side. "Titus always says the fates don't like it when we treat others like crap and will throw it back at us three-fold."

"Huh." I sipped my tea. "Sounds about right. So, no more fighting with strangers on the internet, or all the hate will bounce back at me. Got it."

Emine cackled. "Let me set up these holograms so you can watch the raids. I need to check on the mages. They're having too much fun helping humans, and I have to reel them in."

"Good luck. Even the leaders are overenthusiastic about our new mission."

"Yeah. It's a problem."

After Emine left, Verity shifted in her seat. "Don't dial it back because of me."

"Except I think you may be right. The goals are to retrieve our kids, root out the demons and remaining Bellicose, find the guys with strange magic, and reach a co-existence treaty with as many governments as possible. It was fun while it lasted."

A projection spell lit up, showing the face of one of Olwen's elves. He did a two-finger salute and repositioned it so we could see a heavily guarded building. Olwen's people rushed inside.

We waited in silence for them to return. When they did, the same elf shook his head. "Not here." The spell went dead.

I blinked and waited for something else to happen. When it didn't, I dissipated it. "On to the next, I guess."

Verity activated the next spell, and a large facility came into focus. Several vampires surrounded the building late at night, staying in the shadows as a team crept in and stopped outside the doors. The two lead elves whispered to each other.

It felt off to me. I leaned forward and searched the scene until something in the window caught my eye. As the team lined up, a blinking light on the security box went out. It caused the pale orange light in the window to blink faster. I leaped out of my chair. "No!"

The group rushed inside.

I stood in my protected office and swallowed back bile as the last person crossed the threshold. "No. They need to leave. Get them out of there!"

The building exploded with a roar.

Our monitoring spell went white, and I plopped back into my chair, unable to speak or control my violent shaking. The flames from the explosion obscured the view for what seemed like hours, but it was probably only a couple of minutes. When the smoke cleared enough to see, the building was gone, and in its place stood a cube of ice. My shoulders relaxed. "Olwen sensed it?"

"It's possible," Verity unattached herself from my arm. "He considers every angle before deploying his troops."

A few blurs zipped in and out of the ice sculpture, and dragons popped into existence to extinguish the fire before the shield melted.

The two elves I recognized as Olwen's guards flanked the front door, their muscles bulging with the strain of holding the barrier. After several minutes, more people emerged in groups and were whisked away. After the evacuation, Olwen stepped out, waved his hand, and the icy structure collapsed.

"Damn. Were you aware he had so much power?" Verity asked.

"Yes. But I've never seen him use it. It's beautiful."

"Yeah."

Similar incidents happened at other locations. Two of the five buildings sat abandoned, and the others collapsed as soon as our teams entered them. Olwen's preparations saved several lives. His actions made me feel smart for choosing him as an advisor and a general, even though I did it on a whim.

When the human media showed up, our architectural mages had already rebuilt the buildings. I drummed my fingers on the table. "This isn't a viable strategy."

"I agree. So much for relying on random internet strangers." Verity stood. "I need to make a few calls."

We were missing something. And I'd almost bet it had something to do with the Bellicose. Or demons. Either way, we had to move faster.

Chapter Twenty-Five

A distant wolf pack howled at the full moon. A deafening roar drowned them out as they reached a crescendo. There was only one person who roared at such volume and frequency. I marched to the property line where the shifter woods met the palace grounds. Several dark shapes skittered through the trees. When I sent out my senses, more than a hundred shifters registered.

"Are you ready?" Alex asked from beside me.

"No." I stared down at the white smock I wore. "What if Jonas comes at me?"

"If he doesn't, what's the point? We're trying to teach you how to fight." Alex let out an exaggerated sigh. "Try not to use your magic other than to shift. Use new forms as needed and make sure you don't run out of energy."

I threw up my hands. "You want me to shift into a bunch of animals without practice?"

He patted my shoulder. "You've got this." Alex became a massive American lion and slid through the temporary opening in the castle wall I created.

My entire body shook with adrenaline as I followed. "*Greeaah!*" I squealed when a hand touched my shoulder.

"Great. Now the entire pocket knows where you are." Lily slammed her hands on her hips. "Tell your boy toy if he hurts my brother, he's a dead dragon."

Drake was a few yards ahead of us in what I called his snuffy form. Joy filtered through the bond at her words. "He won't hurt anyone unless he needs to."

It took a ton of concentration to bring Alex's magic forward and morph into what resembled an American Lion. When I shifted, I gave Lily a kitty grin.

"Cute."

I bumped my head against her shoulder.

"Knock it off." She brushed off her sleeve. "I'll shadow you and stop any fights before they get out of hand. Don't piss off my dad or hurt Alex."

I wouldn't test the fates like that, I thought as I padded down a game trail to where I sensed several shifters. My former neighbor Penelope led several smaller, chittering raccoons down a trail. Her head twisted towards me, and she hissed. When I kept going, she returned her attention to her kids. Ha! Fooled her.

I ducked behind a tree and brought forward a wolf. I tried to choose the most common markings. Lily inclined her head when I motioned for her approval, so I padded towards a group.

When I drew near, the three wolves pointed their snouts at the moon and howled. Before I could join, they turned as a group and raced away. Not being used to the body, I tripped over myself as I tried to keep up. They rounded a corner and screeched to a halt. I tried to put on the brakes but couldn't stop in time. My paws skidded on the wet ground, and I smashed into a white wolf.

Jonas noticed and roared a warning before stomping in my direction.

When the ground trembled under my paws, I panicked. The only animal I could think to shift to was an owl. A form I hadn't practiced. I attempted to remember what Drake said about flying, but my mind went blank. I launched into the sky at the last minute in an attempt to escape. My laugh sounded like a gurgle when I lifted off the ground.

Jonas jumped in the air after me and his long jaws snapped close to my butt. Too close, I decided, and flapped my wings, aiming for a nearby tree.

Something smashed into me, and pain radiated through my left arm. Or wing. I tried to catch myself but couldn't, and I racked my brain to find a new form.

The world went dark, and slime covered my feathery body. *I'm inside a mouth!* I screamed in Drake's head. When his only assistance was to laugh, I huffed, turned into a snake, and slithered out the side. I slammed into the ground with a dull thud. I couldn't move, so I lay there naked while I healed. "I promised Lily I wouldn't hurt you."

Alex's hair-raising growl reverberated through my achy bones.

I sat up, created another smock, and slipped it on as Jonas emerged from the trees. "What a disaster." I climbed to my feet. "I have all this shifter magic, but no coordination. And switching forms drains me. Even if it didn't, I can't think fast enough to figure out the right one to use."

In the blink of an eye, a naked, unassuming man stood opposite me. I made him a smock, too, since his kids were nearby, but he ignored it. "I suspect you will build your tolerance and speed with practice." Jonas glared at someone behind me. "Or maybe you're not meant to shift. I don't remember Lissa ever taking an animal form, but she often used shifter magic to make a point."

"She insisted I learn it." I watched a wolf dig out an area and lie in it. "But she also warned me it will take years of practice to master."

"Sounds about right. We'll try again next week."

"Okay." The nearby shadows grew darker near where Drake and Lily hid.

Drake's gigantic green eye appeared, and a massive paw with opposing thumbs stretched into the shadows.

"Damnit!" Lily squealed, and the shadows melted away. He scooped her off the ground, bounded towards us, dumped her at Jonas's feet, and shifted. "Your daughter needs to work on her badassery."

She hopped to her feet and brushed leaves off her clothes. "That wasn't fair. I don't have Jen's senses. You can't cloak and expect me to find you."

"I didn't cloak. You had plenty of opportunities to notice me, but were too busy watching over Alex."

"Whatever." She waved a hand. "One day you'll regret ever starting shit with me."

"No doubt," he drawled. "Just like with Jenella's shifting, perfection will take time."

"Thanks for helping me practice." I directed my comment to Penelope, who sat at Jonas's feet, still in her raccoon form, her kids spread out around her.

She tilted her head and sneezed.

A cluster of griffins appeared on the horizon, shouting an alarm, and I clasped Drake's hand. "What's going on?"

He swung his head in the direction of downtown. "The gates are under attack."

Adrenaline flooded my system, and my hand shook as I reached for my phone, but I'd left it at the palace.

Drake morphed into a dragon, causing shifters to scramble out of his way. *Let's fly in so we can assess the situation.*

I flashed to his back.

Lily and Alex appeared behind me. "No way you're leaving us behind," Lily said.

"If you two cause trouble, I'll flash you to a remote island and leave you there."

"We don't actually cause the trouble," Alex explained. "It's more like it seeks us out. We'd be happy if it left us alone for the rest of our lives."

Drake's warning roar caused them to flinch. Satisfied with the reaction, he let out a dragon laugh and launched into the air. I patted his spine. "Have I mentioned how much I adore this dragon?"

Lily stretched to see the ground below. "He's fucking scary. You don't see it because you're insane."

"Oh, please. You're smart enough not to mess with dangerous beings, yet you tease Drake, who I might remind you is a *First*, all the time."

"He's family, so it doesn't count. Besides, he's the one who starts it most of the time."

Hearing the conversation, Drake went into a barrel roll and plunged toward the ground.

"Whaaaaaa!" Alex's scream peeled through the night sky, startling nearby flying paranormals.

When we leveled out, I glanced back at a green-faced Lily. I couldn't help the wide grin that stretched across my face. "Flying is so much fun."

"You won't think so when I puke on Drake's scales. You okay, Alex?"

"I'm fine. Maybe keep your smart remarks to yourself."

We grew quiet as we neared the gates. Below us, an army of those weak magical creatures filled the dragon landing area and stretched to the parking spell. Inside, dragons, vampires, hundreds of gate guards, and several enforcers stood around in clusters. "Head to Emine." I twisted towards Alex. "You can flash to your mom once we land. She's by the gate."

Drake banked left towards where Emine sat on the wall behind a mounted machine gun. To her right stood the woman training to take over her position as head enforcer. I flashed to an empty spot and strode toward her. "Hey, Emine."

"What in all the realms are you doing here?"

I gestured toward the crowd of strange shifters. "We're being invaded?"

She snorted. "That's a stretch."

Drake lowered himself onto the wall, straddling us with his massive feet. Screams from below made me peer over the edge. It took a few seconds to realize Drake's sudden appearance startled them. I focused on their weapons. "Are those missiles?"

"Yep. Took us less than a minute to disarm them." She pointed to the crowd. "They're still trying to understand what happened to their guns. Ann Marie single-handedly took care of those."

The people attacking didn't look like an army confident they'd conquer their enemy. Instead, they resembled adventurers who walked into a trap. Some wandered around aimlessly with wide eyes, while others tested the perimeter, trying to find a way out. The majority simply stood there, staring at us, while we stared at them. I tucked a stray curl behind my ear. "How many are outside?"

"None. We didn't close off the entrance until they were all inside." The machine gun disappeared. "This is a first-class shit show."

My chest puffed out with pride at our response. "Either they vastly underestimated us, or it's a test."

A streak of white at the edge of my vision came a second before Glacintial landed beside Drake. He blew a line of smoke over the crowd.

Alex flashed in and patted his toe. "Hey, Glac. Have you ever seen anything like this before?"

He shook his massive head.

I sneezed and stumbled into Drake's leg when the smoke drifted into my face.

Emine pointed at Alex. "You better step up your game before everyone realizes you're not the weirdest sibling anymore."

I elbowed Emine as I watched Lily ghost through the crowd below. I sensed Quin near her, but couldn't see him. "You're the only one who thinks I'm weird. If we're judging strange, you're number one on the list. And Alex is happy with his family, and has no desire to be part of mine."

His head whipped toward me. "That's not true."

"It's an observation."

"How is it you can notice the smallest detail of every situation unless it applies to your personal life?"

Drake's laugh made more of the freaks below scream and scoot away.

Emine shoulder-bumped me. "The kid has a point. We're all here, aren't we?"

They were. And it was both wonderful and awkward. "Right." I motioned to the chaos below. "This isn't even a contest."

Lily appeared, causing Emine's replacement to jump. "Those guys are shitting their pants."

My nose crinkled. "Yuck. Tell the witches to spell the wall so the smell doesn't reach our people."

She shot me a cynical look. "Do you not understand a figure of speech when you hear one? It means they're scared." She tapped Drake's foot. "Mind if I sit?"

I've always wondered how far I can kick a puny vampire. His mind voice sounded distracted. Probably because he was communicating with other dragons.

"He won't kick you. Maybe. If he does, he'll have someone catch you." I turned back to Emine and her pale-faced replacement. "What do we do with these guys?"

"If only we had a queen to make such decisions." Quin materialized near Alex.

My lips twitched. "If only."

Lily climbed on Drake's foot and flipped a stray curl out of her face. "Fire away."

"Stop antagonizing him before he follows through on the threat." Alex shuffled closer to me. "They have information about what the humans are doing."

"Thanks." We still had a few Bellicose traitors to sort through. Unlike humans, we didn't lock up our citizens for long periods of time. But we were still sorting through them to determine who volunteered and who got kidnapped. So we didn't have enough jail cells for the weird guys. "Glacintial, have your division separate them into groups of twenty and build barriers. Ensure they're well-fed, clean, and have comfortable bedding. Quin, your troops will guard them. Drake, once they're settled, send your team to read their minds. Emine, gather their phones and send them to the tech mages."

Glacintial launched off the wall as Emine pulled out her phone. "Will do."

I was missing something big. I could feel it. "I'm going to move the gate."

Drake rose and shook his foot harder than necessary. *I'm going to talk to Deva and gather culinary dragons. Keep this flea busy so she doesn't bring down the pocket.*

Lily lost her grip, tumbled through the air, and landed on her ass beside me. She climbed to her feet before her fall registered. "Did he call me a troublemaker and an infectious pest in the same sentence?"

"Yep."

"Respect."

Lily and Alex stayed close after I flashed outside the gates to Allure. I sensed several shifters, dragons, vampires, and elves in the area. "Any sign of more humans?"

A regal-looking vampire in a black catsuit came from the shadows. "Will all due respect, Your Grace, those aren't humans." She spoke to me, but her eyes stayed on Lily.

I stepped in front of Lily. "If you address me, you look at me. And don't start a fight with my sister. She will crush you."

Lily smirked as she ran her hand along the perimeter of the gate.

The woman bowed her head. "My apologies. I heard a rumor you threw her out of your family."

"You shouldn't believe everything you hear." I moved to where the gate clung to a cliff. Drake and I scouted a place to move it and picked a spot near a more well-traveled road. We suspected humans caught on to our illusion, hiding tire tracks from where cars drove off the cliff.

I tossed a hologram ball to the vampire. "A map to the new gate. Share it with the others." When she melted back into the shadows, I examined the area.

Lily stood. "I understand this spell, but can't duplicate it without setting a trap."

"Maybe we need a trap so the humans stop sending us their experiments."

Alex leaned down and examined the bottom of the gate. "There's no way I can tune my magic to this spell."

"You need ruling magic, dummy."

I leaned closer to the gate. "He's probably smarter than both of us combined."

Lily raised a finger. "Yes. But I'm the older sister, so I can call him all the names I want. It's the law."

"Okay, dummy." I shielded myself as I plunged my hand into the gate. "I'm going to hold as much magic as I can. It's a lot more than the other gates I moved, so I doubt I'll be able to contain it for long."

Alex stepped to my side. "Can you transfer the overflow to us?"

"You're not a mimic. I can, but who knows what it will do to you." I examined it again and shook my head. "Too risky. I'd be safer transferring the overflow to Drake. But not without his permission."

"How did you do the other gates?" Lily asked.

"I absorbed the power and put it elsewhere. Alex monitored my sanity while I moved the first ones, but didn't touch the magic. This gate is more complex and more powerful." Mat's desperation to keep me alive was written all over it. I wondered what he did to it and who helped him. It felt like multiple people from different factions. I clenched my jaw against my sudden anger. He'd be there to explain if he didn't sacrifice himself. "Damn grief. I'm going to try. If anything goes wrong, leave."

"Oh, yes. Attempting to harness unfamiliar power with several factions present is always wise." Quin stood in the shadows to the right.

I jerked my hand back. "You're right."

Chapter Twenty-Six

Drake scanned the forest and cocked his head when he spotted the guards who drifted our way. "Even with the unprecedented way we share power, I can't help. The only person compatible enough is Lily."

Lily didn't take her eyes off the gate. "I'll help. Just try not to kill me."

"Right. Everyone, stand back. When I remove the gate, the wards will close, and they're potent." After they took a few steps back, I reached out and touched the edge. My heart thundered when the magic of the pocket latched onto my hand. The last time, the wards sucked my magic dry, and I woke Drake. Back then, I thought Mat's magic was my own, and the ruling magic had a mind of its own. I had no control. "I was a mess," I whispered.

Ignoring Lily's inquisitive expression, I blocked the ward from accessing my magic and wrapped a barrier around it like I'd done with the other gates. Sheer power rushed into my hand, down my arm, and settled into my chest. I drank more.

My whole body ached. I was like a balloon filled with too much air. "Lily, touch my shoulder, please." When her fingers dug into my arm, I relaxed and let the last bit flow into her. After I had every drop, I closed the flow and removed my hand.

Creak.

Lily dragged me back a few steps.

I checked on her and sighed in relief when she stared back with skepticism. “Are you okay?”

“Sure. What the hell is that tickling feeling?”

My forehead creased. “Tickle feeling?”

Whoosh!

Backlash as the wards slammed closed sent us tumbling. I tried to catch my balance, but the push was too strong. Lily’s iron-like grip on my arm stayed in place as we slammed into Alex and Drake. Strong arms caught me. The gate’s magic sloshed around, and I almost lost control. A strange burning sensation stabbed through me and reverberated through the four of us. Someone said something, but the buzzing in my ears was too loud to make out the words. I poured every ounce of concentration I could into holding the gate’s magic.

It wasn’t working. The vibration picked up, and I rubbed my stomach. I could sense Lily’s determination to hold her portion. “Don’t let go of me.”

“Didn’t plan on it.”

I flashed to the area we’d chosen for the gate. It took every ounce of energy I had to reach out and touch the wards. The instant magic buzzed against my fingers, I began reforming it. I pulled the magic from Lily before emptying my own. It tried to rush out of me, so I clenched my jaw and used every bit of control I had to hold it back. The last drop exited my body, and I fought to stay on my feet as I tied the anchors.

It wasn’t until I tried to regain my balance that I noticed Drake still held me. “No.” I squirmed out of his grip and distanced myself enough to examine him. His green eyes had a slight glow, but he didn’t look injured. “Are you okay?”

His lips twitched. “I’m fine. I would have let go if it was too much.”

My shoulders slumped in relief, and I spun back toward the gate to examine it. It seemed a little off. Like a puzzle where the last piece didn't fit right. Or someone added an extra piece. I extended a finger and lightly touched it. Lily's night magic was laced through it and acted as a safeguard. I turned toward her with a devious grin. "Did you do that on purpose?" When I saw her crouched over an unconscious Alex, my heart sank. "No." I raced to his other side.

"He's okay physically. But he won't wake up. And yes, I set the trap. If those guys try to get inside, they'll end up on my dad's doorstep. Let's see how arrogant they are when a dinosaur comes at them."

Pure genius. I took Alex's hand and assessed him. There were no injuries, so I sensed his magic. It wasn't altered, but it seemed hyperalert. "He's okay, but his magic is off."

Drake rested a hand on my back. "Can we move him?"

Bright light almost blinded me as Cavil appeared nearby. He scanned the scene and rushed to Lily's side. "What happened?"

"He's not injured. Something is off about his magic." I cocked my head. "I can't explain it. Hopefully, he won't be like this for long."

Drake's eyes lit with a type of power I'd never seen. "He feels like a dragon."

Lily lifted him. When Cavil reached out to help, she pushed him away. "He's a shifter mage hybrid. Always has been, always will be. You're not taking him from me."

"It's merely an observation. I mean no offence."

I shuffled towards the new gate. "Maybe it's magic overload. If so, it's temporary."

He shrugged a massive shoulder. "I have a kinship with him like I feel with other dragons."

"He's not a dragon." Lily's voice cracked. Her face was as hard as stone, but the fear rolling off her told another story.

"Right." I grasped at ideas about how to change the subject. "Let's take him to the palace and have your mom assess it." I texted Ann Marie.

Lily relaxed a little when we reached the palace. "Where do we put him?"

I motioned towards the elevator. "You have your own suites in the family wing."

She went fluid and disappeared up the stairs.

After she was out of hearing range, I swung towards Drake. "Besides the kinship, what makes you think he's a dragon?"

"Instinct."

"Does Deva know? Is it why she's so obsessed with him?"

"I doubt it. My aunt has long been obsessed with mental mages."

George came from the public area. "The First Jonas and The Sorceress Ann Marie are here to see you."

"Thank you, George."

We filled them in on Alex's condition as we led them to the family wing. Alex lay on a sofa inside the suite Helen assigned to him. His eyes were open and glassy, but he wasn't conscious. The amber in them glowed, as if he were reading minds. I poked at the magic.

Ann Marie crouched by his side and brushed his hair away from his face. "The gate magic is powerful. Maybe he's stunned."

Jonas leaned over him. "No. Something woke up inside him, and it's not shifter magic."

"What do you mean by 'woke up?'" I asked.

"It's hard to explain. The lion shifter part of him is okay, but there's something else."

Drake's hand dropped to his side. "I need to inform my aunt." At Jonas's nod, he raced out the balcony door.

I watched him go. "Drake thinks he's a dragon."

"Well, he's wrong," Lily insisted. "Alex doesn't need to obey Deva, so he can't be a dragon."

Ann Marie stood and pulled her close. "Let's not worry about it until we learn more, firefly."

The area surrounding The Cauldron was packed with paranormals trying to see the people who attacked us. Dragons stood in a loose circle, explaining what the strange guys looked like to people who asked. I darted up the stairs and told people to stand back so Drake had room to land if he wanted to. "They aren't here?"

Emine's replacement, whose name I couldn't remember, pulled her attention away from the crowd. "No, Your Grace. We set up a makeshift camp for them in the field between the mage and elven lands."

Drake joined us and kissed my temple. "You go ahead. I'll help the enforcers clear out some Bellicose sympathizers to make more room."

I squeezed his arm and took one last look at the crowd before I flashed away.

The field outside Elven territory once had traps that were so sensitive that they caught a bunch of rat demons. I landed inside the flashing circle nearby, amazed at how many people were in the area. Navigating through them became a gauntlet of greetings and head nods. Several paranormals trailed behind me as I approached the ward holding the strange men.

They'd changed from their more grotesque forms and, other than a trickle of magic, registered as human. Some sat on the bare ground and watched us, while others stood in clusters, talking. Following the same behavior pattern they showed at the gate, some tried to poke at the heavy wards that held them in the field.

When I spotted Tracy's dad talking to a man with aqua hair, I drifted in his direction. As President of Covens, he must have been called in to create the containment spell. As I made my way to him, I stopped a few times to talk. There was nothing I loved more than mingling with regular people. The other man flipped his aqua hair over his shoulder and glared at me. He radiated a strange power I chose not to deal with right away, so I focused on Tracy's dad. "The spell doesn't need to be this strong. Their magic barely registers."

Calvin's booming laugh rang through the field. "Hello, Jenella. We wanted to ensure they understood the power structure."

My grin couldn't have been bigger as I watched the prisoners. "It looks like most of them understand." The smile melted off my face when the other man moved closer. "You must be Brogan."

"At your service." His ocean eyes narrowed. "And you must be the new Queen of Ahl."

"I'm Jenella, yes. Thank you for answering my call."

He rubbed his bright beard. "Call, was it? It seemed more like an order."

Calvin moved closer. "Jenella sometimes forgets her strength."

"I do. But that wasn't the case here. I needed to find out if you were still around or if my bitch of a mother got to you."

He threw his head back and laughed. "I heard you are causing quite a stir to kick off your reign. It is good to have a passionate leader once again."

The guy was trying to flatter me. And it would have worked if I hadn't been raised by such a hard-ass brother. Even though he isolated and educated me on lies, Mat kept me humble. "Let's cut the crap, Brogan. I've had reports that you're helping with my campaign to win over the humans. Why?"

Humor danced in the depths of his eyes. "Because it's a damn good idea. Have you ever read the human legends about my people? They're downright horrific."

"Uh, huh." I spotted Tracy weaving her way through the throng of paranormals, and I relaxed. I trusted Calvin, but knew without a doubt she had my back. "Thank you for helping."

Tracy didn't hide her skeptical look as she approached. "Hey, Jen. Dad."

Calvin motioned toward Brogan. "Tracinia, this is the First, Brogan. Brogan, this is my lovely daughter, Tracinia."

Brogan bowed. "It's nice to meet you."

Her eyes narrowed. "Why did you wait until now to answer Jen's call? I mean, the least you could have done is send a minion with a message saying you'd contact her later."

My heart fluttered at how fast she defended me.

Brogan waited a beat to answer her, as if gathering his thoughts. "I spent many years trying to evade the second queen. It taught me to deal with Lissa's descendants on my terms."

I crossed my arms. "I'm not my mother."

"Jenella is quite unique," Calvin agreed. "She and my daughter have traveled the world in search of the Firsts. We suspected you also fell victim."

"I see." He gazed toward the elven territory. "My apologies. The next time I hear your call, I will appear right away."

Tracy glanced at the prisoners when one touched the spell with a claw. "We hoped you could tell us the truth about the First, Celia. We pinpointed her sleeping location to be somewhere near Mahri, but Jen couldn't sense her."

"No, Milady. If Celia still exists, she is nowhere near the sea."

I texted Verity the information: "Thanks, Brogan. Do you plan to stick around?"

His hair spilled over his thick shoulders, as if it had a mind of its own. "I must return, but would like to visit the other Firsts before I go."

I told him where he could find them and watched as he strutted toward the elven sanctuary to find Razazia. "That guy is trouble."

"Yep," Tracy agreed. "But he needs the sea, and we don't have one."

"Yeah." I blinked to clear my thoughts. "Have dragons screened the prisoners?"

Calvin motioned towards a group on the far side of the enclosure. "Yes. They are reporting their findings to Bastien."

The dragons stopped talking when we drew close enough to hear. By the grave look on Bastien's face, the news wasn't good. He patted a woman on the shoulder and joined our group. "They're products of a government experiment."

Not a surprise, but my stomach still turned. "How did they learn how to harness magic?"

"They didn't. Someone is helping them. These men, and they are all men, were handpicked to take part in the experiment. Someone infused magic into their bones. Many suffer chronic pain from the infusion and are sure they'll die soon, while others believe themselves invincible." The predatory smile on Bastien's face when he said the last part sent chills down my spine. "They believed they were fighting for their country when they entered our gates to conquer us."

"They feel like shifters, so I assume Morten and his siblings are responsible. Since none of them could transfer magic, maybe a demon helped. Or the person with the foreign magic. Why all men?"

Calvin cleared his throat. "Because many human societies believe men are stronger than women."

"It's hard to wrap my head around because it's so far removed from our culture."

"Understandable."

Bastien scanned the prisoners with an unreadable expression. "What would you like us to do with them, Jen?"

"Nothing. The army and enforcers will guard them. Humans are fragile, especially in cold weather," I said it like I hadn't once struggled to regulate my body heat. "Will the wards keep them warm?"

"Yes, but they will need toilets and bedding."

The army crossed the wards and cleared an area on one side of the field, and I created a long row of a hundred bathrooms with outdoor showers.

When three architectural mages joined me, we moved through the area and created a thousand cots with comfortable bedding. After we finished, I thanked the mages and led my group out of the wards. "Have clean clothes and regular food delivered."

Tracy squeezed my arm. "Text if you need help."

I hugged her. "Sure."

Bastien shifted, stretched his black head over the prisoners, and roared. A satisfied dragon grin spread across his face when they screamed and cowered. He picked Tracy up with his tail and tossed her on his back.

I turned to Calvin. "I need tell Jonas about this. Would you like to come with me?

"I would." He walked by my side as we neared the flashing circle. "Why do you allow the dragons so much leeway?"

"Because Deva tied them to me to ensure their loyalty."

He shrugged. "Many factions would never betray you."

"Most wouldn't. But if I learned one thing from the Bellicose, it's to be careful about who I trust. Gabe and Linda were Mat's closest friends and betrayed us. The signs were there, but we missed them."

"Many dragons have betrayed their own."

"True. But Deva's pledge was a hundred times more potent than a magical contract. It ensured her dragons are physically incapable of betraying me." I led him into the circle. "I'm aware the Pixies, Elves, Dwarves, and even your coven are trustworthy. And I trust you to bring the other witches around. Not because of some magical oath, but because you have integrity." And I no longer hesitated to read the other leaders. But how I went about it wasn't his business. "It will take time before I trust everyone again."

Chapter Twenty-Seven

The entire family gathered around Alex, including Helen and George. I leaned over and tested his health. "He's still stable."

Jonas shook Calvin's hand. "Hello, Calvin. What brings you here?"

"Jenella requested I accompany her."

"When Alex stabilizes, I'd like you to assess our prisoners," I explained. "Cavil can help, too."

"Help them how?" Cavil asked.

"They have shifter magic. Someone infused it into their bones, and many are in pain because their bodies are trying to reject it. Since Jonas created shifters, I thought we could work together to either remove it or complete the transition. I want you to help me assess it."

"I've been thinking along the same lines." Jonas's expression seemed almost conflicted.

"No hurry." My head tilted when sand-colored magic swirled across Alex's skin and faded. "Does that happen often?"

Ann Marie slid her chair closer. "No. It's the first time."

"Calvin, have you seen it before?"

"No. What happened to him?"

"We think Allure's wards gave him magic shock. Drake says he senses a dragon, but to me, he still registers as a mage shifter hybrid."

Lily huffed from the shadows, causing Cavil to grin and move to her side.

Calvin blinked at the display. "It is not uncommon for a victim of magic shock to register differently for a short period. But he should not bleed power. May I assess him?"

Jonas's eyes flashed. "Assess him how?"

"I only wish to place one drop of potion on his skin. Jenella and Drake are both very skilled. If they disagree on the effects of the shock, the potion can help clarify."

"Go ahead."

I'd only ever read about magic shock, but Calvin and Ann Marie had witnessed it. If Ann Marie, one of the oldest paranormals, couldn't decipher his change, then I doubted Calvin could. I went to the balcony and peered out where I sensed Glacintial lurking. "Hey, Glacintial, will you come inside and assess Alex?"

A flash of white, and he appeared in his human form. "My apologies for lurking, Jenella. Alex and I have become quite close. I am not ignoring my duties to the army."

"Of course not. No one cares if you pop in and check on Alex. Drake noticed something earlier, and I want to see if you agree."

He bowed his head to Jonas and Ann Marie. His eyes settled on Alex as Calvin placed the potion on his hand. It settled on his skin for a beat, then flew out so fast he couldn't catch it.

I trapped it in a bubble and lowered it into his hands. "Can I release it?"

"Yes. Thank you." I released the drop, he rolled it around. "It didn't work."

Beside me, Glacintial shifted his weight. "Because he is a dragon."

Ann Marie paled. "Is that even possible?"

I didn't know. "Deva might have more insight. If I remember right, she helped create this pocket. Alex might return to normal when the shock wears off."

The icy looks sent my way made me shiver.

Calvin tucked his potion into a pocket. "Please keep me updated on his status. My daughter is rather fond of him."

Jonas nodded. "Will do."

The sun kissed the horizon when Drake returned. I sat on his landing balcony, a blanket wrapped around myself, and my feet dangling over the edge. He hovered for a minute, neither of us saying a word. I didn't move as he maneuvered his massive feet around me and shifted.

He sat next to me and pulled me close. "Long day?"

"Long and puzzling. This is the only place I could think without being interrupted."

"Want to spend the evening working through your puzzle?"

"No."

He buried his nose in my hair. "Very well." Goosebumps coated my arms as his breath brushed against my skin. "Do you need an ear?"

"No, but I might later."

If there were ever a specific point in time to describe our love, it was that moment. We understood and supported each other, even when we disagreed. "Let's talk about our match ceremony. When should we have it?"

"In the late summer or early fall, if we've made enough progress with the human governments. Afterwards, I'm taking you to my horde to have you to myself."

"Sounds amazing." I rested my hand on his thigh. "We're taking too long. Will the kids be okay when we find them?"

"Physically, yes. But they'll most likely have emotional scars."

"Good thing working through horrific emotional injuries is our specialty."

His warm laugh echoed across the palace grounds. "Considering my fear of rejection and your fear of being trapped, Helen is probably the best resource."

"She has her own issues, but griffins are always supportive of the people they claim. It's who they are when they're not cursed."

Drake stood and lifted me with him. "Let's have a private dinner and get some sleep. I have a feeling we're going to need it."

"Sounds good to me."

The crowds had cleared when we landed near the prison encampment the next morning. Quin, along with several weak vampires, lurked in the shadows on the other side. By the black insignias on the guard's T-shirts, his army division was on duty. I stopped and talked to several of them. They were eager to serve and incredibly well-trained. It was hard to keep my chest from puffing with pride at my army. I'd need to thank Razazia later, since she was the one who placed them in their divisions.

Jonas ignored my networking as he and Drake slowly circled the enclosure, anger and frustration rolling off him in waves. Occasionally, he'd pause and speak to a prisoner.

When I reached the area where I sensed Quin and what I suspected were his new vampires, I stopped and sorted through them. "You're training Lily's problem child?"

Quin appeared from the shadows. "Among others." The new vampires popped into existence as he withdrew his power.

I scanned the group. "Half of them have the intention of betraying you at the first opportunity."

"Yes. Let's pretend I don't understand basic vampire turning."

"Okay." When I noticed some of his vampires trying way too hard to hear our conversation, I threw a privacy barrier around us. "Speaking of turning, Jonas is assessing if he can turn some of the less rebellious humans, or if we can remove the magic before it kills them."

"Interesting. I believe Lissa infused each of the first shifters with a sliver of Belnaught's power to ease the pain. She somehow made the magic stick. Unless Jonas explained the process to his offspring, they wouldn't have understood it."

"Did you witness it?"

"No. But my love once saw Razazia create an elf. Lissa did not care if others attended."

"Huh." I glanced at where Lily's vampire extracted and retracted his jagged teeth. They weren't normal, but neither was Lily. "Is that guy ever going to stabilize?"

"Perhaps. However, it may take several years. His ability to learn is even more impeded than yours."

I laughed as I dissipated the privacy bubble. "Sounds awful."

"Yes. Allow me to remove my trainees, and I shall help the First." He and his people vanished.

Quin returned and was hiding in the shadows when Drake and Jonas reached me. Jonas's eyes glowed, and his fists clenched as they approached. "This is cruelty at its finest. They assigned many of these men to the experiment against their will. Some watched their friends die as they endured multiple primitive procedures."

I moved closer to the wards. Verity once said we were overly violent and reactive compared to humans. Mat disagreed. He believed humans were better at deflection and denial, but equally violent. After feeling the pain radiating from the prisoners, I had to agree with my brother. "Can we help them?"

"It depends on you. Lissa could dull the pain as she weaved my magic into humans. I'm unsure how she did it, but they changed fast."

My grandmother's diaries contained a couple of passages about how she learned the skill. "I'll need some time to research, and you should be with Alex. How about I come see him later and we can talk about it?"

"Of course." Jonas took two steps and stopped. "You should brace yourself for the possibility of their deaths."

Tears burned my eyes, but I kept my face neutral. "Sure."

When I met Drake's eyes, the pain and doubt in them almost brought me to my knees. "You don't think we can save them." It wasn't a question.

"I am skeptical, yes. I am also aware you can do anything you put your mind to if you don't start doubting yourself."

"Text me if anything changes, Quin." I flashed us to my office, completely skipping the flashing circle. A triumphant smile spread across my face. "The ward breaker pixie dust is amazing. I wish I had it back when I was a detective."

"George is going to throw a fit when he learns you can bypass security."

"Then I won't make a habit out of it." I thumbed through the papers on my desk until one caught my eye. I held it up. "A petition for the Troll King and Kelpie Queen to match."

Humor danced in his eyes. "Those two enjoyed bickering too much for there not to be chemistry."

"I should deny it to pay them back for all the headaches they caused."

Drake wrapped an arm around my waist and squeezed me. "That's my petty queen."

I tried not to sigh as I touched the magical signature to approve their request. "Maybe we can all have some peace once they're matched."

"I doubt it."

Me, too. I pushed the papers aside. "I think I'm ready for a conversation now."

"Oh?" He motioned toward his office. "Let's have it where we're less likely to be disturbed."

We settled into seats beside the fire, and he conjured snacks and soda onto the table between us. I filled a small plate and sat back to gather my thoughts. "The hybrids had it rough before I came along, so I don't blame them for their resentment, but it still frustrates me. Especially when we lost so much defending them. I kind of took my frustration out on Lily."

"You did. But she was treating you like an inconvenience, so it wasn't undeserved."

I nodded. "I don't want to play games with the U.S. government anymore, but we're already committed to a strategy, so I feel pressure to see it through."

"Understandable. What would you rather do?"

"Honestly? I fight the urge to crush the arrogant pricks and take over their people. But it wouldn't work, and it's not who I want to be."

"Lissa once had a similar dilemma. She ultimately decided the humans weren't our business."

"Aren't they? Because we live in this world, too. We use their technology, and other than those of us born of Firsts, we're made from humans. Many of the people I heal tell me we're doing god's work. If so, why doesn't their chosen god step up and take care of them?"

Amusement sparkled in Drake's eyes.

"I understand their perception of a god is different from ours. It's just..." I shrugged.

"It's frustrating, and you're losing your patience."

"Yes. I can see we're making a difference with our good deeds. It's even drawing the factions closer by forcing them to work together. Most human governments see the value of our help. But then there are the others." I grew silent while I ate. After I set my plate down, I met his eyes. "It makes me sick how they experimented on their people."

"You, along with every paranormal who's seen them."

"But we're not any better, considering we infused them with magic to create paranormals."

"Perhaps not." Drake leaned forward. "Say what you really think."

He knew me well. "I want the paranormals they took returned immediately. And I'm not willing to negotiate for their release. Our most innovative people need to be focused on it while another group of operatives goes in and flushes out the wielder of the strange magic and find out how much influence the demons have over the situation. Because the suffering we see...." I jabbed a finger toward where we held the prisoners. "Looks like their handiwork."

When Drake started to say something, I stood and paced. "It's not the coalition's job to fix human screw ups. We can keep helping people because it's the right thing to do. But I'm inclined to withdraw our help from countries that kidnap our kids and turn their people into grotesque creatures."

Drake rested his elbows on his knees. "You're saying you wish to wield your power over them?"

A chill ran down my spine. "Not necessarily."

He raised his head and met my eyes. "Are you lying to me or yourself?"

"Both." I stopped pacing and tapped a foot on the hardwood floor. "Am I being unreasonable? Or worse, a tyrant for thinking we should step up our efforts?"

"What you're proposing isn't stepping up our efforts but showing our hand. If they learn what we are truly capable of, it will ruin the progress we've made. They will respond by attempting to eliminate us. And it will undermine the trust we've built with the citizens."

I retook my seat. "Says you."

"I'm right and you know it."

He was. It didn't make it easier to hear. I rubbed my gritty eyes. "What do you propose?"

"We've already alerted all vampire houses and dragon settlements to search for the kids. In addition, some humans have agreed to inform us if they notice anything odd about an area. I suggest we wait it out."

"Are you in charge of the initiative?"

"I am. And I didn't do it to undermine you. I want the kids back, too."

"So, you're saying I'm being too impatient. Funny how not long ago, I wasn't deciding fast enough."

"Your concerns are valid. But you should give the people who work for you time. Focus on Alex and work with Jonas to help the half-turned human prisoners. Distract yourself from obsessing over it."

"Thank you."

He lifted my hand to his mouth and brushed feather-light kisses across my hand. "Anytime, my petty tyrant."

Chapter Twenty-Eight

As Jonas and I approached, the human man's chest puffed out as he used his confidence and conviction to hide his sheer terror. Not even his eyes gave away his fear, as he kept them unfocused and locked straight ahead. His arms were rigid and rested behind his back in a military pose. The self-discipline it took to accomplish such a calm demeanor was impressive.

Jonas rubbed his nose to clear the scent of fear. "Why did you volunteer to let us test our magic on you?"

"I'm in constant pain, sir. I no longer wish to endure it."

"*Achoo!*"

The guy took a step back before catching himself.

I locked my knees to keep from doing the same. Jonas's sneeze was as terrifying as his roar.

He pretended not to notice the new shockwave of fear rolling off everyone except our dragon guard. "You're not a very good liar."

The man clenched his jaw.

"This one's trying to protect his friends. He doesn't believe he has a problem."

"There are plenty of others to choose from, but the magic in his bones is stronger than the others, and I'm impressed by his bravery."

"As am I. It would be a travesty to lose him."

"I think he's stubborn enough to live." My eyes and senses stayed glued to the courageous human. "He has integrity."

The guy cleared his throat. "May I speak, ma'am?"

"Sure."

"It's my understanding you want to use magic to heal us. I volunteered because I've already endured months of severe pain to become this way. Do what you must. I'm at peace with the decision if it doesn't work."

It took all I had to keep from showing emotion at his heart-wrenching confession. Unlike Jonas, I wasn't concerned we'd hurt our first turn. I read my grandmother's diary and visited her for clarification. She walked me through the process and cautioned me not to use it beyond the scope of saving the captured humans. It wouldn't surprise me if she were in her observation room looking down on us while we worked.

"Let me have your hand, please." When the guy complied, I assessed him. As I suspected, it was pure shifter magic. An odd mixture of several animals, and the infusion was half-assed. His bones would most likely disintegrate if I dissipated the magic. I withdrew my hand. "How many sessions did you endure?"

"Too many to count, ma'am."

I nodded. "It's weak. He can't fully shift because they used different animal types, infusing it with what feels like experimental spells into his bones. He might not make it if I dissipate it while he's human."

"We never infused magic into bones. Only blood. If we attempt to do it the right way, will it make him worse?"

"Good question." Jonas could decide which animal shifters they turned into when he created them. Since the guy already had shifter magic, we'd need to be careful. "It's a mixture of wolf, tiger, and bear. I can isolate it until we're done and then heal him, but it's still risky."

"Which one is dominant?"

I retook the guy's hand. "Tiger."

The man's mouth twitched throughout our conversation. After I dropped his hand, he stared at it. "How can you tell what they used?"

I offered a professional smile. "It's a gift."

Jonas ignored him. "Then we'll make him a tiger. Once he shifts, try to save him."

I motioned to a cot. "You should lie down."

After he settled, I laid a hand on him and held the other one out to Jonas. "Wait until the scent of ozone touches your nose, and push your power and intentions towards me."

"Will do." Jonas dropped to his knees. "Relax, kid. This will only take a minute."

I had to hand it to the human. He was brave and hid his nerves well. A slight tremble was the only sign of fear. I sent healing magic through him to numb the pain. The second it activated, I sipped Jonas's magic.

A flood of powerful shifter magic blasted me, and I fell on my ass. I struggled to concentrate on the task. Lissa explained that acting as the connection ensured loyalty to the crown, but with the flood of shifter magic, I wondered if I had any influence over it. Throwing the thought out of my mind, I directed it to his blood. The magic clinging to his bones reacted by attempting to escape, so I sealed it off as a temporary fix.

Jonas cut off the flow, and I focused on his bones. It seemed insignificant compared to the tiger shifter magic flowing through his blood. I anchored Jonas's magic to his heart before I withdrew.

The guy opened his eyes. They flashed orange, and he blinked.

"How do you feel?" I asked when he didn't speak.

"Like I need some raw meat."

I swung toward a dragon guard. "Will you please get him a large, rare steak?"

The dragon flipped his wrist and handed me a plate while Jonas helped the guy sit up.

He devoured the meal. When he was done, Jonas walked him through shifting. He looked like a regular Bengal tiger, though his movements were far from graceful.

After I directed him back onto the cot in his Tiger form, I dissipated the weak magic in his bones. Three ribs shattered the second I unsealed it. I restored him and stepped back.

The man stretched his shoulders after Jonas forced him to shift again. "I feel better than I have in months."

"Any pain?" I asked.

He stretched. "No, ma'am. The pain's gone."

"Great. If it comes back, speak up. You don't need to live with pain here."

Jonas handed him another steak. "You're a normal shifter now. Which means you're mine. I'm Jonas First, the Shifter King. I've been around for thousands of years, so don't fuck with me."

"No, sir."

"Good. Bring us back five of your buddies. Preferably, the ones in the most pain."

"Yes, sir." The guy gave our dragon guards a wide berth as he left.

Jonas patted my shoulder. "You did good, kiddo."

A laugh burst out of me. "Kiddo?"

He shrugged. "It fits."

We transformed twenty shifters before exhausting our energy. My eyes drooped as I led Jonas through the palace to check on Alex. "I'm tired."

"It'll get easier. Lissa's endurance grew as she became used to using transformation and creation together."

"Other than healing, I didn't realize we used my magic, but you're right. I can't imagine how tired you are."

"I could use a hearty meal and a rest."

We fell silent as we entered the suite. Lily lounged in a chair, scrolling through her phone. Across from her, Deva snored where I'd last seen Alex. I felt him and Ann Marie in the bedroom.

Lily tucked her phone away and stretched. "How did it go?"

"Well," Jonas said, never taking his eyes off Deva. "Why is the Dragon Queen asleep in Alex's apartment?"

"She wanted to confirm what Glac and Drake sensed."

"What did she say?" I asked. If anyone could figure out what was happening with him, it was Deva.

"Nothing. She touched his forehead, grunted, stumbled to the sofa, and fell asleep. Weird, eh?"

"Yes." I couldn't imagine Deva letting her guard down in front of so many people on purpose. "Don't tell anyone she's here. I'm cutting off access to this room until she wakes up."

"You honestly believe I'm going to let anyone near my brother right now?"

"No. But this is out of character for her."

Two weeks later, we turned the final shifter. I watched as the wolf bounded toward the others. Almost three-quarters of them were wolves. The rest were black bears, except for fifteen tigers and three horses. Which meant the humans had access to at least four shifters. Probably more. And they had figured out a crude way to extract magic. And I'd bet my crown one of our own helped them.

I tore my eyes away from the new shifters. "How's Alex today?"

"He said something in his sleep last night."

"Has Deva explained her trances?"

"No. She shows up every night, touches his forehead, and takes a nap. When I ask her about it, she says, 'When I have answers, I'll share them, love.'" He used a high-pitched voice to quote her.

Laughing, I pulled out my buzzing phone and sighed. "It's Travis. The guy never leaves me alone."

"He likes to feel important." Jonas shrugged. "And you make people feel important."

I sent the call to voicemail. "One of the many reasons I hesitated to be queen was because it irritated me how people kissed my ass."

"No shit? Huh. I always thought you were a coward."

"My childhood trauma mixed with Mat's coddling made me an anxious mess, yes. Luckily, I surrounded myself with people who aren't afraid to call me a coward instead of a bunch of ass kissers."

He chuckled as he mussed my hair. "You remind me so much of Lily sometimes. You're more polished, but it's hard to miss the family resemblance."

"Thank you. But I'll never reach her level of snark. It's a true gift."

"She mastered it as a coping mechanism. There was a time when Ann Marie and I believed it would make her more of an outcast. Especially if she ever met you."

"Because of Mat's public version of me. I've always gravitated towards the scarier paranormals."

"I see that now. And share your admiration."

Travis waited outside my office. He paled when he spotted Jonas, but recovered fast. "Sir First. Jen. You need to see something."

My shoulders slumped. I could sense bad news hovering over my head, waiting for the opportunity to drop. "Sure."

The TV in my office was already on, five human talking heads yapping away. I collapsed into a chair at the conference table. "What now?"

"They're accusing us of abducting military personnel."

My spine straightened. "The shifters?"

"Yep. One of their top military guys announced he sent them on a reconnaissance mission, and they never returned. He's saying we slaughtered them."

"Of course he is." I tapped the table. "Go to the camp and record yourself interviewing them. Find the lead tiger and ask him about his experience in their shifter trials. Talk to anyone who wants to share their experience and flood the internet with videos. Don't hesitate to contact the tech mages for help."

"Hold up," Jonas said before Travis reached the door. "Those wolves are low to mid-level and don't have shifter families beyond their brothers in arms. They'll be drawn to your power, so tread carefully. You cannot allow them to see you as their leader unless you're willing to declare them family and take an alpha test."

A spark of excitement lit in Travis's eyes. "Of course." He strutted out.

I picked up the remote. "You saw that, right?"

"Yes. He will be their alpha soon."

"You want him to lead?" I realized how the question sounded. "Never mind. It's not my business."

"He takes pride in his heritage. Since his whole family is dead, he's inherited a ton of power. He needs those wolves as much as they need him."

I shot him a flat stare.

"The shifters will not be mistreated again." Jonas's certainty reminded me why I shouldn't involve myself in faction politics.

"Right." Red-hot anger flooded me, and I launched out of my seat. Since Drake's bond had settled, he was always like background noise. I focused on it several times throughout the day to check on him, and he did the same with me. But most of the time, we let each other do our thing without interference. The only exception was when one of us lost control. *What's wrong?*

We found a facility.

Where?

It is too much information to convey while dealing with the sarcastic vampire. I'll explain when I return tomorrow morning.

It didn't surprise me that Quin took it upon himself to investigate the kids' disappearances, even when he was supposed to be in Allure, commanding his army division. *Okay. Stay safe.*

The usual amusement he sent when I told him to stay safe was absent, which made me wonder exactly what he found.

Chapter Twenty-Nine

Drake landed on the balcony outside our apartment as Lily broke through the ward on the front door. The sun wasn't up, so I refused to acknowledge them.

"Wake up, sleepyhead. I brought coffee." Lily's voice called from the sitting room.

I sat up and stretched. "What are you doing here so early?"

She poked her head in as a naked Drake stepped inside. Lily didn't even glance in his direction. "Alex turned over in his sleep. I need you to check on him, so I brought you a bribe." She wiggled the mug.

"Bribe accepted. Give us a minute?"

"Hurry, please." She vanished.

Drake fell face-first on the bed and snaked an arm around my hips. "You're a popular woman these days."

I ran a hand over his stubbly jaw. "Yeah. Turns out, a powerful title means people want things from me. Who knew?"

His body shook with laughter. "Mind if I sleep before you interrogate me about what we found?"

I trailed kisses from his shoulder to the scar on his face. "Sure. I understand how important sleep is to senior citizens."

He flipped me onto my back and tickled me. "You think you're funny."

I squealed and pretended to struggle. "I'm kind of funny."

His soft lips touched mine, and sparks ignited. The second I sank into him, he pulled back. "Go help your sister before she dies trying to kick my ass." He flopped onto his back.

I brushed the dark hair from his face. "Get some rest. I love you."

Drake murmured something I couldn't hear as I left.

Alex's color had returned, and hope ignited inside my chest. I rushed to his side. And released a heavy sigh. "No change internally."

Lily crossed her arms. "How can that be?"

"I don't know. If I did, I'd do something about it."

She poked him in the shoulder. "You better wake up before I lose my temper."

I backed away. "The gate's magic is fading, so he won't stay like this forever."

"I have an entire house to run and can't always hang out here. Can I take him home?"

"No, love." Deva sauntered in wearing a silk jumpsuit. She pulled her bronze locks to the top of her head and glamoured a hair tie. "He must stay near me until he hatches."

"Hatches?" we both screeched.

The Dragon Queen ignored our alarm. "It seems the gate woke his dormant magic."

"There is no dormant magic," Lily said with certainty.

"I suspect his mental magic is so strong because he has a touch of dragon blood."

I linked my arm with Lily's to stop her from launching at Deva. "You never sensed it before?"

"I sensed something from the moment he stepped foot inside my hotel, love. At first, I wondered if Alex is a multidrakelandarnarian."

If Lily weren't a vampire, I would have crushed her elbow with my grip. Only one multidrakelandarnarian lived in the realm, and he was mine. Since I was his only match, he couldn't have had a son. I tried to remember what Drake said about them, but my mind was spinning too fast. "You said dragons don't abandon their children."

Sadness filled Deva's eyes. "We don't. Which is why I have been extracting his thoughts at night and researching his heritage during the day. A dragon-lion sired him, and a mage birthed and dumped him on the American Lion pack. He wasn't family, so they used it as a reason to treat him so terribly."

"Bullshit." Lily jerked away from me. "He's shown no signs of being anything other than a mage and a cat shifter."

"Hasn't he? Because there are no mental mages like young Alex."

Tears filled Lily's eyes, but she kept her thoughts to herself.

Excitement bubbled inside of me at the prospect of him being able to fly with Glacintial. "Will he be able to shift?"

"I'm afraid not, love. He is only a quarter dragon. A form requires at least half."

My excitement drained. "Who is his biological dad? Do I need to summon the heritage mages?"

"No. I have opened an investigation. The mage who abandoned him died not long after giving away her son." She refocused on Lily. "His mental magic is as strong as a dragon's. The awakening will help him with control. He will remain a hybrid, and I will not claim him unless he files a formal request."

Lily didn't bother finding a chair. She lowered herself to the floor. "I'm never going to hear the end of this. He'll lord his greatness over me every day for eternity."

I pointed at her. "Drake would defend you if you befriended him instead of poking at him all the time."

"No thanks. It's too much fun." She was across the room in the next breath. "I need time to think."

"Of course, love." Deva waited for her to leave the apartment. "This is big news for my dragons, and they will want to celebrate. I'll explain it to Jonas."

"Okay." I concentrated on Alex as she left. When we were alone, I took his hand. "Lily loves you. She's worried about what this means for your relationship. If it were up to her, you'd never change because she's afraid she'll lose you. But here's the deal. I've learned several lessons over the last few years. One of the most important is how you can't let others clip your wings. Promise yourself that no matter how much resistance you face, you'll still fly. And never forget how much your family loves you." I released his hand. "If you need to talk, you can always come to me. I'll do everything within my power to free you from the social cages life tries to trap you in. I swear it."

The magical contract settled over me, and I blinked the tears away. I understood what sudden, massive changes would do to his emotional state. And the changes barreling toward him were big ones. I didn't want him to relive his time as a helpless kid in a cage. "Not on my watch," I whispered as I left the room.

Drake leaned against the wall, his face carefully blank. I stopped and tried to gather myself. Before I could, he reached out and pulled me to his chest. "He has always had dragon abilities."

"Yeah." I stepped back. "Lily didn't take it well."

"She needs time to process."

"She's been through a lot lately. Change is good, but this is a lot."

"Since when did you become the reasonable one?"

I chuckled. "You're right. I need to stop before it becomes a habit."

"Not necessarily. But at least let me be the wise one."

"No problem. Aren't you supposed to be sleeping?"

He squeezed my hand. "I have news."

"Good news or bad?"

"Both." Drake waited until we were in my office before he continued. "We've pinpointed a facility where our kids are being kept."

I rubbed my quivering stomach. "Where?"

"In Virginia. The tech mages are working to hack the systems and learn more."

"Then let's call in my advisors to figure out how to retrieve them."

When he didn't respond, I lifted my head to find a thoughtful expression on his face. I tuned into the bond. Pure predatory hunting instincts greeted me. When I gasped, he blinked, and it melted away. "I think you and I should go in with a reconnaissance team first."

"Weren't you the one who said I don't need to rush out and solve all the problems myself?"

"I believe you should trust people to do their jobs, yes."

"Except this one?"

Drake kept his face blank as he thought about how to answer. I closed the distance between us, took his hand, and pulled him toward the seating area. I tugged him back towards the conference table right before we reached it. He dropped my hand. "What are you doing, Jenella?"

"You need to pace so you can gather your thoughts. I'm helping."

His smile didn't reach his eyes. "I don't need to pace."

"Huh. Okay. How can I pry those thoughts out of your mind?"

"You can't unless you use my own magic against me, which you won't." He retook my hand and continued pacing. "But I like how you include me in your nervous habit."

"Feel free to use it when you need to."

"When I strategize, I think in direct routes and minimal damage. Sometimes, the easiest way to accomplish a goal is to intimidate with my size and status. Other times, it's to encourage others to solve their own problems. But the best solution to retrieve our people and make a statement is more manipulative."

"Ooooo. I'm going to like it, aren't I?"

"Yes. Which is why I hesitate."

I pulled him to a stop. "Tell me."

"I believe we should form a small, yet mighty team to infiltrate their facility and find out what they're up to. When we have information, we bring in just enough force to shut it down and retrieve our people. Make a statement without displaying our full power. Also, it may be wise to use observation spells for Travis and Sheila to post."

"So, not manipulative at all. But I like it better." I lowered myself into a chair. "Is the source of the strange magic there?"

"Unknown."

"Can we win if they are?"

"If we choose our team wisely."

"Did you sense demons?"

"Yes. But they have integrated with humans, and we couldn't reach them."

I tapped the arm of the chair while I thought it over. "If we use your idea, let's include the Leadership Council. They're beginning to work together, and I don't want to ruin it."

"Whenever we alert them to our activities, someone leaks the plans."

And it would put the kids in more danger. "If we don't tell them about it in advance, we'll need to explain why we went behind their backs later. It will destroy the trust we've built."

He lowered himself into the chair beside me. "Then we will inform them and use those who want to be involved as our backup. As for the reconnaissance team, I would like Bastien and Tracy to come with us."

I waved a hand. "That's a given. Quin needs to come, too. He's handy in a fight and capable of things the rest of us aren't."

"Agreed. As is Lily. I would like to include her and Cavil."

"We'll leave their level of participation up to them. I'd love to have Alex with us, too."

"Perhaps he will recover in time. What about Razazia?"

"Olwen's better."

"I disagree. She's good in tough situations."

"Point conceded. Sylphira can help us scout."

"She's the perfect choice. What about Emine?"

"I'll ask her, but she might not want to go."

We spent the next few minutes brainstorming. I wasn't the best strategist because I always assumed Mat would be there to do it for me. But Drake wasn't too bad. And we had others who could help us before we acted. When we ran out of ideas, we sat in silence, thinking.

A spell near my desk lit up, and Verity's voice came through. "Sorry to interrupt, but Ann Marie needs you in Alex's room."

My heart skipped a beat as I scrambled to my feet and flung the door open. "Is he awake?"

"She didn't say."

I didn't wait for Drake as I flashed to the family wing, raced to his apartment, and pounded on the door.

It swung open, revealing Jonas. "Is he awake?"

He shifted his weight. "Yes, but his head is fuzzy."

Confusion and dizziness weren't good for someone with Alex's mental skills. I sped to the bedroom and skidded to a stop inside the door. Ann Marie sat on the bed, clutching Alex's hand while Deva rested two fingers on his temple. Lily stood in the corner with her fists clenched.

I shuffled forward. "Let me check him."

Deva shook her head. "I am feeling for his inner dragon."

"He doesn't have an inner dragon," Lily grumbled.

I moved to Ann Marie's side while we waited. A few seconds later, Drake arrived, inclined his head at Jonas, and leaned against the wall beside Lily.

Assessment complete, Deva stepped back, a puzzled expression on her face. "It seems I was right. Alex is not a dragon shifter."

"Ha! I knew it." Lily zipped to her side. "He's far too reasonable to be a dragon."

"Your impression of us is skewed, love. We are very reasonable in most situations." Deva patted her arm. "Alex has dragon blood, but his mixed heritage is unique. He truly is a work of art."

Lily shrugged. "Same difference."

I examined Alex's unfocused eyes. When he didn't register my presence, I assessed him. Once again, I found nothing wrong. "What's running through his mind?"

"Nothing," Drake said. "It's as if he's keeping it intentionally blank."

"Because there are too many people crowding him." Ann Marie stood. "Everyone out." She nudged me to the door.

The small sitting area felt crowded with so many strong personalities shoved together. Helen breezed in with a tray of drinks and set them on the small counter in the kitchenette. "Help yourselves when you're thirsty." She busied herself tidying up.

After what seemed like forever, Ann Marie stepped out and scanned our hopeful faces. "Lily, he wants to see you."

She turned into a blur, and the door slammed shut.

"Is he lucid?" Deva asked.

"Yes. He claims his magic is fine."

My forehead creased. "He still has the echo I assumed was magic from the gate, but it's more settled."

Deva waved a dismissive hand. "It's slight and will fade. But he feels more like kin now."

"There's no point in speculating, so don't." Ann Marie rubbed her eyes. "He's still our son."

She had a point. We all wanted to claim Alex because he was such a fantastic person. But in truth, we didn't have the right. The most we could hope for was a friendship.

The door opened, and Lily poked her head out. "He wants to see Jen."

Alex's eyes were more alert, but still a little glassy, as I approached his bed. "You scared the shit out of us."

His lips twitched. "I scared myself."

"Don't do it again, or it will send Lily and Jonas on a rampage, and I don't want to clean up your mess."

"Again."

"What?"

"You've been cleaning up our messes since we met. And trust me when I say we're not proud of it."

I waved a dismissive hand. "What's a little damage control between friends?"

"You're trying to make me laugh."

Lily shoulder-bumped me. "Except she's not funny."

He rubbed his eyes. "The wards did something to me, and I need you to tell me what it is."

"It's dragon magic. Deva said you're a quarter dragon. Your mental abilities can only come from them, so she always suspected. The backblast from the wards gave you magic poisoning and triggered something inside you."

"Great. But what does it mean?"

"Unknown, because you're too unique." I leaned forward. "Don't let anyone push you around. Including me."

"I won't." His eyes landed on the door. "Dragon blood, huh? That explains why I'm so good with money."

"You're good with money because you're a nerd," Lily said. "But it explains why you're so stubborn and like to hang out at the bar."

Chapter Thirty

It didn't take Alex long to recover and return home. Without the distraction, Drake and I polished our plans. We chose our team members, leaving Lily and Alex out. Drake still believed they'd be assets, but I wanted to give them a break from our problems.

The morning sun hadn't risen when we loaded on my private transport. Deva planned to stay behind to run the summoning room's controls if we needed an emergency exit.

Tracy yawned and stretched. "I do not miss waking up at the crack of dawn to chase you around."

"Hmmmf," Drake agreed.

"Don't pin this on me. I wanted to attack at night. Mr. Grumpy-pants here insisted on daylight for the sake of the monitoring spells." I patted Drake's stomach.

Bastien peered inside the transport. "How many people are going with us?"

Drake pried my hand away from his abs and laced his fingers with mine. "We only invited a few. The rest will meet us in Ferine."

The transport was packed. Cavil, Lily, and Alex sat on one side with what looked like their entire household. Behind them, Jonas and Ann Marie stood with several shifters, including my bear-shifter friend, Colonel Ballard. Quin and Ara sat near my designated seats. We hadn't invited Ara, but I was relieved to see her.

Near the back, Sylphira and a swarm of pixies buzzed around the Minotaur King's head. The First Gorman peeked out from behind the Ogre Queens. Razazia lounged on a chair behind Quin and Ara, with Olwen and a few elves. The entire gaggle of Dwarven princes waved at us. Prince Leebol from the Conservatory winked at me. Members of the Leadership Council filled the remaining seats.

Bastien's shrewd eyes ran over the crowd. "Your idea of a few and mine are vastly different, cousin."

My throat tightened at the sheer amount of support we had from the paranormal community, and it took me a minute to snap to my senses. "Why are they all traveling with us?" I swung to face Drake. "Could this compromise our plans?"

Quin appeared. "Everyone here is loyal. Do not ruin it."

"Loyal like Gabe and Linda? Or loyal like you and Deva?"

"I will not entertain a question designed to be a snotty comment."

So, it was Quin who gathered people to help. I dropped Drake's hand and headed to my seat. "Fine. But anyone who compromises the mission dies."

"Of course."

My glare landed on Lily as I took my seat. She raised her middle finger. It took Cavil a second to notice the exchange and cover her hand. The crude gesture eased my nerves. "Okay. Let's brief them on the way."

The pocket of Ferine hadn't changed since Tracy and I found the Bellicose facility nearby. The sun blinded me as we passed the park, where Quin and I fought a bunch of mind-controlled shifters. I broke out in a sweat as we walked to a more expensive hotel nearby.

We were a large group, and the locals stopped and gawked as we passed. A vampire appeared in front of Ara and said something. She shook her head, said a couple of words, and he ran off.

I rubbed the nape of my neck and ignored the buzzing of small wings as Sylphira led pixies through the crowd and shouted, "Keep up, pixies! We don't slow down and we don't show pain."

The red dragon who came with Lily staggered towards me. "Not to sound like a coward, but why are the local dragons lining the rooftops?"

I fought not to smile. "Flintous, right?"

"At your service."

"Deva sent them to ensure we made it to the hotel." My spine itched from so many eyes watching us, and the tickle intensified.

He groaned. "So they'll think I'm an ass kisser, rather than a coward. I'm unsure which one is worse."

Drake's hand landed on my back. "Flirting with my mate, Flint?"

"I wouldn't dare." He examined the distant complex. "We're discussing the local dragons and their impressions of us."

"Of you." I glanced at the gate as we turned down the street to our hotel. "Anyone else's senses going haywire?"

"What do you mean by haywire?" Alex asked from behind me.

I stopped in the street and tore my eyes away from the gate. I hated Ferine after our last experience, and half convinced myself it was past trauma, causing me to feel uncomfortable. But my senses didn't lie. "Something's off. People watch me all the time, but it never feels like this."

Drake's eyes glowed, and a few dragons launched from the building and moved towards the gate. "Perhaps you should explain to the other leaders."

"Yeah." I took two steps left, then shuffled two steps forward. "Ara, do you have vampires monitoring this pocket?"

"Of course, dear."

Tingles erupted across my shoulder blades, and a stab of panic made me shiver. "Evacuate the pocket." I turned to Drake as the panic faded. A second later, white-hot anger burned in my chest and dissipated. "Someone's trying to screw with my emotions."

"Demon?"

Overwhelming sadness came next, and it took everything I had to swim through it. "Anyone else feeling too many emotions?"

A chorus of 'no's' sounded around me.

I became impatient. "It's targeting me. Anyone sense demons?"

No one did.

Something clicked inside me, and my eyes widened. "It's a distraction."

"From what?" someone asked.

Lust ignited in my core, and I pressed my legs together as I imagined pouring cold water on it. "Something's off here. Evacuate the..."

The ground shook.

Drake scooped me into his arms and barked orders at the others. "Bastien, Ara, use your influence to clear the pocket." He shifted into his dragon form and shot towards the gate so fast I didn't have time to recover from the fake emotional overload. We emerged inside a garage, and he shifted back and set me on my feet. "Talk to me, Jenella."

"I..." Locals stampeded out the gates, along with several leaders who came with us. I flashed to a corner, so we were out of the way. The emotional manipulation diminished. "I can't pinpoint what, but there's something wrong."

"How wrong? Should we continue this evacuation as a precaution, or clear the area?"

A shimmer of something raced across the surface of the pocket's wards, and I gasped. "No!"

Drake gripped my arms and gave me a light shake. "No, what?"

A tidal wave of magic exploded and swept through the garage. I tried to flash Drake away, but it overtook us before I could. I slammed into a cement wall, and pain blasted through my head. A series of thunderous noises erupted, and something hard smashed into my side. A brick, I decided as I attempted to wipe blood from my eyes. I couldn't see, so I used my senses. Another round of soul-sucking sadness rolled through me, and I gritted my teeth against it. "Drake!"

The world flew by, and the sadness lifted. I couldn't hear, and my entire body ached. It was a pain unlike any other I'd ever felt, and I cried out. Dust filled my lungs, and I coughed and sputtered. The next thing I knew, I was on the ground on my back, staring up into a clear blue sky. A puffy cloud floated by, and I couldn't help but think how wrong it was for the sky to be so happy.

Lily's filthy face filled my vision. "You alive?"

I blinked and tried to think. "You're bleeding."

"It's not my blood. Can you move?"

No. "Give me a minute to heal. Drake?"

Her eyes darted to the left. "He's around."

I sputtered and tried to sit up, but something in my spine wouldn't let me move, so I hit the ground with a 'thud.' "Not healed yet."

"How long will it take? We've got to go and I've never been here."

"Where's everyone else? Did they make it?"

"It's too chaotic. I only found you."

A tear rolled down my temple. "Okay." I concentrated on healing. When the pain melted away, I sat up. Lily hid us in a filthy alley where I couldn't see much. "We have to go back."

"Nope." She helped me up. "You almost died, and I'm not in the mood for an encore. We need to move."

The bond with Drake lit up like a light bulb, and by the throbbing in my head, he was trying to talk to me. Sheer panic radiated from him, and

I had to swim through it to gather my thoughts. *I'm okay. Lily saved me, and we're in an alley.*

Relief replaced the panic. *Leave the area. The pocket is gone. I'm going to help rescue the survivors and recover our dead.*

How bad is it?

Bad. Take Lily and go somewhere far away. I will find you.

"Drake wants us to leave."

"No shit." Lily linked her arm with mine. "Flash us somewhere."

I had moved a gate at a nearby pocket after humans made it impossible for the locals to use the gate, so I flashed there.

Lily groaned when she realized where we were. "The Vampire Master in this pocket is a dick."

"He's no match for you."

"No, he's not. But I'm not in the mood."

Neither was I. We ignored the alarmed stares as we dragged our bloody, dirty asses down the street, heading towards the witch district. When a vampire appeared and opened her mouth to say something to Lily, I slammed her against a wall. "Unless you're here to update us on Ferine, we don't want to hear it."

She swallowed. "Visiting vampires must check in."

"Then it's a good thing we're not vampires." My eyes trailed over her. "Tell your master if he interferes with us, then he's interfering with crown business. He will not like the consequences."

The vampire swallowed and nodded. "Of course, Your Grace."

Lily was silent for a few heartbeats. "Damn. It never ceases to amaze me how everyone melts at your feet."

"It irritates me, but I'll use it when necessary." I pointed at a boutique hotel. "If you embraced your title, you could do the same."

"No thanks. I like being underestimated."

We showered, and I created some baggy clothes. They were comfortable, but not durable. Lily liked them because she had her full range of movement. As we ate crappy food from the magichef, I felt a tickle on the back of my neck. My eyes went wide, and without thinking, I dove on Lily and flashed outside the pocket.

"What the hell?" She shoved me away.

I craned my neck to see the wards and gate, but didn't see a shimmer. "Tickle. Same as in Ferine."

She sighed. "How are they tracking you?"

"My magic is like a beacon. I've muted it, but it's not the first time it's made me an easy target."

"Then let's keep moving. We'll find a store and dress like humans. Work on muting your magic, and I'll watch your back."

I reached for my phone for the millionth time. "We need phones."

"Nope. Too easy to track."

"The phones the tech mages make for me aren't trackable. This isn't how I saw the day going."

"No shit?"

"No shit, what?"

"You expected today to go well? You're such a snowflake."

"If you want to tease me, you're going to have to do better because I have no idea what that means." I let out a breath. "I hoped for once we could win without losing anyone. I wanted to go in with an overwhelming force, rescue our kids, banish demons, and be gone before humans noticed us."

"This isn't a fairy tale."

"It was a little optimistic, yes. But we still need to find the kids."

"I agree. But we can't help them if we're dead. Come on."

"We need to go back. Whoever blew up Ferine is looking for me, and I don't want to endanger anyone else."

Before she could object, a flash of light blinded us. I flung my hands over my eyes, and Lily whipped around to face the other way. When the light dimmed, I cracked an eye open.

Drake shook off the dust coating him and set Cavil on the ground. "He needs healing."

Cavil's torso was bare and cut open from collarbone to navel. His face was black and blue. One leg faced the wrong way. I winced at the amount of blood covering him.

When Lily appeared beside him, Cavil attempted to raise his hand to touch her, but it flopped back down to his side. "Jen! Do something." Lily's eyes were wide with fear, and her fangs poked over her lips.

Right. I touched his filthy arm and skipped the assessment as I restored him.

He sighed in relief. "Thank you."

I stood. "How bad is Ferine?"

Drake avoided eye contact. "Bad. It will take time to assess the total damage."

"I'm going back."

"No!" the three of them protested.

I clenched and unclenched my fists. "Only a cowardly leader runs away and hides. And I'm a lot of things, but a coward isn't one of them."

"And only an idiot walks into a death trap," Lily said. "If you go back, we might not be lucky enough to save you this time."

Drake dumped a cleaning potion on Cavil. "I agree with Lily. You need to steer clear until our team figures out what happened."

Solid logic. "It was the complicated, strange magic that blew up the pocket. Demons tried to keep us inside by manipulating my emotions. It proves the two are working together."

"No offense, but it doesn't," Cavil said as he slipped on a neon green T-shirt. "Human authorities, dragons, and hundreds of other paranormals clog the area around Ferine. The pocket no longer exists, but there is still a thick coat of evil in the area."

My shoulders slumped. "I need to do something." A vibration from under my feet made me lose my train of thought. "What was that?"

All three of them dove at me as the ground gave way.

Chapter Thirty One

"Don't let go!" Lily's voice shrieked in my ear as the ground fell away.

I flailed my free arm as we tumbled into the darkness. Drake grabbed hold of me as I sent a spell to slow our momentum. My heart pounded out of my chest when it didn't work. Cavil's sun magic lit, but there was nothing to see besides dirt and rock as we dropped.

Lily's arm slammed against the wall, and my shoulder smashed into it. "Damnit! You're healing that."

I flung out my arms and tried to create a barrier around us, but struggled to anchor it. "I can't hold it!" We began spiraling, so I abandoned my efforts and tried to sense what awaited us below. I caught a glimpse of Drake's face and cried out at the look of utter devastation. A second later, pain ripped through me as if I were being torn into a million pieces. A gust of air so hot it seared my soul whispered across my skin.

The wind increased to a gale force until it pried us apart. I scrambled to focus as I tried every kind of magic I'd ever absorbed. When nothing worked, I formed a barrier around myself and frantically searched for someone else. Only darkness greeted me.

Bone-chilling fear overtook me when my connection to Drake cut off. Crushing loneliness from the loss had barely set in when every trauma I suffered in my entire life sprang into my head. The anger and pain I'd worked so hard to purge blasted through my chest, and my self-doubt amplified to where despair set in. Grief so overpowering I couldn't think overtook me and mingled with a sense of helplessness.

The ripping pain disappeared, and I landed on a hot stone floor with a 'thud.' Tears streamed down my face as the unsettling insecurities and their accompanying emotions whirled around me. I fought to control them. When I couldn't, I tried to tread to the surface. A dam broke when I realized I couldn't. Somewhere in the mixture of painful emotions, I understood that if I didn't pull myself together, I'd be lost forever. The realization only increased my ugly sobs.

It never dawned on me until that moment how much I'd relied on the giant ball of anger. It motivated me in ways no other emotion could. By dealing with it, I'd emptied my fuel. And never replaced it. I hadn't realized that I needed to. It was a big mistake.

The revelation barely surfaced when, white-hot anger washed over me. It pulsed and melted into bone-crushing guilt. Somewhere in the whirling mass of trauma and emotions, a realization surfaced. Someone or something was toying with me. It wasn't real. Not a single emotion I'd felt since falling into the hole was my own. So, I used an old trick and dissociated. I tethered the strings to my emotions with a level of indifference I hadn't used since Jacques's death.

"It won't work."

The raspy voice startled me. "What?"

"I said it won't work."

I turned my head toward the voice. What remained of a man lay on the stone floor, naked and filthy. Someone had shackled his wrists and ankles with thick metal cuffs. Heavy chains snaked across the floor and wall, anchoring him at several points. I hadn't heard or smelled him.

"Can you speak in coherent sentences yet?" he asked without bothering to open his eyes.

"Who are you?"

"King Emiron of Gartolia at your service. I was once a big deal around here." A ragged laugh disappeared into the void.

When he didn't clarify, I returned to concentrating on my emotions.

"I wouldn't if I were you. They feed on them."

"Is that so?" I didn't care if they fed on my emotions. It would buy me time to find the others and leave.

"Aye. The more negative the emotion, the higher the quality of food."

I'd read a lot about demons, so I ran through what I'd learned about the ones who fed off emotions. "Love," I whispered. "What about trust and hope?"

"Dangerous emotions, those."

"You sound like Drake." The mention of his name helped flood my system with love and joy. I grasped it and held on for dear life. My head cleared a little, so I expanded on the feeling until I felt nothing but love. When I had it locked in place, I glared at him. A set of intelligent gray eyes stared back. "What?"

"Who is this Drake?"

"My match."

Another rusty laugh escaped him. "Is that what you call forced bonds? I'd rather stay here fighting for what's left of my mind than fall into a dragon's trap."

The statement offended me far more than it should have, and it forced me to pause long enough to replace the hatred with love. A difficult task. "I doubt one would want you." When he didn't reply, I took the opportunity to sense the area. The stone corridor had a few glowing red rocks scattered throughout, in no discernible pattern. A yawning well of darkness took up the other end, and I reached for Drake to see if he was inside. I gritted my teeth against the ripping pain that sliced through my chest.

After it cleared, I injected vampire magic into my blood and tried to listen. The place was so silent, my ears ached. I realized the entire place felt like a lie, so I injected shifter magic into my nose and sniffed. Yep. Pure deception.

A pulse of something came from the darkness. It felt like average demon magic with a booster injected into it. Which meant I could leave. "How long have you been here?"

"Could be a few days or an eternity."

I concentrated on my love for Tracy as I stood and shuffled to the end to peer out. The darkness disguised everything except a series of pale paths snaking around a black mass. A puff of putrid air blew in my face when I wandered too close, and I gagged. When I regained my composure, I examined the ceiling. "A gate."

"I wouldn't," the man warned. "It's one-way. In only."

"Damn." I replaced frustration with love as I spun in a slow circle. "Where's the exit?"

"Do you think I'd still be here if there were a way out?"

"Your realm prides itself on war, and you don't have an exit plan?"

"We've always prevailed in our invasions."

"So, you didn't bother."

"How was I to anticipate my daughter would sell me to demons?"

"You probably raised her to eliminate the competition."

"Of course I did. However, I somehow struggle to feel pride in her methods. Tell me, Jenella of Ahl, who sold you?"

My heart skipped a beat. The guilt and doubt amplified, and I had to bend over to concentrate on my love for Helen and George. "No one."

"Liar. Only with a contract will the gate take a soul." His words barely left his mouth when the ceiling shimmered. The shimmer turned into movement.

I stepped back. "There is no contract."

"How can you be so sure?"

"Because I killed the person who had the authority to make one. And then I killed her allies."

"Smart. I wish I had thought of that."

I didn't respond as I tried to hold on to love for my friends and family. A tough task when talking about my mother. The black swirling picked up, and a sudden wind blew my hair back. Lily landed under it in her vampire form.

I rushed to her. "You're alive!"

A golden-red sheen rolled across her eyes. "Move!"

I dove to the side as two more bodies dropped from the gate. Our bond snapped back online, and I clutched my chest as I scrambled to my feet. "No." Crushing fear tried to paralyze me, and I rushed to Drake on shaky legs as I flooded our bond with love.

His fiery green eyes landed on me. "Jenella."

I dropped to my knees and took his face in my hands. "Concentrate on love. It's the only emotion it can't eat."

The inferno in his eyes died to a flicker as the roaring anger withdrew. He touched my cheek. "I thought I lost you." The fire relit.

"Love. Think only of love. No other emotions." When he managed it, I turned to help Lily. She stood over Emiron. The red glow from the rock reflected off Cavil's blonde hair as he crouched beside her and touched a cuff. With a burst of light, it turned to dust. "The emotion magic doesn't affect you?"

"Nope. Rolled right off." Lily pointed at Cavil. "He can borrow my immunity."

"It is the god bond," Cavil said, as if it explained everything. "Lily will not test hers to discover what gifts she's received."

"Right. I don't know if we should free him. He's the source of the strange magic."

Cavil paused and cocked his head. "He doesn't belong here."

"I don't belong here, no. I will make you a deal, Queen Jenella of Ahl. If you and your...friends help free me, your realm will be safe from a Gartolian invasion for eternity."

"Our realm has too many non-magical users for you to invade." They liked to conquer realms with a lot of magic and enslave the more useful beings.

When Cavil released his other hand, Emiron rubbed his wrist. He was so skinny, I half expected to hear bones clacking. "True. You may consider it insurance."

I crossed my arms. "I'll take your deal if you provide every detail about the magical traps you've made for the Bellicose."

His brow furrowed. "Never heard of them."

Cavil paused before freeing the last shackle. "You lie."

He sighed. "Gods are such killjoys. Since being trapped in this hellscape, the only goal I've had is to survive. I may have enchanted some objects and set a few traps."

I raised an eyebrow. "And how did humans learn to infuse magic into bones?"

"Since when are you concerned with humans? Besides, I only helped enough to provide them with a false sense of security."

"You were with Morten at the battle. I felt your magic."

"Not mine. The daughter who sold me became indebted to the demons. She requested a favor and paid with two reciprocal favors and me." When the last shackle dropped, he stumbled to his filthy feet. "To sweeten our deal, I shall ensure you escape from this pocket realm and give you a full account of her involvement."

"And yours," I added.

"Very well. I shall try to recall the enchantments my captors forced me to complete."

Lily zipped through the barrier and returned a second later. "It reeks of demons out there."

"Thanks." I examined Emiron. "Do our magical contracts work on you?"

"I wouldn't be here if they didn't. Aside from my freedom, I would like one more thing from you."

"Of course you do," Drake mumbled.

"Hush, little dragon. The royals are talking." He ignored Drake's growl. "There is a mage named Amanda. She is perhaps what you call a match. I wish to see her."

It took all I had to keep my emotions from surfacing when I read what he intended to do to her. "I've never met a mage named Amanda." But I'd find her and make sure she was well guarded.

"She's still around." He beat his chest. "I can feel her and wish to apologize before being expelled from this realm."

"If she wants to see you."

Lily tugged on my arm. "Which I doubt. We need to move, so can we hurry these negotiations along?"

"Of course." Emiron limped to a wall and leaned against it as he stated his terms.

After adding a few safeguards and talking the whole thing over with Drake, we sealed the contract. When the tingling settled in my scalp, I dispelled the demon magic blocking us. "Show us to the exit, King Emiron of Gartolia."

A deep frown formed on his face. "I've been trying to break the barrier for ages, and you accomplish it with the wave of a hand."

"Sometimes trauma comes in handy."

Chapter Thirty-Two

Emiron led us to the right around a massive pit filled with bones and ash. As we left the area, the emotional manipulation melted away, and my muscles relaxed a little. Rocks ignited into red and orange flames as we passed. The darkness swallowed their light so fast that I still couldn't see. I rested my hand on Drake. Behind me, Cavil stumbled. Lily guided his hand to her shoulder. "Stay close."

I injected vampire magic into my blood. My focus sharpened long enough to see we were on a narrow trail as we skirted around the endless pit of death in the center. A black hole lined with discarded bones and chunks of something I didn't recognize. Not wanting to freak myself out, I focused on Drake's back.

After what seemed like hours, we reached the far side of the pit and turned down a twisting corridor with smooth black walls. I didn't see a single door. Demon magic coated the smooth surfaces. It didn't touch us or react as we passed, which made me uneasy.

Ahead of us, something skittered in the dark. "Spider demon," Emiron murmured.

Lily leaned past me to see. "They're easy to kill. Mat and I took out a bunch of them."

The look our new friend gave her was both speculative and respectful. "The spiders and the small rat-like creatures are low-level demons. It's the humanoid ones you need to worry about."

"We've banished a few of those, too."

He didn't speak until we started moving again. "Eliminating demons is a rare skill. Tell me again why you are not winning this skirmish?"

"Because some of our own teamed up with them, and you, to enact a coup," Drake said. "We won. You and this pocket realm are merely loose ends."

"Ah, an ancient dragon who still lies to himself. How unique."

When Drake's expanded aura almost choked me, I started to second-guess whether the contract with Emiron was a good idea.

We moved along in silence, stopping when we heard distant movement. The air became more stagnant, and the putrid sweet smell of death more pungent. The hair on the back of my neck raised, and I tried to pinpoint the crushing feeling of impending doom. Lily must have felt it, too, because she moved closer and pulled shadows around everyone except Emiron.

A rumble shook the ground, and I grabbed the waistband of Drake's pants to steady myself. "I don't like this." My voice was barely audible.

Nor do I. It feels like another trap. Drake's mind voice sounded almost subdued.

I don't trust Emiron and may regret making a deal with him.

The problem is not his intentions, but his knowledge. He isn't sure if this is a way out.

Our conversation ended when the ground shook under our feet.

I reached for Lily's hand, but she pulled it away. "If we fall, we'll break our arms. Or, if something creepy pops up, and it will, I can't fight."

The ground under our feet gave way, and we plummeted.

My hand slipped from Drake, and I flung my other one in his direction as I tumbled. Again. "This is stupid!"

Something flashed by my eyes. "Take it, Jenella."

I tried to stop spinning long enough to reach towards the voice. Our fingertips touched before our weight difference separated us, dragging him out of my grasp.

My ass bounced off something hard, and I slid down a slimy, wet surface at a breakneck speed. A thousand scenarios rushed through my mind. I fought to use my magic to stop the fall, but it bounced off the slippery goo coating the walls and dissipated. Not wanting to waste energy, I leaned back and crossed my arms over my chest.

"Damn fucking shitty bullshit slide." Lily's voice came from somewhere behind me.

"Be ready to fight." Cavil's command seemed to come from everywhere.

My back left the slide, and hot wind brushed my cheeks as I went into a free-fall. As soon as I spotted the platform below, I flashed. I misjudged the distance and smashed into something both hard and soft. Someone crashed into my back and rolled away while I lay there, stunned.

A hand reached down and yanked me to my feet. I shook my head to clear it and fought to reorient myself. When the room came into focus, I gasped. A legion of demons of all shapes and sizes surrounded the platform we stood on. To my left, Lily stood with her claws and fangs out, her eyes glowing. Cavil's white light surrounded her as he calmly examined our predicament.

To my left, Drake's skin gleamed with scales as he held Emiron in a headlock with one arm and steadied me with the other.

Our platform ascended. I braced myself until I realized I didn't need to. When I noticed the slime coating us, I used my anti-Jacques magic to dissipate it. The stuff felt like a lame attempt to dull our magic. Where it somewhat worked on me and Cavil, it slid off Drake's scales and didn't even faze Lily. But it did work on Emiron. Interesting. Since demons lacked critical thinking skills, I figured if I didn't advertise our anti-demon tricks, they'd never notice.

The platform came to a stop high above the demon horde. Drake yanked Emiron with him as we drifted closer to the center.

Another platform lowered, carrying five of the biggest, nastiest demons I'd ever seen. A gnarled gray finger, tipped in a putrid-yellow claw, extended towards Drake. "Unhand my pet."

The voice reverberated through my bones, and my knees almost buckled. I swallowed back the bile and lowered my head. "It's Jacques' other dad, I think."

Lily moved closer to me. "You met him?"

"He liked to torment me when I was a kid. I repressed it until..." I trailed off.

"Are you sure?"

"About seventy-five percent."

She considered the demon. "I remember Anitta meeting with a big, scary man a few times. It might be him."

I tried not to vomit. "If so, it means she summoned and worked with demons long before we were born."

"And he knows what we're capable of."

"No, he doesn't. Because we didn't even understand our capabilities until we went...to class."

The demon lost his patience with Drake's noncompliance and slammed a staff on his platform. A piece of the stone broke off, and one of his demons tumbled to the ground. It clamored to its feet and raised a fist with a series of grunts.

After a few seconds, the leader morphed into a dark-haired man with chocolate brown eyes. If I didn't have magic, I wouldn't have noticed the red sparks in them. He clasped his hands as if he were civilized. "Very well. It won't matter soon, because you will be dead." He flicked the rest of his entourage off the platform. "Before I kill you, we have some business to discuss. How are you, my sweet Jenella? Still tormented?" He licked his lips.

I kept my face neutral as a couple of awful memories surfaced. "I am neither sweet nor yours."

"Of course not." His laugh made my skin crawl. "How about you, Liliana? Fucked any excommunicated gods lately?" His overenthusiastic laugh echoed through the cave.

"All the time. As a matter of fact, I think we invented a new position the other day."

Cavil slapped a hand on her shoulder.

The humor drained from the demon's face. Demons weren't exactly sane to begin with, but this guy was so far gone it surprised me one of his buddies hadn't killed him and stolen his power. He rolled his massive shoulders. "I see you have a sense of humor. Pity."

"How long did you work with Anitta?" I kept my voice calm and authoritative.

"Anitta?" He snapped his fingers. "Oh, yes. That sweet piece of ass with the golden hair and dreams of grandeur." He smirked. "She gave me the best son. Someone took him from me." An evil glint flashed in his eye. "But I avenged him. Tell me, is Mathias resting well?" He burst into maniacal laughter again.

Drake and Lily squished me between them. "Who gave you permission to be in this realm?"

The demon straightened to his full height. "We do not need permission. But if we did, it wouldn't be hard. Send a few demons to a summoning, support your enemies, cause chaos, feed, repeat." He whirled his staff in circles. "There seems to be an abundance of paranormals willing to deal with demons. But summoning isn't necessary with an anchor in the realm."

"What kind of anchor?" Drake asked.

"I am not speaking to you, dragon!"

I cleared my throat. "What kind of anchor?"

"The kind your soft little heart won't allow you to kill." He licked his lips again. "I can send my legion of demons anywhere in this realm, and you can't block me. It's quite handy. You should ask my pet about the practice."

"This anchor allows you to build pocket realms?"

"No. This masterpiece was my idea. Brilliant, is it not?"

I refused to believe demons built the pocket themselves and were behind the entire coup. Though if Anitta had made a deal when she conceived Jacques, they would have demanded payment. I shuddered at the thought. But if she paid by creating the pocket, I could not only dissipate it, but also build a gate leading anywhere. I relayed the revelation to Drake.

While I was contemplating my mother's quest for power and trying to decide how to banish an entire legion of demons, the head demon seethed at my lack of reaction. "We have made promises to certain members of your society who still live. I had hoped you'd find and eliminate them for me like you did the others. But we can't always expect things to go our way. And now I must end your life."

Lily, who'd been examining every corner of the room and every demon in it, turned her attention to the leader. "You think you can best us, eh?"

His eyes flared with anger. "Are you challenging me, little halfling?"

I held up a hand. "Do you have more children in my realm?"

He shrugged. "Only anchors."

What in the hell did he mean? If not children, then I was right, and he'd collected enough souls to let him in. I read somewhere that very few demons could remove and hold souls. It made me sick. My eyes swept over the ones below. A few fights broke out, and the surrounding ones didn't bother to stop them. Most of the legion were lower level, except for the guys kicked off the platform. When my eyes landed on Emiron, an idea formed. I no longer wanted to escape until every demon left my realm, including the people who sold their souls to anchor them. “Distract him for a minute, Lily.”

When her eyes narrowed, I pointed at Emiron. She crossed her arms. “So the dumbass who called herself our mother summoned and fucked the ugliest, dumbest demon in all the twelve realms, had an anchor baby with him, and struck a deal to build a pocket?”

He flinched. “You are rather crude.”

“Yeah. It’s kind of my thing. Even after your demon spawn died, she kept summoning you until you got sick of her and sent her to her death. Am I right?” When he didn’t answer, she continued. “Being unable to maintain a presence here, you used her minions to keep summoning you and your legion of idiots. It’s a miracle that this pocket hasn’t imploded from the stupidity.”

I snuck a hand behind Drake’s back and touched Emiron’s shoulder. A second later, the oozing wounds on his ankles and wrists healed, and his muscles filled in. His eyes widened in shock, but he didn’t move. I leaned closer. “You destroyed Ferine.”

“Ferine?”

“A pocket realm.”

“No, no. I only provided the magic.”

The demon clenched his fists, his angry eyes locked on Lily. “I am the strongest demon in the twelve circles. You will not diminish my status!”

Lily shook her head in disbelief. “I doubt you’re even in the top five. Especially with all these weak ass fuckers following you. I should know, since I eliminated more than half of the ones you sent to enslave the hybrids.”

Another chunk of the broken platform broke off when he stomped his foot. The demons below squealed but didn’t dodge the debris. The lead demon didn’t even notice. “You will stop talking to me like I’m weak!”

“Struck a nerve, eh?”

His platform ascended. “Kill them and spill forth into the human world, my children. The time to feast is upon us.”

The second he was out of sight, our platform lowered. Drake grabbed Emiron by the scruff of the neck and yanked him to his feet. “Stay together and use every dirty trick you have.”

Chapter Thirty-Three

Three black blobs formed in strategic places among the mass of demons as I coated our group in anti-Jacques magic. It slid off Lily but stuck to the rest of us.

"I cannot use my best skills when coated in foreign magic. Release me from this shell," Emiron ordered.

"Sure." I wiggled my fingers, and it dissipated. "Cavil?"

"I am a god. Therefore, I am not vulnerable like the puny Gartolian."

Smiling, I tapped into my full strength.

Lily pulled me back. "You're our secret weapon. Let the rest of us work, then you can come in and flatten them."

"I doubt I can flatten this many."

"You can, but it will deplete your energy, so don't," Drake said. "If you must, wait for the right moment. Our buddy here can atone for his crimes by leading the charge." He squeezed the back of Emiron's neck. "Say you understand."

"No need for violence, dragon. I wish to be free of this place, so I will fight."

Smoke billowed from Drake's nose. "I will hold you to your word."

When the platform lowered enough for the demons to reach it, Cavil handed Lily a pair of dark glasses and crouched. "Protect your eyes."

I covered my eyes a second before he lit up like the sun.

Demons screeched and backtracked, trampling their friends. A few didn't move a muscle. The stronger ones revealed themselves as they shoved the weaker demons away and raced towards us.

Lily formed a box around one. When the whirring of blades started, I turned away. I'd seen enough of her methods in the last battle.

She took Cavil's hand. "I'll take a lap and plant some traps."

I boxed in a stronger demon and nodded. "Be careful." She disappeared.

Drake shifted into his snuffy form and swung his massive head toward me, and I flashed onto his back. As soon as I took my place, he picked Emiron up and tossed him over the crowd's head. The guy flipped at the last second, so his feet landed on the wall. He used it to keep his momentum going and threw a net of his odd magic towards a gaggle of demons with long orange snouts and stubby red arms and legs. They screamed and fell to the floor.

"The king has some moves," I said, as Drake turned toward the thickest part of the crowd.

I'm going to thrash through the crowd. See if you can unravel the pocket.

I wasn't sure I wanted to unravel it and set so many demons loose. "Not a good idea." I created an aura of anti-demon magic around us. I didn't sense Emiron's nets until our magic clashed. His net lit up with a silvery glow, while my mist turned bright yellow. My eyes widened as one of Lily's blobs rolled toward the two. Heart pounding, I pulled the anchors and tried to dissipate mine.

Emiron dove to the side as the three magics met. The mass of volatile, swirling, tangled magic swept around the room, knocking Drake off his feet and launching me from his back. I flashed at the last second and landed against his back leg. He twisted to protect me and his butt swung close to my face. "Wha!" I flashed to his front. "As much as I like your ass, that's gross."

When he didn't laugh at my quip, I refocused on the fight. All the weaker demons were on the ground. Small stripes of Lily's red magic swirled around them. Emiron's head was bleeding. Lily and Cavil huddled against a wall on the far side, surrounded by the more powerful demons. Cavil's light magic didn't repel them, but they were weakened.

I dug my hands into Drake's fur, preparing to flash their way. The floor shook, and I held on tight so I didn't fall. "What the hell?"

A hole opened in the ceiling, and a demon dropped through. His body looked like someone had mashed a bunch of those red glowing rocks together. He landed in a crouch, and his red eyes fell on me. His flat forehead tilted up, and a bone-chilling moan came through the single tusk that replaced his mouth. His hands and feet turned into whirling blades as his whip-like tail cracked above the other demons. He charged.

I formed a wall.

The demon stopped, sniffed it, and blew another grotesque tune through his horn. My magic shattered.

Drake morphed into his dragon form. His ear-splitting screech echoed off the cave walls as he wrapped his tail around me. The ceiling opened again, and several similar demons dropped around us.

Lily zipped around the original one, boxed him in, and sliced off his tusk. The creature melted to dust before the tusk hit the ground.

She pointed at me. "You gonna stand there with your mouth hanging open, or help me kill these fuckers?"

"Right." I sent a shredding spell towards the tusks of the closest ones. Drake bit off a head, spit it out, and shot a stream of green fire across the chamber. Several demons crouched in fear when he roared.

My anti-demon magic was useless against the stronger ones, but the lower-level demons didn't stand a chance, and several disappeared when I sent a blast of it through the crowd. Screams, groans, and battle cries echoed off the walls. I took advantage of the distraction to shred some tusks. As soon as a few of them turned to dust, I flashed through the room, trying to pelt them in their ugly, flat faces.

Strobe lights pulsed from Cavil as he glided through the room, his blonde hair coated in dust. His magic was so precise and effortless, it made me wonder if he was holding back. Burning pain tore down my right side as something heavy smashed into me. I fluctuated between using anti-demon and shredding magic until I realized it was the leader. I gripped his hair and flashed towards the wall, smashing us both against it three times.

His putrid sulfur breath blasted in my face when he laughed. "You are mine." He tried to push his claws into my stomach, but couldn't get past my barrier. When he turned to summon a demon with immunity, familiar magic swam across the wards. "Emiron! Now!"

My mother's magic barely registered as I picked at the threads. Unraveling them was too slow, and I couldn't rely on the Gartolian King. The demon sensed what I was doing and tried to pull me away. He made the mistake of using his nasty magic. I coated it with mine, injected unraveling intentions, and shoved the mass into the frayed web of pocket wards.

Emiron slammed into them beside me, his whole body glowing orange. "As per our agreement." His strange magic coated the wards as mine unweaved my mother's magic.

I didn't know what I expected to happen. But it wasn't a plume of sparkly dust, the scent of ozone and sulfur, and an entire mass of weaker demons squealing so loud they blew out my ears as the unraveling of the magic banished them. I landed hard on my back and raised my knee towards the leader's balls, but he was up and running before it connected. I coughed and sat up.

Drake stood a few feet away, naked and filthy. Lily crouched over an enormous pile of dust, her left hand clutched in Cavil's. Several demons littered the area, still stunned by the transition. Movement from the corner of my eye cleared my mind, and my senses came back online. A massive army of paranormals surrounded us.

I spotted Quin front and center, his sword in his hand. Beside him, Tracy held a large potion in one hand and weaved a spell with the other. Glacintial stood on his other side. Several members of my inner circle fanned out behind them. The group we brought with us, along with what I assumed were some local paranormals, dotted the perimeter of the green field, holding humans back.

"Now!" Tracy ordered.

Alex morphed into his lion form and bounded towards Lily, using his mental magic to drop demons as he went. Tracy flung the spell at the head demon as she sprinted towards me. Bastien lowered his massive black head behind her, drew in a breath, and lit up the ones who moved to stop her.

Quin vanished from sight, barely missing being crushed by Glacintial's tail. It didn't surprise me when he appeared in front of me. "Perhaps refrain from entering strange portals in the future."

"Great idea." I shredded one of the flat-headed demons who tried to sneak up on him. "How did you figure out where we'd land?"

"Tracy cast a location spell that led us here." He swung his sword so fast that the demon trying to grab me didn't have time to duck. "It is always Tracy who saves us."

True. If it weren't for her, the coalition would have fallen before we even killed Anitta. "We owe her our lives." I didn't get the chance to elaborate because Drake gathered the surrounding dragons and went on a rampage. A sharp tug on my chest came a second before green fire laced with my anti-Jacques spell coated the field. The demons immune to my magic lit up with fire as the other ones turned to dust.

Tracy flung her potion as she approached. "Take that, you stinky parasite!" She threw the bottle at a flathead one and weaved another spell. "Jen! Do the sleeping spell thingy! Cover us, Quin."

Without hesitation, I weaved my tried-and-true sleeping spell. The second she released hers, I added mine. Our combined magic smashed into a horde of demons and exploded. We didn't have time to celebrate before chunks of demons blasted us. I threw up a barrier a little too late and took Tracy's hand, desperately searching for a place to flash.

The Ogre Queens raced past us, clubs flying, using the same magic I'd felt in the palace while they were supposed to be breaking the curse. It made me pause and consider them. Human screaming pulled me out of my thoughts, and I flashed to where two demons had pushed past our line and dove into a crowd of human bystanders.

A bug-like demon had a man pinned by the shoulder with its razor-sharp leg. Two women beat it with their bags. I threw anti-demon magic into it and turned towards the thick, monkey-like one chasing people down the street.

Tracy released a spell, and it vanished. I took a second to flash around and heal everyone, and turned to the fight.

Demon dust coated the charred field. Paranormals of all types raced through it, collecting the stragglers. In the middle, a black void about two feet in diameter pulsated. I drifted towards it.

Tracy's hand landed on my arm. "It's how we found you. That thing was lodged in the grove of trees and felt like a pocket entrance. It's not demon magic. It's yours."

My forehead crinkled. "Not mine. Anitta's."

"Yeah. I mean, I think it's kind of like the controls to the gates of Allure. It's small and portable. It might even be how demons entered the pockets without us noticing."

I clenched my jaw as I tried to control my anger. Even dead, the woman still figured out ways to abuse us. After a few deep breaths, I shoved Tracy behind me, reached out with my magic, and blew the controls to pieces. The backblast smashed into us and we skidded into a group of humans who had already fallen on their asses.

The ground shook as I climbed to my feet and tried to help them. Drake and Bastien roared in unison as they approached. I swung my head towards them. "That better not be directed at me." I spotted Quin standing over the lead demon in his full vampire form, and his sword pressed to his neck. I stumbled towards him and stood over the guy. "What were you saying about us never winning?"

The demon's guttural laugh made my ears ache. "An illusion is always an illusion, even if you don't wish to acknowledge it."

My spine straightened, and I moved to face the crowd of humans.

"What did your mother call you? Oh, yes. I remember now. Fake queen. A failure. Useless." More laughter.

The dense crowd of humans shifted enough so that I spotted a group of humanoid demons in suits strutting towards a government building.

"My people will be well-fed for years. You can thank your incompetence and the lack of faith your people have in you."

I refocused on the demon. "This entire coup was a scheme to feed on humans."

"It wasn't even hard. Give Anitta what she wants, spread some rumors, recruit a disgruntled shifter king, feed some egos, and let the feast begin. They even helped me capture my pet and create anchors here. And you!" More grating laughter. "You and your overconfident brother were too stupid and inept to stop us. Cat and mouse. Cat and mouse. Too easy." His voice turned serious. "Now, it's too late. We're everywhere, and you'll never stop us." The demon melted into dust.

Quin had his sword at the neck of the culprit before it settled.

Drake held up his hands. "Jenella has far too many nightmares as it is. No need to pile on."

Heart pounding, I raised my head and zeroed in on the government building. Before my thoughts registered, I sprinted towards an opening in the crowd.

"Jenella, no!"

I ignored Drake's pleas to stop and the alarm he sent through the bond. When I made it through the crowd, I flashed to the sidewalk leading to the building and raced up the stairs.

"Gah!" I jumped back and would have fallen on my ass if Quin hadn't grabbed my arm.

"Perhaps a bit of thought is in order."

"I'm with Jen. Let's get those bitches," Lily said from behind me.

I climbed the steps and turned. Tracy stood next to Lily and a half-naked Alex at the bottom. Behind them, Cavil, Drake, and Bastien fought through the thick crowd of humans to catch up to us. The dragons wore nothing but sweats. Human women behind them swooned. One whooped out of her car window. I refocused on Quin. "Several demons are inside."

He didn't react for a beat. When he did, it was to open the door and wave me inside. "It seems there is no cure for your stupidity, so I shall embrace it."

It wasn't stupidity but determination pulling me forward as I stepped through the door. A large front desk manned by a woman in a business suit blocked access to the elevators. I steered our group around her.

"Ma'am. We're on lockdown, so you need to check in."

I paused. "Lockdown?"

Tracy read the directory. "They could be anywhere."

"I bet this is the ideal toxic workplace." Lily ran her hand over the names.

Alex moved towards the front desk. "Why are you on lockdown?"

The woman shook her head. "There's a disturbance down the street, and several men came into the building without clearance. I can't let anyone else through."

Lily appeared behind the woman and tapped her shoulder. My sister's eyes took on a slight glow. "You will direct us in the direction where the men went and take a nice, long lunch break."

The woman pointed to the elevator as she gathered her things. "Fourth floor."

After we piled into the elevator, Quin reappeared. "When using persuasion, one must be specific."

"I'll keep that in mind next time Jen takes us to a government building to slay demons." Lily pushed the button.

Quin didn't respond, but the respect rolling off him said he appreciated her snark.

When the doors opened, Alex arm-barred Tracy and me. "This floor stinks."

"It smells like their pocket." I peered out, but didn't see anyone. "I wonder if their anchors are places."

"Doesn't matter." Lily shoved Alex out. "It won't be an issue when we're done with them."

We found ourselves in an alcove between two offices with glass doors and long bureau names I didn't read. "They're to the left."

Quin pulled off his tattered suit jacket and tossed it in a corner. When his eyes met mine, the concern in them almost brought me to my knees. "Do not die." He vanished.

Chapter Thirty-Four

As we neared the door, the putrid scent of sulfur and unwashed bodies was so strong, I covered my nose to keep from gagging.

"Here." Tracy shoved a potion in my hand. "One drop to mute the smells."

I dabbed a drop on the end of my nose and gave it to Alex. "Thanks."

The reception counter had a gap torn through it. Papers were scattered and blood splattered across the walls. A woman in a business suit lay in front of it, unconscious and in a pool of blood. As we slid inside the door, her mask slipped to reveal a green, potato-shaped head with sharp, jagged teeth. It was gone so fast, I would have missed it if I blinked. "Demon," I whispered, as I zapped her into dust. If my senses were correct, we were about to encounter at least twenty more. I pointed to the right. "They're down there."

"Then let's go left first." Tracy began weaving a spell.

"There are only humans to the left, and they're scared." Alex peeked around the corner. "Let's evacuate them first."

Lily pushed past us. "I'll evacuate the humans. You two check the cube farm."

"The what?"

She pointed to the open area separated by cloth dividers. "The cubicles. Desks. Check under them and evacuate people."

Alex slunk around the corner. "I'm going with Lily."

Two heads popped up over the dividers, sheer terror reflecting in their eyes as Tracy and I made our way to the center aisle. "Evacuate. Take the elevator, not the stairs." When they didn't move, I pushed the command with a little power, and they scrambled to follow my orders.

As we made our way through the office, we found fifteen humans hiding. Some were brave enough to explain what they had witnessed. Apparently, the demons came in, took some high-level government officials hostage, and were holding them in the conference room.

We waited for Lily and Alex to catch up before we approached the door. When they did, Tracy weaved a spell. "How many humans, Alex?"

He shrugged. "Seventeen. Their thoughts are suppressed."

"Be ready." She tied off a spell I'd never seen before and released it. The thing floated to the solid wooden door. "Go!"

Lily flung the door open, and I hurled anti-Jacques magic towards a cluster of three demons. Before the dust from their banishment settled, I had a box around the humans, who huddled together in the middle of the room.

A dozen demons charged us. I formed a wall at the same time Lily did. A familiar roar from outside the building made me flinch. "Drake and Bastien."

Tracy pulled out a potion and uncapped it. "If Bas needs to break in and save me, I'll never hear the end of it."

"Insist he's nothing more than our backup. Even when he gloats in his arrogant way, say he was our Plan B. I'll declare it if you need me to."

A laugh bubbled out of her as she flung her potion in the face of a square-headed demon. "That will go over well."

I blasted magic towards a cluster of three demons and coated the dome protecting the humans. "If you don't want to go the manipulative route, there's always the butterfly option."

Another laugh. "You are such a good friend, Jen. But you can't fix our relationship. It's up to us, and we're at an impasse."

Lily created one of her death boxes around the remaining demons. "These are toast. But stronger ones are heading our way."

"We can't evacuate without putting the government officials in danger." I swiveled my head, looking for a way out. But there wasn't one. "We need dragons to help evacuate. I'm calling Drake." The second I told him where we were, a roar shook the building. We braced ourselves to keep our balance and sprinted towards the incoming demons.

Tracy opened a door marked 'authorized personnel only,' and I created a barrier as we charged inside. The demons lined the window in their human forms, a row of guys in expensive suits kneeling at their feet.

Alex clutched his stomach. "What they do to these humans is disgusting. You don't even want to know."

"No, I don't." I shuffled sideways while I tried to decide the best way to save the humans and expel the demons.

A dark-haired one stepped forward almost lazily. "Ah, I wondered if you'd discover our little secret."

An auburn-haired demon smirked. "It took you long enough." He kicked the man kneeling in front of him. "We were becoming bored with our toys. They're so fragile." He winked. "Unlike you."

Adrenaline shot through me, and I threw a wave of knockout magic in his direction.

He easily sidestepped and brushed off his suit. "That wasn't very nice."

I dissipated it before it hit one of the many dragons I sensed outside and created a box around the humans. The dark-haired demon leaned over to examine my work, and a sense of dread washed over me. It reminded me of the emotional fuckery in the pocket, so I surrounded it with love. "I'm not here to be nice."

His smile melted, along with his human persona. His height grew by at least two feet. Thick, curly horns grew on his head, and his face elongated. His eyes turned to slits and became almost snake-like, and his shoulders widened. He charged.

I braced myself as I threw a wall between us. Lily didn't hesitate to set a trap and add it to my magic. They merged and sealed, becoming strong and lethal. Silvery-black spikes jutted from it. Unfazed, the demon smashed into it. We backed up when the other demons joined him.

Lily shook out her hands. "These are even stronger than the cave demons."

"Yeah. We need Deva or Ara to banish them. They use ancient chants."

Heavy footsteps pounded down the hallway, and Tracy swung toward the door. "Brace yourselves!" She flung a potion.

The explosion knocked me forward, and I slammed into Alex. Lily caught herself and spun to help Tracy.

The demon horde slammed into our wall, and the anchors holding it cracked.

"Oh, shit." Lily's words barely registered before the wall exploded. I clung to Alex as Lily slammed into me, and we tumbled. Debris rained down around us, and I flung my free arm over my head.

A foot stomped next to my head, a split second before a scorching sensation spread through my side. I coated myself in anti-demon magic. Burning oozed from the demon's claws, as if it had injected some kind of venom. Gnarly gray teeth snapped in my face. I switched tactics and shoved shredding magic down his throat. When he reared back. I flashed to where I sensed Tracy.

She threw another potion at a demon with ten-inch claws. I grabbed her arm and flashed to Lily. Another one appeared the second we landed. His snake-like tongue snapped out, as if tasting the air. The guy's lumpy brown head was too small for his massive body and wobbled in strange ways every time he retracted his tongue.

"This fucker doesn't even have eyes," Lily said as she jammed a spear made of pure shadows through his chest. When Alex, now in his lion form, nipped at her elbow, she backed away.

The ugly lump tore the spear out, hissed, and charged.

Both hands shot up as I created a love-laced shield. He spewed venom.

As a group, we sprinted away. As we rounded the corner, I threw my arms out, intending to flash the second I touched everyone. Before I could react, sharp teeth sank into my shoulder, and pain ripped down my back.

Tracy screamed from somewhere nearby, and I started cycling through my magic tricks, trying to remove the thing before it crushed me.

A dragon roared so close that I recoiled. The demon's swollen hands latched onto the back of my neck and squeezed. I panicked. Raw silver power smashed into him, and a shrill scream joined another ear-splitting dragon roar. The demon's weight lifted, taking a chunk of my skin with it. As I stumbled to my feet, a steel band wrapped around my shredded ribs. I sensed dragon magic, so I beat at the arm.

"Will you knock it off?" I recognized the voice but couldn't place it. I stopped fighting when I saw the demon was on the floor in the fetal position. The one-eyed Ogre Queen stood over him, beating him repeatedly with a spiked club. "For the queen!" she yelled it like a war cry. A mage slid past her meaty foot, grabbed the demon's wrist, and began chanting.

The dragon pulled me away before I could see what happened next. I beat on his arm again. "Let me go. I need to find Tracy."

"No can do. If anything happens to you, Lily will never drink with me again. And don't get me started on how much pain your mate will inflict on my person." He dumped me in an empty cubicle, his red eyes glowing. "Stay."

I opened my mouth to argue, but a giant paw came out of nowhere and landed in the center of my chest. Alex's massive cat head lowered so our faces were only inches apart, and he growled.

"Don't you tell me what to do, Alex First."

"Holy hell. Will you quit your bitching?" Lily appeared beside her brother. A chunk of her hair was missing, and deep gouges ran across the side of her face.

The building shook as more roaring drowned out the sounds of fighting and human screams.

A blur came out of nowhere and slammed into my side. I crashed into Alex and grasped for his fur. His cat form was massive, but he couldn't stop our momentum. Red scales flashed when Flintous shifted into his dragon form. He straddled us as we tumbled as a group and bounced off his leg. He kicked us back under him and created an umbrella as debris rained down.

I extracted an arm from Alex and beat on Flintous's chest. "Let me go! I need to find Tracy."

A clawed hand casually covered my mouth. "Bastien has her." Quin wouldn't have tackled me unless he had to.

I coughed and buried my face in Alex's side to keep from breathing in dust. "Does anyone need healing? Or should I flash us out of here?"

Two nos and a warning growl later, the feeling of utter helplessness settled in, and tears sprang to my eyes. Visions of Mat dying to save me flooded my thoughts, and my breathing became shallow. I'd never forgive myself if I got Lily and Alex killed, too. My whole body shook uncontrollably, and my chest tightened so I couldn't breathe. To make it worse, Drake's fiery anger, mixed with fierce hatred, burned through the bond. I needed to help him.

I squirmed as I tried to find a way out from under the Flintous cage. Alex flung a paw over my chest, so I considered where I could flash, where I wouldn't hurt him. My brain shorted out from the added weight, mixed with Drake's utter hatred, and I wheezed.

"Jen." Quin's voice sounded like it came from the other end of a tunnel.

When I didn't respond, Alex sent images of a strong, fierce Jen into my head. I grabbed onto it with everything I had.

When I got my breathing under control, I patted his paw. "Thanks."

Quin tugged me in his direction. The lighting stressed his sharp features and deep lines around his tight eyes. "You once called me a good man."

"Because you are," I croaked, unsure why he made the statement.

"It takes great effort to fight my instincts."

"What?"

"When you made the statement, I could not admit I had improved for many reasons. I still deny it because of my base instincts."

It wasn't the best time for a story, but I trusted him. "Okay."

"My love and I have always watched over you. When you were in that wretched cage...."

"You were there?" A million explanations and accusations floated through my mind.

He bared his fangs in disgust. "I kept the worst of the dungeon rats away while I tried to figure out how to remove you from the situation without tipping off Anitta. When your sanity slipped, I regulated your memories with persuasion. It was I who helped Mathias kill Jacques and plan your escape. As you and Mathias fled for your lives, I slaughtered many pursuers. I have always watched over you and protected you, as if you were my child. It is one of many reasons you cannot die.

I swallowed and nodded, expecting him to clam up.

"When I witnessed the woman you were becoming, it occurred to me I would soon lose you to your power. I became your mentor to ensure permanence in your life. Those actions alone are enough to prove I am not a good man. Still, I would like to see you live despite your naivety. You are a queen, not a foot soldier or a detective, and it is time to behave like one.

Trust your people to handle missions. It is not your job to be the hero, but to lead the heroes."

The last words brought me back to reality. I caught glimpses of destruction raining down around us through our dragon umbrella. "I'm working on it."

"Do not lie to yourself. You have no desire to work on it. If you were, you would not have almost allowed your family and friends to be slaughtered while an army waited outside. Since you do not have an ounce of self-preservation, I beg of you to think of those who love you."

The rumbling stopped, and Flintous's red body lifted. He made a screeching sound and launched himself out the window.

Quin and Lily were already on their feet when Alex and I sat up.

Lily avoided eye contact. "Let's search the building."

Quin didn't even glance in my direction as they disappeared.

I used Alex's shoulder to climb to my feet. "Well, I guess he told me."

He sneezed and trotted after his sister as Drake's massive green head loomed inches away. He sniffed and bared his teeth in a smile. It was an attempt to lighten my mood. Although I appreciated his efforts, it didn't work. I flashed to his back and rested my forehead against my favorite spike. All the grief and pain and trauma poured out of me as a flood of tears trickled down my face. The first tear hadn't even fallen when Drake cloaked us.

When my emotions drained enough to function, I created a handkerchief and wiped my face, squared my shoulders, and patted his scales. "Thank you. Have I told you how much I love you?"

He uncloaked us and growled with frustration.

"Sorry." I stood and frowned at the building. The top floor was gone, and large stones and debris littered the ground below. "Who figured out how to banish the powerful demons?"

Deva and Ara passed along two ancient, banishing chants.

"But not to me or Tracy."

We didn't expect you to run off and take matters into your own hands.

"Liar. It's kind of what I do. Thanks for the save."

Drake shifted, and I flashed to the ruined office. "The demons had manipulated many government officials. Deva suspects the leader of their legion was among the ones we banished."

"Yeah." I didn't sense a single demon in the area, so I moved to the broken window and peered out. During our fight, human authorities flooded the area. "We don't have much time. Who's looking for the kids?"

"We have several teams searching."

Chapter Thirty-Five

Drake and I were almost to the ground floor in the stairwell when Sylphira fluttered towards us. "They're in the basement."

"Thanks." I picked up my pace. "Where are Lily and Alex?"

"They're the ones who found the kids. Lily and Cavil have requested pixie dust to break the locks."

A large group of paranormals clogged the hallway. When the two-eyed Ogre Queen spotted us, she shoved people aside. "Make way for the queen and the consort."

Those two were ass kissers. I thanked her as Drake tugged me through the crowd. We found Lily and Tracy with their heads together, arguing. Bastien leaned against a wall, his arms crossed and his eyes glowing. Cavil crouched near a blockade of mustard-colored magic that reeked of sulfur.

I headed in his direction, my senses on full blast. Several hybrids were behind the wall and intended to either escape or die. "Why keep the kids?"

Lily glanced my way. "Who, the demons or humans?"

"Both. The Bellicose leaders are gone, and very few demons can use paranormals as food. The ones who can prefer humans."

"Unless they were using them as currency," Bastien said.

"You think they're using hybrid kids as bargaining chips with the humans?"

"Not only hybrid kids. The Bellicose took anyone they thought vulnerable, including you, when they assumed you were a weak mage of Ahl."

The first demon we banished wasn't nearly as powerful as the ones we found there. "The demon in the pocket said they have anchors in this realm. I assume he meant humans who willingly gave up their souls."

Cavil stood. "He also said he learned to anchor from the warmonger Emiron."

"It doesn't help us recover our kids." Lily motioned towards the nasty magic. "Any ideas on how to break through this stuff?"

"I mean, it's not so different from their usual magic." Tracy placed a spell at the bottom corner. It bounced off and dissipated. "With extra protection."

"Let me see if I can reverse it." I hovered my hand a few inches from the barrier.

"Be careful, Jenella." Drake's frustration with me was apparent in his tone.

"I'm careful. Be ready, Tracy." It wasn't only demon magic. I closed my eyes and concentrated on dissipating it. With a whoosh, the protective layer vanished.

The second it was gone, Tracy unleashed another spell. The demon magic shuddered, and the center melted. As soon as it did, remnants in the corners started weaving themselves back together.

I moved closer. It didn't move towards me as it fought to reform. When I zapped it, it dissipated. "It has some of the same qualities as bug magic. Demons are not the most creative beings."

Bastien dropped his arms. "Which means someone more innovative has been working with them. Someone who can withstand manipulators and accomplished liars."

"Emiron?" Lily asked as she stepped beyond the barrier.

"Possibly. Or someone we haven't met yet."

Lily shrugged and appeared before the first door. "They can't hide forever. How many do you sense, Jen?"

"At least fifty kids spread throughout the basement." I motioned down the corridor. "More in that direction."

Alex shifted. "Does anyone have clothes?"

Cavil handed him a set of electric blue sweats.

Lily ignored the exchange. "These locks are magic, too."

"Hang on." I raced to the door and peered out. One of the many dwarven princes leaned against the wall as he cleaned blood and demon ash off his axe. "Can you help us with some locks, please?"

Razazia pushed through the crowd with Gorman on her heels. "Perhaps we can help."

I tried not to scowl at a squeaky-clean Gorman. "Sure. Ask the local pockets to send architectural mages to repair the building. We need dwarven magic to help us inside."

Razazia's eyes flicked towards Gorman for a split second, and a shrewd expression settled on her face. "Of course."

The dwarven prince squared his shoulders and marched forward. "Prince Lancaster, at your service." He slid past everyone and leaned over the lock. "It's a mixture of witch and dwarven magic. Stand back in case it blows."

Drake blocked me, and I leaned to peer around him. Lancaster touched the keyhole, and a buzzing sound, followed by loud clicking, echoed through the basement.

The second the lock gave way, the door burst open. Paranormals poured out, magic at the ready. One threw a spell at Tracy that she blocked. Another tried to fling magic at Lily, but it rolled off her.

Cavil's glow almost blinded me.

My ears rang when a roar tore through the basement. Bastien stomped towards them. "Line up against the wall and do not attack my mate."

The bravado drained out of the group. A few of them shook as they complied. A witch peed his pants.

"Not kids," I mumbled. Of the ten, only two were hybrids. The rest were shifters and witches. Most likely, Bellicose soldiers who the demons exploited. I scooted around Drake and followed the Dwarven Prince to the next room, creating a shield between the door and my friends.

Alex sneezed. "This group stinks."

Drake swung the door open the second Lancaster picked the lock. Inside, humans in various states littered the room. The stench of body odor and human excrement assaulted my nose, along with the faint tinge of sulfur. "Not entirely human."

Drake inclined his head. "Weak demon magic. These may be the anchors."

"I doubt their the only ones." It didn't make sense to keep their keys to the realm all in one place.

As we worked through the basement, we found a mixture of paranormals. There were so many that we had to enlist help from the crowd in the corridor to sort through them. A few hybrids were mixed in, but none were kids.

The Dwarven Prince paused near a solid brick wall. "There's no door here."

"I can sense hybrids just beyond the bricks."

"There's no door and no magic." He examined the ceiling. "If I dissolve the bricks, the building may come down."

Bastien pushed me aside a bit too hard. "What if we remove them slowly and reinforce the ceiling with magic?"

"Magic will hold it for a while, but it isn't a long-term solution. It would be safer to enter through the adjacent building.

"We can't. It's crawling with human authorities," Drake said.

"Then I need my brothers and the queen to reinforce it. When the recovery is done, we'll rebuild."

More dwarven princes arrived and slowly removed the bricks. After several minutes of watching them work, I grew impatient and infused the top ones with a solid ward.

Leebol chuckled. "Inventive as always, Queen Jenella."

When they cleared enough bricks, Lily disappeared inside and returned. "Three doors. One is on this end, and the others are further down. Hybrids in all three, and the doors are guarded by the same weak magic I sensed in the building I destroyed."

We filtered into the hallway. Bastien nudged us aside and kicked the first one. The metal doors bent, but didn't break. Before he could recoil, Lily charged, leaped with an unnatural grace, and drove her feet into the dent. It crashed open, and she shot him a smug look.

Childlike shrieks came from inside the room, and I leaned past Lily to look inside.

The room was massive. Several kids peered at us from the wall-to-wall bunk beds crammed on one side. Cribs lined the other wall. A coven of emaciated witches cowered in a group in the center play area, their hands up.

My stomach soured when I spotted a giant-troll hybrid baby, not even a year old, sleeping on the hard floor. The anger I'd worked so hard to eliminate ignited, and I saw red.

Drake's arm snaked around my waist. "No time for anger."

I took a deep breath to calm myself. It didn't work. I glanced towards the paranormals who'd followed us in. The dwarven princes stood in front, blocking others from entering. Quin stood behind them, rubbing his chin. "Have Deva summon the kids. Take the adults to the closest transport station. Don't lose track of a single person." I shook Drake loose and stormed out.

Tracy followed me. "Where are you going, Jen?"

"To put an end to this bullshit right now."

She tugged my arm. "There are still two more rooms."

When my glowing eyes settled on her, she flinched. "The humans need to learn about the consequences of dealing with demons." Drake and Bastien blocked the doors, not allowing anyone in or out, including me. I would have flashed away, but something about the look on Drake's face made me check the bond. He was pissed. *Why are you annoyed with me?*

Because you charge into situations without thinking and never consider how it may affect the people who care about you. If you wish to confront the humans, send an envoy, but you do not need to take on the task alone. Especially not when you're angry.

A stab of grief replaced my anger as I formed a privacy spell around us. "You sound like Mat."

"Perhaps he was right to remind you of your importance. Because I don't believe you understand what your loss would mean to the world. To me." His face fell. "I thought I lost you when our bond cut off."

I knew the feeling. It wasn't so long ago that I thought he had died. "We need to end this now."

"If we try, it will not go well. The human authorities outside are already scheming about how to trap and kill us. And now you want to hand yourself over to them before we even secure the children."

"Don't lay that shit on her," Lily said as she slid past the privacy barrier, dragging Alex with her. "Jen has done nothing but fight for the coalition, even though you treat her like a child incapable of making sound decisions. Even my dad is impressed at how hard she fights. And believe me, impressing him isn't easy."

"She takes too many risks."

Lily flung her hands out. "Life is a fucking risk, you overgrown lizard. Besides, you like that about her." She squeezed my arm. "My sister is a badass bitch and rarely reads a situation wrong. If you can't handle her badassery, there's the door." Lily stabbed her finger towards the exit.

"Erm." I tried to squirm away from her, but she tightened her grip. "I don't think Drake means to..."

Alex tossed an arm across my shoulders. "Maybe if you people supported her efforts, rather than underestimating and doubting her, this whole coup would have ended a year ago."

Tracy nodded in agreement. "Jen's impulsive actions have saved a lot of people. Or did you forget how she almost died saving your aunt?"

"I didn't forget. Nor have I ever doubted her skills."

"Never?" I asked. "What about how I'm not making decisions fast enough one minute, but too impulsive the next? Or how I should stop and think things through, but still be my impulsive self?"

"Being effective as a leader is about balance."

Lily pulled me away. "Then you should work on your balance and stop acting like she's incompetent. Come on, Jen. Let's find the other kids."

I dissipated the privacy bubble. "The power I feel is coming from the right."

Quin met us at the door. "Separating deep inside enemy territory is not wise."

"I agree," Cavil said. "Deva has secured the children and is ready for the next group."

"Thank you." I sensed twenty kids inside. None were in duress. I said as much.

Drake reached around me and broke the lock. "It's not magical."

As the others disappeared inside, I glanced at the people who crowded the hall, watching us. I didn't sense a single demon. The humans we rescued from the conference room were in the crowd. "What are we going to do with them?"

"Nothing." Drake's eyes glowed as he assessed them. "Some hold high-level positions in the government. Rescuing them may be our chance to negotiate."

"Have them taken to their authorities and start clearing our people out. Send them back to Ferine to help with recovery."

Tracy pulled me through the doorway. The conditions were much better. The central part of the room was a playroom designed for kids. A counter to the right held large containers of water and a cloudy substance, which I assumed was lemonade. Several alcoves with comfortable furniture and bright colors lined the walls. About twenty children occupied them, playing video games or with toys.

A door to the right stood open, revealing a bedroom with bunk beds. Unlike the demon area, the kids were treated well.

"Jen! I told them you'd come for us. No one believed me." Tasha sprinted from a room on the left, and I barely had time to drop my barrier before she embraced me. "You came."

I hugged her back. "We've been looking for you forever. Where's Olivia?"

"I'm here." Olivia stood at the edge of an alcove as if protecting the younger kids beyond. "They take our blood and do scans. One man insisted I shift, but I didn't. We would have left if we could have taken all the babies."

Drake moved in her direction. "You did the right thing by staying. Gather the kids." When she didn't move, he leaned down, so he was on her level. "Please."

She shrugged and turned to a group of smaller children playing with toys. "We're leaving. Come with me." She took the hands of the two youngest ones.

We searched the rooms, but they were sparse. There weren't even spare clothes in the bedrooms. The second we joined the kids, the summoning sucked me backwards and the sense of being stretched like taffy started.

Dark spots danced in front of my eyes after we landed. The summoning room was massive and packed wall-to-wall with the bodies of kids and my army. I shook myself free and flashed into the control room.

Deva grinned. "Hello, love. Welcome back."

"Will you help sort them out? I'll send some griffins and healers over to care for the kids, if you don't mind."

"Of course." Her head whipped towards the door. "Should you wish to escape your argument, I suggest you leave now."

"Thanks. I'll be back later."

"I'm sure you will." I flashed to the palace.

Chapter Thirty-Six

WITH OUR LITTLE DISAGREEMENT came the realization that I didn't have a clue how to communicate when all I wanted to do was punch someone. It renewed my urge to run away, which was impossible when bonded to a dragon. So I did the next best thing. I went to my sister's house and dragged her to the bar.

I sipped my drink and squeezed the glass to keep from throwing it out of frustration. "Why couldn't I have fallen for a nice mage or a harmless deer shifter?"

Lily's face puckered as she tasted her beer. "Because you'd never respect a match that wasn't powerful and dangerous. Though matching with a First was a little much."

True. I gulped down my vodka tonic and admired the bar. "I love this place."

Flintous tossed some peanuts in his mouth and leaned around Lily, his red eyes so serious that I flinched. "I hope you don't expect me to protect you when he shows up."

"I don't need anyone's protection, especially not from Drake. But thanks for offering."

June's purple eyes flashed as she elbowed me. "Don't let all the fake concern fool you. Flint is only worried about saving his own ass."

"I'm not fighting a First, either," Elsie, Lily's second and self-appointed guard, said.

I pushed my glass away with a sigh. "No one's asking anyone to fight Drake. Can we talk about something else?"

Alex strolled through the door, waved at Dale, and slunk to our table. "Hey, Jen. What brings you to Eldritch?"

"She's moping," Lily answered for me.

"I am not."

"Are too."

Alex held up his hand. "Never mind. How are the kids doing?"

"Some are doing better than others. The ones the humans bought were treated well. The others need more time. Dale is working with our mental healers to help them. The Firsts have taken in the ones who are part of their factions."

"What were the humans doing with them?"

"The kids gave us mixed answers when we asked. Razazia took some laptops. It looks like the demons were kidnapping the kids and selling them to the government. The rogue hybrids tried to circumvent them, but we found their operation before they could. Dale believes we've found most of them, but your mom is double-checking."

Alex frowned. "Let's hope there isn't another pocket of demons." He thanked Darla when she dropped off his drink. "What about the government? The media says they're baffled."

"We sent them a detailed explanation and offered to meet. They haven't responded. I plan to descend on the highest authorities if they don't contact us soon."

June pointed at Alex. "Ask her."

Alex shifted his weight. "Now's not the time."

"Ask me what?"

"Since the magic poisoning, Alex has been different." Flintous tapped the table. "He has questions we can't answer."

My eyes narrowed. "Different how?"

Alex pointed at his friends. "It's not your business." He spun his glass. "I keep having dreams of flying. When I wake up, I'm naked and my skin is too hot. Like a human fever, only more intense."

I leaned forward. "You think you're shifting in your sleep?"

"No. I think I'm glamouring in my sleep."

"You're a quarter dragon, so creating glamour is normal. You should see if you can do it while you're awake." I motioned to June and Flintous. "These two can guide you."

"Dreams of flying are also common, but usually end with shifting," June said.

I wondered how that worked, but didn't ask. "You might want to ask Deva."

Alex closed his eyes. "I'll text her. It wasn't a big deal until Flint found out."

"He's a dragon, dummy, so he understands more about it than you," Lily said.

Shouts outside the bar interrupted our conversation. Dale snapped a towel onto his shoulder and pointed at me. "You better corral that big son of a bitch before he trashes my bar."

"He's not going to ruin your bar," I said with confidence I didn't have.

Drake strode through the door, anger and frustration radiating off him in waves. His eyes bore into me and flared as he stomped in our direction.

Flintous and June scrambled away from me as he approached. Lily spun her chair around so she could launch from it more easily.

I held out an arm to stop them. "Don't."

Drake ignored everyone at the table except me. "You're avoiding me."

"I'm having a drink with my sister. Besides, I'm not the one who didn't come home last night."

His eyes narrowed. "Because you locked me out."

"Semantics."

"Petty."

"And satisfying." I stood. "What do you want, Drake?"

Pain flashed through his eyes. "Better communication, for starters."

"No can do. I'm too busy making terrible decisions without thinking. In my spare time, I'm looking for new shoes." I shook my head. "They wear out fast when you drag your feet."

"That's not what I said."

Lily chuckled. "Not my business, but it's almost exactly what you said."

Alex sipped his soda. "You purebloods never give Jen credit, even though she's accounted for or woken all but one First, began healing the scars caused by the anti-hybrid movement, and ended a decades-long coup."

"I didn't do it alone. It was a team effort."

Lily kicked me under the table. "It boggles the mind."

My heart warmed at their defense. "Several leaders despise me for how I've handled things. But I never expected my match to join in the hate fest."

"I don't hate you." He pulled out June's abandoned seat and lowered himself into it.

Darla rushed over and set a plain glass of water in front of him. "Would you like another drink, Jenella?"

I grinned as I sat. "Please."

Drake stared at the glass. "Is the drink some kind of insult?"

"Hard to tell with Darla," Lily said. "If Dale served it, I'd say yes."

"It should be," I added.

He took a sip. "I thought I lost you and haven't felt fear like that in a very long time. I apologize for being overly critical."

"At least you didn't have to watch me die while being attacked by a dinosaur shifter with an over-inflated ego."

"I didn't die."

"No, but it looked like you did at the time. Did I criticize every little thing you did afterwards out of fear? No, I did not. Not even when you whisked me away at the worst possible time. But you don't see me taking it out on you, even though Verity will never let me forget it."

"I already apologized."

"And I heard you. Doesn't mean I'm done being mad."

"And hurt," Alex added. "Jen counts on you and Tracy to always be on her side."

Drake studied him for a beat too long. "You allow him to read your thoughts?"

"There's no stopping Alex from reading my mind, so why bother trying?" A fresh drink appeared, and I thanked Darla. "It's kind of like how I came here to escape, yet you found me."

"You're my mate. It's not the same."

"Says you."

"You're being purposely difficult."

"Yes. It beats admitting I gave you the power to rip my heart to pieces."

He sighed and sipped his water. "It wasn't my intention."

"Bullshit." Lily leaned forward. "You want to stuff her into a box the same as every other asshole in her life. The only difference between them and you is that you're better at making it look like it's Jen's idea."

He didn't explode in anger at her accusation, to Drake's credit. Instead, he considered her for a few seconds. "Untrue. I only want the best for Jenella."

Elsie, who hadn't reacted to our too-public argument, rested her elbows on the table. "You only care about the dragons. Always have. Jen has given them everything you've ever wanted and more." She pointed at him. "Or did you forget I was present for most of your discussions with Mistress Ara and Queen Deva?"

The table went silent, and tears burned my eyes. I struggled to blink them back. "You used me?"

"Of course not." The guilt flowing from our bond told a different story.

My mind raced through every single conversation we had about it. He never once pushed me in a direction. Still, because of him, I felt comfortable elevating their status. When I met his eyes, every single betrayal and lie over the last several years exploded through my head, and I shook so hard that the entire table vibrated. Worse, the bubble forming in my chest told me my magic was about to explode. "I need to leave before I wreck Dale's bar." I threw a couple of hundred-dollar bills on the table and flashed away.

I landed in the main flashing circle in Allure and took my time picking my way past the crowds. Several people greeted me and I tried to nod at them, even though I couldn't bring myself to smile. Before I registered where I was going, I found myself at the deli.

Thaddeous didn't call out a greeting like usual. Instead, he took one look at me, named a sandwich, and began making it while I stood there in silence. He said something to his daughter and motioned me to follow him to a table. After I sat, he pushed the food closer to me. "Go on, then."

"Thank you, Thaddeous." I took a bite to appease him. "You said I was lucky."

He tipped his hat. "Yes, I did. And I meant it."

"I feel more used than lucky these days."

"The perils of being queen, I suppose."

I didn't respond. We weren't close enough for me to dump my baggage on him. I stared at the door, wondering if I should have tracked Tracy down. "Sorry. I'm a little off today."

"You're heartbroken, is what you are. What broke your lucky streak and your confidence?"

"I can't talk about it here."

He ran his hand over his beard. "May I be honest, missy?"

"Might as well."

"You are a kind soul in a ruthless position. The world always tries to break those who are lucky enough to have deep empathy for others. No matter who or what has hurt you, fight it. Don't let this world harden your heart so much that you become indifferent or cruel."

"That's easier said than done."

"Being kind in a vicious world is a struggle for everyone. But it is crucial to keep the luck balanced. Don't tell anyone I said so, but it's even more important than gold." He patted my hand and stood. "Eat and go find your friend."

I didn't find Tracy. Instead, I wandered through several districts, greeting people and listening to them when they stopped me. I loved spending time with paranormals. And it beat running away and wallowing in my problems. Eventually, I ended up at Mat's grave. I sat there for a long time in silence.

Anger burned inside me as I thought about my current predicament. "You didn't need to sacrifice yourself. All those times you lectured me about how important I was to the coalition, and you never once realized your own worth? That's total bullshit! You left us on purpose and never considered what it would do. Emine's a shell of her former self, and I'm barely holding on. We loved you, and you just hopped through the escape hatch without considering what it would do to us." I stood and pointed at his grave as if he were standing there. "Fuck you, Mat! Fuck you and your sacrifice and for leaving your match without a second thought. And fuck you for not being here when I need you most. You didn't need to die like that!"

I sensed Drake hovering nearby, but didn't acknowledge him as I stormed away. After thinking it over, I realized Elsie's accusations were from a skewed perspective. Sure, Drake cared about the dragons. His loyalty was part of the reason I loved him. It didn't mean I was done being mad. And I could end the criticism I received from the leadership council with a flick of the wrist. But I chose not to. It was their right to have an opinion, even if I disagreed with it. Same as Drake. Their open criticism made me tame my selfish tendencies, which made me a better person and queen.

Mentally exhausted, I flashed back to the palace. I didn't lock Drake out, nor did I respond when he slid into bed, pulled me close, and kissed my forehead.

Two green jewels greeted me the next morning when I woke. Drake hadn't slept again. He leaned forward, and his soft lips brushed across mine. "Good morning."

I rubbed my eyes. "When did you become a morning person?"

"I've been awake, thinking."

"You should sleep more often."

"So, you say." He paused. "Am I allowed to apologize now?"

"No. Because you didn't do anything wrong." I wiggled out of his arms. "When you first explained our bond, I warned you I was a hot mess, but you refused to listen."

"You've come a long way since then, and our argument wasn't your fault."

"Correct. But my reaction to the argument was terrible." I swept my hair away from my face. "I wish Mat had told me the truth about so many things. But more than that, I wish I had listened to him when he explained the perils of ruling. And now I can't talk to him." A tear slid down my cheek, and I swiped it away. "The decisions I'm presented with are usually equal to choosing piles of shit, and someone is going to be mad no matter which pile I choose, including you. But I won't stop doing what I think is right for the coalition. I'll just need to learn to live with the consequences of my decisions."

"I fail to see where diving into danger is good for the Coalition."

"It's not. But when I saw those demons, I had to do something."

"And you chose the pile of shit that pissed me off."

"Not on purpose. Quin was pissed, too. He confessed to protecting me my entire life. All those missing memories from my childhood are because he tried to minimize my trauma."

Drake's head lifted, and fire lit in his eyes. "That crotchety old vampire stole your memories?"

"Yep. And he can keep them. The stuff I do remember is bad enough, and I'm no longer interested in living in the past."

"You will need to work through it at some point."

"Sure." I slid out of bed. "But not today. Today, I need to visit Ferine and pay respects to the paranormals who died when it collapsed. Then, I plan to persuade the U.S. government to meet with me." I stopped at the bathroom door. "Even if you don't like it."

"Believe it or not, I agree with you on the matter. But you shouldn't race off by yourself to solve the problem."

"Uh, huh."

"If you plan to invade their territory, I will go with you." He slid out of bed and ran a hand through his hair. "Before you learned about our bond, I watched you often, while I puzzled through how I would fit into your life."

"You fit."

"What I learned is that you don't need me. No matter what obstacles you face, you will always handle them without help. Even though you have given me a worthwhile purpose, I still struggle to make myself relevant."

My arms were around him before he finished speaking. "I need you in more ways than you know. Without you, I'd still panic over every little thing and view my title as a cage. No one else could ever understand and support me like you do." I pulled back. "You're my rock and my soft place to fall. No one is more relevant to me than you. But that doesn't mean I'll agree with you about everything or handle our arguments better."

His lips brushed across mine. I sank into the kiss, savoring the love and trust flowing between us. Drake lifted me off the floor, and I wrapped my legs around him. We devoured each other as he somehow maneuvered to the bed. When my back hit the mattress, he broke the kiss. His emerald eyes burned with desire as he met mine. "You have healed me, too, Jenella."

Chapter Thirty-Seven

"You're late." Verity trailed me to my office.

"I'm the queen. My schedule is what I say it is."

"As Lily would say, 'har har.'" She shoved a tablet into my hands. "Who is that guy?"

A picture of King Emiron stared back at me. "He's the King of another realm."

"The warring realm?"

I nodded.

She slammed her hands on her hips. "Well, isn't that just peachy?"

"So, you figured it out."

"I look just like the guy!"

I sighed and lowered myself to a chair. "It doesn't mean he's your dad."

"Oh? Deva said his magic feels like my oath breaker power. At the very least, I'm related to him."

I didn't dare tell her my theory. "If you want to meet him, I'll go with you."

Her eyes narrowed. "What aren't you telling me?"

"Nope. Whatever I say will shape your impression of him, so I'm keeping my thoughts to myself."

Verity dropped her hands to her sides. "This is too much."

"And not something you should have discovered from a picture on a tablet."

She took a deep breath. "Let me think about it. If I decide to meet him, I'm taking an army with me."

"I'll send all three divisions if it makes you feel better."

She strode toward the door, letting out a ragged laugh. "You would. You might want to check your messages. Travis has been blowing up my phone."

Fifteen messages and six texts, all from Travis, waited for me. I read the texts but didn't bother listening to the voicemails. They all stated that a high-level U.S. government official had contacted us.

Travis came through the door a few seconds later, his suit disheveled and his hair sticking up. "Where have you been? This is big."

His arrogant tone irritated me, and it took quite a bit of self-control not to slap him down. "I saw your many texts and messages."

"But did you read your email?" He pointed at the tablet on my desk. "I sent a report."

Drake appeared at the adjoining door. He didn't come inside, nor did he make any noise. Instead, he crossed his arms and waited.

I bit back a smile as I scanned my email. Travis had forwarded an invitation from the U.S. Secretary of State's office, inviting us to a meeting in three days. The details were vague, but the time and place were clear. "They didn't reveal what they want to discuss."

"Take the meeting. Some officials are calling for your arrest for wrecking those buildings and killing innocent people. It's a PR nightmare."

I waved a dismissive hand. "The building has been repaired. We only banished demons, and not one innocent person was hurt. We have observation spells showing how we protected them, so you should already be ahead of the story."

"They don't believe in demons. Even the news is reporting how we killed people and incinerated the bodies. You need to clear this up fast."

I set the tablet down. "Flood the internet with the observation spells showing them shifting into their true forms. Explain how demons work. Give humans pointers on how to spot them."

"Take the meeting."

"I'll think about it."

When Travis turned to leave, he almost ran right into Drake's chest. Drake leaned down to meet his eyes. "Do not tell Jenella what to do."

Travis froze, as if he were prey, before nodding. "My apologies, Consort. I have videos to make."

The big, bad dragon winked at me. "When do we leave?"

"We can flash to the closest pocket on the meeting day and drive from there. The question is, who do we take with us?"

"Too many and we'll look weak. Too few and we look arrogant."

"Agreed. Let's bring four people who understand diplomacy and can help if it's a trap."

Drake glanced towards the window. "Ara, Deva, Calvin, and Razazia."

"Ara, Calvin, Razazia, and Cavil."

"Too many C's."

"What do names have to do with diplomacy?"

"Nothing."

"Ara, Jonas, Cavil, and Razazia."

"Razazia likes to cause trouble."

"Then we substitute Olwen."

He paused, the humor draining from his face. "Olwen is among the missing in Ferine."

I flew out of my chair. *"What?"*

He sighed. "Glacintial is there looking for him. The recovery has been slow."

Without a second thought, I flashed us to the area where the entrance to Ferine was located a few days earlier.

So many paranormals guarded the garage that I had to pull my senses back. The dragons guarding the rubble of the building stepped aside. What looked like a picture-perfect garage from outside the wards turned into a big pile of blackened rubble as we crossed through.

Mages and Dwarfs worked together to sort through the destruction. An enforcer spotted us and raced to greet us. "Your Grace, Consort. What can we do for you?"

"How many are missing?" I asked.

Utter devastation radiated from him. "Seven hundred and sixty-two are missing. We can't find the outer wards of Ferine or any deceased. We've switched strategies and are looking for sparks of magic that might give us a clue as to where they went."

There were no sparks of magic. Nor were there any living paranormals, aside from the rescue crew and guards. "Do we know what caused the implosion?"

"We don't believe it imploded. It's more like someone stole it."

Beside me, Drake shifted his weight. "Stole it how?"

"Unknown. Several witnesses said they saw a shimmer. The gate exploded, but not the pocket. We've launched a worldwide search."

I thought back to what happened when it exploded, and hoped he was right. After all, I saw the shimmer. "I might have an idea about how to find it. My assistant, Pablo, will contact you."

He bowed. "Thank you, Your Grace."

I flashed back to my office.

I struggled to stay focused as everyone argued. It was a difficult task with Ferine missing. My advisors all wanted to meet with the government. It wasn't the worst problem, but it didn't help me choose who to take. And all I wanted to do was wrap up loose ends from the coup and find answers about the demons. But we had to meet with the government, too. So, I shoved everything else aside. "Each of you can contribute in a unique way. But only four can go."

Deva shook her head. "Untrue, love. Tarquin, Ara, and I can remain unseen."

Tracy raised her hand, then lowered it. "My dad and I can also use potions to hide a few of us."

Drake leaned forward. "Emine needs to stay here and relay information between us and the tech mages. Jonas, you still have too many new shifters to leave them unsupervised. So, you two stay behind."

"Nope." Emine's eyes lit with crazy. "If Jen's going to stir up some shit, I'm going. It's been way too long since I've had fun."

I grinned. "Humans have strange ideas about gender. Devious me wants to take only women to spite them. Diplomatic me says take two women and two men."

Ara folded her hands. "It is odd to be considered diplomatic, rather than deadly and violent."

"We're all deadly and violent," Jonas pointed out. "But so are humans. What's your ultimate goal, Jen?"

"To reach a peace agreement where we coexist. Our kids shouldn't fear being snatched off the streets by demons and forced into some secret government program."

"We need to ensure the demons can no longer enter our realm. I've assigned five army platoons to search for their anchors," Drake added.

"The humans don't see us as equals. We are merely tools to them." Cavil tapped Lily's fang, which hung from a chain around his neck. "If the government didn't recognize the threat we presented when they took Lily and Alex, they do now. You may need a larger entourage."

Good point. "What do you think, Quin?"

"It is unwise to disregard valuable skills in the name of diplomacy."

That's how we ended up with my entire advisory committee, plus Bastien, Lily, and Alex, riding on a human plane to meet with government officials. The amount of power in the aircraft made my hair stand on end.

Cavil and I flashed everyone to a pocket called Misset just outside Chicago, Illinois, and we flew the rest of the way. It wasn't a long flight, but also not an experience I wanted to repeat.

Several government officials waited on what the pilot we hired called a tarmac. We agreed that the Firsts, Ann Marie, and Cavil would descend the steps ahead of Drake. Then me, Emine, and Tracy. Quin, Ara, and Lily would stick to the shadows and scout ahead. Deva cloaked herself so she could follow us in and snoop through the building. Alex planned to stay with the plane to ensure no one messed with it and call in backup if we needed it.

When Drake reached the tarmac, he tried to pause and wait for me, but a man rushed forward to greet him. "Welcome, sir. Or should I call you Alpha?"

Jonas's low growl made Emine snicker as she joined him and Razazia. When I stopped to examine the man, Tracy shoved me towards the group.

Drake took his time answering. "I'm not an Alpha, no."

The man nodded. "I heard you were more of a king." When I moved to stand beside Drake, the man glanced my way and dismissed me. "Will everyone join the meeting?"

"We don't waste resources." Drake's answer was intentionally cryptic.

"Of course. But perhaps your wives could wait outside?"

It wasn't the first time a human leader had dismissed me, but it sounded almost patronizing the way he said it.

Drake wasn't nearly as forgiving of the dismissal. He pulled me closer. "Jenella is not my wife, nor is she to be dismissed."

"Right. And the rest of the...your group? Will they be joining us?"

Razazia sniffed as she butted into the small circle. "Perhaps I can assist with this."

Excitement bubbled inside me to see what she'd come up with, so I inclined my head.

"We are a power-based society. This means that unless you can sense power, you don't know who the deadliest person in the room is, male or female. If you were to dismiss Jenella inside one of our pocket realms, you would die. And no one would care." She bowed in our direction. "My apologies for interrupting, Your Grace."

The man's face paled as she spoke. "Thank you. We have arranged transportation."

The guy insisted on riding with Drake and me. He even took on a tour guide role as we navigated the congested city. We nodded in the appropriate places, but didn't say much.

When we entered the meeting room, I sensed Lily, Quin, and Deva spread out around it. The man guided us to the center of a long rectangular table. As Drake and I took our seats, Tracy and Emine hip-checked each other to sit beside me. Several of the men stared at them with either lust or disgust as they silently bickered. Emine won, so Tracy grumbled as she settled on her other side.

A man across from Drake pried his eyes away from Tracy. "Thank you for meeting with us." He introduced everyone at the table, but I didn't bother to remember their names. I was too intrigued by their mannerisms. Some seemed bored, while others were almost bouncing in their seats with excitement. No one had magic, though I could sense someone with immense power somewhere in the building. Deva left the room and drifted towards the source.

After the man finished his introductions, he fell silent. When we didn't fill in the silence, he leaned forward. "Would you like to introduce your group?"

When I didn't speak, Drake sighed. "Of course. The man on the end is Jonas. Ann Marie, Cavil, and Ara are beside him. On the other end are Razazia, Bastien, Tracy, and Emine." He took my hand and kissed it. "I am Drake, and this is Jenella."

Another dismissive look. "Is it necessary everyone stay for this meeting?"

"Yes."

The man nodded. "Very well. Let's discuss the building you destroyed."

I folded my hands in my lap. "We had our people rebuild it."

The man's beady eyes flashed with anger. "And killed several people."

"Demons. And we banished them, which creates a lot of dust. To kill them, we'd need to travel to their realm, which is not recommended. No one died. Several humans can testify to seeing the demons' true forms, and we have released videos showing how well-protected your people were during the skirmish."

"And you are the foremost authority on demons?"

"No. But I can sense them."

"Do you have proof of their existence?"

I held his gaze, trying to understand why he was so arrogant. The only reason I could think of is that they learned nothing from our little power display. "Show him, Tracy."

Several humans flinched when a hologram spell appeared on the table. A demon morphed into its true form and attacked us while we protected people.

After it played, the man refocused on Drake. "The video wasn't fabricated?"

"It's impossible to alter Tracy's observation spells. And even if we could, we wouldn't bother trying simply to impress you."

"I see." He shared a look with the man on his left. "We have orders to gather as much information as possible and detain you and your people for murder."

Drake's eyes flashed. "I'd like to see you try."

"Oh, we will not only try."

"How many of our kids did you buy or kidnap?" I asked. When no one answered, I continued. "You don't need to answer, of course. We have recovered them and brought down the group selling them to you. However, if you bought others from the demons, it would be easier for everyone if you returned them to us."

"I don't recall." His arrogant smirk said otherwise. He refocused on Drake. "May we talk man to man?"

Drake's white-hot anger radiated through the room. "You are far too ignorant to display such confidence."

"What my colleague means," another man interjected, "is we witnessed the destruction you're capable of and do not plan to cut a deal with you until you offer us some concessions."

The doors to the meeting room burst open, and several armed men in uniforms filed in. They surrounded us and aimed their guns at Drake.

The original speaker leaned forward. "You will comply, or we will force you to, Mr. Drake."

Every gun in the room fell to pieces.

The humans panicked. Some hopped out of their chairs, while others shouted.

I leaned towards Emine. "Thanks."

"No probs."

I threw a barrier between my people and the soldiers as I stood. "I brought my most trusted advisors to negotiate with you in good faith. Silly of us to hope you'd come to your senses after you bought and imprisoned our kids and catered to the whims of demons."

Drake pushed his chair back. "Had you done an ounce of research, you would have saved yourselves from this humiliation."

I nodded. "We have helped solve many of the problems your country refuses to address. And you repay us by kidnapping my sister, sending some half-baked version of shifters after us, and stealing our children. If you don't set aside your egos and see the reality before you, the demons will take over your government. And we won't be around to stop them next time."

"No one asked for your help," the man said. "We were thriving without you."

Jonas sneezed. When the shrieks died down, everyone's attention landed on him. He shrugged. "Lies burn the nose."

I pushed my chair in. "These humans aren't worth a nose burn."

The man's face turned red, and he leaned towards Drake. "Are you going to let her talk to me like that?"

"Leeeet herrrr." Drake's voice was too mild and controlled. "You've made some wrong assumptions, puny human. No one in this room is powerful enough to stop our queen."

With the wave of a hand, I separated the soldiers so we could leave without flashing. "If you ever invite us back into your web of lies, do more research."

"Wait!"

I paused and focused on the man who escorted us to the meeting.

"It's my fault for not confirming your titles."

Emine disarmed the next set of men who rushed through the door.

"I don't care whose fault it is. These men didn't invite us here in good faith." I used magic to push the group blocking the door aside. "Your people have rebuffed my efforts for diplomacy at every turn because you think you have the key to magic."

"We do have a solid program."

"Your program is shit," Jonas said. "The queen and I spent days fixing your mistakes."

"They're still alive?" The dishonest man asked.

I nodded. "And thriving. Your attempts to inject them with magic left them disfigured and in chronic pain. Since you do that to your own people, often against their will, I should have realized this meeting was requested in bad faith." I sighed. "I hoped to negotiate a truce because we like this country and admire its people."

A man at the end of the table motioned towards our empty seats. "We would also like to negotiate. Please, sit."

"The head of homeland security," Emine whispered.

I scanned the faces of the men at the table as I shoved everyone else out of the room. Ann Marie set a ward when the door closed, and I retook my seat. "Very well. Let's negotiate. But I am disinclined to believe a word you say."

The man tried to pretend my magic didn't unsettle him. "If you had this information, why show up today?"

"My consort believes that hope is a dangerous emotion. I wanted to prove him wrong for once."

He rubbed his forehead. "You hoped we'd allow you free rein over our country."

"No one is interested in taking over your country, but we do hope to co-exist."

"I see. How long have you lived here?"

"Since long before you were a nation."

"And you hid from us the entire time?"

"We like to mind our own business," Jonas explained in his lecturing tone. "Unlike you, we have no use for world domination or petty political games."

That was a stretch. "We've made coexistence treaties with several countries and plan to keep our promises."

"We have assessed your agreement and rejected it because you are a national security risk."

Razazia's laughter silenced the room. When no one joined in, she lifted a finger and rubbed her stomach. "Sorry. But I find it ironic you consider those willing to help enemies while allowing demons, who prey on chaos, to influence your government."

Emine nodded. "It's bonkers. Especially since demons destroy their food."

The man took a sip of water. "We don't believe in demons."

"So you're willing to sacrifice your country to maintain your naivety." I drummed my fingers on the table so I could think. Several countries we allied with reached out and offered us a place among them, so if the negotiations failed, I could move the pockets. It would take time and disrupt the lives of many paranormals. But it was oh so tempting. I tossed it out of my head because it wasn't about the smug government officials. It was about regular people who needed our help.

He smirked. "We have secured three of your healers. They are not as strong as you claim."

I stared him down until he dropped his eyes. "You're not qualified to assess their strength. And I guarantee you won't be able to hold them." Healers were Forte mages, so they'd flash away at the first opportunity.

Emine's anger flared, and she conjured a knife under the table before dissipating it. "If you continue to harass our humanitarians, it won't end well for you. Know what I mean?"

"Emine is right, and this meeting wastes our time." Jonas leaned forward to address me. "It's the same old story. You give humans an inch and they take a mile. It's why I encouraged the hybrids to refrain from helping them."

"It's also why we withdrew from their society. They are greedy and ungrateful," Razazia added.

"My advisors are right. This discussion isn't productive."

Drake rubbed small circles on my back. "We will present you with a solid contract. If you choose not to negotiate, or cannot meet our deadline, we will withdraw our support from your people."

The man who ran Homeland Security rubbed his chin. "Very well. We will consider your treaty, but only if you allow us to visit the magical troops we sent after you."

When everyone fell silent, I turned to leave. "We'll consider it."

Chapter Thirty-Eight

We flashed to the area where I sensed Deva.

"What in the actual fuck?" Lily emerged from the shadows when we landed in a stark room with a hospital bed on the far wall. She motioned to a woman hooked to several medical devices. "Who is she?"

Jonas ran a hand through his hair. "How in the hell did they find Celia?"

I sensed the turbulence inside her, as if she were aware. "A question for another day."

When Deva pulled a wire away, a machine screamed. Her shrewd eyes focused on the offending machine, and it went quiet.

Ann Marie rushed over and helped her remove them. "We don't have much time."

Deva nodded. "The humans are gathering outside."

Banging on the door, followed by the loud cracks of guns, proved her point.

My head swung towards the commotion. "Tell Alex to evacuate and pull our people from the area."

"Authorities surrounded our plane right after we left. Glacintial has already evacuated him and the human pilot," Drake tilted his head. "Move!"

"Holy hell, you're bossy." Lily moved at vampire speed as she fought to free Celia. "Can you wake her up now?"

I raced to her side and threw the blankets off the bed. "Anitta put her to sleep. I'll need to wake her like I did the others, but not here."

Boom!

An explosion rocked the room, and dust rained down. I leaned over Celia to protect her at the same time as Lily, and we bumped heads. "Ow. Hands on me."

Once everyone was accounted for, I flashed to the enforcer station in Misset.

The vampire shifter who berated me for calling Emine during my first visit to Hospa poked his head out the door. "Your Grace. Mistress Ara."

"We'll only be here a minute." I didn't like the guy because of my bad first impression.

Drake pushed Lily and me back and lifted Celia. "We will leave for Allure momentarily."

Two days later, Drake dragged Emiron into Deva's office and slammed him into a chair. "Stay."

"Were you not banned from this realm a thousand years ago?" Deva stood at her usual window, watching over Allure. She didn't bother facing him.

He tried to be brave, but the wariness in his eyes and stiff posture gave him away. "Hello, Queen Deva. As per my agreement with Queen Lissandra, I should not be here. The demon who kidnapped me brought me against my will, and I will leave as soon as Queen Jenella releases me." He offered her a plastic smile when she sauntered to her desk.

"How many children have you spawned here?"

"It is hard to tell. At least one."

I held up a hand. "You can have kids without a match?"

Emiron shook his head. "I can declare anyone my match for as long as I need."

"Perhaps it's best to keep him here and under surveillance." Drake must have read my mind.

"Of course, love." Deva's intelligent bronze eyes lit with something I couldn't read. "Let's have a nice long chat about how you stole Ferine, shall we?"

Before he could answer, Verity stormed in.

When I moved to intervene, Quin tugged me back. "Do not insert yourself."

She stomped up to Emiron and punched him in the face. "You fucking slimeball!"

"Uhm." I shook Quin loose. "What's going on?"

"He kidnapped me and gave me to humans." When she cocked her arm to punch him again, Titus appeared behind her and pulled her away.

The strange magic emanating from Emiron didn't match his solemn expression. "I am sorry. Your existence in this realm is quite inconvenient."

"How?" I asked.

His heavy sigh and remorseful eyes seemed almost too polished. "One of my many children spawned her. Had I left her with paranormals, Prince Mathias would have caught on to my plans. A wasted effort, considering my daughter stole my throne to create a more peaceful realm. When I challenged her, she sold me to demons." He shook his head, as if erasing a memory.

"Lie." Titus tried to shove Verity behind him, but gave up when she wouldn't budge.

"Not a lie. She is half mage, half Gartolian royalty."

"My magic says otherwise."

Emiron threw his hands into the air. "Fine. I'm unsure who spawned her. It could be one of my kids or another noble. But it doesn't matter because she's an anchor. I had two choices when I found the kid. Either kill her or hide her. I chose the more civilized route."

I shoved Verity and Titus across the hall and into Bastien's office. As soon as we had privacy, my fierce assistant melted into Titus and sobbed.

I rubbed her back. "I'm sorry. If I had known, I wouldn't have brought him here."

She pulled me into an awkward group hug. After she gathered herself, Verity released us and stepped back. "That asshole."

"Yeah. I should have let the demons kill him. Or killed him myself."

She blinked. "You would, wouldn't you? And you wouldn't even feel remorse."

I met her swollen eyes. "I'd feel bad, but if it's what you want, he's dead."

"Our people are so violent."

Titus threw an arm around her shoulders. "You said *our* people."

"I did. I'm unsure when it happened, but I've moved to the dark side."

My brow furrowed. "Another reference I don't understand?"

"You never understand human references." Verity eyed the door. "Can you banish him like the demon he is?"

I bit back a smile. "No. He taught the demons how to create anchors here, which means he has at least one and can come and go as he pleases."

"Unless you put him under a magical contract," Titus said. "An air-tight one."

"I will after he tells us what he did to Ferine." I sighed. "Will you write the contract for me?"

Verity closed her eyes. "We'll work on the right wording together."

"Are you sure?"

"Yes. I have a good life now and want to preserve it."

As I returned to Deva's office, my mood soured. I leaned against her desk in front of Emiron. "Tell me about the Bellicose and your involvement with Anitta. When you're done, explain why your magic shimmered across Ferine before it exploded."

His lip curled in defiance. "Demons lie."

"I am aware."

Emiron stared at his feet as if contemplating what to say. When he raised his head, he met my eyes and nodded as if agreeing with himself. "Anitta used the demons as if they were nothing but tools. And they used me in the same way. She had a child with the mid-level one and built him a demon pocket. I believe he tormented you as a child?"

My fists clenched at his amused look. "Explain."

"My sole mission was to stay alive during my captivity. At first, I bargained with them. It's how they learned about anchors. But instead of having children like an honorable Gartolian would, they collected souls from the gullible." He ran a hand through his long, dark hair. "I didn't understand demons well when we discussed it. One day, Queen Anitta came calling. She was as easy to read as an open book. Unlike her daughter, her motivations were clear. She craved power and influence. I offered her my magical services for my freedom.

"My elation at her agreement was short-lived. She moved me into the demon pocket where I slaved away on inventions. My unique power does not mix well with yours, so she had me experiment with mixing my power with that of her demon lover. The only successful experiment was a set of cuffs to syphon magic. When our combined magic failed to create more powerful weapons, she had me infuse a set of three inescapable pyramids, among other things. Anitta never mentioned how she planned to use them, but was gleeful about the success."

"How did she keep you from escaping?" I asked.

"When I stepped out of line, she would dump me inside a frozen realm where the magic gave me terrible headaches. The pain seemed intentional."

No doubt my grandmother's doing. "Your magic isn't part of the wards holding the pocket realms."

Emiron's eyebrows slammed together. "Correct. I only researched them because Anitta did not allow anyone control over things she deemed important. Many paranormals believe she built the realms to save her people. But her motivations were quite the opposite."

Drake had theorized it was to isolate paranormals for better control. The logic didn't add up to me. I leaned forward. "How so?"

"She created them so when the fates inevitably removed her magic, the paranormal community would be left leaderless, and you would eliminate each other. The only faction she expected to survive was the dragons." He barked out a laugh. "Imagine my glee when she showed up ranting about how her eldest son thwarted her efforts and saved her heir. She didn't realize the rapport he'd built with the community's leaders.

"From that point forward, her plans became more unhinged. She dragged me to Ferine to laugh in my face and inform me that my daughter's agreement superseded my own. The woman forgot about me until the mid-level demon arrived and chained me to that wretched soul-sucking pocket. But not before she explained her motivations." He met my eyes. "She didn't care about you, your brother, or your throne. Her goal was revenge against her mother."

"The demon disclosed her plans," Drake said.

"Correct. She had a way of convincing others that they held power. But the only authority she considered was her own. The demons believed in her because they'd never met another race as good at lying as them. After her death, the alliances she built fell apart. Then, one day, I overheard the demon discussing their takeover of this world with a former shifter king."

"Let me guess. They planned to replace me with Morten?"

"Wasting so many resources in their failed attempt to steal the Dragon Queen's power made them skeptical. But the former Shifter King convinced them he could steal yours." He tapped the arm of his chair. "When the demon returned half banished and without his shifter friend, I knew if I waited, you would arrive to rescue me.

Deva's entire body took on an eerie glow. "Ferine."

Emiron clenched the chair so hard it creaked. "You cannot read my mind, Dragon Queen, so don't try."

"You overestimate yourself, Gartolian King." The glow was replaced with a satisfied smile. "And unlike you, I have allies."

Drake had gone unnaturally still during the exchange. When Deva's glow died, he squared his shoulders. "He stole the entire pocket and moved it to San Diego, California. He planned to move his forces into it and prepare for an invasion."

Emiron paled. "Those were my plans before I was dethroned. I gave them up long ago."

"False," Drake said in an even tone. "When he realized Jenella might save him, he manipulated the demons into taking him there. He plans to regain his throne and return Gartolians to their warring ways."

Deva waved a hand. "I will have a map to Ferine ready by today. Do you have any more use for this sorry excuse for prey?"

"Not right now. Will you secure him and keep his magic dampened until I decide his punishment?"

"Of course, love."

"Thank you."

I stormed out of her office without looking back. The entire coup was senseless, dumb, and predictable. Too many lives were lost so big egos could satisfy their hunger. And it pissed me off. I needed to walk off my anger.

A mane of aqua hair caught my eye as I stepped off the elevator at my office. Brogan sat in the waiting room, one ankle crossed over a knee. Beside him, a selkie clutched a purse to her chest and watched me approach with wide eyes. I sensed her skin inside. "Brogan. What can I do for you?"

He stood and bowed. "Your Grace."

I sipped his power. "We don't bow anymore."

"Good." He glanced towards the selkie. "May we have a moment of your time?"

"Sure." I led him to Drake's office. When Drake spotted Brogan, an eyebrow shot up. I grinned. "Brogan, you remember my consort, Drake."

"Consort," he ground out.

I motioned for him and the selkie to sit and created a chair for myself next to Drake.

Brogan's eyes bore into Drake's. "My friend here has information about Celia."

We secured Celia in the guest wing, but I wanted to hear what she had to say. "You know what happened to her?"

Her eyes darted to Brogan and settled on a spot on Drake's desk. "The Second Queen removed her the week before your coronation."

I fought to keep my face neutral. "You saw her?"

"Yes, Your Grace. I dove into the water when she appeared. She didn't see me, so I watched her extract the First Celia and disappear."

I leaned back and nodded. "Thank you."

Brogan rubbed his chin. "Why does it seem irrelevant?"

"Because it is," Drake said. "She gave or sold Celia to the humans for experimentation. We have secured her, but Jenella hasn't had time to wake her."

"May I be present at her awakening?"

Alarm bells went off in my head. "Why?"

"We were close friends. I wish to ensure she's okay."

Since I planned to bring in all the Firsts to wake her, I didn't feel right about denying him, so I agreed.

Which is how we ended up with five Firsts gathered around a bed in the last room of the palace's guest wing. Like the other Firsts, Celia's immense power made the hair on my arms stand up. Unlike them, she had several holes and scars from human experimentation. "Should I heal her now or offer it when she wakes up?"

"Now," Brogan said, without hesitation. "Her looks were important to her."

I could see why. Unlike her creations, she was petite. Chestnut hair framed a beautiful heart-shaped face. I touched her hand. When she was restored, I changed the intention to wake and increased the flow.

She didn't wake up fighting. Instead, her eyes fluttered before they opened, and her forehead crinkled. "Who in the fates are you?"

Drake swept me behind him before she finished the question. I peered around him. "I'm the Third Queen of Ahl, Jenella."

Her eyes locked on Brogan, and she sat up, the blankets falling away. "You promised if I allowed her to place me by the sea, you'd guard me."

Brogan's strange hair swayed back and forth as he hung his head. "I watched over you for many years. The day she came for you, I was called away briefly. When I returned, you were gone."

"Promises made, not kept. But I do not wish magic to exact its price, so I consider your contract fulfilled." Celia threw off the rest of the covers and swung her legs over the side of the bed.

Gorman and Brogan lunged to catch her, but she waved them off. "Thanks to the humans feeding me through a tube, I am as strong as a Centaur." Her feet hit the floor, and she wobbled. "Now, where are we and how do I return to Italy?"

The Firsts made her stay in Allure for a week so they could show her around and give her a crash course in modern times. According to Jonas, she was polite and quiet. I wouldn't know because she avoided me like I was my mother. Instead of informing me when she left for her homeland, she sent a missive to Drake's office. Fine with me. There were too many Firsts in my life, and if she didn't cause trouble, I didn't care where she settled.

Chapter Thirty-Nine

I STROLLED INTO THE council building and took my usual place. Most of the leaders already occupied seats or were present by hologram. Several looked eager for the meeting to begin. "Thank you for your hard work finalizing the treaties. I'm pleased to announce we've finalized agreements with nearly half of the sovereign human countries. I want your updates. We should also discuss those who don't want peace with us. If we can't reach an agreement, we need to consider moving our pockets."

The hologram of the Siren Queen stood. "I've negotiated treaties with three more smaller countries."

Her voice created a throbbing ache, and it took a few seconds for me to respond. "Thank you. I'll look at them today."

As the other leaders briefed me on our humanitarian efforts and contract negotiations, I felt pride swell in my chest at how well they worked together. Some did it for selfish reasons, but it was a tremendous improvement considering how they fought so hard for status before I took the throne.

I folded my hands. "The federal government hesitates to sign a treaty with us after we ruined their magic program. It may be time to move our gates to countries where we have agreements in place. Since we're well-established here, it will be difficult and time-consuming, so I'd rather not. Ideas?"

"We should not even consider such a preposterous idea." The Troll King said.

"Moving millions of paranormals will destroy the trust we built in our people and the humans," The Chimera King said without his usual disdain. "If we withdraw, it will crush many of our businesses and anger the very people we are trying to help."

"I agree." Those were words I never thought I'd say. "But unless their government negotiates, it's unsafe for us here. My advisors suggested giving them an ultimatum."

The Kelpie Queen cleared her throat. "There is always a magical solution."

I almost hid my flinch. "If we go that route, we're no better than the Bellicose."

"We've already used their people against them, so I fail to see the difference."

"You would," The Troll King mumbled. "The difference is that by helping their people, we're manipulating on their level. They don't have magic, so they can't defend themselves against it."

His words kicked my mind into gear. As they argued the point, I had a revelation. "Wait." When everyone fell silent, I lifted my head. "They don't realize we have other levels."

Ara rested her chin on her hand. "Perhaps you should explain, dear."

"Right. Aside from banishing demons and rescuing our kids, we've stayed on their level. The government officials we met didn't understand us. Even when we disarmed their guards, they seemed almost arrogant about it. What if they believe we're them with a little magic? If so, they don't understand how much restraint we've shown."

"How can we show them?" Sylphira asked.

"Let's invite them here. We can give them a little tour to open their eyes. Maybe even ask our citizens to play it up," The Fairy Queen suggested.

"The hybrid pocket would be more ideal," Dale said. "Hybrids understand humans better than you."

The Minotaur King rubbed his beard. "Which is precisely why we need to bring them here. The culture shock alone may shake some sense into them."

"Not to mention our sheer numbers." I twisted in my seat. "Verity, what do you think?"

She raised her head from the monitoring spell. "I almost had a heart attack when you dragged me to Hospa back when I thought I was human. If you bring them here, warn them about what they might experience and keep some healers on hand. Maybe instruct everyone to hide their violent tendencies around them."

"Invite them to see the half-formed shifters they sent to our gates," Jonas said. "It's a good example of us accomplishing something they can't."

We discussed the idea for a while and decided on a guided tour that would begin with a visit to the former humans.

As I returned to the palace, Quin caught up with me. "You understand there is no turning back from this decision."

"I do. It's a chance I'm willing to take. Especially if we can avoid displacing millions of paranormals."

"Interesting." He went into one of his vampire stupors. "Perhaps they should also see their lost agents."

"No. Humans fear vampires, and I don't want you or Lily to be bigger targets than you already are."

"By design. Before Anitta was spawned, ensuring humans feared us was my life's work."

"You did a good job."

"Of course. Do you wish to know my current life's work?"

"Not really, no."

"It is ensuring you and Lily not only survive but thrive."

"Great." I didn't know what to think about Quin hyper-focusing on us. "How's that going?"

"Abysmally. Lily cannot avoid trouble, and you tend to make questionable decisions."

"Sounds about right."

"The decision to ensure our peace is not one of them." He disappeared.

Late that night, I sat on Drake's launching balcony, waiting for him to return. He'd been monitoring the agents who still milled around the valley and helping Lily convince hybrids to relocate. The longer he was gone, the more anxious I became. I checked on him through the bond and tamped down my worry. Without him, my nightmares plagued me, and the feeling of the walls closing in around me returned. The open balcony helped a little, but for some reason, I still couldn't shake the feeling of being trapped, alone, and helpless. I pulled my sweater tighter to shield myself from the cool spring night. My trauma irritated me, more than hurt, which I supposed was progress. But I still couldn't help but wish I could turn it off like a light spell.

Griffins were on their patrols, swooping low and checking every shadow and corner. Palace guards paced the wall as if we were expecting another Bellicose invasion.

Drake's massive form descended from the sky like an avenging angel. He circled the palace grounds, tucked his wings, and shot towards me. At the last second, he shifted and crouched beside me. "Hello, Jenella. Did you miss me?"

"Always." Relief and warmth flooded me as I kissed his chin. "We have a fresh idea."

"I heard."

We sat in companionable silence, and my anxiety melted away. A pleasant warmth radiated from him, and in that moment, a deep sense of belonging washed over me, as if I were finally home.

I bit my lip and forced myself to stand still as we watched paranormals work together to drag Ferine away from a strip mall and out of the city. Razazia's shoulder brushed mine. It felt odd for her to be so close, but because of the nervous energy rolling off her, I didn't comment.

Fifteen minutes. Drake's voice rang through my head.

Is anyone alive inside?

Alex senses brain patterns, but I do not.

I relayed the message to Razazia.

"He's alive."

"Why are you so nervous?"

"None of your business."

"It is if you're going to help me build a gate."

She sighed. "If you must know, he's my third-born."

Her heir. Though the two looked and acted nothing alike, I somehow wasn't surprised. "Why is it such a big secret?"

"Must I remind you of my long, involuntary nap?"

"So, you're trying to protect him?"

"Correct."

"Where's your match?"

"Nosy little bitch today, aren't you?"

I let it go and focused on my senses. The glow of magic was immense as thousands of paranormals navigated the pocket to an abandoned warehouse. As soon as Drake gave me the signal, I laced my arm through Razazia's and flashed to it. The wards still felt the same, but Emiron's shimmer of magic was more pronounced. The only way I could remove it was to either convince him to fix it or eliminate him. Either option was fine with me.

The massive crowd couldn't fit in the warehouse, so they surrounded the building, peeking through holes in the walls and ceiling to see what had happened.

I shook out my hands. "Okay. Here goes nothing." I sipped Razazia's magic as I formed the gate. With each one, I got better, so it didn't look so lopsided when I finished.

Before I could step through, Drake pulled me back. "You may want to let the people who located the pocket have this moment." His whisper tickled my ear.

Razazia rushed inside, and about a hundred paranormals rushed around us to follow. A few minutes later, Olwen stepped out, scanned the crowd, and bowed. Razazia followed, a gleaming smile on her face. As person after person left the pocket, alive and well, a thundering cheer from the crowd roared through the room.

I turned to the enforcer, who worked to clean up the mess in Pennsylvania, and led the search for the missing pocket. "Thank you for everything, Colonel."

He inclined his head. "We still lost too many." Three hundred and forty-three paranormals were lost, including several from Olwen's army division. We planned to have a remembrance ceremony as soon as we accounted for the survivors and the families were ready.

After the crowd thinned, I texted Pablo and instructed him to buy the warehouse. It would allow people to move their things before I destroyed it, along with any chance Gartolians had of moving troops into my realm. We already sent inspection teams to all the other pockets to look for his magic and found none.

The only way to bring non-magical people through our wards was to use the summoning room. And as much as I hated the thing, it had come in handy. I assigned Pablo to help Travis plan a visit from a few high-ranking government officials. We'd made the offer so intriguing that several representatives requested to tag along, so we waited for fifty people. "What do I call the spare president again?"

Verity's laugh filled the control room. "Vice President, just like the witches. Or are you joking?"

"I'll use the association from now on. Thanks." I wrung my hands. "What about the others?"

Tracy linked her arm with mine. "Maybe you should calm down."

"I really want this to work. We're out of ideas, so if it doesn't, we're screwed."

"Nonsense, love. We only need to become sneakier." Deva's eyes lit as she communicated with her dragons. "Five minutes."

Drake and Bastien stood outside the steel doors, wearing replicas of the most expensive suits humans could buy, as they waited for the officials to arrive. I smoothed my charcoal jacket. The color was awful, but everyone assured me it was appropriate. Quin leaned against the wall nearby, examining his nails. He hadn't spoken a word since he arrived.

"Keep your concentration laser-focused." Deva stuck her hand into the summoning room's controls.

"Right." I placed my hand next to hers.

The screaming was to be expected. There wasn't a paranormal alive, including me, who didn't scream the first time they were summoned. The group appeared inside the solid white room, looking wide-eyed and disheveled. We warned them about the travel method, but it didn't look like a few believed us. "Do they need healers?"

"Give them a minute to adjust. We have some on hand if they do." Verity leaned forward. "Five women. That's what I call progress."

I understood it was a dig at their patriarchal society, but I didn't care about it when the stakes were so high.

Drake, Bastien, and several council members entered the room. They made their way through the group, shaking hands and greeting them. I dragged my eyes away and grinned at Deva. "Are you ready for the show?"

"Always."

The humans grew silent as Drake led them into the dragon-sized room. I stood in front of Deva, who had shifted and lounged behind me, her head hovering above mine.

Sylphira perched on my shoulder, a crown of multi-colored pixie dust swirling around her head. I placed Calvin and Tracy to my right, and the two Ogre Queens to my left for contrast. They were all beautiful in their own way, but I understood humans would consider the Queens ugly and gravitate towards the Cordalias.

Drake stopped a respectable distance away and bowed his head. It was jarring, considering he'd never once bowed to me or anyone else. "Your Grace. May I present the Vice President of the United States?" He motioned towards Deva. "I present my aunt, Queen Devarkalara of Dragons, and my match, Queen Jenella of Ahl."

"All?" The man's muddy eyes assessed me. "Is it a formal title?"

"It's A-H-L. And yes." I remembered humans liked to shake hands, so I extended mine.

He shook it too hard as he watched Deva. "A real dragon?"

Deva huffed, and smoke rolled out of her nose.

"Yes. As Drake explained, she's their queen." I leaned in as if sharing a secret. "I wouldn't recommend making her angry."

A man from our previous meeting shuffled forward. "Who is in charge?"

Drake motioned towards the other leaders. "These are the leaders of the various paranormal factions."

The one-eyed ogre queen grinned, her pointy yellow teeth on full display. "We are pleased to meet you. Should you need someone to pummel demons to banishment, call me."

A few humans flinched, while others stepped back, their eyes wide.

I introduced the rest of the Council. We'd planned long introductions, so the dignitaries had time to get used to our strangeness before we hit the streets. Deva loomed over me in warning the entire time, which didn't help calm their nerves.

As soon as the introductions were complete, most of our leaders left. I motioned toward the door. "Let's start by taking you to visit the deformed shifters you sent to us for safekeeping."

"We sent them to attack you," a man behind me said.

I waved a dismissive hand. "Had you not sent them to us, they would have died from the magic poisoning." Not exactly true, but it got their attention.

The city was bustling when we gathered on the steps of Dragon Headquarters. Flying paranormals circled the downtown area, fighting to see our human guests. A group of fairies clashed with a swarm of pixies for the best spot in a nearby tree. Two human-sized fairies stood below, their bright pink and green wings fluttering. Vampires zipped by in large groups, resembling a mass of black shadows. Elves milled around the grassy areas, growing unneeded plants, while dwarves made unnecessary repairs on nearby buildings. Shifters of all shapes and sizes strolled in animal form or naked. Trolls and ogres pretended to sweep the streets.

A human man gasped when a well-endowed donkey shifter strolled by, his junk swinging in the wind. "Do you people have no decency?"

"Rarely," Razazia drawled.

"I read about this," a woman said. "It's so they don't ruin their clothes, right?"

I pasted a professional smile on my face. "Exactly. We are monogamous and only have sex with our match. So nudity doesn't bother us." Not exactly true. We had sex before we found our match, but never a relationship. I was already racking up the lies, so I figured one more wouldn't hurt. "This way." I pointed to a line of platforms floating above the street.

As they settled in their seats, some requested seat belts. Razazia flapped her wings, and vines formed across their laps. After their gasps ended, she hovered above them. "Should you need to release your seatbelt, pull the end three times."

When our slow procession approached the field where we kept the new shifters, Jonas and Ann Marie stood outside, waiting for us to arrive. They wore business clothes and oozed power.

Drake hopped off the platform and offered me his hand. "Think we should dial it back?"

"We'll see how it goes. So far, they're thrilled by our scariness."

His lips twitched. "It will wear off."

"For fates sake, I hope so." Tracy wiped her hands on her pants. "Their ogling is creepy."

I made eye contact with an older man who hadn't taken his eyes off her since they entered Deva's throne room. His face flushed, and he looked away. "Yeah. That's gross. How long before Bastien steps in?"

"Not long." She scanned the skies. "He's organizing some stuff, but feels how uncomfortable it makes me."

Our entire plan would fall apart if Bastien showed up to protect her. "Make yourself scarce." I turned my attention to Calvin. "Go with her. Stay close enough to act, but out of sight of the humans."

Tracy's shoulders slumped. "Why do I feel like I'm letting you down?"

"You shouldn't ever feel inadequate, considering how many times you've saved me." I nodded an acknowledgement when Jonas motioned for me to join him. "Stay close, but out of sight. And tell Bastien not to lose his temper, or I'll follow through on my butterfly threat."

Chapter Forty

The new shifters brimmed with disdain and resentment as they met the delegation. The humans pretended not to notice and maintained their manners. Vampires hid in every shadow, listening to conversations, while several dragons scanned their thoughts. We'd have a lot of intelligence soon.

A man strode towards me. "How did you complete their transition? The reports from our scientists said it was impossible."

"We're blessed by magic and abide by its rules. It is impossible for someone without a concept of how magic works to wield it unless it chooses you."

"You speak of it as if it is a living thing."

"It is, in its own way. You and your scientists are immune, so you can't feel it."

"I see. And when will these men be able to return to their duties?"

"They're paranormals now, so they can't return to their human lives. We have strict rules around it."

"You can't keep them here. They have families."

"Yes." I pointed at Jonas. "The Shifter King is helping them to maintain a relationship with their friends and families."

"You're not going to isolate them?"

"It depends on how this meeting goes."

The man looked thoughtful. "I see. We still need them back. They swore an oath."

"A human pledge. They've been reborn with magic, so it's no longer relevant."

"You can't keep them. If you do, we will never agree to this deal."

I shrugged. "If you choose not to sign the treaty, we'll move our people to less hostile territory."

His chest puffed out. "We need our soldiers to return to duty immediately. Return them, or we will make things difficult for you."

The man thought I was stupid and easily intimidated. "If you wanted to keep them, you shouldn't have left them on my doorstep like a neighbor offering a gift."

The Vice President, who stood nearby listening, stepped in. "My apologies, ma'am. We would like them back, but it is a conversation for another day."

"No, it's not. You left them in our care, and we adopted them. You can visit if they consent, but they're paranormals now, and you aren't going to use and abuse my people."

The Vice President maintained a blank expression, but he was as determined to take the shifters as the other man. "We will see about that."

My magic pulsed. "Humans, gather around!" The power-laced command had them scrambling. I maintained eye contact with the Vice President the entire time.

He took a step towards me before catching himself. "What did you do?"

I allowed my eyes to glow. "You are trying to wield power that is not yours to wield. The shifters are ours."

His eyes darted to Drake for confirmation, but whatever he saw there didn't ease his nerves. "Very well. I won't insist they return today, but I can't guarantee we won't negotiate it later."

I nodded. "If you deal fairly with us, I might agree to discuss it."

He swallowed. "Of course."

We spent the rest of the day as tour guides, and the humans never lost their sense of wonder. This both reassured and unsettled me.

When we returned to Dragon Headquarters, we filed into a banquet hall, where I sat between Drake and the Vice President. Dragons of every color entered with trays of soups and salads. Some conjured drinks and condiments and soaked up the admiration.

The Vice President watched them. "Is it safe for us to eat the food?"

I frowned. "If we wanted you dead, we wouldn't need to poison you."

Drake covered his laugh with a cough. "I believe the Vice President is referring to fae legends."

My forehead crinkled. "I still don't understand."

He patted my leg. "This isn't a fae realm, and the food is safe for human consumption. There is no poison, and it won't bewitch or entrap you."

The Vice President nodded. "Thank you. You have been very gracious hosts."

"We have coexisted beside humans for centuries, and adore your kind," Deva said from across the table. "Our combined histories go back to the dawn of man."

"Interesting." He sipped his wine. "Have you always lived in these realms?"

I moved food around my plate as I considered the reasons for his question. "No. We established them a few centuries ago."

"Are they all like this one?"

"Like your cities and towns, each one is unique. But I wouldn't recommend coating humans in magic and sending them inside like you did when my sister escaped her torturers."

"What happened to the platoon of soldiers we sent?"

"They killed three paranormals and injured many others. My people reacted. I'm sorry, but they are no longer with us."

"Can we have their remains to return to their families?"

"We returned their remains and offered them support and compensation," Drake said. "We skipped the government involvement so you couldn't use it as propaganda against us."

The man tilted his head as if considering something. "Very well. How can we, as humans, identify demons?"

"The easiest way is to sniff them. The scent of sulfur is often subtle, but always present. Another is to look for sparks of red in their eyes." Drake pushed his plate away. "Though they often convince humans to ignore it."

"I wouldn't recommend confronting them yourself," I added. "They'll trap you and use you for food."

Drake nodded. "Contact us if you encounter one, and we will identify and banish it for you."

After the meal, the humans mingled with our leaders, no doubt trying to find more information about us. When their time was up, they gathered in the summoning room in a tight group and braced themselves for the pain. I slumped against Drake as soon as they disappeared. "Will they negotiate?"

"They will," Deva answered.

I hoped she was right.

Verity's spine snapped straight as she glared at the man trapped in Deva's most powerful magic. "Hello, Emiron."

Emiron stood. "Hello, Verity. I take it you're here for answers?"

"No. You and I have terms to negotiate."

"No terms will keep me from this realm while my anchor lives. Blood is stronger than magical contracts."

"I don't care. We're going to come to an agreement, and Jen will decide your fate."

He raised an eyebrow. "Oh?"

"You will leave and never come back. Your realm will not attack us. If you try, your family forfeits their reign over Gartolia, and you will end up back inside this cell."

Emiron stepped closer to the containment spell. "Disregarding you as weak was a grave error on my part. You're everything a Gartolian should be. Strong, brave, and decisive." He made eye contact just a tad too long. "I will agree to these terms."

After they sealed the contract, Emiron pulled a golden thread from his pants. "Thank you for freeing me, Queen Jenella. It has been a most enlightening experience." The string glowed and expanded as it wrapped him in a cocoon before he vanished.

Verity tapped her foot. "Too easy. There's no way that guy is going to stick to our terms."

"Don't worry. He didn't go far. What is that?" A small package rested on the bed. I waved at the dragon guard. Can you open the ward?"

Verity crossed her arms. "Good. He can rot for all I care."

When it opened, I shuffled closer. "It has your name on it." I pointed at the tag on top.

"Verity of Gartolia is not my name."

"If Emiron reinstated your birthright, then it's your official title."

"It doesn't matter if he shouted it from the mountaintops. It's not my name."

Not wanting to argue, I used my magic to probe the package. "It's safe."

"Should I open it?"

"Only if you want to."

She took the tag off, peered inside, and shoved it towards me with a groan. "Nope."

I moved the cloth-like material aside, revealing a small golden tiara. It even had her name engraved on the side. "Looks like he's acknowledging you as part of his family."

She yanked the crown out of my hands with a huff. "Don't start with me. That man and his motivations can't be trusted."

True. "As you wish, Princess Verity."

She slugged me in the arm. "I mean it, Jen. This is ridiculous."

I thanked the dragon guard and pulled her towards the stairs. "Fine. But it's going to be hard not to tease you."

"No, it won't. You simply keep your mouth shut when you have the urge."

"Keep my mouth shut? Have you even met me?"

We burst into laughter as I flashed us back to the palace.

Travis waited for us outside my office. Drake's assistant, Charlotte, hovered in front of him, blocking him from going inside.

"What is going on?" Verity asked.

Travis spun towards me with the practiced grace of a shifter. "The U.S. Government wants to negotiate. They sent an outline of their terms."

I spent the rest of the day with Pablo, Verity, and Charlotte, pouring over the three-hundred-page document. They wanted us to defend them should they go to war, to help them identify and banish demons, and to register with them as citizens, among other things. The only term I agreed to was the one about demons. No way would I give humans control over my people. Nor would we fight their wars for them. We condensed and rewrote the entire agreement to resemble the ones we had with other governments and returned it.

It took a week before their second offer arrived. They agreed to the co-existence treaty but still wanted us to help their military. I took that part out, added a note about how we were a neutral society and would not take part in human wars, and returned it one more time with the most dangerous emotion attached.

Chapter Forty-One

The salty scent of blood mixed with festering rot assaulted my nose as Ara led me and Lily down some hidden stairs deep inside the vampire mansion. My muscles stiffened as we drew closer to a door radiating pain and suffering. She stopped and clasped her hands. "Before we enter, you must brace yourselves. Vampire discipline is not always torturous, but this situation warranted a slightly more brutal solution."

Lily examined every inch of the door. "I'm okay with it, but you're already freaking Jen out."

"It's not you. I've seen a torture chamber before as a resident. I have scars."

"Precisely." Ara pulled out an old-fashioned key. "Though you never should have been in a dungeon, one never forgets the lessons learned." When the lock clicked, she met my eyes. "Will you be able to restrain yourself, dear?"

I didn't have to worry about restraining myself. I had Lily with me, who would die for the people she loved. Ara and Quin would remove me from the situation if I couldn't handle it. I had Deva and Bastien, who would tear the world down if anything happened to me. And Sylphira, who would gladly zip in and be the hero. I had Thaddeous, who insisted I was lucky even if I couldn't see it. Most of all, I had Tracy, who would come up with the most inventive spells to help me, and Drake, who flooded the bond with reassurance, strength, love, and support. I wasn't trapped and alone anymore. And I would be okay.

I linked my arm with Lily's. "I'll control myself long enough to address the traitors."

My sister shook herself free. "You lose badass points by being clingy."

A laugh escaped as I swallowed the bile threatening to rise and worked up the courage to square my shoulders. "I'm ready."

Ara's torture room was as stark as her office if I disregarded the multiple vampires pinned to the walls in various states of decay. The entire thing was made of spelled cement. Magic containing a cleaning spell pulsed at even intervals. There wasn't a single piece of furniture, and the only door was the one we came through.

Lily's hand shook as she touched the wall. "Interesting."

"You will find this is the most effective way to contain grievous offenders. I would not recommend it for more mild discipline." Ara motioned for us to follow her across the room.

"Wouldn't dream of it," Lily mumbled.

I only recognized one vampire. Jedediah hung by his wrists, his face gaunt. His entire body was covered in dark bruises and dried blood. He'd lost a lot of weight and barely resembled the arrogant vampire who left us in a field in Alabama.

Ara closed her eyes and concentrated. "It seems my son has not learned his lesson. As much as it pains me, I must eliminate him and his loyal followers."

My heart ached for her. I couldn't imagine killing my own child, no matter the circumstances. "Can you influence him to change?"

"I have tried many times. He believes Anitta's vision was the correct one. If I release him, he plans to kill me and Lily to take over."

He couldn't. Jedediah was powerful, but he had nothing on Ara, Quin, or Lily.

"What happened to Vesna?" Lily asked.

It took me a minute to place the name. "Isn't that your daughter?"

Ara nodded. "I released Vesna with conditions. She did not partake in the coup and has accepted her punishment for keeping Lily's existence a secret."

By the look on Lily's face, she wasn't happy about it. "Should I be worried?"

"Certainly not, dear." Ara pointed at Jedediah. "This pains me. I do not wish to facilitate your death in front of the queen or my heir. Lily, please release your bond to the vampires whom Roman unwisely placed with you."

"Not sure how to release a bond."

I laced my fingers to hide the shaking and concentrated on convincing myself the walls weren't closing in as Ara walked her through it. Lily was a fast learner, and her sigh of relief was audible when the bonds released.

The woman to Jedediah's right began to thrash and yell in Gaelic.

Her words cut off when Ara turned her glowing red eyes in her direction. "Please read their sentencing so I may proceed with the executions."

I locked my trembling knees. "The Crown of Ahl finds Jedediah Umbra and his loyalists guilty of treason against the crown and sentences you to death."

The room whizzed by, followed by the stairs. Before I could blink, I got dumped on my ass. "What the hell?"

Lily leaned over me. "We both know you can't handle her version of a death sentence."

I climbed to my feet. "Weren't you worried about badass points?"

"Badass points don't matter when everyone is dead."

"You scare me sometimes."

"Same." She motioned towards Ara's human-style kitchen. "We'll wait in there until she's done."

Before we could move, a man with dark hair entered the room and froze. "Oh, my. I'm terribly sorry to interrupt." He slammed into a black wall when he tried to leave.

Lily launched herself across the room and smashed into him, her wall crumbling when they hit it.

Unsure what to do, I took two steps back.

Elsie appeared beside me. "Huh. I wondered how long it would take her to run into Roman. Aren't you going to stop her?"

I side-eyed Lily's second. "Nope. It's out of my jurisdiction."

"She's going to lose."

"Maybe."

Roman jammed his claws into her side. "I do not wish to fight you, niece."

"Too fucking bad." She wrapped a wisp of night around his throat. "You should have thought about that before you manipulated me.

He released her and tried to run away.

She caught him by the collar and spun him around so fast it made me dizzy. "He's going to let her win again."

They crashed into an antique table, and a priceless vase teetered. I caught it as Roman steered their fight in a new direction.

"Probably," Elsie agreed.

Ara appeared as they smashed into the back of a sofa, shoving it forward a few feet. "Oh, my."

Lily jammed her claws into his chest and squeezed. I couldn't see what Roman did, but it made her release him.

"Thank you for saving my furniture, dear."

"Sure." I leaned to the side to try and focus on the punches they threw, but the fight moved too fast.

When they came close to a bookcase. Ara sent a torrent of skin-crawling magic into the mix. “That is quite enough.”

Lily rolled head over ass and landed at my feet, while Roman was slammed on his face. I healed her without asking and trailed Ara to Roman’s side.

She poked him with her foot. “You are not so injured that you cannot stand and apologize for your meddling.”

He raised his head. “Oh. Hello, Sister. Your Grace. I didn’t see you there.”

Ara helped him to his feet. “You will clean up this mess.”

“Yes, yes. I am sorry for ensuring you took your rightful place, Niece. It won’t happen again.”

“Gee, thanks for such a heartfelt apology.” Lily poked at the holes in her shirt.

“You’re very welcome.”

My head ached from the odd conversation, yet I was so invested, I couldn’t help but stay and listen.

“You will offer a proper apology.” Ara directed her statement to Roman. “And Lily will accept it.”

“Very well. I am sorry for meddling in your life.”

“Uh huh.” When everyone’s attention turned to her, she huffed. “Fine. Apology accepted.”

It sooooo wasn’t accepted, but at least Lily wouldn’t start a fight next time she saw him.

“Good. Now, let’s move to the kitchen and enjoy some tea.”

I burst into the council chambers and dumped my things on the desk. Several leaders were already seated, but there were some stragglers, including Drake. He laughed at something Jonas said as they sauntered in, like the meeting revolved around them. *Damn Firsts*, I thought with affection. Those two were becoming close friends, and I was all for it. Drake deserved to be accepted and loved.

Sylphira landed on my desk. "Hello, Jenella."

"Hey. Did you get your colony settled in the new trees?"

"Some of them, yes." She shook her little head. "It's going to take time."

"Well, if anyone can herd the swarm, it's you."

She studied me. "You really believe in me, don't you?"

"Yes, I do. You're an outstanding leader and one of the best critical thinkers on the council. I love how you make yourself relevant, no matter the situation."

"Pixies are small. Many paranormals will dismiss me as insignificant if I don't make myself relevant."

"Then they're idiots. Because you're one of the most resilient, creative factions in the coalition."

"You think so?"

"I wouldn't say it if I didn't."

Her smile stretched from ear to ear. "And here I thought you were using me to prove a point. But you're not, are you?"

"No. I approached you because I needed allies. But I consider you my friend because I like you. No hidden agenda here."

"Ha! I told you friendship was the key." Her wings hummed as she flew away.

Drake slid into his seat. "What was that about?"

"I don't know." I patted his thigh. "How's the demon hunting going?"

"I need a break. How is Emiron's imprisonment going?"

"Swimmingly. He is not a fan of the cold and hates Olwen. The idiot doesn't even realize I placed him in my grandmother's care and keeps whining about how the pocket is painful. He's whiny when his evil plans are thwarted." I watched Gorman argue with the Kelpie Queen.

"We've almost sorted out the last of the Bellicose soldiers. How about a spring picnic after the meeting?"

"Sounds perfect." My stomach flipped at the thought of spending time alone with him. I activated the projection spell. "We did it. We made a coexistence agreement with the U.S. government."

Cheers rang out, and conversation erupted. When it settled down, I went over the details, pleased at how excited everyone was to succeed. I wasn't stupid enough to believe it would last, but it was a good start, and I couldn't help but puff with pride.

I paused before I ended the meeting, trying to find the right words without sounding cheesy. "Thank you for putting aside your differences, for taking care of your people, and helping me through this painful transition. Because of you, we defeated the Bellicose and removed most demons from our realm.

"But we couldn't have done it as isolated factions. I encourage you to keep working together, because we still have work to do. Some demons still have anchors in our realm and could come back unless we find and eliminate them. But I'm confident that we can accomplish anything if we work together." Drinks appeared on the desks, and I raised my glass. "Here's to the new era of peace."

Epilogue

I WRINKLED MY NOSE at my image in the mirror. "I like yours better."

"It's too sexy for my taste." Lily ran her hands down her sleek black gown. "It would look better without the stupid tiara."

I straightened my own crown. "I look like a jar of grape jelly."

"Har har. It is a lot of purple, but it works for you."

"The slit is too high."

"Drake will like it."

Butterflies erupted in my stomach. "I wish we could skip the ceremony."

"It's in the job description," Emine said from behind me. "Does this knife make my ass look fat?"

A devious smile formed on Lily's face. "Absolutely. As a matter of fact, the entire ensemble is hideous."

"I like leather." She brushed her hand down her knee-length leather skirt. "Anyone who has a problem with it can get bent."

I couldn't help but laugh. "It's you."

The smile melted off her face. "I wish Mat were here."

I blinked back the tears that threatened to fall. "Yeah. I don't know how I'm going to make it through this without him lecturing me about being a responsible adult or threatening Drake."

"He would, too. You'd throw a fit, and it would be a glorious show." She sighed. "I miss him."

I pulled her into a hug. "Me, too. It feels like a piece of my heart is missing."

"Half my soul." She gave me an awkward pat on the back and stepped away. "Enough of that. We're supposed to be happy."

I smoothed my too-sexy purple gown. "Yeah."

Helen stuck her head in the tent. "We're taking our places, so activate your viewing spell."

"Thanks, Helen." I stretched out a shaky hand and activated it. "I'm nervous."

Emine pulled me towards the screen. "Nice. Maybe you'll trip going up the stairs. It'd be a hoot."

In most match ceremonies, friends and family came in from opposite sides, intermingled, and took seats at the back of the platform. After they settled, the two closest family members met in the middle to present the couple. Usually, their parents. Since our lives were so entwined, our friends would come down the center aisle. Deva and Bastien would present Drake, while Emine and Lily would present me.

Butterflies took a lap around my stomach when Quin and Ara emerged from a tent near the back of the massive crowd. Quin wore a pristine tuxedo and black tie, while Ara wore a short red dress. They didn't acknowledge the crowd.

Jonas and Ann Marie stepped out as soon as they reached the stage. Ann Marie's tea-length navy dress fluttered in the wind. She raised a hand to place a spell on her flower crown when it tried to fly off, as Jonas waved to the crowd. Travis and his new wolves began to howl. Other shifters joined in as they let out whoops, chirps, growls, trumpets, and cheers. They were so much happier with their first in charge again.

Tracy's gold dress stressed her good looks as she looped her arm around Alex's. He slicked back his mop of brown hair, revealing the too-handsome face he always tried to hide.

I nudged Lily. "I adore your brother."

"You've hijacked my entire family."

"I knew Quin and Ara before you did. Besides, I tried to cut you out of my life, but you wouldn't leave."

Lily linked her arm with mine. "Because I'm an idiot."

I rested my head on her shoulder. "You're going to lose badass points."

She shrugged so hard my head dislodged. "It's the price we pay for family."

Razazia came next, wearing a deep green dress without a back, her wings shimmering in the light. She said something to make Cavil turn beet-red as she took his arm.

"You should have let me pair Cavil with Tracy."

"It's for Razazia's safety. Alex would have retaliated if she tried that shit with him, where Cavil prides himself on self-control."

"I'd pay good money to see a showdown between the two," Emine said.

Sylphira buzzed down the aisle solo, dropping shiny dust ahead of George and Helen. George's suit was a bit too loose, and Helen's light gray dress had pleats in the skirt. Broad smiles lit their faces as they floated towards the stage.

As soon as everyone settled, trumpets played the coalition anthem.

"You sure about this?" Emine asked. "Because it's not too late to run."

"I'm done running, but thanks."

"Good." Lily released my arm and fixed one of my curls. "Give 'em hell."

I couldn't see the other side of the stage where Drake's tent was located, but his anticipation and overwhelming joy calmed my nerves.

The four reached the top, and I wiped my sweaty hands on my dress as they came together on the stage. Deva wore a chocolate brown long-sleeved dress, while Bastien wore a black suit with a charcoal shirt and tie. A thundering cheer came from the crowd as the four bowed to each other.

A projection spell lit above them, and Bastien stepped forward. "I present my cousin, my protector, and my closest friend, Drake, as a match for my friend and our queen, Jenella."

Emine dipped her head. "Don't tell Jen, but she is the best friend I've ever had, and I consider her my little sister, even though I get on her last nerve." She took a deep breath. "My beloved match, Prince Mathias, became responsible for a little girl he barely knew. He fell in love with her and could not have been more proud of the kind of person she grew to be. I present you with his heart, Queen Jenella, as a match to the biggest dragon on the planet, the First, Drake."

Her words enhanced the hollow ache his absence left.

Lily rested a hand on Emine's arm. "The fates blessed me the day I met my big brother and sister. They not only accepted me, but also treated my entire adopted family as their own. I'm proud to present Jenella, a good friend and kick-ass sister, as a match for the big oaf of a dragon, the First Drake."

Bastien's jaw clenched as the crowd erupted in laughter.

Deva's smile lit up the stage. "Many years ago, I took a discarded nephew into my home. Many dragons claimed I was a saint for the act. That I saved him. I assure you, it was quite the opposite. He helped me raise my children, nursed me through the death of my match, and has stood by my side for centuries. I am proud to present the most unique and loyal dragon, and my beloved nephew, Drake, as a match to the most caring and brave Queen of Ahl we have witnessed, Jenella.

My heart pounded in my chest as I stepped out of the tent. I kept my head down and focused on the stairs as I walked in tune with the trumpets. When I spotted Lily's shoes, I raised my head.

I forgot to breathe as I fought the urge to run into Drake's arms. He wore a dark suit and purple shirt. My family's color. He didn't bother with a tie, but he styled his hair, revealing his rugged face. His lips twitched as his emerald eyes lingered on the slit in my dress.

Emine and Lily bowed to him, while Deva and Bastien bowed to me, and the four stepped out of the way.

The world disappeared when he took my hands. I couldn't help but stare at his beautiful, sincere, rugged face. Love, respect, and a sense of belonging rolled back and forth through the bond.

When the crowd's cheers died down, he cleared his throat. "They sent me to this realm to become a First many years ago. When my family followed me and destroyed the gate, the other Firsts shunned me. I remained an outcast for centuries. So long, I forgot I could be anything else. One day, while in a sleeping stupor I didn't want, the most extraordinary woman I ever met reached out with her amazing magic, woke me, and changed my life forever. She gave me a purpose and ensured others give me a level of respect I never had. She accepted my family, fought for our people, and gave me millions of little things I didn't know I wanted or needed. I have lived thousands of years thinking very little of myself. But in one wave of her hand, Jenella changed the course of my life and has spent every day since convincing me to have faith. She is my entire world. I am pleased to announce Queen Jenella Lissandra Andreas Ahl is not only my mate, but my match in every way."

So many emotions swirled inside me. I'd prepared a gracious speech to present in front of everyone, but couldn't remember a word of it. My eyes trailed to where Quin and Tracy sat. The slight narrowing of Quin's eyes almost made me laugh. Even when silent, the guy chastised me.

I returned my attention to Drake and swallowed. "The first time we met, Drake shook me like a rag-doll, and I slapped him. Twice." The crowd laughed. "I was a mess back then. A giant ball of pain and anger that my loved ones had attempted to heal for years. Even with their best efforts, it never occurred to me it was possible to heal until Drake crashed into my life. He stood beside me and, with a deep well of patience, guided me through every step in my journey. I'm a better friend, sister, and queen because of him. I've had many paranormals ask what I saw in a grumpy dragon. But what he only shows those of us he loves is that behind the façade, this man is the most wonderful, caring, funny, and thoughtful person on the planet. I thank the fates every day for bringing him into my life. With great joy, I declare Drake Deslaurian Ahl my match and my King Consort." I waved a hand to dissipate the spell hiding his crown.

He leaned down to kiss me as the crowd roared so loudly, I couldn't hear myself think. His soft lips grazed mine before settling on my ear. "I will cherish you always."

Jonas stepped forward. "Coalition members and honored guests. I am honored to announce that the matching of Queen Jenella and King Drake is complete. Please proceed to the banquet."

Emine leaned against my left side as we watched a massive crowd dance in the open field. Drake swung a barefoot Deva around in a practiced move as a group of dragons stood to the side, cheering them on. "He would have been proud of you today."

"He'd still give me a bunch of shit."

"It would have been so much fun to watch." Her heart wasn't in the teasing.

I swung to Lily's friend, Flintous, who stood nearby. He wore a pair of spelled black shoes. "Why are Deva and Bastien always barefoot?"

He shrugged. "We have scales, so shoes are optional. If I had to guess, they're more comfortable that way."

The answer was too easy but made sense, so I chalked it up to a mystery I may never solve.

I took Emine's hand as I stood. "Come on. Let's dance and have a little fun while we can."

As I danced the night away with my friends, family, and my people, I couldn't help but think Mat was staring down at me from above, his golden hair blowing in the wind as he judged my impulsive, manipulative ways while breaking all the rules to protect me. Just like he always did.

The End.

One More Thing

THANK YOU SO MUCH for reading my first series! It's been so much fun to write, and I hope you enjoyed it.

Reviews mean everything to authors, so if you haven't already, please leave one. Not a fan of reviews? Then a few stars are fine.

I've seen too many authors complete a series, only to return to it later, so I'll never say never when it comes to checking in on this world. It might be fun to see what Jenella's up to in a few years. I also have a few ideas about stand-alones featuring some side characters, including Alex.

Later this year, the first book of a new series in a new world will be released. You can find the full description on the series page on my website. While you're there, sign up for my newsletter at www.mlconklin.com to stay updated on upcoming releases.

Thanks again to everyone who helped me with this book. The editors, proofreaders, beta readers, and ARC readers were all amazing to work with and continue to make me a better writer, one criticism at a time. The cover designers at getcovers.com do a great job.

As always, thank you to my furry assistants for dealing with only receiving partial attention while I write, and keeping me from going insane.

And once again, thank you. Don't tell anyone, but I have the best readers and I appreciate every single one of you who took a chance on a new author and read to the end.

ML Conklin

Email: mlconklin@mlconklin.com

Website: www.mlconklin.com

Here's my socials:

I'm most active on:

Threads: https://www.threads.com/authormlconklin

Facebook: https://www.facebook.com/author.mlconklin

Instagram: https://www.instagram.com/authormlconklin

I also have accounts on:

Bluesky: https://bsky.app/profile/authormlconklin.bsky.social

TikTok: https://www.tiktok.com/@authormlconklin

X (Twitter): https://www.twitter.com/authormlconklin

Series Info

Reading order for The Paranormals of Ahl series:

The Dragon Problem (Book 1)
Bug Magic (Book 2)
The Mage Vampire Hybrid (Book 2.5) – Lily's POV
Crowns and Curses (Book 3)
The Hybrid Heir (Book 3.5) – Lily's POV
The Queen of Ahl (Book 4)

Printed in Dunstable, United Kingdom

67898067R00245